LOOK FOR THE SILVER LINING

When Nellie marries a man who does not meet with her mother's approval she is cut off from her family, and with her soldier husband Teddy away, a pregnant Nellie is forced to face the horrors of the Blitz alone. Bitterly angry and grief stricken at news of Teddy's death, the church is the last place Nellie would turn to, but when her brother asks for help tending a man who has sought the sanctuary of St Joseph's, she complies. The man mysteriously disappears, but the end of the war sees his return, and a new challenge for Nellie.

LOOK FOR THE SILVER LINING

LOOK FOR THE SILVER LINING

by

June Francis

Magna Large Print Books
Long Preston, North Yorkshire,
BD23 4ND, England.

British Library Cataloguing in Publication Data.

Francis, June
 Look for the silver lining.

 A catalogue record of this book is
 available from the British Library

 ISBN 978-0-7505-2545-9

First published in Great Britain in 2006 by Allison & Busby Ltd.

Copyright © 2006 by June Francis

Cover illustration © The Old Tin Dog by arrangement with
Allison & Busby Ltd.

The moral right of the author has been asserted

Published in Large Print 2007 by arrangement with
Allison & Busby Limited

Magna Large Print is an imprint of Library Magna Books Ltd.

Printed and bound in Great Britain by
T.J. (International) Ltd., Cornwall, PL28 8RW

Part One

1941 to 1942

Prologue

'Up, children! On your feet!' Out of the corner of her eye, 21-year-old Nellie Lachlan could see the giant crack in the wall widening. 'We're going to march out of the classroom, along the corridor, then outside. Dennis, you can lead the way.'

'But it's raining, miss,' Dennis moaned.

'A bit of rain won't hurt us.'

'Is this a game, miss?' asked one of the four-year-olds.

'Sort of.' She began to sing 'The Grand old Duke of York' and hustled the children, whose attention had obviously been elsewhere when she had ordered them up, outside to where their class-mates were already lining up. 'Come on, Dennis,' she urged, 'or someone else can be leader.'

'No. You said I could be leader but do we have to go outside?' he asked.

'Just get going!' ordered Nellie, glancing at the wall. Bits of masonry were starting to fall. She knew that she mustn't panic the little ones but they had to move fast. Who would have believed the bomb that had exploded in the next street last night could have had such an effect on the old school? She remembered Teddy, her husband, saying the effects of a bomb blast should never be underestimated. He had wanted her to get away from the bombing but so far she had stuck it out, not wishing to leave the job she adored and also

9

hoping to heal the rift between herself and her family.

'When they were up they were up,' she sang, gently pushing children through the doorway and counting heads at the same time.

Was it her imagination or was the floor really quivering? Is this what it felt like to be involved in an earthquake? She shoved five-year-old Johnny out of the door, thinking, 'Thank God, the last one!' when she remembered there was a new girl, Audrey.

She turned back and her gaze swept the room. Where was she? Could she have sneaked out to the lavatory? No! She spotted a foot sticking out from behind the sand tray. The child must be hiding, thinking the marching was just a game, and one she didn't want to join in.

Nellie wasted no time and raced over to the sand tray with the sound of shifting masonry and the singing of the marching children in her ears. She dragged the startled girl to her feet and ran with her towards the doorway. They were almost there when Nellie heard a rumbling and the floor shook violently. Audrey screamed. The urge to look behind them was overwhelming but Nellie resisted and swung the girl in an arc and then let her go. Momentum took her out into the corridor and Nellie flung herself after her as the wall caved in.

Chapter One

Nellie sat at the end of a row of children with a three-year-old boy on her knee. She could feel his skinny body shake as he giggled at the antics of a child puppet performing a jerky dance as it tried to escape a mother puppet attempting to get a miniature gasmask on its head. A smile lit her blue-green eyes as she watched another tiny puppet blundering about with its arms held out in front of it because its gasmask was on backwards. The performance went on for a few minutes longer and then ended with the message: *Don't forget your gasmask!* It was greeted by a storm of clapping and a shouted request for 'More, more!'

Nellie echoed their sentiments, thinking the poor loves had been through so much that it was good for them to forget the horrors of the bombing for a short while. Gradually the noise died down as the puppet booth was cleared away and the area set up for a game of musical chairs.

Miss Jackson, the headmistress of the Central School on the outskirts of Liverpool, crooked a finger at Nellie. With a feeling of trepidation, she eased the boy off her knee and stood up. She was aware of being the focus of numerous pairs of eyes and prayed that she did not look as nervous as she felt. This would be the first time she had played since her arm had been broken when the wall had collapsed. The librarian smiled encouragingly. He had initiated the Saturday morning hour and also arranged for lessons for those children who had not been evacuated to take place in the library after the primary school had been closed due to bomb damage.

Nellie settled herself on the piano stool and her fingers felt for the black and white keys. She tried out a few scales. It was her Great-great-aunt Adelaide who had allowed her to 'mess about making a bloody din' as her seafaring father, Bernard, called her playing on the upright piano in the parlour of Adelaide's large Victorian house, a short distance from the LeedsLiverpool canal. Sadly, the old woman had died last year shortly after Nellie's sailor brother Joseph had been killed. It had been just six months before Nellie had eloped with her brother's best friend, the Protestant Teddy Lachlan.

She began to play 'The Teddy Bears' Picnic' and relaxed a bit when she heard the children singing as they skipped around the chairs, slowing down as they came to the end of a row, ready to scramble for a seat if the music should suddenly stop. She thought how her husband would have found pleasure in watching the tots enjoying themselves. They both wanted a family but it was too early to tell whether she was pregnant from their too-short honeymoon. He had been so tender and thoughtful on their wedding night that all her trepidation had vanished. She sighed, wishing that she could relive those few days in Southport, but she did not know when she would see him again now that he had disembarked for Libya.

She stopped playing and there was a mad

scramble for the chairs. Nellie watched, her ready sympathy roused by the plight of the two littlest ones who did not reach the chairs in time. One cheerfully went and sat on her mother's knee but the other stamped away to lean against his grandfather's leg and glower at the other children.

Another two chairs were removed and Nellie began to play again. Her gaze wandered to the rows of books displayed in the children's department. It was Adelaide whom she had to thank for her love of stories. Nellie's mother, Carmel, had never told them fictional tales for fun; she made her children focus on stories of the saints' lives and daily readings from the Catholic missal first thing in the morning and last thing at night. The rest of the time, Carmel spent keeping house for Grandfather Callaghan, visiting her sister in Bootle or attending church while her seafaring husband was away for months on end. It was Nellie's paternal grandfather who had inherited Adelaide's house and the rest of the family, except her brother Francis who served as a curate in an inner city parish in Liverpool, still lived there.

Nellie lifted her hands from the piano and watched, again, that mad scramble of children trying not to be left out. Suddenly it occurred to her that the little girl with plaits and a quivering lip, who had been pushed off a chair by a larger boy, reminded her in a peculiar way of herself. Since her marriage, she had been cut off from her family. For once, her parents had presented a united front when Teddy had asked for her hand in marriage. Her father, who was home on shore leave, voiced his disapproval in no uncertain terms and refused to grant his permission.

Her parents' antagonism had shocked the young couple. Nellie had never imagined her mother would be so against her choice of husband. Teddy, despite being a Protestant, had been made welcome in their house since boyhood and she had often heard her mother and Aunt Josie saying what a nice, charming young man he was. He'd had a steady job working in a shipping office until being called up. It was just before he'd left for an army training camp in Scotland that he asked Nellie to write to him. She had done so and, over the months, their affection for each other had grown. On his first leave, the friendship forged by their correspondence had blossomed into a real love affair.

Nellie took her hands from the keyboard and eased back a strand of chestnut hair from her eyes, watching again the children's rush to secure a seat. She decided musical chairs was not a nice game but at least it served the purpose of teaching children at an early age that life was not a doddle and one had to put in effort to get what one wanted. She and Teddy had wanted each other desperately but, even so, it had taken some doing going against her family's wishes and running away to get married on his embarkation leave.

Nellie launched into 'Run, Rabbit, Run' and felt that ache inside her as she thought of her younger sisters, Lottie and Babs. She loved her sisters dearly but, although she had written to them several times since her wedding, she had not received one answer and it hurt.

'Miss Callaghan, can you spare half an hour

14

after we've finished with the children? We're having a meeting and want you to be there,' said Miss Jackson.

Nellie nodded. She had kept secret her marital state, knowing that normally a married woman would not retain her job once she left spinsterhood behind. 'Can you tell me what it's about?' she asked.

'You'll be told at the meeting, dear, which will take place at the far end of the Adults' section of the library.' Miss Jackson hurried away.

Nellie hoped the meeting wouldn't go on too long. She had shopping to do and her rented room to clean.

Fortunately for Nellie, her part in the proceedings was dealt with first. 'Miss Callaghan, we wondered if you would be willing to accompany a group of mothers and their pre-school children to Cumberland?' she was asked.

Nellie blinked at the man. 'You mean they're being evacuated?'

'Voluntary evacuation.' He peered at her over his spectacles. 'It is not the same as the government's scheme for school children just before the outbreak of war; it is being offered to mothers wanting to escape the recent bombing. The Luftwaffe might have left us alone for a short time but, no doubt, they will be back. Their intention is to destroy the docks if they can and the morale of the people.'

Nellie remembered that day when she had almost been flattened because of a German bomb and knew what her answer would be. 'So would I be going to teach the children?'

He tapped the tips of his fingers together. 'These are pre-school children so your task will be to prepare them for school.'

'How many children will there be?'

'A dozen in your charge but there will also be younger siblings who will be in the care of their mothers. You will be staying in a large detached house called High View, which has been loaned to us by a colonel who has come out of retirement and is now at the war office in London. The house is situated a couple of miles from Ambleside.' A slight smile relaxed his rather thin lips. 'Beautiful country, and I'm sure it will do your good self and the mothers and children nothing but good. Of course, you will have some help. A Miss Finch from Kendal, who is a qualified nurse, will be responsible for the children's health, and the Colonel's housekeeper, with the help of the mothers, will see to everything else to do with their welfare.'

'Will there be other such groups going elsewhere?' asked Nellie, her face showing interest.

'Yes, but that is not your concern.' He waved a hand dismissively. 'Will you accept this job? I know the care of pre-schoolers was not what you were trained for but it is becoming increasingly obvious the care and education of this age group will take on more importance on the home front in the future.'

Nellie felt a rising excitement and was flattered that they should ask someone as young and inexperienced as herself to take it on. She would have a roof over her head and be fed and paid a wage, which meant she could save money for the day when she and Teddy would have a home of their own.

'Yes, I would like the job,' she said firmly.

The committee looked pleased and she was told they would be in touch with more details soon. Nellie thought the departure could not come quickly enough for her.

Within days, Nellie gave her landlady notice and thought about what she would need in the way of equipment. She was fortunate in that her list met with the education suppliers' approval. She was looking forward to the challenge but she knew that she could not leave without trying to heal the rift with her family, so she decided to visit them.

As she reached the front gate, she was stopped by a next door neighbour, Mrs Wainwright, who liked to have her nose in everyone's business. Silver-haired with baby-blue eyes, she looked the picture of a cuddly granny.

'What are you doing here, Nellie? If you were hoping to see your sisters, they're out.'

Nellie felt a deep disappointment. 'What about Mam and Grandfather?'

'He's at a retired seamen's meeting, I believe.' She gave Nellie a sharp look. 'So what made you leave home? You haven't joined the Forces.'

Nellie's pretty mouth tightened. 'Mam didn't tell you?'

The woman looked frustrated. 'No, but I did wonder if you'd got yourself into trouble.'

'Well, you were wrong. I did something much worse: I married Teddy Lachlan, a Protestant.'

Defiantly, Nellie walked away, forcing open the gate to her grandfather's house and heading up the path. Her heart was beating fast at the thought of confronting her mother. If Aunt Josie was with her then the meeting would be more than a little fraught. She went round to the back of the house and let herself in by the washroom door and into the kitchen.

Her mother glanced up from the book she was reading and Nellie saw that it was *The Life of St Francis*. Carmel's auburn hair was greying and her face was lined. Her lips tightened when she saw her daughter. 'You've got a nerve coming here when I told you to never set foot in this house again.'

Nellie felt tears prick the back of her eyes. 'I'm going away, Mam. I just wanted to try and make up our quarrel. Teddy and I are married now, so it seems pointless carrying it on.'

'You're not married to him in the eyes of the one true Church, Nellie, so you're living in sin. A daughter of mine behaving in such a way! I'm ashamed of you,' she said scathingly.

Nellie felt the colour rise in her cheeks but she tilted her chin. 'Then you're wrong to feel like that. You know Teddy's a good man but he has his own faith and he's entitled to it.'

'Rubbish!' cried Carmel. 'There is only one true faith and he needs to turn or he'll go to Hell.'

The mention of Hell angered Nellie. 'Well, rubbish to that,' she said. 'If there's a hell I believe it's on this earth. Think of all those soldiers who were killed in the Great War.'

'He's turning you his way,' gasped Carmel, putting a hand to her bosom. 'Now get out of this house before I throw you out.'

'I'm going. I'm sorry you feel the way you do, Mam. I'm off to Cumberland in the morning. I'm going with some children and their mothers, so if you ever did worry about me and the bombs you can stop worrying. Give Babs and Lottie my love, and Grandfather, too.'

Her mother pointed at the door. Angry tears almost blinded Nellie as she turned and walked out of the house. She would have to be asked back before she returned to this house again.

The next day Nellie left Bootle. It had been decided to ferry the party to Cumberland by charabanc because the journey by train would have entailed several changes and a bus trip at the end, which might prove too difficult for mothers with little ones.

The children were excited as they climbed into the vehicle.

'Dad said I'll see cows in fields, miss,' said one little boy, his brown eyes shining as he looked up at her. 'Is that right?'

'I'm sure we will,' said Nellie, seating him next to the window before helping his mother and baby sister into the place beside him.

'I'm gonna miss my fella,' said the woman, settling the baby on her knee, 'but the kids have got to come first.'

'Works at the docks, doesn't he?' asked Nellie, giving another mother a helping hand.

'That's right,' said the first woman, lowering her voice and adding, 'I'll worry meself sick about him, knowing there'll be more air raids, but he said if we were on a sinking ship it would be women and children first.'

Nellie took his point and determined not to worry about her family. Besides, her grandfather's house was at least a mile and a half from the docks and not in an industrial area.

Within less than an hour they had left bomb-damaged Merseyside behind and were roaring along the main road heading north into the Lancashire countryside. One of the mothers began to sing, 'We're off, we're off, we're off in a motor car, sixty coppers are after us and we don't know where we are.'

The simple refrain was taken up by most of the women and several of the older children. Nellie smiled, wondering where the song had started. Perhaps it reflected the mothers' visits to the picture house when they were girls, watching silent films in which the Keystone Cops featured. When all were sick of singing that ditty, Nellie started them off with 'Ten Green Bottles Standing on a Wall'. It was another simple song but it would help teach the children how to count down from ten to one. When that ended someone suggested 'Run, Rabbit, Run'.

Nellie loved singing and proceeded to lead them into such popular songs as, 'Look for the Silver Lining', 'Life is Just a Bowl of Cherries' and the odd children's Sunday school chorus, which she had learnt when, unknown to her mother, she had visited the Methodist chapel on Linacre Road with a Protestant friend. The building was almost opposite to where Babs worked in the office of the Diamond Match-works. 'This Little Light of Mine' kept them going for five minutes and the mothers remembered other choruses.

So the miles sped by. There had been no snow in the city but here, in the countryside, lay odd patches in the fields and on the summits of the distant mountains. She remembered once when there had been a fall of snow in the city and Teddy had told her that if you were to put some snowflakes under a microscope they looked just like stars. He had gone on to liken the stars to those in her eyes and she could still feel the thrill his words had given her. She had teased him, saying that he was a real romantic.

'I'm all in favour of a bit of a romance,' he'd responded, kissing her and then twirling her round in an impromptu dance and singing against her ear, 'Wait till the Sun Shines, Nellie'. It was a song about being happy and sighing and going down Lovers' Lane. He had reminded her of an evening in her great-great-aunt's house, when she had picked out the tune on the piano and the old lady had told them that the music was written by Harry von Tilzer in the early years of that century before the Great War.

A tiny sigh escaped her, thinking of all those young men who had lost their lives in that so-called 'war to end all wars'. She feared for her husband, missing him terribly, but knew, like many another wife and sweetheart, she just had to bear it. At least she would have his letters, and her ex-landlady had promised to send on any that might come for her after she left. Nellie had already written to Teddy with her new address and reminded him to write Miss Callaghan on the envelope.

They had several stops on the way when mothers and children scurried behind a handy hedge to relieve themselves. It was far too cold to have a picnic, so they ate meat paste and jam butties on the charabanc. As they drew closer to their destination, Nellie noticed the sweep of Morecambe Bay.

A mother cried excitedly, 'The sea, the sea!'

Then it was gone, but ahead loomed the mountains of Cumberland. By then, some of the children had fallen asleep, while others had got fed up of having sheep and cows pointed out to them and were getting fractious. Nellie drew several of them to the back of the charabanc and played 'Pat-a-Cake' with them and told them the story of 'The Three Bears', putting on a gruff voice for Father Bear and a lighter one for Mother and Baby. She wished that she had thought to keep some crayons and paper from the boxes she had packed, but they were in the luggage compartment of the vehicle. By the time Lake Windermere came into view, she was beginning to sag, but the dipping sun reflecting off the surface of the water, turning it to apricot and gold silk, raised her spirits.

'Not long to go now,' called the driver over his shoulder.

Mothers perked up and so did the children. Several of the older ones began to ask, 'Are we there yet, miss? Are we there?'

Nellie had no more idea than they did but said, in what she hoped was a reassuring voice, 'Nearly.'

To her relief they were soon making their way through Ambleside. Nellie gazed at the grey slate houses and the tiny shop windows but the light was beginning to fail, so she could see little detail. Soon they left the village behind to wend their way along a winding road, fringed by trees. Eventually they stopped near a gatepost that bore the name High View. 'All out here,' said the driver. 'I won't get up there.'

They got down from the vehicle, stretching and groaning, wanting to see exactly where 'up there' was. On the other side of the gatepost, a drive led up a hillside only to disappear round a bend but, between the bare branches of the trees, a large grey house could be seen.

It took some doing getting everyone with baggage and boxes up to the house. Some of the mothers complained about the steepness of the hill before they'd even started the climb. The noise brought forth a man, a boy and two women. The man and boy instantly started to carry in the baggage. One woman, in a nurse's uniform and with greying hair, introduced herself as Miss Finch. The other one was plump and said that she was Mrs James, the housekeeper. Nellie put both women's age in the late forties.

'Hopefully the worst of the weather is behind us now we're into March,' said Mrs James in a northern burr. Her gaze swept over the group of women and children in front of her before returning to rest on Nellie.

'January was so cold that Rydal Water froze over and we had skating on the lake.'

'What a pity we missed it,' said Nellie brightly. 'It would have been a sight worth seeing for the children.'

'It's much too far for the little ones to walk but you can take the footpath over the fells. The weather can change dramatically. You must never go out alone or without telling someone where you're going.'

'I'll bear that in mind,' said Nellie, having no intention of traipsing up mountains and getting lost. She was a city girl and if she decided that this Rydal Lake was worth having a look at, then she felt sure there would be a bus that would take them there.

'Right! Let's get them all in, Mrs James,' said Miss Finch briskly. 'You lead the way and I'll bring up the rear. I'm sure the mothers would like the children to have their suppers and to get them to bed as soon as possible.'

Supper and bed are just what I need, thought Nellie, picking up her holdall and gasmask and following mothers and children indoors. While Mrs James saw to them, Miss Finch dealt with Nellie.

'I'll show you to your bedroom first so you can leave your bag and gasmask there. Then I'll take you down to the room we've allocated as a playroom for the children. I'm sure you'll want to see what we've done as soon as possible.'

Nellie agreed and followed her up several flights of stairs to an attic bedroom. She was reminded of the ones in her grandfather's house. They were slightly smaller than this one and were full of junk. She had once suggested when her father had been on shore leave, that it would be good if the rooms were cleared out so Babs and Lottie would not have to share. He had pointed to the damp in one corner and the peeling wallpaper and the assorted leftovers from several generations. 'You going to sort this out, girl? I doubt it. And I'm not going to bloody waste my leave doing it either.' He had hurried downstairs and out to the Red Lion.

'I hope this will do you?' said Miss Finch. 'We've given the bigger rooms to the mothers and children.'

Nellie nodded. She had a room to herself and, although there was not much in the way of furniture and the bed was narrow, she saw no point in complaining. The blackout curtains were drawn, so there was no use in looking out of the window at the view. Tomorrow would do. She felt a momentary homesickness, wanting the comforting sight of familiar houses and shops and the sound of a foghorn on the River Mersey. Well, she was going to have to forgo those things for a while. She wondered what Teddy would make of the place. Most likely he would love it, having spent months in the Scottish countryside and having written of his liking for lonely, wild places.

'If you leave your things and follow me down,' said Miss Finch, standing in the doorway, tapping the wall with her fingers.

Nellie dropped them hastily on the narrow bed and hurried after the nurse as she vanished from view.

Nellie had no complaints, though, when Miss Finch showed her to the room designated the playroom. It had a large bay window with a padded window seat and, except for a grand piano, space had been cleared of what she presumed was most likely dark, heavy furniture, similar to the pieces she had noticed in the hall and on the landings. In their place stood several small tables and chairs and surprise, surprise a sandbox, which rested on a huge sheet of tarpaulin. Next to it was a cardboard box containing buckets and spades. 'Golly,' said Nellie, smiling. 'I never expected that.'

'It was the gardener's idea. He thought with the children coming from the coast they'd like it.'

'I must tell him how much I appreciate it,' said Nellie, wandering over to the boxes that had come from Liverpool. Her fingers itched to unpack them and see if she really had been supplied with what she'd requested.

'You'd best leave them until after supper,' said Miss Finch, as if reading her mind.

Nellie nodded and followed her out of the room. Yet when supper was finished, tiredness overcame her and instead of heading for the playroom, she went upstairs. After unpacking, she pulled on her fleecy pyjamas and got into bed. The sheets were cold but did not feel damp. She forced herself to lay still and prayed for Teddy, her family, the children and mothers, and, lastly, herself. Her thoughts drifted over the happenings of the day, before she fell into a deep sleep.

The next morning Nellie woke feeling a bit groggy and, when she climbed out of bed, nausea overcame her. With a handkerchief held to her mouth, she had to rush downstairs to vomit in the toilet next to the bathroom. She put her sickness down to the macaroni cheese they'd had for supper.

When she went down to breakfast, she did without porridge and ate just toast smeared with butter and a cup of tea. Then she gathered her children together and took them to the playroom. There were a couple who wanted their mothers to stay with them but Nellie decided that she had to be firm from the start and insisted they left. She knew from her brief experience of primary school that most children stopped crying after a short while.

She told the children that they would say a prayer first and then practise putting on their gasmasks. After that the older children could help her unpack the boxes that had come from Liverpool while the younger ones could play in the sand tray.

She saw that a couple of the four-year-olds were torn between curiosity of what was in the boxes and making sand-pies, but when she told them they could play in the sand tray later, they appeared satisfied with her decision.

Once the boxes were unpacked, Nellie soon discovered most of what she had asked for was second-hand. Even some of the paper had been written on the back. It was annoying but she reminded herself that there was a war on and so there were bound to be shortages. She handed out individual blackboards and chalks to the oldest children, thinking that if by the time they were five they knew their alphabet, could write their names, count to ten and distinguish red from yellow and blue from green, they'd cope with school better. Not that she expected all of them to develop at the same rate.

She thought of her younger sisters; Lottie was almost eighteen and Babs was a year younger.

Lottie, plump, short, with mousy hair, had always been slow but thorough. As for Babs, she was like quicksilver, wanting something finished almost as soon as she started. Even their father made some time for his youngest daughter when he was home. She had flaming red hair, dancing green eyes, dimples and a smile that made you want to smile yourself. It was as if the good fairy had waved a wand over the youngest in the family and dished out most of the charm and good looks. Folk might say that inner beauty was more important, but from Nellie's experience of life, good looks were what made that first positive impression on people. Perhaps for that reason, she'd always had a soft spot for those children not so fortunate as Babs. She had her eye on one already who would need drawing out. She also felt music was a good place to start and, that afternoon, planned to involve all the children in being part of a band.

The morning sped by and Nellie enjoyed her lunch of cottage pie and sponge pudding and custard. While the children spent time afterwards having a break, she unpacked the box containing not only proper musical instruments: triangles, drums, cymbals and tambourines, but also blocks of wood, spoons and a small washboard. She smiled, thinking that the music they would make would definitely not be to everyone's taste but at least they would enjoy themselves.

She gathered the children together as soon as they began to drift back into the playroom. She handed a drum and sticks to Ronald, a dark-haired, thin-faced boy, who showed signs of scurvy. 'This for me?' he asked, looking amazed.

'Yes. And I want you to bang it nice and loud.'

'But Mam says I've to be quiet and behave meself,' he said.

'Not during music time,' said Nellie, giving him a brief hug.

She gave out the rest of the instruments and told the children to make as much noise as they wanted and to march once she started singing. This time she did not mind being the focus of at least ten pairs of wide eyes as she seated herself at the piano and began to play and sing 'We're Soldiers of the King, Melads'.

Slowly but gradually the noise level increased as the children banged, shook, chimed and got into step. Several bumped into each other but no harm was done and soon they were marching in some semblance of order. She thought that in the weeks to come she would teach them a few simple songs, as well as so many other things. They could draw and paint, do jigsaws. She would read them stories and take them on nature walks as the weather warmed up, just short ones around the garden at first. For the first time in weeks she felt content.

What Nellie called 'real spring' arrived in the Lake District sometime towards the end of April. By then she had something else on her mind besides her small charges. She had missed a couple of periods and had suffered from morning sickness since her arrival. While delighted to be having Teddy's baby, she was determined to keep her condition a secret as long as possible for fear that, once it was out, she would be sacked. The thought of what she'd do if that happened worried her enormously.

She had written to her sisters and brother telling them where she was living, but had not heard back from them. She had refrained from pouring out her hurt to Teddy, thinking that he had enough on his plate with having to face the Italians and Germans in Libya, but she wrote to him about the baby, knowing that he would be just as thrilled as she was. In the meantime, she would carry on working and saving as much money as possible. She sighed, wishing she could talk to someone about her situation. As it was, despite making good use of her time in the countryside getting to know the mothers, she still felt something of an outsider being 'miss' to them.

The women spent their time helping with the housework and cooking, knitting for the men in the Forces whilst listening to the wireless, as well as looking after the babies and tiny tots amongst them. Some made the effort to go into Ambleside and brought back sweets and newspapers. Others 'oohed' and 'aahed' over the films and dances taking place in Kendal or Morecambe advertised in the local *Gazette*. Nellie would have enjoyed seeing Ivor Novello's *The Dancing Years* at the Winter Gardens in Morecambe but had to forgo that pleasure because of the distance and cost.

It had taken Nellie some time getting used to the country sounds at night: the screech of an owl, the baa of a sheep, the wind in the trees when a storm blew up. Despite the beauty of the countryside, the war could not be forgotten: occasionally the noise of aeroplanes could be heard and Mrs James spoke of the shipyards at

Barrow being their target. Nellie would pray for the people there, as well as her loved ones. Posters went up in the village promoting Ambleside and Windermere's joint fundraising effort for War Weapons Week, and there was news of a war casualty – the pilot grandson of a Mr Lupton of Ambleside.

Then, on a beautiful morning towards the end of the second week in May, Nellie received a letter. She had been hoping for one from Teddy in response to her news about the baby but this was addressed in her brother's sprawling hand. The sight of it caused her a mixture of delight and apprehension and she was about to slit it open with a finger when someone called her and she remembered that the children were assembled in the hall for a nature walk.

She pocketed the letter and ushered them outside. The smell of wood smoke was in the air, mingling with the scent of hawthorn blossom and gorse. Birds twittered and warbled and she pointed out birds on the wing, carrying scraps of tawny dried grass or grubs in their beaks, explaining to the children that this meant they were building nests to lay their eggs. She thought how different these surroundings were from the city streets and felt a pang of homesickness. She asked the children what they missed most about home.

'I miss my dad,' said Ronald.

'The shops and the river,' put in another boy.

'What do you like about the countryside?' she asked.

'No bombs to blow us up,' said a rosy faced girl called Ruth, jigging about.

Nellie agreed. 'That's why we're here, isn't it?'

They nodded solemnly and a couple said, 'Yes, miss.'

Nellie suggested they look for wild flowers and see if they could spot any bees, butterflies or other insects. They ran off happily and she settled down on a fallen tree trunk and took out Francis' letter.

Dear Nellie,
There is no easy way of telling you this, so I might as well get straight to the point. Mam and Aunt Josie are dead.

She stilled, conscious of the thud, thud, thud of her heartbeat, and reread those last six words. *Mam and Aunt Josie are dead.*

'I don't believe it,' she murmured, and read them again before continuing.

I don't know if you're aware but Liverpool has suffered a week of devastating air raids. Mam and Lottie were visiting Aunt Josie when a raid started. You know how stubborn Aunt Josie was. Anyway, she refused to go to the shelter and a high explosive went off right in front of the house. They were both killed but thank God Lottie survived, even though she was buried for several hours. She is in Southport hospital now, her hip is broken and so is her left leg. She's been asking for you and so I told her that I would write.

Lottie apart, you're going to have to come home to look after Grandfather and Babs. She's of an age when she needs an eye keeping on her and the old man can't do it. She'd have him running round in

circles trying to keep up with her and that won't do.
Also, the match-works received a direct hit so she's
going to have to find another job.

I can guess how you must feel about the loss of Mam
but from what Babs told me, you mustn't reproach
yourself. It seems Mam had kept the letters you sent to
the girls and hid them away before they could see
them. Both have been waiting to hear from you,
certain you'd have kept in touch, and were hurt when
you didn't write. Anyway, Babs found your letters in
Mam's insurance policy box and that upset us all.

I'm hoping I can depend on you, Nell, to do what I
ask. Your marrying outside the church without coming
and talking to me beforehand caused me pain.
Mother wanted you excommunicated but I couldn't
do that to you. Besides, I've been stretched to the limit
dealing with the sorrow caused by the bombing in my
own parish and that is why I put off writing to you.
Yours,
Francis.

Tears welled up in Nellie's eyes and she returned
the letter to its envelope. There was no doubt in
her mind that she would have to do what her
brother asked. She did not want to leave the
children in her care, but family came first. She
would have to serve her notice and go. Calling
the children, she spent a few minutes inspecting
and commenting on the wild flowers and odd
beetle they had found, before hurrying them
back to the house.

Chapter Two

It was June before Nellie was able to get away but she wrote to Francis and Babs telling them when she would be home. Tears were shed when it came to her taking leave of the children, but she said that she hoped to see them when they returned to Liverpool.

'Some of us mightn't be long following you,' said a mother. 'My fella said there hasn't been any raids worth mentioning since the May blitz.'

'See you around, then,' said Nellie, smiling as she climbed into the pony and trap taking her into Ambleside, from where she would catch a bus to Windermere railway station. She had quite a journey before her and planned to go into Southport, where Lottie was convalescing, before going home. She intended on writing a letter to Teddy on the train, bringing him up to date about her movements. She was worried about her husband because she had not received an answer to the letter she had sent telling him about the baby. Of course, letters did go missing during wartime. The German U-boats were still wreaking havoc with British shipping. She could only pray that was the problem, terrible as the thought of ships being blown up was, and Teddy was OK.

Once settled on the train at Windermere, Nellie took out her fountain pen and pad and began to write:

Dearest Teddy,

I am sitting on the train, watching the beautiful countryside go past, on my way back to Liverpool. I've become used to the hills and the fresh country air, so it's going to feel strange being back home again. As I haven't heard from you for several weeks, I don't know if you received my letter telling you about the baby or the one I wrote after Francis got in touch. If not, the good news is that I'm having a baby, which is due in October. I am thrilled to bits and now the morning sickness is over, I'm in the pink. As soon as I get home, I'll have to register with a midwife and find out what help I can get from the government when it comes to nourishing food, large clothes to cover my bump and the baby's layette. With the need for clothing coupons starting this month, I'm hoping there'll be extra for this expectant mum. I only wish you were here to share in the excitement with me because we've talked about having a baby, haven't we?

I have to confess to having had some worries about where to live once the time came for me to leave High View. As you know, Mam had told me not to darken the doors again. Hopefully, Grandfather will be pleased to see me but I'm getting ahead of myself.

Mam and Aunt Josie were killed in the blitz and Francis says I'm needed at home. I was so shocked I couldn't believe it at first. Well, I just hope the pair of them get into Heaven. I won't say anymore on that score.

Poor Lottie was injured but I will soon be seeing for myself just how bad she is. Babs says she can't walk but hopefully that isn't a permanent state. Babs has found herself another job as an invoice clerk because the match-works was blitzed, but I don't know how long she'll last there as she said there's only old women in the office and they boss her around. By 'old' she probably means twenty-five or thirty.

How are things with you, sweetheart? I hope you're not suffering from the heat too much having spent so many months up in Scotland. I do so miss you and even the memory of that lovely honeymoon in Southport can't make up for not having you with me, my handsome, wonderful husband.

At least I feel my time in Cumberland has not been wasted. All that I've learnt about small children will stand me in good stead when I have ours. Boy or girl, it does not matter to me as long as he or she is healthy and all there. If it's a boy I can just imagine you taking him to Goodison and cheering the Blues on, and if it's a girl I know you'll want her dressed in pretty frocks and for her to have the best things in life.

I love you lots and wish we could be together. Kisses and hugs and keep your head down,

Your very own,

Nellie.

XXXXX

There were tears in her eyes as she folded the letter and placed it in an envelope, which she kissed after sealing it. Hopefully, there wouldn't be too many delays on her journey and she would reach Southport in time to post it.

Nellie was in luck, arriving at a handy time in the resort where the sun was shining. She followed her brother's instructions to a T and found the convalescent home, which was a requisitioned hotel adapted for helping the wounded recover for the duration of the war. She expected the meeting with Lottie to be an emotional one and was not mistaken. As soon as Nellie walked into the small ward and saw her sister sitting in bed, looking, if Nellie was honest, rather like a stranded whale, her eyes filled with tears.

'Oh, love,' she said unsteadily. 'What a thing to happen!'

'Nellie!' Lottie's plump cheeks trembled and her chins wobbled as she held out her arms to her. 'I thought you'd never come.'

Not wanting to hurt her, Nellie hugged her sister as best she could. Lottie wept on her shoulder and it was some minutes before she gained control of herself. 'I couldn't even get to the funeral,' she said, sniffing and wiping her damp face with the back of her hand, 'but Francis said all was done as it should be. They've been buried at Ford cemetery. I'd have liked a marble angel for their grave but he said that Grandfather wouldn't fork out for it and Dad definitely won't.' Anger twisted her face. 'May the Holy Mother and our Saviour forgive me but I don't think either of them has a heart.' Her grey eyes filled with tears again.

Nellie fumbled in her pocket and produced a crumpled handkerchief. 'Here, use this, and stop getting worked up about them. You should have realised by now that the only member of the family Dad cares about is Babs. Francis said he's yet to have a reply to the letter he sent telling Dad about Mam and Aunt Josie's deaths.'

'That doesn't surprise me,' muttered Lottie, mopping her face with the handkerchief. 'I don't know how he and Mam ever came to get married. They certainly didn't have time for each other when he was home.'

Nellie nodded. 'It's a mystery to me, too. But maybe they loved each other once.'

Lottie handed the handkerchief back to Nellie and pushed back her lank mousy hair from her forehead. 'You must love Teddy Lachlan a lot to go against Mam and Grandfather the way you did and marry outside the faith.'

Nellie's blue-green eyes lit up as she pocketed the handkerchief. 'I love him to bits. He's a good man. Remember how he bought us girls ice-creams from the Italian ice-cream cart at the Pierhead years ago? It must have broke him but he was a generous soul even then.'

Lottie sighed. 'It's just a pity he's not a Catholic soul.'

Nellie frowned. 'Don't start on religion, Lottie. Teddy has his way of worshipping God just like we do. The main difference, as you know, with Proddies is that they have no time for the Pope ... or priests for that matter ... although, Teddy and Francis used to get on OK years ago.'

Lottie's eyes widened. 'It's not just that, Nellie, some of them don't have any respect for the host.'

Nellie groaned. 'Forget it, Lot. You're never going to convince Teddy that bread and wine becomes the flesh and blood of our Lord. Now stop this or I'll walk out of here right now and I won't give you the chocolate I bought you. Although, perhaps I shouldn't have done so but there's no bananas or oranges to be had.' As she produced the bar of Fry's Chocolate Cream, Lottie almost snatched it out of her hand.

'My favourite. You are generous, Nellie, especially as you'd have had to use some of your sweet ration for this.'

'You're my sister and I was willing to make the sacrifice because I don't want to put on too much weight myself.' Nellie placed a hand against the material covering the soft swell of her belly.

Lottie stared at her. 'There's hardly anything of you.'

'There'll be a lot more of me soon.'

'Why?'

Nellie rolled her eyes. 'Never mind. I'll tell you another time. So do you want to talk about what happened or don't you want to think about it?'

Lottie was only too ready to discuss the experience of being buried alive. The awfulness of feeling as if she had the weight of most of the house pressing down on her. She said with a shiver, 'I was terrified when I could smell leaking gas and then there was the drip, drip of water and shifting of rubble ... not knowing if I would ever get out alive was awful. As for Mam and Aunt Josie ... I don't want to think about them being blown up.' She swallowed and offered a piece of chocolate to Nellie.

She shook her head. 'You enjoy it.'

Lottie sighed. 'I wonder if you can get Fry's Chocolate Cream in Heaven.'

'God only knows,' murmured Nellie, amused.

'I suppose not,' said Lottie, looking doleful. 'Gluttony's one of the seven deadly sins, so it'll probably be forbidden. I did pray, Nellie, to Our

Lady, Saint Joseph and every other saint I could remember to get me out, and they did.'

'I hope you thanked your rescuers.'

'Of course, between screams. The pain, I'd never felt anything like it. I thought I'd die when they moved me.'

'Well, you're here to tell the tale,' said Nellie, and continued to listen to her sister filling her in on her operation and what had happened after that. Nellie, although wanting to hear her sister's tale, was exhausted and only just about managed to prevent herself from nodding off by getting up off the chair. 'I don't want to leave you, Lot, but I'm going to have to. I've been travelling for hours and I'm whacked. I've got to get home yet.'

Lottie's face fell. 'I wish I could come with you but they say it'll be a few weeks yet.'

'Me too,' said Nellie, bending to kiss her. 'But as soon as you're on your feet I'll be back for you.'

'Thanks, Nell. But you will come to see me again before then?'

'You bet,' she said.

On reaching the door, Nellie turned and waved to her sister.

Lottie waved back.

Nellie left and headed for the railway station.

An hour later she got off the train at Seaforth and crossed the road, passing the auctioneers of Litherland and Outwaite, the Railway Arms and the Litherland Boys Club as she made for the Lift Bridge over the LeedsLiverpool canal. It was situated right by her father's favourite drinking house when he was home, the Red Lion.

As Nellie crossed to the other side of the canal,

she remembered her great-great-aunt telling her that in the old days before the lift bridge and a proper road was built to Ford cemetery, the coffin would be carried across a wooden bridge. The mourners would trail after it and what with the weight of them all the bridge would creak and groan as if in sympathy. No wonder some called it the Bridge of Sighs. She chided herself for thinking of coffins and burials and making herself miserable.

Of course, it was natural she would be thinking of such things, knowing her mother and aunt were buried at Ford. She would need to visit their grave and pay her respects and leave flowers. Perhaps Babs would go with her. She strode past the shops situated opposite the newly built town hall, which housed the council offices, remembering when farm cottages had stood where the shops were now. The need for more homes, promised to those who'd fought in the so-called 'war to end all wars', had resulted in the cottages' destruction. It was an attempt to turn Britain into a land fit for heroes. In the Thirties new housing had sprung up on farmland and the young couples who had moved in had needed shops: a bakery, a fishmonger's and greengrocer's, a Co-op, a hairdresser's, a chandler's, a chemist and a cobbler's-cum-shoe shop. A park had even been laid out with bowling greens, a paddling pool and swings for the children.

Her grandfather's house was a short distance away in a crescent known as Litherland Park. There was a chestnut tree either side of the front gate and, predictably, the house was called The

41

Chestnuts. Having been away for several months, Nellie viewed it with new eyes and thought it could do with a coat of paint. Not much chance of that, though, with there being a war on, she thought.

The front gate was warped and not easy to open. She placed her holdall and gasmask box on the ground and was struggling with the gate when a familiar voice said, 'So, you're back, about time too!'

Nellie spun round, saw Mrs Wainwright and groaned inwardly. She recalled that the old woman had been widowed during the Boer War and knew she should be more tolerant of her.

The old woman scurried towards Nellie with hands tucked mandarin-fashion in the sleeves of a pink cardigan. Freeing one of them, she pointed at Nellie. 'Francis did say you were coming but it seems ages ago. Your grandfather won't let you in, you know!'

'They had to find a replacement for me,' said Nellie. 'So tell me why won't Grandfather open the door?'

Mrs Wainwright's lips tightened. 'He's become very suspicious of people.' She raised thinly pencilled eyebrows. 'His language is atrocious, to put it mildly. He seldom goes out, has the groceries delivered by the messenger boy from the Co-op. Surprisingly, he's also employed the boy to work in the garden digging for victory. Although, no doubt he'll soon be going off to fight.'

'What about Babs? Surely Grandfather opens the door to her?'

Mrs Wainwright snorted, blowing down her

nostrils just like a horse. 'She has to go round the back. Sometimes the door's locked and it's bang-bang-bang-bang. Occasionally it's been after ten o'clock in the evening and the noise is enough to wake the dead. Sorry about your mother and aunt, by the way, you'll know Lottie's in a convalescent home.'

'Of course. I visited her on the way here. Now if you'll excuse me it's been a long day and I'm tired.' Nellie pushed the gate with some force with her hip and that did the trick. She bid Mrs Wainwright a good evening and picking up her baggage, made to go up the path, pausing when she heard her name being called. She turned and watched Babs running towards her and blinked back tears, determined not to cry. She'd had enough emotion for one day. Her younger sister, who bore a striking resemblance to the singing star Deanna Durbin, was looking attractive in a green jacket and matching skirt. Babs not only possessed a figure that would have looked good in a sack but also had great hair beneath the yellow and green patterned headscarf; she could have posed for the artist Titian with that red hair of hers.

Nellie dropped her baggage and held out her arms. Babs flung herself at her, squeezing Nellie so tightly that she could scarcely breathe.

'Watch it,' gasped Nellie, remembering the baby. 'You'd think you hadn't seen me for a year.'

'It does seem ages,' said Babs, freeing her and stepping back. Sparkling green eyes scrutinised Nellie from head to toe. 'You look well. You've put weight on. It must be all that country air and good farm food.'

Nellie smiled. 'Don't make me laugh. Some of the mothers couldn't cook for toffee. I look fatter because I'm having a baby.'

Babs' jaw dropped and, for several seconds, she did not speak. Then she took a deep breath. 'I wonder what Mam and Aunt Josie would have made of that news.'

Nellie's expression sobered. 'It's something I haven't dwelt on. I'd like to believe that it would have softened their hearts, but I never could tell which way they would take things I was made up about, so I gave up trying to please them. Remember how they were both completely against my training to be a kindergarten teacher?'

'That was because Great-great-aunt Adelaide was in favour of it. You know she and Mam hated each other.'

Nellie was shocked by her sister's use of the word 'hate'. 'I know they didn't get on. I put that down to them being so different.'

Babs picked up Nellie's holdall. 'You're too nice, Nell. I would have thought working with children would have made you realise that most human beings fight tooth and claw to be top dog and get what they want. Mam was jealous as hell of our great-great-aunt for owning this house. She was mad when the old woman left it to Grandfather and thought Dad should have got it. She'd have been in a different position then but, instead, he ruled the roost and she continued to fill the role of housekeeper.'

'How do you know all this?' asked Nellie, grabbing her gasmask box and following Babs up the path.

'I didn't have my nose in a book half the time I was home, or playing the piano the other half.' Babs chuckled. 'No offence meant, Nell. But I watch people and keep my ears open.' The light in her eyes died suddenly. 'Pity I wasn't home when the postman called when your letters were delivered: I never thought Mam could be so sneaky.'

Nellie sighed. 'We can't know all there is to know about people.'

Babs nodded.

'So how has Francis taken Mam's death? Although he's written to me, he hasn't said anything about his feelings,' said Nellie.

'He didn't seem to take it in at first but I think that was down to his already being exhausted and shocked by the sights he'd seen in his parish after the Luftwaffe tried to beat Liverpool into the ground. In a way, I think he was glad to be on what he called "the frontline" for once. I think he feels it not being in the Forces.'

Nellie's heart sank. 'You don't think he'll go and volunteer?'

Babs shrugged. 'I've no idea. He's always been one for playing his cards close to his chest. Anyway, let's not think about it now. You've got Grandfather to face.' She stopped in front of the house.

Nellie knocked on the door. The sound echoed through the house and she listened for her grandfather's footsteps, but all was still. She banged with her fist on the wood again, louder this time, but still there was no response. 'Mrs Wainwright said he's been refusing to open the door to people,' she said, turning to Babs.

Her sister giggled. 'He wouldn't open up to her ... thinks she's got her eye on him since Mam went ... but he has been acting peculiar ... the old biddy's right about that. He locked me out last night, so I ended up staying at a friend's.' Babs went over to one of the bay windows and, standing on tiptoe, she peered inside before signalling to Nellie. 'Come and have a look in here.'

Nellie followed her over and stretched up to look through the window. Her eyes widened as she saw newspapers spread over the sideboard, on the sofa, easy chairs and the piano. 'What on earth is he playing at?'

'God only knows. When I ask he says it saves money.'

Nellie moved away from the window. 'Is he in, d'you think?'

'Probably. I think he's going deaf as well as daft.'

'Shall we go round the back?'

Babs nodded. 'I generally do. Although, he might have the door locked.' Her pretty face darkened. 'One of these days I'll give him a fright by smashing a window pane and unbolting the door and breaking in.'

They walked round the side of the house and the setting sun dazzled Nellie as she came out of the shade onto the back of the house. Shielding her eyes with a hand, she gazed over the garden. The lawn had been dug up and rows of sprouting plants showed above the soil. At the bottom of the garden there were several fruit trees. But there was no sign of her grandfather.

46

'He must be inside,' said Nellie, absently stroking the ginger tom that sat cleaning itself on top of the bin.

'You go and look,' said Babs, placing the holdall on the ground. 'He might want a few words with you on your own. I'll have a ciggie out here. He goes mad if he sees me smoking.'

'I should think so, too,' said Nellie, becoming the big sister. 'When did you take that up?'

Babs grimaced as she reached into a pocket and produced a packet of five Woodbines and matches. 'It hasn't been much fun here on my own with him, you know? He chunters on to himself and I don't know what he's saying then. Sometimes it's been a bit scary. I'm really glad you're back.'

Nellie squeezed Babs' shoulder lightly and, picking up her holdall, walked past the outside toilet and outhouse towards the washroom door. She did not bother knocking but turned the knob. To her relief the door opened and she stepped inside. All was quiet. She hurried across the red quarry-tiled floor to the door that led to the kitchen, opened it and went through.

The kitchen was large and bright and Nellie had loved it since she was a little girl. Her great-great-aunt might not have done much in the way of housekeeping and cooking the main meals but, on occasions, she had encouraged Nellie to help her make gingerbread men and lemon cheese and jam tarts, and in autumn the sweet fragrance of stewing apples and plums had filled the kitchen. They would bottle the fruit or make pie. Suddenly she felt like crying because those times would never come again.

47

There were signs of occupation. A coal fire glowed in the black-leaded range and on the draining board was a dirty saucepan filled with water. The sink was piled high with crockery and cutlery. Nellie frowned, remembering Babs had been locked out last night. Like most men, Grandfather had never lifted a finger on the domestic front.

She sniffed. Something smelt rotten.

Following her nose she went over to the walk-in larder and there on a shelf were several plates. She peered closer at one; what was that moving? She gagged. Maggots! Her stomach heaved and she backed out of the larder in a hurry.

Something pressed between her shoulder blades. 'I'm armed. Make any sudden move and you're dead,' rasped a voice.

Nellie's heart was already beating fit to beat the band and now she thought it would burst from her chest. 'Grandfather, is that you?' she gasped.

Whatever was digging into her back was removed and, turning, she saw her grandfather holding a walking stick. 'Helen, what are you doing poking about in my larder?'

She did not answer immediately but gazed at his unkempt figure. His white hair was shaggy and he badly needed a shave; his navy-blue trousers were shiny with age and baggy at the knees, his soiled blue shirt was minus several buttons and revealed a grubby buttoned-up vest underneath. She swallowed a sigh, thinking he was a lot untidier than last time she had seen him. Since his Aunt Adelaide's death he had started to let himself go. 'I was looking for you.'

'In the larder?' he said, leaning on the walking stick.

'Something smelt horrible.' She shook her head at him. 'There's maggots in there. Whatever they're eating should have been got rid of.'

'Frightened of a few maggots, are you, girl?' He chortled. 'I'll just put a match to them and that'll get rid of them. The meat will be OK.'

Nellie gazed at him in horror. 'You've no intention of eating it? You'll poison yourself.'

The amusement ebbed from his weather-beaten features. 'If you'd had to eat what I've had to eat to survive, my girl, then you wouldn't be so fussy. Sixty years I served under sail and steam and often we went without sight of land for weeks, existing on worm ridden biscuits and dried up salted meat. When we did fetch up at an island, we had to hunt and kill our food, that's if we weren't hunted ourselves by the natives and eaten.'

Nellie had never heard her grandfather speak of such things before, but then, just like her father, he had spent most of his time at sea. 'You're saying you nearly ended up in a cooking pot?' Then immediately she shook her head. 'No! You're having me on.'

Grandfather looked injured. 'Saying I'm a liar, Helen, isn't the way to worm yourself into my good books.'

She was unrepentant. 'You must have a stomach like a goat if you can eat that meat and survive.'

He grinned, showing a set of dentures that needed a good soak. 'I'm as tough as old boots but never mind that now. How about making me a cup of tea?'

Nellie was not averse to making tea. She was desperate for a cup herself but she made sure she washed the crockery thoroughly first. She was putting milk into cups, when Babs appeared in the doorway. 'So here you are, Grandfather. Didn't you hear us banging on the front door?' She placed the gasmask holders on the table, pulled out a chair and sat down.

He scowled at her. 'Get to your feet, girl! You don't sit in my company until I tell you,' he rasped. 'The trouble with you young ones today is that you've no respect for your elders.'

'I've plenty of respect, Grandfather, but I'm tired and my sitting down isn't doing you any harm.' Babs smiled up at him. 'Anyway, aren't you pleased that Nellie's back?'

He glared at her from beneath bristling eyebrows. 'I bet you are. You don't do a tap in this house ... think you can twist me round your little finger. I'm not our Bernard, you know? He spoilt you.'

Babs folded her arms and said challengingly, 'You know that's not true. I might be his favourite but he's never spent enough time in this house to spoil me. A prezzie once or twice a year if I was lucky and he made landfall in Liverpool.'

'All right, you've made your point,' he mumbled, moving over to the table and sitting opposite her. He waved a gnarled, blue-veined hand in Nellie's direction. 'Give us that tea, girl, and sit yourself down.'

Nellie placed cups and saucers in front of him and Babs before fetching her own. Avoiding the chair with a wobbly leg, she sat to the right of

Babs and took a mouthful of tea before saying, 'So, Grandfather, is it OK with you if I come back and live here?'

'I think you'd better. I'll soon be dead if I'm left to the mercies of this one.' He indicated Babs with a jerk of his head. 'Carmel would have done for me if she could. She was trying to poison me, you know? That sister of hers was a bit of a witch, mixed potions.'

Nellie blinked at him. 'Don't be daft, Grandfather! Mam wouldn't have poisoned you.'

'He's said this before,' said Babs with a shrug. 'I've told him Aunt Josie made herbal medicines ... remedies she knew from Ireland.'

Grandfather fixed her with a stare. 'That's what she wanted you to believe, girl.' He was silent for several moments and, when he spoke again, his words stunned his granddaughters. 'Carmel wasn't the wife I wanted for Bernard. She tricked him into marriage but he was too besotted with her to see that at the time. Probably that old witch gave him a love potion.'

'What d'you mean tricked?' blurted out Babs.

'Use your nous, girl,' he growled. 'She led him astray and he had no choice but to wed her.'

'You mean she was having a baby?' asked Nellie.

'It's the only reason he would have married her. She was a handsome woman but she wasn't the right one for him. I could tell you things...' His voice trailed off.

Nellie was annoyed that the blame for her mother's pregnancy should be laid only at Carmel's door. 'It takes two to tango, Grandfather.'

'Yes, but she shouldn't have led him onto the

51

dance floor. Of course, I never let Joseph know he'd been conceived out of wedlock.' His voice cracked. 'I loved that boy. It broke my heart when he was killed.'

'We all loved Joe,' said Nellie, glancing at her sister. Babs rolled her eyes and got up and left the kitchen.

Grandfather wiped a hand across his eyes and then cleared his throat. 'So you're needing a berth. You thought of your old grandfather and are hoping he'll take pity on you.'

Nellie was not having that. 'I married Joe's best mate if you remember? Francis said *you* needed me and that's why I'm here. I had a nice berth up in Cumberland.'

The old man looked uncertain. 'So that's where you went. Where is he now?'

'Libya.'

'Not a navy man?'

'No. I'd best tell you that I'm having a baby,' said Nellie firmly. 'It's due in October. So if you feel that you can't cope with a baby in the house, then you'd better say so now and I'll find some-where else to live.' She crossed her fingers.

He was silent, staring at her. 'According to Aunt Adelaide, you were a good baby, Helen. Joseph was a rascal, into everything. Perhaps you'll have a boy. You can call him Joseph.'

Nellie thought that if Teddy was in agreement and the baby was a boy, she wouldn't mind one of his names being Joseph. Edward Joseph; she liked that. 'It is a nice name,' she said diplomatic-ally.

'A saint's name. Which reminds me ... your

52

sister ... the ugly one, is in hospital somewhere.'

Nellie almost snapped his nose off. 'Lottie is not ugly! And she's in a convalescent home. I've already seen her and you could have visited her, too, had you a mind to!'

He nodded his shaggy head. 'Don't shout. You'll keep the place tidy, Helen, do the washing and cook the meals. There's the garden ... although, I have a lad, Billy, who comes in. I'll want every penny accounted for. At least you being married and having a baby means you won't have to go out and work for the war effort.'

Nellie agreed, thinking that he definitely was not as daft as Babs said. She'd be working her guts out, doing an unpaid job that she wouldn't have chosen in a million years. Hopefully, she would feel differently about housework when Teddy came home and they had a place of their own. She went off into a dream, picturing him and her and the baby living happily together after the war.

Her grandfather's voice interrupted her imaginings. 'Teddy will be sending you money, so you can chip in with some. You have your ration book?'

'Yes, I have my ration book,' said Nellie, thinking he had a nerve expecting money from her as well as work. She drained her cup. 'I'll take my things upstairs and then I'll go to the chippie. I'm starving and the last thing I want to eat is a plateful of maggots.' She left the table before he could stop her and, picking up her things, hurried out of the room.

Nellie climbed the stairs to the first landing, which was long and wide with six doors opening on to it. Once the wooden floor had been varnished and highly polished, but now it was dull and scratched and the carpet runner needed a good beating. She deposited her things on the landing, then went into the lavatory and had to hold her nose as she put down the seat. The pan was stained and she knew her first job would be to clean it. Her feelings towards Babs were not warm at that moment. How could her sister put up with such filth! There was a toilet brush in the corner but Vim was needed. After pulling the chain, she went into the bathroom where there were double cupboards from floor to ceiling. She opened the bottom one and found a half-empty container of Vim and a couple of cloths. She scrubbed and wiped the lavatory bowl and seat and then went into the bathroom and cleaned the sink and washed her hands again. When she emerged Babs was calling her name.

Nellie found her sister in one of the back bedrooms, which was crammed with a double bed that had been passed down from their parents and shared by the three sisters until Adelaide had died, when Nellie had taken over her room. There was also a tallboy and a chest of drawers, on top of which stood a Madonna and Child, mantled in a layer of dust. Nellie did not mince her words. 'You lazy so-and-so! I can't understand you. I'm not interested in housework but I couldn't put up with the state of that toilet.'

Babs' face reddened. 'I know it's terrible. I kept meaning to do it but he made such a mess every morning and was in there for a heck of a long time that, in the end, I got into the habit of using the outside one. Sorry, Nell. I told myself Mam would have had a fit if she'd seen it but that only made me feel worse in a way. I was so upset when she and Aunt Josie were killed I did go a bit to pieces. Now you're here, I will try and pull my weight.'

Nellie's anger dissolved. 'Sorry for shouting but I don't like cleaning toilets either. I know someone has to do it but it was always Mam in the past. Maybe we took her for granted too much.'

'But she never asked us to do any housework, did she?' said Babs. 'Dad used to say that she had a martyr complex.'

Nellie nodded. 'I remember her complaining that she was the only one who ever did anything round here. I offered to do the polishing.'

'She said that in front of me. I remember the old woman told her that she should be thankful that she had a roof over her head and that she and Grandfather were prepared to feed us all and help buy our clothes.'

Nellie frowned. 'Dad must have kept her short. I suppose we shouldn't be talking about Mam in such a way. She worked hard all her life. None of us are perfect and she did do a lot for the family.'

Babs nodded. 'I wouldn't talk about her to anyone outside the family. Which reminds me, what did you think of what Grandfather said about Mam and Dad having to get married? You could have knocked me down with a feather.'

'I was stunned. She was always so religious. Poor Mam.' She glanced about the room. 'Are you OK sleeping on your own? Or would you like me to share with you for a while?'

Babs smiled. 'I'm glad you offered. I'll be

happy to share the bed with you. I never thought I'd miss our Lottie's company but I've had nightmares since Mam was killed. We can rethink when Lottie comes home.'

'Lottie's more likely to need a bed to herself because of her injuries, and she's put on more weight,' said Nellie. 'She can have my room because there's a three-foot single bed in there.'

'That's generous of you,' said Babs.

Neither suggested using the bedroom that had been their parents', while their father was at sea, both certain he would not like them doing so.

After collecting Nellie's few possessions, they discussed their sister's condition, wondering when she would be home.

Nellie took bedding from the drawer at the bottom of the tallboy. The sheets were old and darned in several places. One had been turned outsides in and sewn up the middle. Make do and mend, she thought, remembering seeing her mother sew them. Sadness swept over her and she wished that they could have been closer, but Carmel had always kept her daughters at a distance; it was the younger of her sons she had chosen to be her favourite.

'Does Francis visit much since Mam was killed?' asked Nellie.

'Not really. He's kept busy in the parish. I should think we'll be seeing him soon now you're back. He'll have things he'll want to say to you.'

Nellie hoped he would not go on at her about having married a Protestant. Once the bed was remade with clean sheets, she told Babs that she was going to the chippie and went downstairs.

She could hear the wireless, so popped her head into the parlour and saw that Grandfather had removed several sheets of newspaper so he could sit down and listen to *In Town Tonight*.

When she asked if he wanted any chips, his response was, 'Who's paying?'

'Me,' she replied.

'I'll have some, then,' he said with a grin.

She had thought as much, and, leaving the house, headed for the fish and chip shop in School Lane, where the Catholic parish church of English Martyrs was situated. It was months since she had been to church and thought it was unlikely she would set foot in this one for a time. No doubt her mother had confessed to the priest that Nellie had married outside the church. Perhaps *he* had excommunicated her? How would she know if he had? If she went to another church and did not confess what her mother would have called the error of her ways to a priest, how were they to know she'd married a Proddy? She smiled at the prospect. If she felt like going to church at some time, then she would go and not worry about being excommunicated.

Of course, when she told Francis about the baby, he would certainly have something to say about the need for it to be baptised in the Catholic faith. If her mother and grandfather had played their cards right, then Teddy probably would have agreed if Nellie had wished it. As it was, her mother had put his back up by calling him a heretic. She then got to wondering if Francis might turn up tomorrow. If he did, then she'd best be prepared and have her answers ready.

57

Chapter Three

Nellie woke to the sound of birdsong and, for a few seconds, thought she was back in Ambleside. Then the memories of yesterday trickled in and she turned her head to see if Babs was awake, but the space beside her was empty.

Nellie rose and went over to the window. Moving aside the blackout curtain she gazed down at the back garden. Most of it was in shadow but the sun was shining on the fruit trees. How peaceful it looked. Thank God that the Luftwaffe had gone away. If only Teddy were here instead of in Africa. He had loved this time of year, when a day out meant not having to come back until eleven because of the long summer evenings. She prayed that he would survive the war and her dream of having a happy home with him and the baby would come true. She felt a sudden rippling sensation in her belly and, convinced it was the baby moving, a thrill raced through her. She had been aware of similar tiny sensations but this one was stronger, which meant she must visit the doctor soon so she could be referred a reliable midwife.

She dressed, washed her hands and face and went downstairs. She found Babs in the kitchen, drinking a glass of water as she gazed through the window. The ginger tom came over to Nellie and stropped her legs.

'I think it wants some milk but there isn't any

left,' said Babs, without looking round.

'I should have thought to get some last night when I went out to the chippie,' said Nellie, checking the bread bin and finding only a crust. 'Same with bread.' She smiled wryly.

'I ate the last for breakfast.' Babs paused. 'Remember Mam and Aunt Josie taking us on the ferry across the Mersey just for a change from Seaforth Sands?'

Nellie experienced a flood of nostalgia. 'Of course, I do. I was twelve last time we went. They liked New Brighton because of the fair and it had nice sand. We always had to be careful at Seaforth because of the sinking sands. I remember at New Brighton they'd watch us paddle in the seawater pool with our skirts tucked in our knickers. I'd have to hold yours and Lottie's hands because they worried about you two going out of your depth. I'd want to have a swim but wasn't allowed to. The pair of them would gossip away, handing out jam butties when we said we were hungry and giving us drinks of Aunt Josie's homemade dandelion and burdock.'

'It was always just us girls.'

'Joe and Francis were too old for making sand-castles by then,' murmured Nellie, a catch in her throat, 'and even when Dad was home, he never came with us. Remember getting sand inside the leg of your knickers? It didn't half chaff!'

'Happy days,' said Babs softly. 'When I was a bit older, Dad used to take me places. He took me to see his ship once, and to the park to listen to a brass band. I remember him bringing me a frock home. I think it was from China. It was pink and white and I loved it but Mam told him he needed glasses because the pink clashed with my hair. I'll never forget the look on his face. I hated her for that but because he wanted me to wear it, I did. I loved the feel of the material, it was all silky soft. I wondered if she was jealous because I don't remember him bringing her anything.' Babs turned to face Nellie and a solitary tear rolled down her cheek. 'I hope if I ever marry that me and my fella don't fall out of love.'

'Perhaps they never were in love,' murmured Nellie, going and putting an arm round her sister. 'He probably got carried away and she couldn't stop him. They married because they had no choice. Sad.'

Babs nodded and wiped away the tear with a finger. She glanced at the kitchen clock. 'I should be on my way now.'

'I'll walk with you as far as the shops,' said Nellie.

'Has Grandfather given you any money?'

Nellie shook her head. 'I've still some of my own.'

'I'll get my things,' said Babs.

While she did so, Nellie checked the larder and was relieved to see that the maggoty food had gone. She went in search of shopping bags and found a couple hanging on a hook next to her grandfather's mackintosh and cap in the wash-room. Babs was ready by then and the pair of them left the house.

'So, d'you think you'll stick with this new job?' asked Nellie.

'No.' Babs turned her attractive little face

towards her as they walked along the pavement. 'I decided I wanted to move half an hour ago. When the weather's like this I hate being indoors. I quite enjoy working in the garden.'

A startled Nellie said, 'You never have before.'

'I do now.'

'You're too young for the Women's Land Army.'

'It's something to think about, though, when I'm eighteen. In the meantime I'll try something else. I'm going to hand in my notice today. I wouldn't mind working in a shop or a restaurant, or at the pictures,' said Babs enthusiastically. 'There's a dry-cleaner's in Waterloo advertising for a counter assistant. Apparently, now clothes rationing has come in, they reckon they'll be doing more business because people won't be able to buy much in the way of new clothes. Dry cleaning means people will have to give their old ones the kiss of life,' she added with a smile.

Nellie found it hard to imagine Babs finding fulfilment in a dry-cleaner's, but kept her mouth shut about that and instead said, 'This youth Grandfather's taken on...'

'Billy.' Babs' eyes danced. 'What are you getting at?'

'I just wondered what he's like,' she said casually.

'You couldn't call him handsome but he's a worker. He reminds me of someone but I can't think who.' Babs' heels click-clacked on the pavement and her hips swayed seductively in the tight-fitting black skirt two inches above her knees. She clutched the straps of the bag and gasmask container that hung from her shoulder and glanced at the two men on the opposite side of the road.

'Much too old for you,' murmured Nellie.

Babs' lips twitched. 'I wasn't even thinking about that but you must admit, Nell, there's not much talent around these days with most of the young men in the Forces.'

'There's boys of your own age. Although, perhaps I shouldn't be encouraging you to think about going out with boys. Grandfather wouldn't be in favour and Dad would have a fit.'

'Dad would only get to know if someone told him.' Her green eyes fixed on Nellie's face. 'I can't see you telling him.'

'No, I seldom write to him because he's a lousy letter writer. Even so, I hope you don't start messing about with boys yet. Mam kept a real tight rein on me at your age.'

'Poor Nellie,' said Babs, sounding sympathetic. 'But don't think you have to take her place. You're far too young. I'm really glad you're back, though. Anyway, this is where we part.' They had come to the shops and Babs fluttered her fingers at her eldest sister and headed for the bus stop. Nellie watched her for a moment and then went into the bakery.

Babs climbed aboard the bus and went upstairs, intent on sitting in a front seat. She might not be a kid anymore but still loved gazing down on the traffic and people. If she was lucky, a youth called Ritchie would be keeping her a seat. They'd first noticed each other about a month ago but it had taken him a week to pluck up the courage to say 'Morning!' to her. Another couple of days had passed before he'd commented on the weather. Several more had gone by before he had introduced himself and asked her name. She found his shyness rather endearing, but then Billy had been slow in coming forward when he had first come to work in the garden. She put a bet on with herself that if Ritchie was there today then he would ask for a date.

Her eyes gleamed as she recognised his neatly cut hairstyle and imagined him saying to the barber, 'Short back and sides, please?' His neatness was one of the things she liked about him. He turned before she reached him and smiled. His smile was another thing that she found attractive. As he removed the haversack from the window seat next to him, she said, 'Morning, Ritchie.'

'Morning, Babs.' His brown eyes wore an expression similar to a dog that had spotted a juicy bone. She brushed past him and sat down, causing him to shift a little to give her more space. He took out a packet of cigarettes and offered it to her. 'Cigarette?'

'Thanks.' She watched him flick the wheel on the lighter before placing the end of the cigarette between her lips and lowering her head to the tiny flame. His generosity was another thing that made him acceptable to her. She thanked him again and said, 'So how are you this sunny morning?'

'All the better for seeing you,' he replied.

She flashed him a dimpling smile. 'You say the nicest things.'

He flushed. 'That's because you're nice to talk to and nice to look at.'

There was a pause as they both inhaled and then

slowly allowed the smoke to trickle from their nostrils. She stretched out her legs and crossed shapely ankles. 'So are you doing anything exciting this weekend?'

'That depends on you.'

Her ears caught the slightest quiver in his voice and she warmed even more to him. 'In what way?'

'I wondered if you'd come to the pictures with me tomorrow?' The words came out in a rush.

'Maybe. What film were you planning on seeing?'

'*The Thief of Baghdad.* Sabu's playing the genie. It's on at the Trocadero in town.' He faced her. 'It'll be fun.'

'Sounds good to me,' said Babs, responding to his enthusiasm. 'There might even be a flying carpet. The heroine will be wearing Eastern costume with silky pants and a nice little top and a yashmak ... and there'll be a real nasty baddie with a beard.'

Ritchie grinned. 'So you'll come?'

'Try and stop me,' said Babs with a chuckle, flicking ash from her cigarette. 'When and where shall we meet?'

He suggested seven o'clock at the bus stop where she normally got on this bus. Babs agreed without hesitation, even though it did mean she would be getting in after eleven. She would tell Nellie that she was going out with a friend and there would be no getting locked out tomorrow night because, knowing Nellie, she would wait up until she was safely in.

Nellie fought the temptation to break off another piece of the crusty fresh loaf as she walked round to the back of the house, but failed. She felt very tired this morning and reasoned with herself that not only had she had no breakfast but was feeding two. She ticked off in her mind the food she had bought, thinking she was bound to have forgotten something: porridge oats, sugar, bread, milk, onions, two pounds of potatoes because she was not sure what was in the garden, sausages, a tin of peas, two eggs and tiny portions of bacon, butter and cheese. She had also bought a morning paper for her grandfather.

Hanging up her jacket in the washroom, all seemed quiet in the house. She pushed open the kitchen door with her hip and struggled in with the loaded shopping bags, only to stop at the sight of her brother, who was bent over the fireplace, putting a match to the fire Babs had set last night. He must have heard her gasp because his head turned and he got up from his haunches.

Neither spoke. Not for the first time, Nellie was thinking the priesthood's gain was womanhood's loss. It wasn't that Francis was conventionally handsome, but there was a rugged attractiveness about him that surely caused a flutter in the breasts of many a woman in his congregation. He wore his clerical garb but was bare-headed and she noticed his hat on the windowsill. He had thick hair, which was the same shade of reddish-brown as her own.

'So you came,' he said, coming towards her and relieving her of her burdens.

'I said I would.' She flexed fingers, stiff from

carrying the shopping bags. 'Where's Grandfather?'

'I presume he's still in bed. Babs gone to work?' Francis placed the shopping on the table.

'Yes. She said she's going to hand in her notice today and go after another job.'

'Surely it would be more sensible for her to get the other job first.'

Nellie smiled. 'You know our sister. Mam did her best to keep her in order and succeeded most of the time.'

'So now she's rebelling, you think?'

'We'll see.' Nellie pulled out a chair and sat down. She felt awkward in her brother's company in a way she had never done so before. Was it because she felt guilty?

He sat opposite her. 'So what's it feel like being back home?'

'Well, Grandfather didn't kill a fatted calf or put a ring on my finger.' She smiled wryly. 'His intention is the same as yours, I'm to take Mam's place – just the kind of life I was looking for.'

Francis' mouth tightened. 'Thousands aren't living the life they'd like to, Nellie.'

'I know that! My husband's in the desert fighting the Jerries and the Eyeties!' She paused, thinking what to say next. She could hear the crackling of the wood in the grate and suddenly was desperate for a cup of tea. 'I'm grateful, anyway, that you broke the silence by writing.'

'I would have written sooner but I couldn't understand why the pair of you couldn't come and see me so we could have discussed your situation. I just never thought you believed me such an ogre that you felt you had to run away and marry in that hole-in-the-corner fashion,' he said, riffling his fingers through his hair.

Nellie said stiffly, 'We didn't have time for discussions. He was on embarkation leave. I love Teddy. He's a good man and we wanted to spend his last few days here together.'

'I don't dispute his goodness, Nell, and I do understand your wanting to marry him. It's just that mixed marriages always cause trouble.' His expression was sombre.

'There wouldn't have been any trouble if Mam hadn't thought she was in the right,' said Nellie hotly. 'It's not as if Teddy isn't a Christian, but she called him a bloody heretic as if he was the greatest sinner in the world. I found out yesterday that she was no angel, so what right had she to judge Teddy?'

'What do you mean, she was no angel?' Francis' voice was dangerously low. 'You shouldn't speak ill of the dead, especially after the way she died.'

Nellie wished she had kept her mouth shut and fiddled with the knife on the table. 'I'm sorry. I shouldn't have said that. None of us is perfect.'

'I want to know what you meant by it!' Francis hit the table with his fist causing her to draw away from him.

'That's enough,' growled their grandfather's voice from the doorway, taking them both by surprise. 'A man of the cloth should be able to control his temper.'

Francis stared at him aghast and his hands clenched on the folds of his cassock. 'Forgive me, Grandfather. I've been under a great deal of strain the last few months.'

'I know, I know,' said Grandfather. 'You had to identify your mother's and aunt's bodies and you saw sights in your own parish that were enough to turn a man's stomach.'

'A head! I found the head of a child once,' muttered Francis.

'Forgive me.' Nellie was horrified and reached out a hand across the table and placed it on his arm. She stroked his sleeve.

'Of course, he must forgive you,' said Grandfather. 'It's what Joseph would do. He taught me what can be gained by forgiveness.'

She heard the hiss of Francis' breath and as their eyes met she guessed what he was thinking: Joe had found it easy to forgive people because he was the kind of sinner who confessed regularly and then blithely went out to sin again. She winked and the muscles in Francis' face relaxed.

'Of course, I forgive you.' He squared his shoulders. 'Now, Nellie, what have you got in these bags? I hadn't got as far as seeing if there was any milk for the tea. I'm hungry, too. You wouldn't have a loaf in there, would you?'

She gave him a knowing look. 'As if you couldn't smell it.'

Grandfather leaned across the table and sniffed. 'I can smell it.' He reached for one of the bags. 'Butter. Did you get butter, Helen? The stuff Billy brought has all gone. Crusty bread with butter makes my mouth water.'

She tapped the back of his hand. 'Butter is on the ration, which means there's not a lot.' Getting to her feet, she began to unpack the shopping.

Francis took the bread knife and the loaf she passed him. The expression in his eyes was quizzical as he said, 'I think the mice have been at this.'

'Very funny. I am eating for two.'

He froze a moment before beginning to slice the loaf. 'You didn't mention that in your letters.'

'We didn't jump the gun. It's due October ... and before you start talking about its baptism, I'll tell you now I'll make no decisions about that until it's born and I've discussed it with Teddy.'

He nodded. 'OK. Is there any jam? I seem to remember Mam making some last autumn.'

'It didn't set properly, so it's runny.'

'I'm not fussy,' said Francis, as he disappeared into the larder.

Nellie saw that the fire was still not ready to boil water, so made do with half a cup of milk and more bread. She was relieved that she had managed to get away without explaining to Francis why their mother was no angel.

As the three of them sat at the table eating, Nellie told Francis about having seen Lottie. 'I thought she might have been out of bed by now.'

'She has to rest, Nellie, but they do get her up and I've wheeled her out in a wheelchair. Naturally she's still broken-hearted about Mam and Aunt Josie, but thanking Our Lady and Saviour for her survival. Time will heal but it'll take a while. So many are grieving for the loss of their loved ones.'

'Were there many lives lost in your parish?' asked Nellie.

He gave a sharp nod. 'There's an Italian couple

I've been visiting weekly since the May blitz. They lost a son in the bombing.'

'A child?' asked Nellie.

He shook his head. 'No, but Michelangelo helped out at the boys' club and was the apple of their eye. At the beginning of the war he was put in a POW camp on the outskirts of Liverpool, despite having lived here most of his life but then he was moved. His crime was that he hadn't registered for British nationality.' There was a note of bitterness in Francis' voice.

Nellie's heart went out to the parents. 'How unfair, and how sad that he should die. But how did it happen if he was in a POW camp away from Liverpool?'

'He was freed after a year and he joined the merchant navy. His ship was damaged by a torpedo, so he was on leave. It would have been better if he'd stayed on the Isle of Man.' Francis' expression was bleak.

'I'm sorry. I shouldn't have mentioned the blitz.' Nellie covered his large hand with hers.

Grandfather mumbled, 'No use talking about long ago sad things.'

Nellie and Francis glanced at him, both wondering what he was referring to. They knew scarcely anything about his early life and guessed that now was not the time to ask.

An hour later Francis left, saying he would call again in a week or two. As soon as he had gone, Nellie made a start on the housework. While she polished and scrubbed, she thought about visiting the doctor and the need to buy maternity clothes. She waited until the afternoon before going into the parlour where her grandfather was listening to the wireless and reading the newspaper she had bought. She began to gather the old ones from surfaces.

'What d'you think you're doing?' he asked, lowering the *Daily Post*, and pushing himself up out of his chair and fumbling for his walking stick.

'This is a lovely room and you've got some lovely things. It's a shame to cover them all up,' she said, folding the sheets of newsprint.

His face worked and spittle appeared at the corners of his mouth. 'It saves money having them covered, saves on polish and dusters! I won't have you interfering with my decisions, Helen.'

'Come off it, Grandfather. I won't polish every day. I like to see the things you've brought back from your travels.' She picked up a sandalwood box and sniffed it. 'Doesn't the smell take you back to the Far East?' She put that down and picked up a conch shell. 'What about this?' She stroked the blush pink inside of the shell and then held it to her ear. 'I remember being told that if I did this, I'd hear the sea.'

'Load of rubbish,' he muttered. 'You can't hear the sea in a shell but I do remember where I picked that up. It was in Jamaica.'

Nellie's eyes sparkled. 'You've had such an exciting life. Hiding your things away is like saying you want to forget that life.'

'I'm not going to do that, girl. It's inside here.' He tapped his skull.

'Dad used to always point at this if I was ever in here with him.' Nellie picked up a brass ornament of the three wise monkeys. 'He'd say, "See

71

no evil, hear no evil, speak no evil", and then he'd squeeze my shoulder really hard and talk about the man being the boss of the house and women needing to heed what they said. He'd talk about the dangers of sinning and Hell until I could almost feel the flames.'

'Aye, well, Helen, he had more experience of sin than you did. Foreign ports can be right dens of iniquity, not that I'm saying our Bernard would do more than get roaring drunk,' he added hastily. 'Anyway, if you're going to disturb my peace by messing about with my things, make sure you polish those monkeys ... and you can give some money towards the polish.'

She was indignant. 'I've already paid for the shopping I bought this morning. I do need some money for myself, Grandfather. I'll need maternity clothes and a layette for the baby. I'll need a cot and a pram, although, it probably won't be easy getting the latter.'

He scowled. 'You should have thought of all this before you went and ran off with Teddy Lachlan and got yourself in the family way, girl.'

Nellie rolled her eyes. 'I wouldn't have had to run away if you had stuck up for me.' She thought of the last time she had seen her mother; a lump rose in her throat and she was unable to say another word. Instead, she left the parlour with her arms full of newspapers, thinking that tomorrow she would visit the doctor's surgery up the road.

The next day Nellie's pregnancy was confirmed and the doctor congratulated her, recommended a midwife and told her that she was entitled to an extra pint of milk a day. She would also be allowed sixty extra clothing coupons for maternity wear and to buy the baby a layette. That news came as a relief.

When Babs arrived home at two o'clock the following afternoon, Nellie asked her if she would like to go shopping for maternity clothes with her.

'I can't, Nell,' said Babs. 'I got that job, by the way. The boss said that he thought I'd be good for business. It doesn't sound exciting but at least I'll be meeting different people. Anyway, I'm going to the pictures tonight with a friend and I've also told Billy I'll help him in the garden later this afternoon. I'll need the time to get myself ready to go out that I'd be giving up if I went with you. We can go next Saturday afternoon.'

Nellie was disappointed but decided that next week would do just as well. 'OK. So when will Billy get here?'

'As soon as he finishes his deliveries for the Co-op,' said Babs, and went upstairs to change.

Nellie stood at the top of the garden, listening to Billy talking to Babs. Since setting eyes on the seventeen-year-old, she knew what her sister meant about him reminding her of someone but, just like her sister, she had no idea to whom. He was a well set-up young man with floppy mousy hair and straight eyebrows.

'You want to try and persuade Mr Callaghan it would be a good idea to have some pullets here. He really should have bought them weeks ago but there's some still to be had,' he was saying.

'But how would we look after them? Where would they live and what would we feed them on?' asked Babs, who was kneeling on an old cushion, weeding between the rows of peas and runner beans.

'It tells you in the *Crosby Herald*. I did woodwork at school, so I wouldn't mind having a go at building them a house. They'll need an enclosed run as well because we wouldn't want them digging up the vegetables.'

Babs wrinkled her nose. 'I doubt I'll be able to persuade him. They'll cost money and he doesn't like spending money.'

'Eggs are getting as rare as gold dust. He'd have a ready supply and a nice chicken at Christmas, too,' said Billy.

'It sounds good, but...'

Nellie interrupted her sister. 'I'll talk to Grandfather. Most likely if I offer to go half with the cost and appeal to his greedy nature by painting pictures of yummy yolky eggs with soldiers, he'll agree.'

Billy looked her way and she saw that his eyes were blue-grey. 'I'm Babs' sister,' said Nellie, smiling. 'I'm sure she's mentioned me.'

'Yes, Mrs Lachlan. It's nice to meet you. Just let me know when Mr Callaghan gives you the go ahead,' he said.

'I'll go and ask him now.' Nellie left Babs and Billy alone, convinced by the way they looked and spoke to each other that there was nothing of a romantic nature between them, but then at that age maybe they were hiding their feelings.

She found her grandfather gazing down at the letter that had come that morning. She had recognised her father's handwriting on picking up the envelope from the mat. She wondered what he had to say but knew the old man would tell her soon enough if there was anything he thought she should know. Bernard had written to his wife regularly once a month. Carmel would read them and then rip them up and put them on the fire. Nellie presumed they had been duty letters. It saddened her to think that her parents might have realised very early on in their marriage that it had been a mistake but were trapped because the church did not accept divorce. At least she and Teddy had married for love. She felt a niggle of anxiety, wondering when she would hear from him. It seemed ages since his last letter but maybe with his being in the desert, it wasn't easy to get letters to a ship.

'What is it you want, Helen?' asked Grand-father, without looking up.

'Billy thinks we should buy some pullets. We'd have our own eggs and a chicken at Christmas.'

'Can he get them cheap?'

'I don't know what cheap is. I'll give something towards the cost,' said Nellie.

'Do it then.'

Nellie could not conceal her surprise. 'Are you feeling well?'

He glanced up at her from beneath bristling eyebrows. 'What's that supposed to mean, girl?'

'I expected to have to persuade you.'

He grunted. 'Impudent miss! By the way, Bern-ard's hoping to make it home soon. This letter is dated two months ago. If you ask me, he writes a few lines and then puts it aside and then does an-other couple when he's got nothing better to do.'

'Does he mention me?'

'Of course he does. He'll give you a right earful when he comes home. Wouldn't be surprised if he thinks he can have the marriage annulled.'

Nellie's stomach flipped over but she said defiantly, 'I was over twenty-one when I got married, so he couldn't have stopped me.'

Her grandfather cackled, 'That's what makes him mad. But you weren't married in our church, were you, girl? So you're not married in the eyes of God.'

'We were married by special licence in St Andrew's on Linacre Road, so it's legal and that's good enough for me.'

He muttered, 'Bernard won't agree. His being captain of a ship makes him think he can order things the way he wants. He forgets when he's home that we've all managed to live our lives without him.'

'And we'll carry on doing so, too,' said Nellie, tilting her chin. 'What does he have to say about Mam and Aunt Josie?'

He folded the letter and did not answer her.

Nellie walked out of the parlour, guessing that whatever her father had written concerning the death of his wife was best not being repeated to his children. Could he have referred to what their grandfather had told them the day she had returned from Ambleside? Could be that he was glad to have his freedom. The thought grieved her, but she put it from her mind as she went into the garden and told Billy to go ahead with buying the pullets and building them a home. He looked delighted and promised to get onto it as soon as possible. She was glad that at least she had made him happy.

That evening Nellie wrote a letter to Teddy telling him that she was now at her grandfather's house and that she had seen a doctor and would most likely have a talk with the midwife during the coming week. She told him about Babs changing her job, of her visit to Lottie and of Billy's plan to get them some pullets, adding that he seemed to know only slightly more about gardening than herself but he was strong and a great help when it came to digging and weeding. Both of them had asked questions of Grandfather, but his years at sea meant he knew little more than them, so she'd have to become an avid reader of the advice given weekly for amateur 'Diggers for Victory' in the local *Crosby Herald*.

She made no mention of the conversation she'd had with Grandfather concerning her father's homecoming, deciding it was best not to annoy him with that news.

Having finished her letter, she went and had a bath before joining her grandfather in the parlour and listening to a murder mystery on the radio, thinking she probably would have enjoyed a trip to the pictures with Babs, herself.

'You're a perfect gentleman, Ritchie, but I think it would be best if you didn't see me home,' said Babs, as they stood in front of the town hall that evening.

'But it's dark, Babs. I hate the thought of someone jumping out and hurting you,' he said earnestly.

'You're a sweetie,' she said, planting a kiss on his cheek, 'but I think I'll be safe enough. It's not pitch black at this time of year and we have a real nosy neighbour, who never seems to sleep. If Grandfather knew I was seeing a fella, then I wouldn't be able to go out with you again.' She squeezed his hand before releasing it. 'Now go.'

'But when will I see you again?' asked Ritchie.

She thought about that. 'Thursday. I won't go home but stay in Waterloo. I'll meet you outside the Plaza.'

He hesitated but then nodded. 'OK!'

Babs had not missed that pause. 'We can go Dutch. Or even just have a walk. We'll see what the weather's like.' She kissed him lightly on the lips and left him standing there, knowing he was staring after her. She hoped he would not take it into his head to follow her. She did not want him knowing where she lived because, sooner or later, she knew that she'd have to break it off with him. She liked him a lot but had no intention of things getting too serious between them. She wanted to have some fun while she was young and no doubt he'd be joining the Forces within the year.

Chapter Four

As Babs walked along the pavement the following Thursday evening, she became aware that despite the lateness of the hour, Mrs Wainwright had her in her sights. She was leaning on her gate and Babs knew there would be no getting past her without some comment being made.

'I wouldn't like to be in your shoes,' said Mrs Wainwright. 'I'd get a walloping if I'd dared stay out until this hour when I was a girl.'

'When was that? The Stone Age?' said Babs with an innocent air.

The old woman's hands tightened on the gate. 'Don't you give me your cheek, girl. Your father's just gone into the house and I'll speak to him about you when I see him. The whole family's been far too soft with you. Short skirts, smoking and staying out late! It's asking for trouble.'

'It's none of your business what I do, Mrs Wainwright. Good night,' said Babs airily.

She walked away, humming a tune from the film she had just seen as if she didn't have a care in the world. The truth was that she was going to have to put on an act. When her dad was around, she always felt she had to please him and pretend to be the person he believed her to be. It wasn't that she was exactly scared about how he'd react if she let him down ... no, that wasn't true, she was a teeny bit scared. She just wished his expectations of her weren't so unrealistic. Of course, she was looking forward to seeing him because he was her dad but, in the past, his arrivals had always created an atmosphere in the house that was un-comfortable; perhaps she was worrying too much. With Mam no longer around, he might be com-pletely different. Then Babs remembered Nellie and her heart sank. There was no doubt in her mind that their father wouldn't pull his punches when he faced his eldest daughter.

Babs burst into the washroom to the accompaniment of mild chirping and clucking from the pullets in the wooden crate, waiting to be housed in the home Billy was constructing for them. She hoped Nellie had thought about keeping an eye on the cat where the birds were concerned. There was a dozen of them, eleven hens and one cockerel. They were ugly things, in-between that fluffy and cuddly stage and full-grown strutting birds.

She hung up her jacket, her ears alert for the sound of raised voices but, to her surprise, all was quiet. She opened the kitchen door, only to pause in the doorway, as the first person her gaze fell on was Nellie.

She was standing against the table, her hands gripping the wood. Her face was pale and strained but when she spotted Babs her expression changed to one of relief. 'So there you are! I told Dad there was nothing to worry about and probably you'd missed a bus.'

'I did,' lied Babs. She and Ritchie had walked back from the picture house in Waterloo, taking a shortcut using the lane that ran along the allotments and across the canal via the footpath that came out on Field Lane by the park. They had stood gazing down at a coal barge for a few minutes, and his arm had slipped round her waist as he pulled her to him for a stolen kiss.

'You should have allowed extra time in case you missed a bus,' said Bernard.

She sensed his disapproval but pretended not to have heard him. 'Did I hear you right, Nellie? Did you say Dad's home?' She did not wait for her sister to answer but hurried forward to where she could see Bernard standing by the fireplace. He was a fine figure of man with broad shoulders and a strong frame. He was clad in a navy blue jacket and trousers and had loosened his tie so that his white shirt gaped at the throat, revealing the neck of his vest. He had a Clark Gable moustache and Brylcreem-slicked-back reddish brown hair, flecked with silver at his temples. He was not exactly handsome but he had attractive, if stern, features. 'It's lovely to have you back, Dad!' She stood on tiptoe and kissed his chin.

He hugged her to him and then held her at arm's length. 'You get prettier each time I come home.'

Babs sought for the right word. 'And you get more distinguished looking,' she said.

He looked pleased. 'We're a good-looking pair. That's why I was worried about you being out late. There's blokes around who'll take advantage of a lovely girl like you.'

'I don't let them get close enough, Dad. Mam warned me to keep my distance.'

'As long as you remember what she said, even though she's gone. Nellie didn't heed her and look what happened to her.'

Bernard frowned in his eldest daughter's direction. It infuriated him that she had dared to go against her Catholic upbringing and that, as a married woman, he had no control over her. She had moved away from the table to put on the kettle. He could see the slight swell of her belly and was reminded of his dead wife. Carmel had looked just the same when she had first broken the news that she was pregnant. He had been mad for

81

her then and had willingly married her, but he had soon realised his mistake after Joseph was born. No wonder he felt that women couldn't be trusted. It was the same with Lottie. He had always wondered if she was his child. She had supposedly come early but was so different physically to his other two daughters that he couldn't help doubting his wife's fidelity. Still, he'd been blessed with Babs and had done his duty by her and the church all these years. He hugged her against him.

'I'll never forget Mam,' said Babs, a catch in her voice. 'Or Aunt Josie. Will you be visiting the grave, Dad?' She looked up at him from lovely green eyes, the same colour as his own.

He hesitated, unsure what to say. His mother had died when he was only young and he hated cemeteries. Besides, he was glad to be rid of Carmel and her carping sister and felt it was hypocritical to go and visit their last resting place. 'Not just yet, Babs. I'm still coming to terms with their deaths.'

'I haven't been yet,' said Nellie, wishing she and her father could be closer. 'Perhaps the three of us could go together?'

'Didn't you hear what I said, Nellie? I don't want to go just yet.' Her suggestion exasperated him.

'I thought that visiting the grave would help you to come to terms with Mam's death,' she said. 'But if you don't want to go that's up to you.' She turned away from him and fetched a packet of cocoa from a shelf.

'I didn't say I *didn't* want to go,' he snapped. 'Don't mention this subject again.'

Nellie nodded, convinced he had no intention of paying his respects to her mother. She turned to her grandfather. 'Cup of cocoa, Grandfather?'

His rheumy blue eyes fixed on her face. 'I don't see why not. But remember, Helen, what I said.'

She stared at him. 'About what?'

His brow puckered and his mouth worked and then his face brightened. 'Angels. That was it.'

'Angels!' exclaimed Bernard. 'What the hell are you talking about, Father?'

There was a crafty expression on the old man's face and he tapped the side of his nose. 'Careless talk cost lives. I'll say no more.'

Bernard shook his head in disbelief. 'Please yourself.' He turned to Nellie. 'Have you anything for me to eat?'

She said, 'How about jam on bread? With not knowing when you'd arrive, I haven't much in the larder.'

He looked annoyed and, noticing his expression, Babs said, 'I'll make some jam butties.'

'Isn't there anything else?' demanded Bernard.

'There's a bit of bacon but that's for Grandfather's Sunday breakfast treat,' said Nellie.

'Can't take that away from him, I suppose,' muttered Bernard, glancing at his father.

'No, you can't,' said the old man, hunching a shoulder. 'That's mine. I bet you eat better at sea these days than I ever did.'

'Depends on the cook and the weather,' said Bernard, digging his hands in his pockets. 'I suppose it's too late for the chippie.'

Nellie nodded and Babs went and fetched the jam from the larder.

Supper passed off without anything contentious being said and then everyone went to bed. As she and her sister undressed, Babs said, 'What did Dad say before I came in?'

'What d'you think he said?' murmured Nellie, leaving the bottom two buttons on her pyjama jacket undone and stroking her belly, wishing it was Teddy who was home and not her father. She'd love to relive that short honeymoon in Southport.

'That you're a bad example to me?' Babs sat cross-legged on the bed. 'I wish he'd stop thinking I'm so blinking marvellous.'

Nellie laughed. 'You're not? Anyway, that was the least of what he said. Not only am I a disgrace and a disappointment but also that, most likely, I've been excommunicated and won't be able to go to Mass. I'm wayward, disobedient ... and I'm too much like mother. What do you think of that last one?'

'He's crazy thinking you're like her. You're easy-going. Mam never was.' She changed the subject. 'What did you think of Grandfather going on about angels and careless talk costing lives?'

'Maybe he was thinking about Mam. Remember him saying that she was no angel? She could have been a bit of a girl in her day and only got religion when life stopped being fun. If she did have to get married, it could explain why she was so strict with us,' said Nellie.

Babs yawned. 'Poor Mam. She must have felt the shame of it. I suppose I'll have to go to Mass with Dad tomorrow?'

'What about visiting Mam's and Aunt Josie's

grave with me?'

'OK. Dad hasn't said how long he's going to be home, has he?'

'No.' Nellie prayed that it would not be too long.

Her prayer was to be answered.

Within the week Bernard was back at sea but he had made his presence felt during the days he was home, especially after he'd had a few drinks at the Red Lion. The old man had grumbled his disapproval of his son's drinking and what a thorough waste of money it was as he'd stood watching Nellie mop up Bernard's vomit. She and Babs had also had to help their father to bed one night. Nellie had received a clout on the ear from his flailing arm for her pains. She wondered how he related his religious beliefs to his excessive drinking and his reluctance to visit his wife's grave. She and Babs had wept real tears when they'd gone to pay their respects and Nellie knew she would have to go through it all again when Lottie came home.

A few days after Bernard had departed, Babs let slip the news that she would be working Saturday afternoon and would be going straight out afterwards with a friend.

'I was hoping you'd come shopping with me,' said Nellie, wondering about this nameless friend.

'Sorry, Nell. It's this new job. I have to work Saturday afternoon.'

Nellie was disappointed but understood. Smiling, she said, 'At least that means you won't be spending money on clothes.'

Babs grimaced. 'I don't have money to spend

once I've handed over for my keep to Grand-father.'

'You have my sympathy but we all have to pay our way. Wouldn't it be great if women got equal pay with men ... but even teachers don't get that.'

'Perhaps one day after the war,' drawled Babs, and left for work.

The following morning, to Nellie's delight, several letters from Teddy arrived. Some had been redirected from High View and she wasted no time in putting them in some semblance of order and opening them one by one. They all started with the same words,

My darling Nellie,
I hope you are well. I am OK, so you're not to worry about me. I am missing you more than words can say and wish I was with you.

The letters consisted of only one page but were written on both sides in her husband's neat hand. The most important letter was his reply to the news that she was expecting their baby.

I was so overjoyed to get the news of the baby that I danced around the tent, yipping and yowling like a madman. You couldn't have sent me better news. It's pretty rough out here. Sand gets into everything and it's so hot that ... well, I won't go into how unpleasant it makes things. I have dreams of Britain's cool green fields and woods and strolling arm in arm with you. Now I can imagine three of us enjoying the country-side. Dreams are what I live on, Nellie. When this war's over, we'll find a little place that's just our own.

It would be nice if it had a garden but the main thing is the three of us being together as a family. I know that's what you want too.

I can't really say much about things here ... careless talk costs lives ... but you must take care of yourself and keep the letters coming. They mean so much to me. I have enclosed a photo that one of the blokes took. Lots of love, kisses, hugs,

Yours for ever, Teddy.

With eyes that shone with tears, Nellie gazed down at the photo of her husband. He was wearing shorts and a shirt. His hair was already showing signs of being bleached by the sun and his skin looked tanned. She kissed the picture and propped it up against the statue of the Madonna and child. Then, after reading the letters, she put them in a cardboard box and placed it inside the tallboy. After doing that she sat quietly on the bed, smiling as she imagined Teddy dancing about. She could only echo his wish that he was here with her.

She went downstairs and found the parlour unusually deserted, so she sat at the piano. Memories of days gone by when her great-great-aunt had been alive were evoked as she played 'Come into the Garden, Maud'. 'Wait till the sun shines, Nellie' reminded her of the music hall and Teddy. 'Run, Rabbit, Run' recalled the children she had left up in Cumberland. She wondered how they were getting on and how old they would be when they came home. As the music echoed round the parlour, her anguish at being parted from Teddy eased a little, and after a while, she closed the piano and, collecting her purse and shopping bag, she left the house.

The next day Nellie received a surprise visit from the midwife. It appeared that the doctor had got in touch with the woman and given Nellie's details to her. The midwife examined her and seemed satisfied with Nellie's condition. She talked about what Nellie could expect as her pregnancy advanced and about the birth. The woman was so down-to-earth that Nellie felt reassured she was in good hands.

With that hurdle over, Nellie went out into the garden and found her grandfather keeping an eye on Billy as he put the final touches to the henhouse. He had already enclosed an area of the garden for a run where they scratched about in the soil. First thing that morning, she had made them a mash consisting of a mixture of porridge oats, corn and greens, which they appeared to have enjoyed.

'I'm looking forward to my first egg,' said the old man, rubbing his gnarled hands together.

'Aren't we all,' said Nellie, noticing that he looked a lot cleaner and tidier since her return, although his hair could do with a trim. 'We'll need to give Billy some.'

Grandfather's overgrown eyebrows twitched together like hairy caterpillars. 'Don't be making promises in front of the lad, Helen. We don't know how many eggs there are going to be. After all they're my birds.'

'Our birds,' said Nellie, winking at Billy. 'I paid half the cost. Billy got them for us and is making them a home so he's entitled to a share. Fair's fair, Grandfather.'

The old man seemed about to argue with her but she gave him a stern look and, grumbling beneath his breath, he stomped away into the house. She had been about to mention her trip into town that afternoon but on second thoughts decided it was best to keep quiet. He'd only moan and tell her not to waste the fare and to shop local. She could see the sense in that but today she felt a need to get away. Besides, if she went into town, she could always call in on Francis and tell him of their father's visit. If he wasn't in, then she could slip a note through the presbytery door saying she had called and ask whether he had any news of Lottie, as she hadn't had a chance to visit her again yet.

Nellie got ready and caught the bus into town. She did not have much in the way of money to spend and she had yet to apply for her extra coupons, so she limited herself to buying one maternity smock and skirt, a brassiere and a couple of pairs of big knickers. There was little in the way of cots and prams to be seen, even if she'd had the money to buy new. It occurred to her that it might be worth checking up in the attic rooms before advertising for second-hand items or buying any baby clothes.

She walked from C&A Modes to her brother's parish near Scotland Road. Unfortunately, he was out, but she left a note with the housekeeper and caught the bus home. That evening Nellie showed her purchases to Babs.

Her sister shook her head dolefully. 'Blinking

heck, Nell. I'm never going to get pregnant if I have to wear clothes like that.'

Nellie agreed that they weren't flattering. 'But they're not meant to be and as soon as the baby's born, hopefully, I'll be like Mam and get my figure back dead quick.'

Babs looked thoughtful. 'It'll be strange having a baby in the house. I've never known there to be one.'

Nellie smiled. 'That's because the last baby was you.'

'Was I a good and beautiful baby?'

'There's no need to fish for compliments,' said Nellie. 'You've seen the photograph. All those curls! When Dad eventually saw you he said that your hair should never be cut.'

Babs said ruefully, 'I hated it when I was twelve. Mam thought it was lovely that I could sit on it but it was a real nuisance getting it dry, remember?'

'I remember you hacking at it with a pair of blunt scissors,' said Nellie.

Babs' eyes danced. 'I got you into trouble, didn't I? Mam caught you trying to tidy it up and hit the roof.'

Nellie rolled her eyes. 'I was seventeen but she still whacked me with a hairbrush across the head! I saw stars.'

'I did confess I'd done it myself.'

Nellie nodded. 'You might have been a pest at times but you always did try and make things right.' She folded the maternity clothes and placed them in a drawer. 'I'm going to bed.'

'Me too. Did you remember to get the hens into their little house?'

Nellie gasped. 'No, I didn't.' She headed for the bedroom door.

'Stop, stop, stop!' cried Babs. 'I did it. I was just seeing if you'd remember. Billy made a good job of the henhouse.'

'You can say that again.'

Babs nodded and found herself comparing Billy with Ritchie. She liked them both but neither was her Mr Right. She got into bed, watching her eldest sister put on a spotless white nightdress. 'What's happened to your pyjamas?'

'This is looser and more comfortable. I wore it on my wedding night and I thought I might as well make use of it, rather than keep it until Teddy comes home.'

Babs said, 'It's pretty. You putting the light out?'

Nellie did so. Babs wished life was more exciting. Should she let Ritchie kiss her more passionately next time? She was still thinking about that when she fell asleep.

Babs duplicated the woman's name and address on the bottom half of the slip, tore that off and handed it to her. The other half of the slip she pinned to the jacket and said 'Good morning!' as the customer left the shop, closing the door behind her and setting the bell at the top of the door frame jangling.

Babs went into the back of the shop and hung the garment on a hanger on a rail. She had worked at the dry-cleaner's six weeks now and was fed up. Outside the sun was shining and she longed to be in the fresh air. Her mind was busily working on several thoughts at once. A fortnight

91

ago, she had read in the *Crosby Herald* that due to the government wanting to encourage people not to go away for their holidays and thereby save fuel and pressure on transport, various groups had got together to arrange family fun days and open air dancing in parks. She had celebrated her seventeenth birthday whilst Nellie had been in Cumberland but had never had a proper dancing lesson in her life, although Nellie had taught her a few steps. Babs did not feel very proficient but was keen enough to give it a go, so she had got Ritchie to agree to go dancing that evening in the grounds of Potter's Barn in Waterloo. The name was a local one for a building that was supposed to be an exact replica of the farmhouse that the British troops had used during the battle of Waterloo. History was a subject Babs was not particularly interested in so she could not remember its real name, which was French anyway. She decided it should be fun and could not wait for the evening to start.

The other thing on Babs' mind was changing her job. Without having said a word to Nellie, she had made enquiries about joining the Women's Land Army after remembering hearing stories of youths lying about their age to go and fight in the Great War. Poor lads, thought Babs, so many had died so young. Still, that wasn't going to happen to her and she saw no reason why, at seventeen, she shouldn't be doing her bit for the war effort. She wanted to work on the land. There was something so satisfying about planting seeds and seeing vegetables and fruit grow and picking the fruits of your labour. She had discovered that it was a Lady

Denman who was in charge of the scheme. She had devised a minimum wage of twenty-eight shillings a week for her army of women. Of course, male farm labourers earned ten shillings more, but Babs was not going to get herself worked up about that; it would be the same no matter what job she went for.

Out of the twenty-eight shillings, Babs would have to pay for her board and lodgings, but as she didn't earn much in her present job, and she handed most of it over to Grandfather for her keep, that was something she was philosophical about. She would be provided with a uniform and wearing a uniform appealed to Babs, although she had no desire to go into the Forces and be sent far away from home. The farmlands of Lancashire were almost on her doorstep, so she was convinced she would be able to come home every week and see Nellie. She felt slightly guilty about leaving her sister alone with Grandfather, but no doubt that wouldn't be for long. Lottie would be out of hospital soon and, in October, Nellie would have her baby to look after and so wouldn't have time to miss her youngest sister.

Babs decided to join straight away. She had a perfect excuse for not being able to produce her birth certificate if those in charge wanted to see it because it had been in her mother's capacious handbag, along with other important papers and their ration books, that evening in May when she had stayed at her Aunt Josie's house and the bombers had struck. Hopefully the Land Army would take her on and, if they suggested she get a replacement and send it on later, she would conveniently forget to do so. She couldn't imagine them considering her so important that they would chase the matter up.

That evening as Ritchie taught Babs to foxtrot to the music of the band from the local dance hall, he held her much too close for her liking. The air was tangy with the salty smell of the river and the scent of roses. She could see the faint outline of the moon in the sky and really, she thought, if Ritchie had been her Mr Right her heart would have been beating ten to the dozen with excitement but, as it was, she could only feel his hammering away. She glanced around in an attempt to distract herself from the thought of her breasts being squashed against his chest, certain that her mother would not have approved. But then she would have been shocked at so many couples dancing out in the open air.

'Babs, I'm crazy about you,' whispered Ritchie against her ear. 'I wish we could get married.'

'Married!' squeaked Babs, treading on his foot.

Ritchie winced. 'I shouldn't have blurted it out like that but you look so-so lovely, I couldn't help myself.'

She gazed up into his pleasant face and saw the yearning in his eyes. A sigh escaped her as she decided that it was definitely best for him if she went away. 'It's nice of you to say these things, Ritchie, but I'm only just seventeen.'

'People do get married at seventeen. I'd like us to get married before I get called up.'

'I don't think my father would agree,' she said.

'But he's at sea, isn't he? Does he have to know?' Ritchie had come to a stop.

Babs patted his collarbone and gently drew away from him. 'Let me think about it. Do you have the time? I daren't be late tonight.'

Ritchie checked his watch. 'It's only half nine.'

She pretended dismay. 'It'll be ten by the time I get home. I'm going to have to go. The dance will soon be coming to an end anyway because it's getting dark.'

'I'll come with you.'

Babs knew she had to allow him to walk her most of the way home. On the way, she gave him no chance to bring up the subject of marriage again. It was ridiculous. She was far too young and, besides, she didn't love him. She chattered away about her job and the garden, telling him about the henhouse that Billy had made. Ritchie asked who Billy was and how old he was. 'Ancient,' she said. 'He's Grandfather's old gardener.'

He accepted that because so many young men's jobs were being taken by men coming out of retirement. He stopped her on the footbridge and drew her into his arms. She allowed him to kiss her but when his hand brushed her breast she pulled away. 'None of that, Ritchie. I'm a respectable Catholic girl. Now I must get home.'

She hurried ahead but he soon caught her up. 'Sorry,' he said. She smiled and said that she forgave him. He reached for her hand and she allowed him to hold it. When they came to the town hall, she bid him goodnight.

'But when will I see you again?'

She looked up into his earnest young face and said that she'd see him on Sunday afternoon and arranged a meeting place, but she had no intention of keeping the date. As she walked the rest of the way home, she knew that she should have told him to his face that she did not want to see him again but it was easier to lie rather than see his hurt expression. She thought of Nellie and knew that her sister would try to stop her leaving if she could, so she decided the best thing would be just to go without saying goodbye. She would just walk out of the front door one morning carrying her holdall and use the excuse that she was having some things dry-cleaned. She would leave a note in her underwear drawer in the hope that when Nellie found it, she would understand why she had done things the way she had.

It was a week later, a few hours after Babs had left for work taking some dry-cleaning with her, that Nellie decided to go and pay Lottie a visit. She had received an answer to the note she had left for Francis, telling her that he was going to be staying in Ireland for a fortnight. The first week would be taken up with a series of religious seminars but during the second week he planned on visiting their mother's childless aunt and uncle, who farmed a few acres in County Wicklow. He would visit Lottie before he went but would appreciate it if she could find time to go and see their sister. He was concerned about Lottie's slow recovery and wondered how much longer she would be allowed to convalesce in Southport. Nellie had been wondering about that herself, so as soon as she could, she told her grandfather where she was going and left.

It was a beautiful July day when Nellie set out and she was wearing the maternity smock and skirt that she had bought at C&A Modes. Beneath the blue and red floral smock, she wore a pink crepe-de-chine blouse that she had bought for her wedding. It was a bit tight round the bust and she had been unable to fasten the bottom buttons. The baby was getting more active and often she found herself marvelling at the miracle of life that was growing inside her womb. Because of the heat, she had pinned up her chestnut hair on top of her head, leaving her slender neck feeling much cooler. She took the train to Southport and enjoyed gazing out on the gardens of big houses, the fields and woods, sand dunes and golf course. She thought that on such a day, there was nothing so lovely as the countryside.

When Nellie arrived in the resort, she bought her sister a copy of *Peg's Paper*, which was light reading, and headed for the convalescent home. She was directed to the garden and found Lottie sitting in a wheelchair, toying with her rosary beads. A Catholic missal was balanced on a belly that was as large as her own. She was dismayed, concerned that her sister was putting on so much weight. It couldn't be good for her damaged hip and legs, or her heart for that matter.

'Hello, Lot.' Nellie bent and kissed her sister's cheek.

Lottie looked up at her and there was a fiery light in the grey eyes beneath the straight slashes of her eyebrows. 'I prayed you'd come and here you are.'

'Yes, here I am,' said Nellie, sitting on the

wooden bench a couple of feet away. Taking the magazine from her bag, she placed it on the bench.

'Isn't prayer wonderful?' said Lottie. 'I pray to the Holy Mother and the saints for healing and one day I think I will be healed. Perhaps right now, though, I'm still sitting here because I've indulged in wicked thoughts.'

'Wicked thoughts! You?' Nellie laughed. 'I don't believe it. Hitler's Luftwaffe dropped a bomb, that's why you're here. It would be better if you'd get out of that wheelchair and try walking some more.'

Lottie pushed back a hank of lank mousy hair and screwed up her eyes against the sun. 'But it kills me to walk.'

'I'm sure it does, but you *can* walk.'

Lottie hesitated. 'If I said it hurts, I must be able to walk, mustn't I? I get puffed, though.'

Nellie refrained from saying that was because she was overweight and instead said, 'I get puffed sometimes.' But that was when she forgot she was pregnant and ran upstairs or climbed on a chair to clean windows and the like.

Lottie shielded her eyes from the sun and scrutinised Nellie. 'You've put weight on. You're getting as fat as me.'

'That's because I'm pregnant.'

'Pregnant!'

Nellie nodded. 'I wish you could come home, Lot. I'm sure it would be better and easier for both of us if you were home.'

Lottie was distracted and looked uncertain. 'We don't have a wheelchair there,' she said, as if that was the deciding factor. 'Why haven't you mentioned before that you're pregnant?' she added.

'I thought I'd tell you face to face. Anyway, now you know. It's due in October and hopefully you'll be home by then.'

'I hope to God I will be.' She frowned.

Nellie wondered if Lottie was about to mention her not having married in the Catholic church and the baby being illegitimate, so she swiftly changed the subject. She talked about Babs and Grandfather, the hens and how the cockerel was starting to wake them in the morning.

Lottie had little to say and eventually Nellie rose to go. Her sister stopped her with the words, 'Couldn't you take me out in the wheelchair? We could go along the prom.'

Nellie hesitated and glanced towards the gate at the bottom of the garden. Could she manage the drop to ease the chair down off the step? Perhaps she should ask for help.

She did so and, after a word of warning to come back immediately if she found things difficult, a nurse helped her out of the garden into a back lane. It was hard work pushing Lottie in the wheelchair so Nellie did not rush but took her time. There was quite a crowd along the prom and the sound of a brass band playing dance music floated on the air. Nellie headed in that direction. When she saw people dancing, she wished that Teddy was there so they could dance, too. There was a bench nearby so she sat down, glad to have a rest. The band was playing 'Look for the Silver Lining' and she thought that everyone must be looking for a silver lining to lighten the dark clouds of war.

They stayed for a while, listening to the music until at last the band packed up its instruments and left. Nellie got up and pushed Lottie back to the convalescent home, said her goodbyes and departed.

The train was crowded with day trippers heading back to Liverpool and she was so weary when she got off at Seaforth that she decided to buy fish and chips to save her cooking. She entered the kitchen, wanting nothing more than to kick off her shoes and put her feet up, but her grandfather was not alone. Billy and a strange young man sat at the table.

'Who's this?' asked Nellie, putting down the wrapped newspaper parcel on the dresser.

Billy stood up and offered her his seat. 'Please sit down, Mrs Lachlan.'

'His name is Ritchie,' growled Grandfather, 'and apparently he's been seeing Babs and wants to marry her.'

Nellie sat down on the vacated chair. 'He's been what?'

'We haven't done anything wrong,' said Ritchie, his hands clasped tightly together.

Nellie stared at his unhappy young face and then glanced at her grandfather. 'Where is Babs? Surely she should be home by now?'

Ritchie answered. 'She's gone off. I called in at the dry-cleaner's and they said she'd quit. Not a word did she say to me about that.'

'Us neither,' whispered Nellie, stunned by her sister's duplicity.

'I didn't even know where she lived. She would

never let me see her home.'

'So how did you find this house?' asked Nellie.

'The woman at the dry-cleaner's gave him the address,' rumbled Grandfather.

Nellie did not speak for several moments and then she stood up and left the kitchen. She went upstairs and into their bedroom. Going over to the chest of drawers, she opened the ones used by her sister. It was in the bottom one she saw the envelope and took it out with shaking fingers.

Tearing open the envelope, she spread the sheet of paper flat on the top of the chest of drawers and read,

Dear Nellie,

I know you would have tried to persuade me not to go and that's why I've done what I want this way. After all, you set me an example by running off with Teddy. I've joined the Women's Land Army. It was easy enough to get in because they're desperate for workers. I'm not going far. Up Lancashire that's all. As soon as I'm settled I'll write again. In the meantime don't be too angry with me and take care of yourself and the baby.

Lots of love,
Babs.

Nellie sank onto the bed. Daft! That's what Babs was. As if she would have stopped her if she really wanted to do something towards the war effort. If she had run off with that Ritchie in the kitchen, that would have been a mistake. Thank God, she'd had the sense not to do that. The cheek of her, saying that Nellie had set her an example.

101

She smiled and shook her head.

Her stomach rumbled and she remembered the fish and chips that she had bought. She got up and went downstairs and handed the note to her grandfather. The two young men stared at him as he read it.

When Grandfather had finished, he raised his eyes to Nellie's face. 'Stupid child! Believes because she's done a bit of gardening with Billy that she knows all there is to know about growing things. Probably thinks it'll be lovely working in the countryside at this time of year, but wait until winter comes,' he chortled, 'that'll be another story.' He dropped the note on the table and reached for the fish and chips. 'You lads can beat it. Supper time's for us.'

Billy and Ritchie got up and Nellie followed them out. She felt sorry for the latter. It was obvious he was smitten with Babs and Nellie doubted her sister had been intentionally cruel. Hopefully, he would soon get over his feelings for her. As for herself, she would miss her youngest sister, but at least she had not gone far away. Even so, Nellie bet a pound to a penny that when their father heard about his darling daughter's behaviour, he would find some way of laying the blame not on Babs, but on her.

Chapter Five

'Here, lass, wash that cow down.' The farmer, Mr Rowland, indicated the beast he had just finished milking with a nod of his head and passed Babs a bucket of soapy water and a cloth before moving on to milk the next animal.

She gazed at the cow in dismay, thinking this was not what she joined the Women's Land Army for. The beast was huge and she had no idea where to start her task. Its horns looked really sharp and the sound of its hooves, as it shifted in the cowshed, scared her to death. She could just imagine how it would feel if her Wellington-clad foot got trodden on. She shuddered and knew she had to stay alert. Trouble was that she had been roused at four o'clock that morning and still felt half-asleep. Perhaps she should start at the top and work her way down. It seemed the most sensible thing to do.

Babs soaked the cloth in the water and told herself to show no fear but stare the cow in its surprisingly beautifully fringed eyes and start with its head. She reached up and slopped water over the cowlick between its horns. The cow reacted by blinking water out of its eyes and jerking its head.

'Sorry,' she said, attempting with trembling hands to mop the water away.

'Wha' the hell d'yer think yer doin'?' demanded the farmer.

She stared down at him. 'I'm washing the cow.'

'Yer don't bloody wash all the beast, lass, just its udders.'

Babs could not help but giggle. 'Sorry.'

He looked at her as if she was an idiot. 'Gerron with it.'

Laughter was still bubbling away inside her as she bent down with the dripping cloth clasped in her hand. She stared at the dangling skin bag with its set of teats and stopped laughing. Taking a deep breath, she rested a hesitant hand on the animal's flank and prayed it would not kick out at her as she gingerly began to wipe the teats. To her relief the cow just stood there and the tension seeped out of Babs.

She had arrived at the farm yesterday evening, having been picked up by the farmer in a horse and cart at Ormskirk railway station. Mr Rowland looked to be a man in his late thirties, with a weather-beaten face and a front tooth missing. Beyond telling her to get 'oop' into the cart, he had not spoken to her on the journey to the farm. On arrival she had been shown to a cottage that had looked quite pretty with honeysuckle and a rambling rose climbing round the door and up the wall of the house.

Inside was a different story. The front door opened straight on to a room that was small and dark, and there was no electricity. The only furniture was a saggy-looking sofa and a gate-legged table and two chairs. On the stone-flagged floor there was a rag rug in front of a black-leaded grate, to the side of which was a coal scuttle. A blackened kettle stood on the hob but the fire was unlit. Lighting was provided by a couple of oil lamps. Babs' heart had plummeted as she had put down her holdall and gasmask container.

Mr Rowland had showed her the scullery with its deep white sink and shelves with two of everything in the way of crockery and cutlery, as well as a couple of saucepans and a frying pan. He then pointed to another door in the corner of the living room, which led to a flight of stairs. 'Flo will be back in the morning,' he'd said in a Lancashire accent. 'Come over to the house in half an hour and Sister will have some supper ready for you.'

She nodded, relieved that at least she was being fed that evening because she was starving. Upstairs there was one large bedroom with two narrow beds, a large wardrobe and a chest of drawers. One of the beds showed signs of being in use. On the other was folded bedding and this one was next to the window, which was open at the bottom. She had thrust her head out and gazed at the view. A variety of smells had assailed her dainty nose: honeysuckle, manure and what she took to be the smell of the fields, which stretched towards the distant hills and encompassed several small woods. There was only the odd building and, realising she had really come to the back of beyond, she felt homesick for Liverpool. The other room upstairs was only big enough for a cot and chest of drawers. There was no bathroom. When need had driven her to go in search of a lavatory she had discovered a primitive privy at the bottom of the garden.

Babs sighed as she plunged the cloth into the bucket of soapy water again and wiped the udder of another cow. This was her third and she thanked God that Mr Rowland went in for mixed farming so didn't have a huge herd but just a round dozen. By the time she had washed the last cow, her knees were shaking, her back ached and her hands were red from being in and out of water.

As soon as she had finished, Mr Rowland told her to skedaddle to the kitchen and get herself some breakfast. 'Tomorrow, you'll cook for yerself, lass.'

Babs wiped her hands on her brown dungarees, wondering whether he would take her into Ormskirk to buy food. Then she remembered the other land girl, Flo, and hoped she would bring some groceries back with her.

Once outside, Babs felt a bit better. Dawn had arrived but she was still glad of the brown jacket that covered her working dungarees; there was a definite chill in the air. As she trudged across the cobbled yard, she thought about her 'walking out' uniform hung in the wardrobe upstairs. She could only hope she would get a chance to wear it.

She eased off her wellies at the back door of the farmhouse and entered in her stockinged feet. The farmer's sister looked up as she entered the kitchen. There was a lovely smell of freshly baked bread and the room was warm. The woman said something incomprehensible in a thick Lancashire accent. It amazed Babs that she was only about twenty miles from home and this woman might as well be speaking a foreign language. Thankfully Babs could understand what her brother said much better. Miss Rowland repeated her words and waved a hand towards the sink beneath the window. Babs presumed that she was telling her to wash her hands.

She did so reluctantly, wishing there was a jar of glycerine and almond oil handy to moisturise her skin. She washed her poor mitts and then dabbed them dry on a towel. She noticed Miss Rowland had placed bowls of porridge on the table. Porridge was not Babs' favourite food and she would have liked to refuse it but guessed she might not get anything else to eat if she did. There was a stone jar of honey on the table and Babs reached out with a greedy hand for it. She had just got the lid off when a wooden spoon descended and caught her a stinging blow on the back of the hand. The woman said something but Babs did not need words to get the message. The honey was not for the likes of her.

Miss Rowland pointed to a small dish of salt and one of sugar. At least she had a choice, thought Babs, and while the woman's back was turned, used the sugar liberally. There was also a jug of cream on the table and she made swift use of it, so the lumpy porridge did not taste too bad. As she ate her breakfast, Babs thought of Nellie. Tears pricked the back of her eyes and she wanted to go home. She wondered what her sister had thought when she found her note and what she would say if Babs suddenly turned up on the doorstep as unexpectedly as she had left the house. 'Come in, love,' she'd probably say and would refrain from adding that she had known her sister would find the job harder than she imagined. Grandfather would be a different matter.

107

The farmer sat down at the table and said something about potatoes to Babs. As his sister placed mugs of tea in front of them both, he carried on talking and Babs stared at him with dawning comprehension. It seemed he expected her to begin digging up potatoes that morning. She remembered the potato plot at home and how Billy had done most of the digging. She reached for the mug of tea and knew she was in for a long, hard day.

To her relief, Babs was not to work alone with the farmer in the potato field, which seemed to stretch to the horizon. The other land girl, Flo, was back and he left them to it and went off to do something else.

'Howdo,' said Flo, who was small and lean but soon proved to be much stronger that she looked. 'I'll do the diggin',' said Flo, wielding a spade. 'Yous can pick up the spuds and place them in them baskets over there. Don't be lookin' so worried. We'll get more help. Mams and kids generally turn up with it being the school holidays. Them's glad to make a few bob.'

Looking at the size of the field, Babs thanked God for that.

Potato picking on such a large scale was back-breaking work but, as, the day progressed, Flo was proved right and they were soon joined by an army of women and children. Miss Rowland also appeared and a trestle table was set up. Babs reckoned she had the easy job of weighing out the potatoes and totting up the earnings at the end of the day.

That night Babs fell into her lumpy bed,

muscles aching and fingers bleeding. She went out like a light. It was the same every single night of that first week. Too exhausted to indulge in chitchat with Flo, she ate what the other girl put in front of her morning, noon and evening.

The second week Flo began to lay down some ground rules. 'I know what you're sufferin',' she said. 'I've been there, but you'll soon toughen up and in the meantime, you've got to do your share of the cookin' and cleanin' and everythin' else.'

Babs did not argue but smiled and thanked her for being so patient with her. 'I never thought it would be like this.'

'Naw! Neither did I. I worked at mill and thought what a lovely life it would be away from Bolton in the country.' She gave a wry smile. 'He does a bit of everythin' here, as you'll have noticed. Cows, pigs, poultry, spuds and ... wheat ... you're just in time for harvest, Babs.' She threw back her dark head and laughed. 'It might look luv'ly on the pictures but it's bloody hard work. What we really need is a tractor here and mebbe by the end of the war this bloody tight-fisted farmer will have one, but I've no intention of hangin' around here till then.'

As they lay in their beds that night Flo told Babs about what she'd found out while she'd been away for a couple of days. Mobile gangs of Land Girls were being organised to work in different parts of the country as the need arose. Great swathes of Lancashire countryside that were once farmed but had been left to go wild since the Great War were being dug up to use for crops. 'Bigger fields where they can use machinery will be more productive. The German U-boats are still sendin' merchant ships bringin' food to Britain to the bottom of the Atlantic. The country has to be fed and it's the job of the farmers and the Women's Land Army to make sure nobody starves. The billets will be much better, Babs. I've heard some are in country houses and there's wardens who'll look after our every need.'

That really appealed to Babs. Instead of having the energy to go out to the nearest town to the pictures or dancing, here she had to work until she dropped. Thinking about the pictures and dancing reminded her of Ritchie. He'd have had her letter by now and would know it was over between them. Then she thought of her sister and remembered guiltily that she had not written to her yet. She must do so as soon as she had the time and the energy to put pen to paper.

'Helen! Where is that girl? Helen!'

'Coming!' called Nellie, drying hands that were chapped and sore from washing clothes, before hurrying into the parlour.

The wireless was on and her grandfather was sitting in an armchair with the light from the window falling over his bowed shoulders onto a letter on his lap. He removed his Woolworth's spectacles and stared at her.

'What is it?' She stared back at him, trying to conceal her impatience. Seeing the open sheet of paper reminded her of Babs, who had not yet written. She felt cross with her. Then there was Teddy, who faithfully wrote to her still. The poor love! In his last letter he had mentioned having a heat rash that itched unbearably. He had called her his lovely wife. She thought ruefully that it was a good job that he could not see her right now with her chestnut hair falling in damp wisps about her sweaty face and her body clad in a wraparound dingy pinny that could not conceal her advancing pregnancy.

'Who's the letter from?' she asked.

'Two things,' said Grandfather. 'The Hun has invaded Russia.'

She nodded, thinking poor Russians, although, they should have had more sense than to align themselves with someone as untrustworthy as Hitler. 'And the letter?'

'Your sister, Lottie, who was the least favoured amongst you girls when the looks were doled out.'

'That's not kind,' said Nellie. 'What about her?'

'They want her out. They need the bed.'

Nellie's feelings were mixed. She wanted her sister home but how would she cope? 'When is she coming?'

He tossed the letter to Nellie. 'She's got to be fetched. There's nothing more they can do for her. She's got to leave Friday at the latest.'

'But that's the day after tomorrow,' cried Nellie. Her eyes scanned the page. 'It says here that she won't be able to climb stairs just yet. I'll have to get Billy to bring down the single bed from Adelaide's old room. If you agree, it can go in the dining room as we never use it.'

He nodded. 'I hope you'll be able to manage looking after the house and the pair of us. If her being here means I get neglected, then other arrangements will have to be made.'

Nellie ignored him, thinking, not for the first time, that he was a selfish old man. She left him to his newspaper, wondering how she was going to get Lottie home. There would be the walk from the hospital to Southport railway station and then the walk up from the one at Seaforth and she would need to get the room ready. It was at times like this that she needed Babs, but she was going to have to get help from another quarter. So, that evening, Nellie spoke to Billy when he arrived to help in the garden.

Instantly, he said, 'No problem, Mrs Lachlan.'

Relieved, she almost hugged him.

Between them they managed to move the table and chairs out of the dining room, dismantle the single bed and bring it downstairs. As he re-assembled the bed frame in the dining room, they talked about the beans and peas that were ready for picking.

After Billy had carried the dining chairs out of the way upstairs to the attic, Nellie gave him thruppence and thanked him. He pocketed the money with thanks. She had wrapped vegetables and a couple of eggs in newspaper and now handed them to him.

'There's something else I want to ask you, Billy.'

'Fire away,' he said.

She told him about Lottie having to be brought home from the hospital. He had already heard about her being buried in the blitz and spending months in hospital. He looked thoughtful. 'I could probably give her a ride on my delivery bike up from the station.'

Nellie visualised Lottie, who must be all of twelve stone, sitting in the wicker basket fastened to the front of Billy's bike and smiled. 'It would be a disaster,' she said frankly. 'She'd have the pair of you over.'

He sighed. 'If that's what you think, Mrs Lachlan, we'll have to come up with something else. I could ask my dad. This used to be part of his beat years ago, but now he's a desk sergeant at the police station.'

'I didn't realise your dad was a policeman,' said Nellie.

Billy flicked back a lock of hair from his forehead. 'He wanted me to join the force but I'm going in the army. I might get to see a bit of the world.'

'As long as you keep your head down,' said Nellie, and brought the conversation back to Lottie. 'So will you help me bring my sister home?'

He said that he would speak to his father and let her know tomorrow.

The following morning, Nellie had just finished feeding the chickens and was washing her hands when there was a knock at the door. She went to answer it and found a policeman on the doorstep. He was well over six foot, with a sturdy build and had a cherubic rosy face with grey eyes and thick eyebrows.

'Sergeant McElroy, at your service, Mrs Lachlan,' he introduced himself with a smile. 'My lad Billy told me you have a problem.' He removed his cap to reveal receding salt and pepper hair. 'Your sister, love. What you need is a wheelchair and I can get you one, just for tomorrow, mind,' he said in a low voice. 'I'll leave it at Seaforth Station. Billy can return it after your sister's safely delivered here.'

Nellie thanked him. 'It'll make things so much easier for me.'

'All in a day's work,' he said cheerfully. 'The wife and I really appreciate you having Billy here and the eggs and veggies he brings home.'

She smiled. 'He deserves them. He's a hard worker.'

'Glad to know you appreciate him.' He touched his helmet and strode off down the path.

The journey to Southport was achieved with the minimum of fuss. Sgt McElroy had oiled the wheels for Nellie and she and the wheelchair travelled in the guard's van. She found it hard work pushing her sister through the bustling streets of the seaside resort and it was a relief when Lottie and the wheelchair were deposited on the Liverpool-bound train.

It was only as they neared Seaforth that Lottie began to babble on about how nervous she felt seeing Grandfather again. 'He never liked me, Nellie.' Lottie's lips quivered and her double chin wobbled. 'Is-is he as m-much a whingeing, m-miserable, tight-fisted, old so-and-so as he used to be when Mam was alive?'

Nellie nodded. 'Although, it can't be much fun getting old,' she murmured, gazing out of the window towards the Beach Road allotments as the train approached the station. 'Quick-tempered, unreasonable, autocratic – he's them, too. Just comfort yourself with the thought that he spends most of the time in the parlour listening to the wireless and reading the paper.' She stood up. 'Here we are.' Helping her sister to her feet, she added, 'Chin up, shoulders back, best foot forward ... and, whatever you do, Lottie, don't let him see that you're scared.'

Lottie promised to do her best. Yet half an hour later as her exhausted sister pushed her up the path, Lottie was thinking that it was easy for Nellie to say she shouldn't show any fear of their grandfather. He had been something of a bogeyman to Lottie as a child. Aunt Josie had often threatened that if she didn't behave herself then they'd tell him what a naughty girl she had been. 'He'll put you in a dark cupboard and throw away the key,' she'd warned in her squeaky voice. Holy Mother of God, she had almost wet her knickers when her aunt had said that. She'd had nightmares about being locked away in the dark for years.

'Rouse yourself, Lottie. We're here,' panted Nellie, placing a hand on her shoulder. 'Can you get out now?'

'If you can take my belongings and hold the chair, I think I can manage.' Lottie leaned on the arms of the wheelchair and pushed herself up. Her feet searched for the ground and Nellie took her arm and helped her to stand. Lottie took a cautious step forward and then another. She was walking but there was no way she could scud along the ground as she had once been able to. Before the operation, she had looked forward to being out of pain. Yet here she was almost four months later and still in agony.

'So here she is,' grunted a voice.

Lottie lifted her head and stared from wide,

frightened eyes at the old man with his white hair and straggly moustache. She attempted to speak but could not get the words past the constriction in her throat. Her father had once said that she was no oil painting and, although the words had puzzled her, she had guessed they weren't complimentary. She was suddenly conscious of just how tight the brown frock was and she felt the blood rush to her face with embarrassment. Why couldn't she be like her sisters?

'Cat got your tongue, girl?' he said.

'Grandfather, can you help me here?' Nellie thrust Lottie's bag at him. 'It hasn't been an easy journey and we both need a rest.'

'A rest,' he barked. 'Hasn't she been resting for the last few months?'

Nellie sighed. 'Can't you see she's in pain? Please, get out of the way so we can both get inside. The quicker you do that, the quicker I'll get dinner on and you'll have less to complain about.'

'Don't you be pert with me, Helen. I'm the boss here. You're here because I allow it,' he muttered, ambling up the lobby and dumping the bag outside the dining room before going into the parlour and closing the door.

Lottie glanced at Nellie and accompanied her sister to where her bag had been dumped. Nellie opened the door of the dining room and ushered her sister inside. 'You're to sleep here,' she said. 'Hopefully you'll manage the outside lav without too much trouble.'

Lottie gazed about the sunlit room and whispered, 'It's so much bigger than the bedroom upstairs and I'll be sleeping here on my own. It's going to feel strange without Babs here, too.'

'You'll soon get used to the space, and you can have the cat for company. You can see the back garden from here. I've brought in an armchair so you can watch the garden birds and the hens, as well as Billy when he comes to give a hand.'

Lottie did not ask about Billy because her sister had talked about him before. She limped over to the easy chair near the window and lowered herself onto it carefully. 'Thanks, Nell, for getting me here.'

'No trouble.' Nellie picked up Lottie's bag and carried it over to the bed. 'What have you got in this? Do you want me to unpack it for you?'

'A new ration book and identity card, the missal that Francis gave me.' She ticked the rest of the items off on her fingers. 'A couple of changes of clothes, nighties ... oh, and a medallion from Lourdes that a woman who visited gave me.' Her grey eyes searched Nellie's face. 'Mam didn't believe in accepting charity but giving is good for people's souls, don't you think?'

Nellie smiled. 'I'm sure you're right. After I've done this, I'll make us a cup of tea. Perhaps you can come with me to the kitchen.'

'I'd love a cuppa. Will Grandfather be joining us?'

'Probably not.' Nellie placed her sister's clothes in one of the sideboard cupboards but when she straightened up dizziness overcame her and she had to sit on the bed.

'I don't think he likes me,' said Lottie, heaving a gusty sigh.

Nellie murmured, 'Don't let it bother you. I

117

don't think he likes anybody much. You know Joe's death knocked him for six.'

'I liked Joe. Aunt Josie used to say he was a naughty boy. To be honest, Nellie, I didn't know him as well as Francis. I love Francis. Do you think he'll visit me? You and him used to get on really well before you...' She hesitated.

'Married Teddy,' supplied Nellie. 'Things aren't that bad between us. He's busy, though, so he mightn't be able to get here as regularly as he'd like to.' The dizziness was passing and she changed the subject. 'D'you think you'll manage to do some jobs for me? It'll mean Grandfather won't have as much to moan about.'

'I want to be useful,' she said eagerly. 'I can sew. I can peel potatoes.'

'You can knit, too, can't you? I need things for the baby.'

'Oh, Nell! I've been thinking about your baby. You'll have to get married in the Catholic church now. Otherwise, it'll be a little...'

'Don't you dare say that word!' warned Nellie. 'Besides it's not true. Our marriage is legal. I'll go and put the kettle on. You can follow me when you're ready.' She walked out of the room.

'Oh, Mary, mother of God,' whispered Lottie, feeling for her rosary beads. 'I've gone and upset her now but she has to be told. Help me, Mother, to make her see the error of her ways.' She sat for a few minutes in the silence, aware of the ticking of a clock and the muted clucking of hens. Then she pushed herself up out of the chair and limped across the room.

Nellie looked up as Lottie entered the kitchen

118

and forced a smile. 'You OK?'

Lottie's face was tight with pain but she nodded and made for a chair at the table.

'Don't sit on that one. It's the one with the wobbly leg.'

'A bit like me,' joked Lottie. She lowered herself onto a different chair. Once seated she looked up at her sister. 'I'm praying to St Giles for a miracle.'

'Good for you,' murmured Nellie, remembering he was the patron saint of cripples and beggars. As she placed a cup of tea in front of Lottie, she prayed her sister's devoted religious zeal would not get on her nerves.

As they drank their tea, Nellie filled her sister in on the everyday routine of the household, as well as any other of Grandfather's foibles of which she might be unaware, such as his still covering furniture with newspaper despite her telling him that it should be reused for the war effort.

'What about Mass?' asked Lottie.

'Grandfather doesn't go regularly and the priest doesn't visit.'

'And you?'

Nellie gave a twisted smile. 'Not yet. Now finish your tea and don't say another word about religion.'

'One more thing?' squeaked Lottie. 'Mam's grave?'

Nellie's fingers tightened on her cup. 'What about it?'

'I'd like to visit and put flowers on it.'

Nellie felt a stab of guilt. She had not visited her mother's and aunt's graves since her father had been home. 'Maybe we'll go there in a few weeks' time. At the moment the walk'll be too much for you.'

'What about the wheelchair?'

'I told you Billy's coming for it.' Nellie rose from the table and began the preparations for the evening meal.

Later when Billy arrived, she introduced him to Lottie, realising they were much of an age. 'It must have been scary being buried alive,' he said.

Lottie nodded. She had never had much to do with boys. Aunt Josie had warned her never to be alone with one and if she found herself in a boy's company by accident, she must certainly not allow him intimacies. Lottie had had no idea what her aunt was talking about.

Billy persisted. 'My dad's mate was killed in Bootle during the blitz. He was a hero and was awarded a posthumous medal.'

Lottie managed to mumble something about there being lots of heroes around then. Billy was about to say something else when Grandfather appeared and barked an order at him. Relieved, Lottie limped back into the house and managed to reach her bedroom, where she sat and watched through the window what was going on outside. She felt much more comfortable being an onlooker.

The following day Nellie received a postcard from Teddy. It had a photo of palm trees and pyramids. She told herself that she must not worry about him because that way madness lay. She longed for him and it was only the thought of them being together as a family in the future that helped her keep going when she felt so unbearably tired.

The days fell into a pattern. Nellie would help Lottie to get out of bed and leave her to dress herself. Then her sister would join her in the kitchen and they'd have porridge, toast and tea with their grandfather before Nellie went shopping and did some of the household chores. Lottie was given the task of doing all the darning and mending, as well as preparing vegetables. Nellie went to the library and brought books for them to read.

Lottie spent more time reading her missal, promising herself every day that she would make the effort to get to church on Sunday but so far she had not managed to do so. She was shy of being asked questions about what had happened to her and having to talk about their mother's death. Francis had not been to visit and there had been no letters from Babs.

Every evening when Billy arrived, Lottie would settle herself in the chair in front of the window with the wool and knitting needles Nellie had bought and knit for the baby, watching him work among the rows of vegetables. She found it restful, spending that hour or two in such a way, and gradually the nightmares of being buried alive and the awfulness of losing her mother and aunt began to lessen.

Chapter Six

'There's a letter here for you here, Helen.'

Nellie glanced down as Grandfather dropped it in her lap. Instantly she recognised the handwriting and eagerly slit the envelope with a finger. It was little more than a note but it was from Babs who, it appeared, was not far from Ormskirk. Immediately Nellie was reminded of the article in the *Crosby Herald* about hundreds of acres of land in Lancashire, which had lain neglected since the last war, being ploughed up by the Women's Land Army. It did not appear that Babs was one of them because her note said that she was working on a small mixed farm. She said it was back-breaking hard work and she missed her home comforts and hoped Nellie was well and that she would be able to visit home before the baby's birth.

Unfortunately Babs had forgotten to write her address on the top, which was annoying, but Nellie was relieved that her baby sister had written at last and that she was doing exactly what she wanted. She looked forward to seeing her.

But they were to have a surprise visitor the following week. Nellie had set up a deckchair in the garden, so Lottie could have fresh air while sewing a vest for the baby and she helped Billy pick vegetables. The three of them were gainfully occupied when a loud voice hailed them. Nellie turned and saw a man dressed in a tweed jacket and tan trousers coming towards them. He was bareheaded and smoking a pipe and she did not immediately recognise him.

'It's my dad,' said Billy in a low voice. 'What's he doing here?'

Nellie wondered the same herself. 'Good evening, Sgt McElroy,' she said.

'Mrs Lachlan.' He gazed at her pregnant shape from slightly protuberant eyes before giving his attention to Lottie. 'This your sister?'

'Yes. Lottie, this is Billy's father,' said Nellie.

'How d'you do?' said Lottie, slanting him a look before resuming her task.

'Billy mentioned you were managing to get up and about a bit, so I thought I'd come and say hello. How are you coping after your terrible experience?'

'Fine.' Lottie did not look up.

'Billy was quite concerned about you,' said the sergeant.

'Billy's very caring for someone of his age,' said Nellie with a smile.

'Well, we did our best with him. It wasn't easy.' He was silent a moment and then said, 'If everything's all right then I'll be getting back to the missus. She's an invalid, you know. Good evening, Mrs Lachlan.'

'Good evening.' Nellie watched him until he was out of sight before turning to Billy. 'You didn't say your mam was an invalid,' she said.

'No,' he said tersely.

'Was the wheelchair hers?' asked Nellie.

Billy shook his head. 'She's not sick that way.'

He turned his head away and resumed picking beans.

His behaviour roused Nellie's curiosity but, as it was obvious he did not want to talk about his mother, she let the subject drop.

The Sunday in August when the clocks went back, Nellie arrived home from the shops to find Francis in the kitchen, talking to Lottie and Grandfather. She wondered why it was that priests and vicars wore their clerical collars when they were not working. She said, 'Hello,' and proceeded to unpack the shopping and put it away.

He followed her into the larder. 'Grandfather says you're fine. Is that true, Nellie? You look tired to me. He and Lottie aren't expecting too much from you?'

She was touched by his concern. 'I'm managing.'

'And Lottie? He's not bullying her?'

'He ignores her most of the time.'

Francis looked relieved. 'Better that than have her cowering in corners in fear of him.'

Nellie agreed.

'Pity Babs decided to go off and be a land girl. You could have done with her here.'

Nellie nodded. 'She's young and I think part of her leaving was due to wanting to get away from an overzealous boyfriend.'

'Boyfriend!'

She smiled. 'Grandfather not mention him?'

'No.'

'Probably forgotten. He is getting old.'

He nodded and sighed. 'It's a shame Lottie's

124

still in pain.'

'She's a good help to me, though. She's knitting for the baby.'

He tapped his fingers against the shelf holding packets of oats, sugar and tea. 'She is worried about you both...' He let the sentence hang.

'Ahhh!' murmured Nellie, her body tensing. 'I presume you're not referring to my physical health?'

'You know the church's teachings, Nell,' he said gravely.

She stared into his sober, rugged face. 'I thought we agreed not to mention the baby's need for baptism until after it's born. I know you feel it's your duty to broach the subject but we'll end up at loggerheads if you persist.'

'Have you mentioned it to Teddy yet?'

She shook her head. 'Truthfully, I've so many other things to think about and, besides, the poor love has enough to deal with out in the desert without me giving him that to worry about.'

'He's still safe, then.'

'I hope so,' murmured Nellie, her heart flipping over. 'Africa's such a long way away and it takes time for news to filter through.'

'I'll hold him in my prayers,' said Francis.

She thanked him and asked whether he'd heard from their father.

Francis shook his head. 'Like Mam, he might have been pleased to have a priest in the family but I think he's always resented our closeness.'

'That doesn't surprise me. He's a possessive, jealous man.' She flushed. 'I know I shouldn't have said that but I can't pretend that he's the perfect father.' She cocked an eyebrow. 'Shall we join Grandfather and Lottie and have a cup of tea?'

He nodded and she went to put the kettle on.

A few weeks later, on a Sunday afternoon, Nellie was out in the garden, thinking about Teddy as she washed down a cot she had found, dismantled, up in the attic. She still did not have a pram but it was six weeks until her confinement and she had decided to wait until the baby was born before putting an advertisement in the Wanted column of the *Crosby Herald* for a second-hand one. Billy was up a tree picking apples. Lottie was at the foot of the trunk, taking them from him and placing them in a bucket. Nellie's eyes were dreamy as she thought of the baby, convinced it was going to be a boy. She hoped that when her grandfather set eyes on him her son would take the place in his heart that Joe had once filled.

'Helen, come here, girl!' Her grandfather's brusque voice took her by surprise.

'What is it?' she said, wringing out the cloth into a bowl of water and glancing up at him, where he stood in the doorway of the washroom.

He did not speak but held out a light orange envelope to her. She did not move, staring at it in disbelief. The cloth slipped from her fingers and a pulse began to hammer in her head. The old man's mouth trembled and he moved towards her.

Wordlessly, Nellie took the envelope from him and with shaking hands removed the telegram. The message abruptly informed her that Corporal Lachlan had been killed in action. She felt as if she had been stabbed in the heart, swayed, and had to grip the cot to prevent herself from falling. For what felt an eternity she rested against it as waves of icy desolation swept over. Her vision blurred as she stared down the garden at Lottie and Billy, working together beneath the apple tree. She could not believe that Teddy was dead. She crushed the telegram in her hand as if somehow that would obliterate the news, but the words hammered inside her head: Dead! Teddy was dead.

He was not going to be one of the survivors who would come marching home. Never again would she see his face or feel his lips on hers. Never again would he take her in his arms and make love to her or call her sweetheart. They'd spent so few days of married life together. The dreams they'd had for their future would never come true; they had died in the desert with him.

She felt a hand on her shoulder and looked up at her grandfather. To her amazement she saw that his eyes were moist. 'Come inside, Helen, and sit down. You look as if you're going to faint.'

Me, faint? thought Nellie. She felt dizzy and sick, so perhaps she would just slip to the ground and lose consciousness, at least then she wouldn't have to think or feel. She felt hot and cold, and then blackness descended on her and she knew no more.

'Are you OK, Nell?'

Nellie blinked and stared up at Lottie and Billy. What had happened? Why did they look so worried?

'Of course she's not all right. She fainted,' snapped Grandfather.

The ground was hard and Nellie's back ached. She looked at the cot and saw what looked like a sheet of yellow paper stuck to one of the bars.

'Is it the baby?' asked Billy.

'The baby!' Lottie's fat jowls wobbled. She had no idea what to do if it was the baby that had caused her sister to pass out.

Nellie said nothing but continued to stare at the yellow paper.

'Let's get her inside,' said Grandfather. 'Billy, you help her up.'

Billy placed his arms round Nellie and she clutched at his pullover with trembling hands. She was cold and felt strange. Something terrible had happened but she did not want to think about it. Her baby needed her. Billy carried her into the house and she flopped against him as if the strength had drained out of her. He took her into the parlour and placed her on the sofa on a sheet of newspaper. She did not care about that but was thankful to lie down.

Her grandfather and Lottie had followed them in and Lottie carefully lowered herself onto the edge of the sofa. Her grandfather had told her about Teddy's death and she did not know what to say to Nellie or what to do, but could only pray for guidance. She reached out and took one of her sister's hands and chaffed it. 'You're cold, Nellie.'

'That's shock,' said Grandfather. 'A hot water bottle and a cup of tea are what she needs.'

Lottie looked up at Billy. 'I'll put the kettle on,' he said, and left the parlour.

'You go and help him, girl,' said Grandfather. 'I'll sit with Helen.'

Lottie hesitated and then dragged herself up. She limped into the kitchen and saw that Billy was pouring milk into a cup.

'Best put in several spoons of sugar,' he murmured, glancing at Lottie. 'Mam says that's good for shock.'

'OK,' said Lottie, going in search of the sugar bag. 'I hope she's going to be all right. Her husband's been killed. She ran away and married him, you know? He was lovely even if he was a Proddy. She really loved him.'

'It's a blinking shame,' said Billy, shaking his head. 'Why is it that terrible things happen to good people?'

'It's not God's fault,' said Lottie, spooning sugar into the milk. 'It's the devil, who tempts people like Hitler into wanting power. They think they're somebody great and all they are is evil.'

Billy mooched around the kitchen with his hands in his pockets. 'D'you think Mr Callaghan and Mrs Lachlan will want me to carry on picking apples?'

Lottie was not used to making decisions. 'What do you think?'

'She wanted them all picked by tomorrow.'

'Then why ask me? Go and do it.'

He nodded and made for the washroom, only to pause in the doorway. 'I hope she'll be OK,' he said, before vanishing outside.

So do I, thought Lottie, carrying the cup of tea into the parlour.

Nellie sipped the hot tea, scared silly, fearing she had damaged the baby when she had fainted. The ache in her back was spreading and she wanted to be up and doing something, anything to get rid of the dark thought hovering on the edge of her consciousness. She wanted to scream at it but knew if she did that she would only frighten Lottie and Grandfather.

Lottie brought in a hot water bottle and placed it next to Nellie and then sat at her feet. 'Billy's carrying on picking the apples,' she said.

'That's good,' said Nellie, feeling as if the words were coming from a distance. 'What about supper? Will you be able to make it?'

Lottie said, 'I'll have a go.'

Nellie ate her supper off a tray. She was feeling like a cat on hot bricks and could not relax. Grandfather sat with her, listening to the wireless. The drone of men's voices caused her to grit her teeth. That scream inside her still lurked and she got up, unable to bear doing nothing any longer.

Her grandfather lifted his head and stared at her. 'You all right now, Helen?'

She nodded and carried the tray outside. Her body felt in the grip of one of those monsters of steel she had seen in a sci-fi film with Teddy. A chill seized her heart and she felt a sense of panic. 'Teddy, Teddy, I want you,' she babbled silently as she walked into the kitchen.

Lottie was washing dishes and looked pleased to see her. 'You're on your feet, Nellie. Are you OK?'

Nellie thought, if anyone asks me that again, I'll scream. She made up her mind to go to bed and lumbered out of the kitchen and climbed the stairs, knowing she would be left alone up there. She went to the lavatory and then undressed and got into bed with a sigh of relief. Teddy, she thought, hugging her pillow against her cheek. A tear slid down her face and then another and another, dampening the pillowcase. No, she mustn't cry. What was there to cry about? He wasn't dead! He couldn't be dead! She and the baby needed him.

She tried to shut out the thoughts but the same ones kept coming. Teddy was dead. She would never see him again. Never, never! Stop it, stop it, cried her brain. You'll make yourself ill. Think of the baby. The baby. Generally, as soon as she lay down to sleep, the baby started moving and she imagined her son practising football in her womb. Tonight she could feel nothing, just that ache and cold fear. She told herself that the baby had probably had as big a shock as she had and was resting. 'Look on the bright side. Things are going to be fine,' she murmured, determined to sleep.

But Nellie could not sleep. Every nerve in her body was alert for any movement from the baby. Minutes and then hours ticked by and still nothing. She got up and went to the lavatory and was shocked to see a smear of blood when she wiped herself. Her heart began to thud. What was happening? Oh God! Something was wrong. Outside it was dark and she did not know what to do. She needed the midwife. Lottie would have to fetch her.

Nellie went downstairs and banged on her sister's door. Normally it took Lottie some time to get up and open it but to her surprise it opened instantly and she stood there in a voluminous nightgown with her hair in disarray about her flushed face. She looked wide awake. 'What is it, Nellie?'

'Get dressed. You must fetch the midwife,' said Nellie without preamble.

'But-but where does she live?' stammered Lottie, who had been no further than the garden gate since she had arrived home.

Nellie told her. 'You must hurry,' she cried.

Then she sat on the stairs in her night attire, white-faced with misery.

Lottie wasted no time wishing that Babs was here to run for the midwife, but got dressed and limped out of the house. Fortunately the woman was home and came immediately. She was middle-aged with a hatchet face and a brisk manner. Lottie suggested she and Nellie might like to use her bedroom to save her sister climbing the stairs. Then Lottie went into the kitchen to see if the fire was still burning so she could boil a kettle for tea.

Soon Nellie was lying on Lottie's bed. 'Let's have a listen and a look at you,' said the woman, easing up Nellie's nightie. Her face was grave when she finished her inspection. 'Hospital for you, my girl, and straight away.'

'No,' she whispered. 'No.'

'My dear,' said the woman gently. 'You must be brave.'

'But...'

The midwife shook her head and went in search of Lottie. 'Stay with her while I arrange things.'

Nellie wanted to scream that this could not be happening to her. Within the hour an ambulance had whisked her to the hospital. Various unpleasant things were done to her and then the pain started. It went on and on. A doctor came to visit and spoke to her kindly and after that everything was a blur. Hours later, still gowned and masked, the doctor told her that her baby boy had been delivered stillborn. Despite her utter desolation, she asked to see him, only to be told that was not a good idea. Besides, he had been taken away and disposed of.

Chapter Seven

Babs hummed 'Life is just a Bowl of Cherries' as she brushed her hair in front of the cracked mirror she had bought from the white elephant stall at the local church's fundraising sale in aid of the Red Cross. Flo had shown her the nearest village that lay hidden out of sight beyond a wood and could be reached in twenty minutes by a footpath.

Flo, who had been ready for the last ten minutes, said, 'There won't be any talent there, yer know.'

Babs' red hair whirled about her shoulders as she looked at her. 'How do you know? It could be different from when you went last year.'

'Tradition,' said Flo, inspecting her fingernails. 'There'll be Lancashire hotpot wiv mebbe a choice of red cabbage, beetroot and brown sauce, as well as bread and butter. For pudding there'll probably be apple pie and custard ... and there's the barn dance. Yer knows what that's like.'

'No, I don't,' said Babs.

'Stamping feet and couples charging up and down centre of the hall. There'll be lots of clapping and dosey-doein'. If you get a man to partner yer, and you probably will because yer a looker, he'll do his best to swing yer off your feet.'

'It sounds fun,' said Babs, her green eyes bright with excitement.

'Aye! It was fun last year. Yer can have a laugh if you don't worry about not knowin' what yer doin'. If you can forget yourself and let yerself go.'

'I've been working that blinking hard I'm determined to have a good time,' said Babs, easing back aching shoulders from cutting cabbages and milking. 'Mr Rowland certainly likes his pound of flesh.' She puckered her brow. 'I wish I'd brought a decent frock, but I didn't have any room in my holdall.'

'We're best wearin' breeches and brogues, anyway, as we'll be usin' footpath.'

'I suppose you're right. Besides, I'm getting used to not having a skirt flapping about my legs,' said Babs, glancing down at herself in the WLA uniform of green V-necked ribbed jumper worn over a fawn aertex shirt with brown corduroy breeches and knee length fawn socks. 'Even so...' She didn't finish what she was saying, wondering instead what Nellie and Grandfather would say when they saw her dressed like this. She was disappointed that Nellie had not replied to her note but perhaps she had believed Babs would be visiting in days so hadn't bothered. Unfortunately, Mr Rowland had refused to allow her the time off, saying they were too busy, despite a group of land girls turning up to help gather in the harvest. She and Flo had picked their brains about the new scheme and planned to get in touch with the organiser. But her mind had strayed away from Nellie. She must write to her tomorrow as she was sure the baby was due any day now. Would she have a niece or a nephew? She felt a thrill at the thought of being an aunt.

'Yous ready then?' asked Flo.

Babs reached for her waterproof brown overcoat and felt porkpie hat and put them on before slipping her gasmask holder and bag containing her torch, purse, comb and ticket over her shoulder. 'Now I'm ready,' she said, smiling. 'I hope you know the way in the dark.'

'It's spooky but I'll get us there,' said Flo. 'Mam always said eat plenty of carrots and you'll see in the dark.'

'It's a pity Mr Rowland didn't offer to take us in the pony and trap,' said Babs, leading the way downstairs.

'If we were local he might have but we're only the hired hands and *furriners* to boot,' said Flo.

'Who did you go with last time?' asked Babs.

'Oh, there was a bloke workin' here but he joined up with his mate from village. Both are in army now. I write to Pete now and then.'

Fortunately there was a harvest moon and lots of stars overhead, so there was no need to switch on their torches. Babs was glad to be warmly clad. There was a definite nip in the air and she had noticed that morning it was getting lighter much later and the leaves were beginning to change

135

colour. She thought of Nellie and the time she had spent in Cumberland and wondered if she ever missed the countryside or her job with the children. It had probably been more interesting than being at home looking after Grandfather. She wondered if Lottie was back home and how Francis and her father were, and thought that she must get round to writing to them, too, but right now she wanted to have some fun.

The village hall was already filling up when the two girls arrived. They hung their coats and hats in the cloakroom and entered the main hall. It was brightly lit and the walls were festooned with berry-encrusted greenery. Vases of Michaelmas daises were placed on trestle tables set with white cloths and crockery and cutlery. At the far end of the hall, a female pianist, a grey-haired male violinist and a youth with a penny whistle were in a huddle with a stocky man wearing corduroy trousers, a checked shirt and a red 'kerchief knotted at his throat.

Babs noticed that most of the women and girls were wearing full skirts or frocks and envied them. 'Do we dance or eat first?' she murmured.

'Eat. So they can clear everythin' away for dancing. Man wearing red scarf is master of ceremonies. He tells us what to do when it comes to dancin',' said Flo.

'Will people feel like dancing after eating?'

'Folk don't get up straight away and some have to be dragged onto floor 'cos they worry about makin' fools of themselves. 'Sides, yer not goin' to get that much to eat yer can't move.'

Which was a pity, thought Babs, who had only

136

eaten a jam butty because of the hotpot supper.

They found themselves a place and sat down. Babs glanced at the other people at their table and was pleased to see a couple of young men in uniform. She guessed they were on leave and eyed them up, wondering if either was married, not wanting to go poaching another woman's man. One of them, fair-haired and with a lively expression, had noticed her looking at him and stared boldly back.

'Evening,' he said.

'Hello,' said Babs, thinking he had a cheeky grin.

'Yous must be redhead working on Rowland's farm. Heard about you,' he called across to her above the din in the hall.

'What have you heard?' she asked, thinking that the village gossips must be as busy as Mrs Wainwright back home.

'Don't want to make yous think too much of yerself but they said yous were trouble.'

Babs was indignant and her cheeks flamed. 'I don't know what they mean by that but if you're going to take any notice of them, why bother speaking to me?'

''Cos I fancy a dance with you. Shame, it's wild west kind of dancing but they'll probably throw in a waltz towards the end. Yous fancy getting up with me?'

'I don't mind, although, I tell you now I've never done this kind of dancing before.'

'No problem. Half the fun is having a go. Don't you go letting any other idjit persuade you to get up.'

137

Before she could say that she'd please herself, a man in a clerical collar rose and called for hush. He had to repeat himself several times before the noise subsided. The proceedings were opened with a thanksgiving prayer for the harvest and then a blessing on the food they were about to eat. No sooner was that over than the hotpot was served by a team of middle-aged women.

Babs did not waste any time eating hers and would have enjoyed a second helping but, as none was offered, she had a couple of slices of bread and left room for pudding. This turned out to be what Flo had prophesied, apple pie and custard. She laid down her spoon with a satisfied sigh and placed a hand on her stomach. 'That was lovely.'

'No argument,' said Flo, reaching for her cup of tea. 'So yer've found yerself a partner already. Well, just don't go acceptin' any invitations to go outside and look at the moon. Eric has busy hands.'

Babs got the message but was determined to enjoy the dancing, anyhow. She wasn't looking for trouble.

Half an hour later the tables had been cleared away and the musicians were tuning up. The master of ceremonies was urging people onto the floor and Babs expected Eric with the busy hands to appear at her shoulder but that did not happen, so Babs sat watching the first dance with lively interest. There were several sets of four couples who whirled and skipped backwards and forwards; men twirled their partners and did what the master-of-ceremonies called dosey-doe-ing. She thought it looked really complicated but the music set her feet tapping and she decided that if Eric didn't make an appearance soon, she would accept any offers to dance that came her way.

She did not have long to wait before a distinguished looking elderly gentleman wearing a navy blazer and flannels approached her. 'May I have the pleasure, my dear?' he asked.

He was not the partner she wanted but was aware that several pairs of eyes were watching her and among them were those of Mr Rowland and his sister. She smiled and stood up. 'I'll probably tread on your toes. I've never done this before.'

'Just listen to what I tell you and not that fool in the red handkerchief and we'll do fine.' He held out a hand.

Babs placed her hand in his and was led onto the floor. As the music started, he bowed. She curtseyed and within moments joined hands with the other women and was skipping forward and back, forward and back. Her partner caught her hands and said, 'Swing around.' He continued to give her orders throughout the dance but she still got muddled up and ended up giggling madly.

Yet when the music stopped, he told her she had done wonderfully well and led her back to her seat, where a smiling soldier sat. He stood up and waved her to it. 'So d'yer think yer've got the hang of it now, Babs?'

She thanked the elderly gentleman before saying, 'You have to be joking, Eric,' with more than a hint of breathlessness.

'Prepared to have another go?'

'Once I've my breath back,' said Babs, whose legs were aching too. And talking of breath, she thought, catching the smell of beer on his.

His blue eyes widened. 'Come on, lass. Yer not one of these oldies.'

She laughed. 'No! But I work bloody hard all day, mate.'

'Then yer won't have any strength to resist when I take yer in my arms.'

'You've got a nerve,' said Babs mildly. 'But I'd better warn you my brothers taught me self-defence.'

'Yer've brothers?'

'Only one now,' she said, looking up at Eric, who wasn't half bad looking. 'Joe was killed in the Battle of the Atlantic.'

Eric's smile faltered. 'Sorry about that.'

'It wasn't your fault but thanks. My dad's still out there.'

'Bloody war,' said Eric.

'Yeah.' She decided not to mention her mother and aunt; their deaths were still too raw. 'So are you good at this barn dancing?'

His smile reappeared. 'I'll not make a hash of it.'

'Glad to hear it,' she said.

He proved himself right and, although he laughed when she made mistakes, Babs sensed his laughter was not unkind. Even so, when he asked to see her back to the farm at the end of the evening, she refused and that wasn't only because she'd sensed the farmer's eye on her while she danced. 'I'm with Flo.'

'She could go back with the Rowlands,' said Eric, still holding Babs' hand after the last dance.

She shook her head.

His blue eyes gazed into hers. 'Oh come on, lass. Have pity on a poor soldier! This is my embarkation leave.'

'Sorry.'

'What about the pictures on Monday evening?'

She hesitated. 'I work long hours and I'm whacked at the end of the day.'

He persisted. 'I'll borrow Dad's motorbike and take yer into Wigan. Yer'll hardly have to walk a step and if yer fall asleep during the film, yer can rest yer head on my shoulder.'

The offer was tempting and knowing he would be leaving soon lowered her resistance. 'OK. But you'll have to cut the engine, so Mr Rowland doesn't hear it. I'll meet you at the end of the path leading to the farm.'

His eyes lit up. 'Yer won't regret it. I'll give yer a good time.'

Babs said, 'Does that mean I get a box of chocolates?'

He smiled. 'Mebbe. See yer Monday.'

She watched him walk away and was glad there was no time to get fond of him. He could get killed and she did not want the pain of grieving again.

'You ready to go?' said Flo, appearing at her side with their coats and hats. 'Mr Rowland said we're to go back with him.'

Babs nodded. 'I thought he might.'

On the short journey back to the cottage in the pony and trap, she thought of Nellie and reminded herself that she must write to her in the next few days.

'It's good to have you home, Nell,' said Lottie, her grey eyes concerned as she looked into her sister's strained face. 'I'm really sorry about Teddy and the baby.'

Nellie's eyes filled with tears and, wordlessly, she squeezed her sister's hand and walked slowly over to the fireplace. She felt so down that she just wanted to sleep and not wake up. She rested her head on the mantelshelf and gazed down into the fire. If only she had seen her baby and held him in her arms. Had he been fair like Teddy or chestnut like herself? Had his eyes been blue-green, brown or grey? Would he have grown to be tall or of medium height? She would never know these things and her grief weighed heavily.

'There you are, Helen,' said her grandfather gruffly, entering the kitchen. 'How are you, girl?'

She lifted her head. 'How do you think I feel?'

'Bad. As if there's nothing to live for,' he surprised her by saying. 'But moping about won't solve anything. I remember when I lost your grandmother I felt terrible. But what could I do? I was on the high seas when she died. I was expecting her to be there when I docked but she'd been dead months and I didn't know about it. I could have been killed and she wouldn't have known, either. I've lived on memories ever since.'

Nellie was deeply touched by his words. 'You've never spoken of her before.'

He looked embarrassed and pulled on his moustache with a trembling hand. 'You never knew her, so what was the point? She was a stranger to you.'

'But if you'd spoken about her, I would have

142

got to know her. It's – it's like reading a book. The more you read about people the more they become real.'

'Like reading about the saints,' interposed Lottie.

Grandfather ignored her. 'It was a long time ago. Time goes some way to healing but you have to get on with your life or go under.' He gave Nellie a ferocious stare. 'Work, girl, that will help you. Work.'

Work, she thought. A job. I could do with getting away from this house, but not yet. In her present mood and state of health she wasn't fit.

'Something to eat, Nellie?' asked Lottie, rousing her from her reverie. 'I've managed a bit of shopping and cooking while you were in hospital.'

'That's good.' She managed to sound enthusiastic, thinking that if her sister was able to do more in the house then she, herself, could seriously consider going out to work.

The next day Nellie received a letter from Babs and this time there was an address in the right hand corner. She wondered why her sister had not come home as she had said and, with a lift of the heart, hoped this was to tell her when she would visit. She began to read,

Dear Nellie,
I hope you are well. I thought I might have had an answer to my last letter but perhaps you thought you'd see me before you had a chance to write. I'm sorry I didn't get to see you but we're up to our eyes here and Mr Rowland, the farmer, refused to allow me time off.

God only knows when I'll get home. I had some fun, though, at the village Harvest Supper and Barn Dance. You would have laughed to see me, Nellie. I made a right muck of it. This soldier, Eric, was on embarkation leave and tried his best to teach me, as did some other elderly gentleman, but I think I'd have to take lessons to get the hang of it. The village is one good thing about this place, I don't feel so cut off and Flo says there's an Autumn Beetle Drive to look forward to, whatever that is, and a Christmas Bazaar with a bottle stall and all kinds of things to make money for the church and the Red Cross.

But enough about me. What about the baby? My niece or nephew should have arrived by now. Whatever it is I'll love it. I can't wait to see it and hope you are OK.

A sob burst from Nellie and, crushing the letter in her hand, she ran out into the garden and down to the trees at the bottom. She placed her head against a tree trunk and cried and cried. It felt as if her heart was breaking, not only for her child but Teddy as well. She did not know how she was going to go on despite what her grandfather had said. What was there to live for, if she could not have Teddy or her son to love and care for?

'Are you all right, Mrs Lachlan?'

Slowly Nellie lifted her head and turned round to see Billy's father standing a few feet away. She swallowed and managed to say, 'Where did you come from?'

'I came to see if Billy was here. He spent more time helping out while you were in hospital.' He tugged at his full lower lip. 'Do you think he and

Lottie get on well?'

Nellie wiped her wet face with the back of her hand. 'Yes. I'm glad about that. She's never had many friends. Mam and Aunt Josie always kept such a watch on her.'

His eyes seemed to bulge and for a moment she thought he looked haunted. She was surprised when he said, 'I remember your mother. She was unhappy because she was treated like a skivvy in this house.'

'She never complained. We'd have helped if she'd have asked but often she just seemed to want us out of the way.'

'I'm not talking about you girls but the old woman and your grandfather.' He paused, tapping the fingers of his right hand against his left wrist. 'Anyway, it's all water under the bridge now. Both women are dead and...' He paused again as if remembering something. 'I'm sorry to hear about your husband and the baby. You've had a bad time.'

'Yes.' She resisted screaming at him that she was still having a bad time. Wanting to get rid of him, she added, 'Would you like some apples? Billy's already taken some but maybe your wife would like more. Fruit's good for invalids.'

He thanked her and they walked up the garden together. She put some apples in a paper bag and handed it to him and said she'd see him to the gate.

'There's no need, Mrs Lachlan. I know the way out.'

She ignored his words and began to walk to the front of the house. He followed her and, at the gate, thanked her again, adding, 'If you ever feel Billy's here too often, just send him away.'

Nellie shook her head. 'You don't have to worry about him. I'm always pleased to see him. He's no trouble at all.' She turned and went back into the house.

Making herself a cup of tea, Nellie opened Babs' crumpled letter and finished reading it.

I hope Lottie's home now and is being a help to you. Give her and Grandfather my love. I'll be writing to Dad and Francis. Do, do write, Nellie.
Lots of love to yourself and the baby.
Your affectionate sister, Babs. XXXXXX

Nellie did not immediately reply to Babs' letter. She made several starts but her tears just soaked the page. Eventually, though, she managed to write down the terrible news and posted the letter to Babs.

Somehow Nellie got through the following days. She had a reply from Babs almost by return post. It was brief.

Dear, dear Nellie,
I am so, so sorry. I wish I could be with you but Mr Rowland is a selfish swine. He's got Flo and me ploughing with the horse now and won't give me the time off. He has no sympathy at all but says there's lots of people in the same boat. I wish he'd drop dead. By hook or by crook I'm determined to see you soon.
Love Babs.

Nellie realised she was glad Babs could not get

away, knowing she would have trouble coping with her sister's sympathy.

Francis had already visited her in the hospital briefly but now he wanted to do something more positive for her. She cut him short when he said that the church was there to help her at such times. 'Not now, Francis,' she said, placing a steaming mug in front of him. 'At the moment I'm angry with God and don't want anything to do with him.'

'I can understand your feelings, Nell,' he said earnestly, pausing to take a large gulp of the Camp coffee that she knew he liked, 'but don't separate yourself from the best help you can have at such times.'

Her eyes were sad. 'It's too soon. I'm hurting too much. I know you can say that it wasn't God that caused the war but Hitler but that still doesn't help me. I need to come to terms with this in my own way ... and don't even think of mentioning that perhaps I'm being punished for marrying outside the faith. If you did then I would never speak to you again.'

Tears shone in Francis' eyes and he clasped her hand, which rested on the table. 'What kind of priest do you think I am?'

'Sorry,' she said, tears trickling down her cheeks as she gazed at their joined hands. 'But I need a brother more than I need a priest right now.'

He nodded and, holding her hand tightly, said no more.

A few days later, it came as a shock to turn on the wireless and discover that the Japanese had bombed the American naval base of Pearl

Harbor. Within no time at all, America and Britain were at war with the Japanese and, shortly after, America's declaration of war with Germany and Italy followed. Soon it would be Christmas and Nellie wondered where was that peace and goodwill to all men that so many longed for?

She was in no mood to celebrate Christmas but Lottie was so desperate to try and get to Midnight Mass that, in the end, Nellie gave in and said she would go with her. Grandfather surprised them by accompanying them. Somehow Nellie managed to remain dry-eyed throughout the service but there were those who cried.

It was one o'clock in the morning by the time they arrived home but they were worried when they entered the house by the front door and saw a light in the kitchen. Grasping his walking stick tightly, Grandfather crept towards it, followed by Nellie. Lottie collapsed on the chest in the hall, exhausted by the effort she had made in getting to church after a long day preparing for the Christmas festivities.

Then Babs appeared in the doorway. 'Surprise, surprise!'

Nellie burst into tears.

Babs hurried forward and put her arms round her. 'Is my face that ugly? Please don't cry, Nell.'

'You've got a nerve, girl,' growled Grandfather, stumping past her into the kitchen. 'You should have visited ages ago.'

'I didn't have the money and besides, I wasn't allowed leave. I knew that after twenty weeks I was entitled to a free journey home but that swine of a farmer still kicked up a fuss. I couldn't stand it any longer and so I've walked out.'

Nellie rubbed her damp cheeks and cleared her throat. 'I'm glad you've made it at last. Heck, I'm desperate for a cup of tea.'

Babs smiled. 'I've something better. Home-made wine. I bought it at the bottle stall at the Christmas Bazaar. I thought it might help.'

Lottie called from her place in the hall, 'I don't hold with strong drink.'

'I do,' said Nellie, thinking a strong drink would be very acceptable right now.

Lottie placed her arm through Nellie's and Babs', and the three sisters walked across the kitchen. Nellie could see more clearly now that Babs was wearing a green V-necked, ribbed jumper and baggy brown corduroy breeches with knee-length socks.

'You look a right cut,' she said.

Babs laughed. 'I know. Would you believe I went to a dance in this outfit and was asked out to the pictures. They're lovely and comfortable and warm. Even so, I'm longing to get into a frock.' She opened a cupboard door and took out some glasses. 'Bloody hard work, it is, working on the land. I must have been crazy applying but in summer the countryside looked so lovely and after doing my bit for the vegetable patch, I thought it would be a piece of cake.'

'Serves you right,' said Grandfather, casting a disapproving eye over the bottle of wine. 'You girls shouldn't be drinking.'

Babs ignored him and, having found a tin opener with a corkscrew attachment she drew the cork, sniffed the bottle and filled three glasses.

She handed the first to Nellie, the second to Grandfather and kept the last for herself. 'It's peapod.' Raising her glass, she added, 'Here's to better times.'

'Cheers,' said Nellie, and took a large gulp. It was sweeter than she expected and went down a treat. She drained her glass and held it out for a refill.

Grandfather made a disapproving noise in his throat but Nellie noticed that he'd emptied his glass, too. He did not ask for a refill but left the three sisters on their own and went upstairs.

Clasping her drink, Nellie moved over to the fireplace and sat down. 'So how long can you stay?'

'A couple of days.' Babs followed her over and sank onto the rug in front of the fireplace. 'I'd best go back. If I'm in luck, he'll tell the powers-that-be he wants rid of me and I'll get somewhere better than the cottage. You'd probably think "how picturesque", like I did when I first got there but in winter it's cold and damp. And as for the lav! That consists of a wooden board with a hole over a bucket, which we had to empty into a trench we dug ourselves ... and there's no hot running water. This time of year it's a nightmare.'

'But you managed to go dancing.' Nellie sipped more wine.

'So it hasn't stopped your gallop,' said Lottie.

Babs stuck her tongue out at her. 'We manage the occasional night out but I must admit, if I have any choice in where I go next, I'll make sure it's near somewhere there's more life.'

Nellie was beginning to feel light-headed and

could not hold back a giggle. 'How are they going to keep you down on the farm?' she sang.

Babs chuckled. 'You said it, Nell. But I reckon I'm stuck in the Land Army for the duration and God only knows how long that will be.'

A silence followed her words. Nellie wished she had a crystal ball. The war seemed to have been going on for ages. She yawned suddenly. 'Time for bed. Still want to share the double one?'

'Sure. It'll be almost like the old days,' said Babs.

Nellie knew those days were long gone. They were different people. They had suffered great losses and life would never be the same again.

Having Babs in the house over Christmas and Boxing Day had a beneficial effect on Nellie. Maybe it was because she did not want to upset her eldest sister that Babs avoided the subject of the baby and her husband. Instead she talked some more about her life and mentioned Eric.

'I hope you kept him in order, Babs,' said Nellie. 'He'd have been looking for comfort.'

'I'm not daft, Nell. I know what's what,' she said with a twinkle.

Nellie found herself remembering hers and Teddy's honeymoon and felt a fierce gladness inside that she had defied her mother and married him. Hadn't someone once said that it was better having loved and lost than not to have loved at all?

Chapter Eight

'So, Nellie, what are you going to do with yourself now?' asked Mrs Wainwright. 'You've had tragedy in your life but you're only a young woman and doing something for the war effort will be good for you.'

'You think so, do you?' Nellie clenched her teeth as she dragged the front gate towards her until it jammed shut. 'For once, Mrs Wainwright, I think you're right. Good morning!'

She crossed the road and carefully walked along the pavement on the other side. It was February 1942 and there had been a frost the previous night. The last few months had been the worst of her life but now it was time to move on. Teddy would want what was best for her and that meant not wallowing in misery. He would want her to go out and do some good. She considered how attitudes had changed since before the war. The government was now positively encouraging married women to go out to work. But what was she to do? Could she go back to her job as a kindergarten teacher? She would find it tiring working full-time with children in a proper school. She had enjoyed working with the pre-school children up in Ambleside. Perhaps she should think of repeating that experience here on Merseyside. Not so long ago, she had seen an article in the *Crosby Herald* about the need for a wartime nursery that would enable mothers of babies and small children to work in factories. She had not read anything more about it but maybe it was worth looking into. Perhaps someone at the council offices would know something about it.

So that's where Nellie went and was directed to the Department of Education. There she spoke to a woman who informed her that plans were afoot for a nursery to be built in the Litherland area by next spring.

'That's no good to me. I was looking for a job now.'

'There is a woman, a Mrs Perkins, who has just opened a private nursery in Linacre Road. She was hoping for a government grant but the building she is using doesn't meet with our criteria.' The woman tapped the base of her pen on the blotter on the desk. 'She is a trained nursery nurse and is filling a need, so we haven't closed her down. Could be that she'll appreciate your help.'

Nellie thanked her and asked for the address. She crossed the canal and made her way past the library and sausage factory and along Linacre Road until she came to a bicycle and repair shop. Inside, an elderly man was mending a puncture. She asked him where she would find Mrs Perkins.

'Upstairs, love. But I heard say that she was full up. Lots of young mothers are keen to earn money and can't get the kiddies' names down quick enough.' He fixed her with unblinking eyes. 'Of course, you can always put your child's name down on her waiting list.'

Nellie experienced the familiar pang of loss but managed to say, 'I have no children. I want to

153

work with them.'

His face brightened. 'In that case. You've come at the right time. One of the school leavers she had helping her walked out yesterday. Got herself a job in a factory earning more money. I'll show you where to go. Can't be having the little 'uns coming through here, so you need to go through the side door.' He took a bunch of keys from under the counter and led her outside and opened the door for her.

Nellie thanked him and headed up a flight of uncarpeted stairs to a landing at the top. Several doors faced her but she crossed to the one where the din seemed to be coming from and knocked. There was no response so she knocked louder and tried turning the knob. The door did not yield, so she banged on it. She heard a bolt being drawn and the door opened to reveal a woman in her late twenties. She looked harassed and had a struggling toddler wedged between her knees. 'Quick, say what you want,' she said. 'If you want to enrol your child we're full up.'

'I'm a kindergarten teacher interested in pre-school children. I heard you might be in need of help.'

The woman looked hopeful. 'I can't pay you what you could get in a proper place but perhaps money isn't as important to you as looking after children, otherwise you'd be after a job in a school.'

Nellie smiled. 'You're partly right. I love children but I do need some kind of wage.'

'I'm Polly Perkins.' The woman smiled. 'Hopefully we can come to some kind of agreement because it sounds like you're an answer to a prayer.'

Nellie stepped inside and bolted the door behind her. Almost immediately, a little girl came over and slipped a hand into hers. While Mrs Perkins dealt with the toddler between her knees, Nellie allowed herself to be led over to a corner where two children were building with bricks. They were so absorbed in what they were doing that they did not seem to notice her, that is, until the girl dragged her hand free and tumbled the boy's tower of bricks.

The boy turned on the girl with lightening speed and walloped her one. She screamed so piercingly that the sound seemed to go right through Nellie's head. 'Stop that noise. You shouldn't have knocked over the boy's bricks. That was asking for trouble.'

She did not wait to see the effect of her words but turned to the boy. 'Boys should not hit girls.'

He looked up at her from angry brown eyes. 'Why?'

'Because boys are generally bigger and stronger and it's not kind to pick on someone smaller than yourself,' said Nellie.

'But she was naughty.'

'She was but if she does it again then she won't be allowed to play with the bricks again today.' Nellie knelt on the parquet floor beside him. 'Now let's see who can build the highest tower. I'd like one of blue, one of yellow and one of red.' She smiled at the three children. 'I'll do a green one. Who can tell me which bricks are red?'

The girl had stopped screaming and now

scrambled over to the pile of bricks and picked up a red one. The boy sniffed. 'I don't want red ones. Blue for boys.'

Nellie told him to take all the blue ones and asked the other little girl to take the yellow ones. She hesitated and Nellie nudged a yellow brick towards her hand. Immediately the girl picked it up and soon the three children were absorbed in carefully piling brick upon brick. Nellie felt a hand on her shoulder and looked up at Mrs Perkins.

'Thanks for that. The one screaming is my daughter Daisy. She thinks she can do what she wants because I run the group. I'm sure you can imagine that doesn't make things easy for me.'

Nellie nodded and got to her feet. 'Is she one of your helpers?' she asked, spotting an adolescent girl across the room.

'Yes, she's fifteen years old.' Polly grimaced. 'I'm not sure how long she'll stay. She says she loves children but I don't imagine she thought it would be like this.'

Nellie glanced about the rest of the room. There were two babies in a playpen – one had managed to pull herself up and was rattling the bars – and about twelve other children were involved in a variety of activities. It was not exactly pandemonium but there were several running around, exercising their lungs to their full capacity. 'You have your hands full.'

Polly nodded. 'I was a children's nurse until I married. After I was widowed I decided to do this for the war effort but I've discovered that a group of lively toddlers isn't the same as nursing sick children.'

'I'm Helen Lachlan. Most people call me Nellie.' She held out her hand. 'I'm a widow, too. I can only do part-time because I live with my grandfather and younger sister. She was injured during the bombing and can't get around as well as she used to. So I'm needed at home.'

Polly's pleasant features lit up. 'Part-time will be great. I can only offer you twenty-five shillings a week. Nowhere near what you're probably worth but it's the best I can do.'

If Nellie had to pay all the overheads involved in running a house then the money would not have been enough, but situated as she was, living with her grandfather, the money would do for now. 'I accept.'

Polly looked delighted and, reaching out a hand, squeezed Nellie's. 'Thanks. I'm sure we'll get on fine.'

Nellie said, 'I'm sure it won't be from want of trying if we don't.' She noticed a piano against a far wall. 'Do you have a music time with the children?'

Polly shook her head. 'It belongs to the dancing class that rents the room in the evening. Why, do you play?'

'Self-taught. I've found musical games use up lots of energy, much more than kids running around, going mad. I hope you don't mind my saying that?' she added hastily.

'No! I'm happy with any suggestions you make.' Polly frowned. 'Such as what to do with that little horror over there? He's a real nuisance at the moment.'

'Which one?' asked Nellie.

157

'The one on the rocking horse.'

Nellie gazed in the direction she indicated. The young helper was attempting to drag a boy from the horse but he was clinging to its mane and yelling. As she watched, she saw the girl prising his fingers away from the horsehair. The boy spat at her and she smacked his bare leg. 'You little monster! I don't put up with that from no one.'

Polly sighed. 'She shouldn't smack him. Trouble is that's what she does to her younger brothers at home. There's your second challenge. Separate Jimmy from Dobbin the horse, but in a way that doesn't mean he kicks every child in sight once he's down. He's been through a bad time, poor lad, but we can't encourage such behaviour. Fortunately, he'll be off to school in September but that's some way off yet.'

Nellie nodded and strolled across the room with Poll, avoiding children and passing a table where five older children chalked patterns on blue sugar paper. As she approached the child on the horse, she asked, 'What's the bad time he's been going through?'

'His father was killed at the docks during the May blitz. Jimmy's a twin and shortly after losing his father, his brother was hit by a coal cart when the horse panicked and bolted.'

'No!' cried Nellie, distressed. 'The poor child ... and his poor mother.'

'Yes. It was terrible for them both. There's a baby girl in the family, Irene. She's the younger one in the playpen; she's no trouble. In fact, I wonder sometimes if she's too well behaved. Of course, she never did know her daddy or her

158

other brother but I think babies pick up on the way we adults feel, don't you?'

Nellie nodded. Of course children could sense how their parents were feeling without understanding why they were angry or violent. She thought of her own double bereavement and wondered how the mother coped. Perhaps she had found caring for the baby difficult, so ignored her as much as she could and Irene had given up trying to get her attention.

Nellie placed a hand on the horse's mane and smiled. 'Hello, Jimmy. I see you like Dobbin.'

'Yus,' he said sullenly.

'I can see why. He's got a lovely mane, hasn't he?' she said, stroking it.

He pushed her hand away. 'He's my Dobbin and does what I tell him or he gets a smack.' He hit the horse's neck with the flat of his hand. 'Smack, smack, smack!'

Nellie covered his hand with hers. 'I bet he'd rather have something to eat or a hug than a smack.'

'He's naughty, so he has to be smacked,' said Jimmy, attempting to drag his hand free.

Nellie released him. 'Why is he naughty?'

''Cos!'

Nellie was tempted to ask ''Cos what?' but was certain Jimmy would have difficulty putting into words the grief and angry bewilderment he was feeling. It was difficult enough for an adult to cope with loss, as well she knew, so how much harder was it for a child?

She made a decision and climbed up behind Jimmy and put her arms round him. 'Do you know this song?' she said, and began to sing:

'*Ride a cock horse to Banbury Cross,*
To see a fine lady upon a white horse,
With rings on her fingers and bells on her toes,
She shall have music wherever she goes.'

Jimmy threw back his head and stared up at Nellie. 'I'm not a lady and Dobbin's not white.'

So Nellie changed the words to Jimmy sitting upon a piebald horse. The boy appeared to like the rewrite and smiled, asking her to sing it again. She did so and then said that she wanted him to help her.

'Help you do what?' he asked.

'I'll show you,' said Nellie, climbing from the horse. She lifted Jimmy down and held his hand as she led him away. 'How would you like to do some marching, Jimmy?'

'Like a soldier?' he asked, turning his thin face up to her. 'My uncle Marty's a soldier.'

'Where is he?'

'Somewhere hot.' He sighed gustily. 'Mam's cross 'cos he's gone away.'

Nellie sympathised with her. Aloud, she suggested to Polly that she organise the children into a line while she played the piano. 'That's if you think the dancing group won't mind?'

Polly smiled. 'Why should they mind? It's not going to do the piano any harm. It's locked but I know where the key is.' She went over to a jar on the windowsill and seconds later brandished the key.

Nellie asked Jimmy if he would like to be the leader.

He put a finger in his mouth and looked

worried. 'What's a leader do?'

She told him he was to stand at the front and all the children were to follow him. He seemed to like that idea, so she left him in Polly's charge and unlocked the lid of the piano. She ran her fingers over the keys and after a few seconds, launched into 'The Grand Old Duke of York'.

'The Grand old Duke of York, he had ten thousand men.
'He marched them up to the top of the hill and then marched them down again.
'When they were up they were up, and when they were down, they were down.
'And when they were only halfway up, they were neither up nor down.'

By the time the children had marched round the room three times, Nellie could hear some of them having a go at the words. She smiled, thinking it did not matter to them that they did not know who the Duke was or how many ten thousand men were or that the rhyme was about an event in British history they were learning without realising it. For the first time in months Nellie knew she was doing something she really wanted to do and, whether her grandfather liked it or not, she was going to carry on doing it.

Later over a cup of tea, Polly told Nellie about the need for more toys for the children. 'Trouble is, just like everything else, they're in short supply. I did advertise for second-hand stuff but had no luck.'

Nellie recalled Billy helping her to take the cot up to the attic and, if her memory wasn't playing tricks on her, there was all kinds of discarded

161

stuff there, including a dolls' house. Perhaps it had once belonged to her great-great-aunt. There might even be some other toys in the tea-chests. It wouldn't do any harm to have a look. She decided not to mention it to Polly until she had had a chance to see what there was. Instead, she asked her the hours she was expected to work.

'What if we say ten o'clock to three and I'll throw in lunch?'

'Saturdays?'

'Nine till twelve?'

Nellie agreed, thinking Lottie was coping with walking so much better now that she might be able to manage more shopping and to prepare lunch for Grandfather and herself.

'I'll start tomorrow,' she said.

Polly beamed at her. 'I just know you're going to be the best thing that's happened to this group,' she said. 'I'll see you out.'

Warmed by Polly's words, Nellie hoped she was right. As she passed the window of the bicycle shop, she noticed the old man looking out and waved to him before going on her way. Her heart felt lighter as she walked along Linacre Road, thinking about Polly and the likelihood of her being a war widow. If that was so, then she was certainly working hard at overcoming her loss and supporting her child.

Nellie crossed the canal and did some shopping in the Co-op, buying what she thought they would need for today and tomorrow. Life would be easier once the days were longer and the weather was warmer. Although, that would mean more work in the vegetable garden. Hopefully Billy would still be willing to help there but she could not expect to have him much longer. She would miss him when he was called up and Lottie probably would too.

Nellie had no sooner entered the house than her grandfather appeared in the kitchen doorway. 'Where've you been, Helen? I was starting to believe you'd had an accident and I was stuck here with your sister,' he said in a grouchy voice.

'After a job,' she said, knowing there was no point in putting off what she had to say.

'A job! What kind of job?' he demanded.

'Essential war work. I'll tell you as soon as I've put the shopping away and sat down.' Despite her words, she had to squeeze past him into the kitchen because he stood in her path. She dumped the shopping on the table and smiled at Lottie who was sitting by the fire, darning the heel of one of her grandfather's thick woolly socks.

'I heard what you said, Nellie. What job?' asked Lottie anxiously. 'Will it be full-time?'

Nellie removed her gloves, noticing there was a tiny hole at the base of the thumb. She dropped it in the mending basket next to Lottie's chair. 'Will you mend that for me, please?' Taking a deep breath she said, 'I can't stay at home when I'm fit and healthy. There's a war on and we all have to do our bit in whatever way we can. The government needs more women, mothers included, working in factories making munitions and armaments and other essential things. Some-one has to look after their pre-school children when there's no family to do it, so I'm doing that part-time. It doesn't pay much but...'

'How much?' growled her grandfather.

She did not answer but said, 'I'll still put money in the kitty, Grandfather, but I do need to save some for a rainy day.'

Lottie burst out, 'Is it wise you working with little children, Nellie? Won't it upset you after losing the baby?'

Nellie turned to her. 'Of course I feel it,' she said unevenly. 'But most people aren't having it easy. Why should I be any different? I love children and...'

'What about the housework and the shopping?' grunted her grandfather.

'The house won't get very untidy if we all make an effort to clear up after ourselves every day,' said Nellie pointedly. 'On Sundays I'll try and catch up on the big jobs, such as the washing. Although, I'll only be working from ten until three ... nine till twelve Saturdays.'

'You shouldn't work on the Sabbath, Nellie,' chided Lottie.

Nellie frowned. 'I won't be the only person in the country working on the Sabbath, Lottie. The enemy doesn't take the day off then, I bet.'

'It's not right,' muttered Grandfather, glaring at her from beneath his bushy eyebrows. 'You'll wear yourself out, girl.'

'Not if we all help out in the house as I said,' insisted Nellie.

There was silence and she took that for agreement and got lunch ready.

After the meal, Nellie went upstairs into the attic rooms. Her brothers had slept in the larger one before they had left home. It was in a right mess. A dismantled bed stood against a wall and other stuff had been dumped in there. Damp was coming through the ceiling in one corner, causing the wallpaper to peel off. She couldn't remember when the paintwork had last been done anywhere in the house. As for the net curtains, they were filthy. She decided that, when the weather got warmer, she would take them down and wash them.

She gazed through the window and saw Mrs Wainwright standing in the middle of the road, gossiping with one of the neighbours. She wondered whom she was talking about now. Probably not this household because there wasn't much happening. Although, no doubt she'd pass the word around once the news got out that Nellie had a job.

Nellie turned away and saw the dolls' house on the floor in the part of the room where the ceiling slanted down and ended a few feet from the floor. She knelt and discovered that she could remove the front of the house. Five rooms were revealed: two on the ground floor, one larger one on the first floor and two on the top floor. Only a couple of the rooms had fireplaces and there was no furniture or dolls to be seen at all. Her brow puckered. She could not remember ever playing with the dolls' house. Was it because there was no furniture or dolls? But what use was a dolls' house without furniture or dolls? They must be somewhere in one of the attic rooms.

She went over to one of the tea-chests filled with junk and began to rummage through its contents. She dragged out strings and strings of red, white and blue bunting and dropped it on the floor.

165

There were several old-fashioned dresses and she held one against her. There was lots of material in the skirt which reached almost to the floor; the neckline was high with a mandarin collar. The dresses followed the bunting. Pity the frocks weren't smaller. The children could have had great fun with a dressing-up box. If she and Lottie had more time they could have altered them, but in the circumstances...

She delved further, looking for anything that might contain small furniture or dolls. She found a couple of other boxes that might prove useful. Inside one was what she realised, when she put it to her eye, was a kaleidoscope; the other had 'Shadow Pictures Punch and Judy Show' printed on the box. Inside were black figures with rods attached and tiny screens. Nellie smiled, thinking that perhaps once she'd had a bit of practice with them, then she would be able to show the older children how to use them. She put the puppets aside with the kaleidoscope and, as there didn't seem to be anything else of use to her in that tea-chest, she dumped the dresses, bunting and every-thing else back inside and turned to the other one.

Almost immediately she struck lucky. Besides finding boxes of furniture and dolls, there were also dominos, a tin drum and an odd shaped teddy bear with holes either side of his body and a loop of woven wool attached to his shoulders. She felt certain that the children would like him.

She gathered her spoils together and carried what she could downstairs. She was unsure how to get the dolls' house to the nursery but the rest she felt certain she could manage. But, first of all, she supposed that she had better ask Grand-father if she could borrow them.

To her surprise she found him sitting by the fire listening to the wireless in the kitchen. 'When did you bring that in here?' she asked.

He glanced up at her with her arms full of toys. 'What have you got there?' His tone was sharp.

'Toys. I found them in the attic.'

'You've no right to go rooting up there.'

'Sorry, but I thought you'd want to help with the war effort,' she said, determined to get him to agree to her borrowing them. 'Toys might not appear to be as important as making battleships or guns but children do need to play.' Nellie held out the teddy bear to him. 'He's a funny one.'

'It's a children's muff.'

Nellie's blue-green eyes sparkled. 'The children will love it. Can I borrow these and the dolls' house upstairs for them, please?'

He pulled on his moustache. 'They'll damage them,' he grumbled. 'Can't be letting kids pull them apart ... been up there for years.'

'Doing nothing!' cried Nellie, wanting so much for the children to have them. 'Giving nobody pleasure, forgotten, gathering dust. I don't ever remember seeing them before. Have a heart, Grandfather!'

'Why should I?' he grumbled, gazing into the fire. 'I don't know these kids.'

'You could get to know them,' she suggested rashly. 'I bet most of them haven't a granddad and would like one. I could bring some of them to visit. I'm sure they'd love seeing the hens and...'

'That's enough!' He looked horrified. 'Take the

bloody things. They won't be of any use to me once I'm dead.'

Nellie was so delighted that she did something she had seldom done before and bent to kiss his wrinkled cheek. 'Thanks. You'll get your reward in Heaven.'

'As long as there's no bloody kids up there,' he said, touching his face where her lips had pressed against his skin.

She left the kitchen singing, thinking all she needed now was for someone to take the dolls' house to the nursery. A consultation with Polly would hopefully sort out that problem.

Polly was delighted when Nellie produced the toys the next morning. 'I said you were going to be the best thing that happened to this place.'

Nellie was warmed by her praise and broached the subject of getting the dolls' house to the nursery.

'If it's not too big you could balance it on a pram.' Her eyes met Nellie's. 'Maisie Miller lives near the library. Perhaps she'll let you borrow hers. I'll suggest it when she comes to pick up her two. I'll let you know what she says in the morning.'

That suited Nellie.

Later, Polly suggested that Nellie might like to heat up Irene's bottle and give it to her. It was a bittersweet moment holding the baby in her arms but at least Irene did not kick up a fuss at being handled by a stranger. She simply gazed up at Nellie from curious blue eyes. Tears clogged her throat and she pressed a fierce kiss against the girl's curly fair hair, thinking, if only...

The following day Nellie asked Polly if she had

spoken to Maisie.

'Yes. She said you can borrow the pram. She suggested that you take her kids home, drop them off and take the pram home and then pick them up at eight tomorrow morning with the dolls' house. That does mean you staying here until four and I did tell her that you didn't start here until ten. She suggested that you knock off earlier the next day. I don't mind that if you don't?'

Nellie said that it was fine with her.

So several hours later, Nellie wheeled the pram along the street where Maisie Miller and the children lived. Jimmy was sitting at the foot of the pram, gripping the sides of the handle. His eyes were intent on the front doors of the terraced houses as they passed. Nellie could hear the baby sucking on her fist. Poor lamb, she's hungry, thought Nellie, hoping her mother would have a bottle ready for her. Growing children were allowed two pints of milk a day, although young babies had to have skimmed. Her heart ached, remembering that moment when the doctor told her that her son was dead.

'There's Mam!' cried Jimmy.

Hastily Nellie wiped her eyes with the back of her hand and looked up to see a woman standing on the doorstep.

'So yer here,' said Maisie, eyeing her up and down. 'You don't look a bit like I thought you'd look. Teachers aren't generally young and attractive.'

Nellie laughed. 'I'm not attractive and I feel ancient some days.'

'Well, you don't look it. That's not having

169

children of your own.'

The laughter died in Nellie's face and she lifted Jimmy down from the pram. 'I lost a baby. Still-born.'

Maisie looked mortified. 'I am sorry, luv. I heard you were a widow. This war's a bugger. My brother's been sent abroad. I think he's in the Middle East somewhere.' Maisie reached beneath the hood and unfastened Irene's harness. 'I'd ask you in for a cup of tea, so we could have a chat, only the woman I lodge with has a man friend in.' She lifted her daughter into her arms. 'Sorry.'

'Doesn't matter. I'll see you tomorrow morning.'

'Sure. You take care,' said Maisie.

'And you three.' Nellie glanced down at Jimmy. 'Bye. See you tomorrow, too.'

He half-lifted an arm and then let it drop and ran into the house.

As Nellie pushed the empty pram past the sausage factory, she noticed an indicator for War Week on the wall; the local target was to raise seventy thousand pounds to buy a motor torpedo boat. She thought what an enormous sum that was and wished that instead of it being for weapons it could have been spent on houses and hospitals and schools. She did not notice the policeman until he was a couple of feet away and only just managed to avoid him.

'Mrs Lachlan, isn't it?' he said, peering down at her from beneath the rim of his cap.

'Sgt McElroy! You startled me.'

'What's this we have here?' He bent his large burly frame and peered inside the pram before straightening again and looking down at Nellie.

'No baby. For a moment I thought...'

'Thought what?' asked Nellie, staring at him.

He flushed brick red.

She realised what he was thinking and was shocked. 'You thought that I'd stolen a baby.'

'Losing a baby can do queer things to a woman. So what's with the pram? No black market goods or bottles of booze hidden inside?' he said with heavy humour.

'Very funny,' said Nellie, pulling a face. 'I've borrowed the pram to carry a dolls' house. You can search it if you like.'

'I'm sure there's no need for that.' He rocked back and forth on his heels. 'It's my job to uphold the law. There's too many people around ready to break it. They think because there's a war on that it's an excuse for all kinds of things.'

'I'm sure you're right ... but I haven't broken the law. So if you don't mind, I'll be on my way.'

He nodded. 'You mind how you go.'

Nellie pushed the pram in the direction of the Red Lion but stopped at one point and looked back in time to see the bobby turn into the street where Maisie lodged. Remembering Billy lived near the library, she guessed that the Millers and McElroys were neighbours. She crossed the canal, wondering if he really had believed she was desperate enough to steal a baby. What had he meant 'losing a baby can do queer things to a woman'? No. She could imagine only too easily the child's mother's grief. She had to accept that she would never have her own child because no man could ever take Teddy's place. She would spend the rest of her life looking after other people's children.

Chapter Nine

Nellie picked up the letters from the coconut mat and turned them over. She was pleased when she saw they were from Babs and Francis, but wondered what her brother was writing to her about. She decided to open his letter first and read it over breakfast. Lottie and her grandfather were still in bed, so she would have the kitchen to herself.

She sat at the table and took a gulp of tea before slitting open the envelope.

Dear Nellie,
I thought I'd best write and let you know that I'll be bringing a solicitor to visit Grandfather on Friday afternoon. Last time I visited, you were at the nursery and I don't know if he's mentioned what we discussed that day. He is getting forgetful. He must have been feeling his age because he wants to make a will. You don't have to be there but I thought you should be aware that he's taking this step. It seems he appreciates what you do for him and wishes to provide you with some security for the future now you are widowed. I had mentioned to him that one of my parishioners, widowed when her husband was killed at Dunkirk, had said her war pension was not enough to live on. I hope you are feeling much better and not working too hard. May our Saviour bless you.
With love,
Francis

Nellie was astounded and read the letter again. She had presumed that when her grandfather died everything he possessed would automatically go to her father. It seemed that she was wrong. She remembered his uncharacteristic behaviour when she had not only lost Teddy but the baby too, and found herself wondering how her grandmother had died. She imagined him as a young sailor away at sea for months on end and thought how awful it must have been to arrive home to be greeted with the news that his wife had been dead for months. She remembered the tears in his eyes. Perhaps he had never married again because he couldn't bear to put another woman in her place. She recalled her father's reaction to her mother's death and her eyes darkened. Why couldn't he have pretended to feel some affection towards her memory and regret for her untimely death? It would have cost him little to have shown some respect by visiting her grave. Her feelings towards him hardened, and, not wanting to think about him anymore, her thoughts returned to Francis' letter.

Should she mention it to her grandfather? Should she try to get home early from the nursery? Or should she just carry on as usual as if she didn't know anything about the will or the solicitor? She decided on the latter and naturally wondered how much money her grandfather would leave her. A hundred pounds would make a nice little nest egg. She vowed she would be more patient with him, feeling warmer towards him. Who knows, maybe he might even leave some money to Lottie and Babs.

Thinking of her sisters reminded Nellie of Babs' letter. She glanced at the postmark and saw that it said Warrington. So Babs had left the first farm. Was she finding her new billet any more exciting than her last one?

Nellie stretched out a hand for her cup and drained it to the dregs before beginning to read,

Dear Nellie,

Sorry I'm late in answering the letter you sent me at the end of February telling me all your news. Would you believe that I'm living in a mansion? It makes the cottage on the farm seem like a dog kennel. I'm sharing it with nineteen other land girls and you want to hear the noise when we all sit down for supper in the huge dining room! It has oil paintings on the walls of hunting dogs and horses. Flo moved with me but we're making other friends, so are not as close as we were at the cottage. Some of the older girls can already drive tractors and this is something I want to learn. Today work's been back-breaking and it makes planting seed potatoes in the garden look like a doddle. We've planted thousands on some of the land that had lain fallow and was ploughed up last year. But you don't want to hear about work. Guess what the big news is here right now? The Yanks are here, Nellie! I mean they're here at Burtonwood, the airbase. So far we've only seen a dozen or so of them strolling about town but rumour has it that there's going to be thousands of them coming over. I've never met a Yank before and I'm expecting them to speak like they do in the pictures. I'll keep you posted to when I actually speak to one.

174

Anyway, enough of them. How are you, Nell? How are you getting on with the kiddiewinks? I bet it's hard work. How's Grandfather and Lottie? Is he still as much of a grouch as ever, and is Lottie any better? It must be tough being in pain the way she is. Has she lost any weight since she's had to help in the house and garden? How's Billy? He can't have much longer to go before he gets called up. Do write and bring me up to date, Nell.
Lots of love,
Babs. XXXXX

Nellie smiled as she folded the letter and replaced it in its envelope. She loved the way Babs wrote, could almost hear her voice in her head as she read her words. She pondered on whether she should tell her youngest sister about Francis' letter but decided not to count her chickens before they were hatched. Who was to say Grandfather might not get a cob on with her and change his mind? She thought about what Babs had said about the Yanks. Would she keep her head or lose it to a handsome American airman? A timely bit of sisterly advice might be in order. She could also tell her about Lottie and Billy and how they seemed to get on well. Most likely he would be calling round this evening, now the days were starting to draw out.

Nellie placed the letters in her handbag and, putting on her jacket, left for work. She looked forward to seeing the children and having a chat with Polly. She supposed that she would also have to give thought to who could replace Billy when he was eventually called up.

175

Lottie looked out of the window and saw Billy come out of the outhouse with a spade. A bag of seed potatoes had been delivered that morning and she had been waiting for him to come all day to dig the trenches, planning on helping him plant them out. It might give her hip gyp but she was prepared to put up with the pain to spend time in his company.

As Lottie limped through the kitchen, Grandfather glanced up from his newspaper. 'Where are you going?'

'To help Billy.'

'Billy? Who's Billy? Can't have strangers here.'

Lottie sighed. She had noticed that her grandfather was getting forgetful. 'Billy's not a stranger. He's been coming here for the past year. Not that he'll be coming much longer. He'll be eighteen soon and is going to be a soldier.'

Grandfather scowled at her. 'Nobody's told me that. A soldier, you say? Handy having the armed forces around the place. There's a war on, you know, and there could be spies around.'

'Spies! There's no spies here,' she said, wondering if he was going doolally as well as forgetful.

'That's what you think,' he said, rustling the newspaper. 'They're crafty, them spies.'

Lottie decided to humour him. 'If you say so. I'm going out in the garden.'

She left him to his newspaper and went outside. Billy looked up as she approached and smiled. 'Hi, Lottie. You coming to give me a hand?'

She smiled shyly. 'If I can be of use.'

'Of course, you can. There's nobody I'd rather

176

have in the garden helping me.'

She blushed. 'You mean that?'

'I wouldn't say it if I didn't. Shall we get cracking?'

She nodded, glad that he never seemed to stare at her as if he found her fat and unattractive. He was kind and helpful and she would never forget how quickly he had reacted when Nellie had fainted and how, later, he had asked her for her opinion about what to do about the apples.

Billy began to dig. Lottie watched him, wondering if he could ever fancy her. Of course, she was older than him and probably looked it too, she thought sadly, limping over to the potato bag and taking out some sprouting potatoes and going over to where he was digging the trench. He indicated exactly where he wanted her to put the potatoes and the distance between them. As they worked together as a team, she said, 'It's a miracle, isn't it?'

'You mean a whole load of potatoes growing from each little one you plant?'

'Yeah.' That was another thing she liked about Billy. He seemed to know exactly what she meant without asking her to explain herself. 'How is it you're so good at this, when you only have a back yard at home?'

He smiled down at her. 'It's like anything. You learn about it by having a go. No other way of going about any job in my opinion.'

'You think I could learn about things the same way?'

Billy rested on his spade. 'Practise makes perfect. Although, I reckon if your heart's in it, then you're more likely to make a good job of things.'

Lottie nodded. That made sense. 'What would you like to do when the war's over, for a living, I mean?'

He resumed his digging. 'I don't think that far ahead. Your grandfather was telling me about your brother Joseph. I wonder what plans he had for after the war, if any?'

She realised what he meant. If you were a young man and had to go and fight, what was the use of making plans when you might be killed? She shivered at the thought of Billy being killed. She liked him a lot and didn't want anything bad to happen to him. She decided not to think about the future either. 'D'you like potatoes?' she asked, getting on with the job in hand.

He nodded. 'Chips. I love Mam's chips. She makes them the gear.'

'I thought your mam was an invalid,' said Lottie, and was surprised to see hot colour stain his cheeks. 'Have I said something I shouldn't have? I'm sorry if I have.'

He said roughly, 'You've got nothing to be sorry about. Mam is sick and what makes her sick does mean she's laid out flat sometimes, but she can get about.'

'You mean her illness comes and goes like the pain in my hip and leg?'

'Exactly like that,' he said, smiling, and leaning forward, he brushed her lips with his. Lottie's lips tingled. She could scarcely believe he had just kissed her and wanted him to do it again because it had felt so nice. She held up her face, closed her eyes and puckered her lips. 'I shouldn't,' he murmured, but he did.

This time it was a proper kiss and lasted until a voice startled them apart with the words, 'What's going on here?'

Lottie almost fell over the bag of seed potatoes but was steadied by Billy's hand on her arm. He helped her to straighten up and they both stared at his father. Sgt McElroy did not look pleased and Lottie was scared.

'What are you doing here, Dad? It's like you were checking up on me,' said Billy, an angry note in his voice.

'Don't be impertinent, boy! I'm – I'm here on police business,' he stated.

'What kind of police business? This isn't your beat,' said Billy.

His father said sternly, 'More cheek. You get on with your work and keep your distance from Miss Callaghan or I'll be having words with her grandfather. I can't see him approving of you taking advantage of this young lady here.'

'He hasn't done anything wrong! I – I'm not a little girl. I – I liked him kissing me,' said Lottie boldly.

Billy hid a grin and got on with the digging.

Sgt McElroy stared at Lottie and she stared back defiantly. He spoke quietly as if to a child, 'I'm only thinking of what your grandfather and Mrs Lachlan might say if they knew you'd been canoodling with the hired hand. They might tell him not to come here anymore. You don't want him sacked, do you?'

Lottie certainly didn't want that to happen and

shook her head.

'I knew you were a sensible young woman,' said Sgt McElroy, smiling. 'And how is your grandfather and Mrs Lachlan keeping? I saw her a short while ago pushing a pram.'

'She'd borrowed the pram to take the dolls' house to Mrs Perkins' private nursery. She's helping with the children.'

'Now that's good.' He nodded his head several times. 'She's showing sense by doing something useful to take her mind off her loss. My wife lost a baby and ended up with a form of paralysis.'

'That's sad,' said Lottie.

'You can say that again,' he said, a grim smile playing about his mouth. 'You tell your grandfather to be on his guard. There's been a few break-ins round and about. I'll be going now but don't you forget what I said, Miss Callaghan, if you don't want Billy to stop coming here.'

She nodded, thinking that perhaps kissing wasn't the good thing she had thought it.

Later when Nellie came home, Lottie told her that they'd had a visit from Sgt McElroy.

'What did he want?'

Lottie pursed her lips. 'He said it was on police business and there'd been some break-ins.'

'Where?'

'Round and about. I was to put Grandfather on his guard.'

Nellie's brow furrowed. 'How did he react?'

'He talked about guns. He doesn't have a gun, does he, Nellie?'

'I shouldn't think so. He talks about spies but we haven't seen any, have we?'

Lottie chuckled. 'No. It would be funny if Billy's father came round again and Grandfather thought him a spy.'

'That man does have a habit of popping up when one least expects it. What else did he have to say?'

'He asked how you and Grandfather were keeping. He mentioned having seen you. He also said that his wife lost a baby and ended up with some kind of paralysis. Billy told me, though, that she can get about a bit.'

Nellie nodded, thinking perhaps she might make a point of seeing Maisie Miller and asking her about Mrs McElroy. With them living in the same street Maisie might know something about her.

She did that two days later after telling Lottie and her grandfather that she would be late home that afternoon. She had completely forgotten that it was Friday and the solicitor and Francis were coming to call.

To save Maisie Miller picking up her two children, Nellie had said that she would drop them off at the house. She was invited in for a cup of tea and as they sat in the kitchen, Nellie brought up the subject of Mrs McElroy.

'My sister's been told that she lost a baby and it resulted in some kind of paralysis. I feel really sorry for the woman.'

Maisie said, 'Save your energy. She drinks.'

Nellie's eyes widened. 'What!'

'She's a boozer.' Maisie looked disgusted. 'Don't ask me how she can afford the amount she gets down. Poor Terence! He's had to put up

181

with it for years. So she lost a baby but she had Billy and we all have to get on with life as best we can. We both know that as well as anyone.'

Nellie nodded. 'They must be embarrassed by her drinking and that's why we were told she's an invalid.'

Maisie agreed. 'Trouble is she depends on Billy a lot, so she'll miss him when he's called up. Still, we all have our crosses to bear and have to cope as best we can.'

Nellie agreed and left soon after.

When she arrived home it was to find Francis sitting in the kitchen drinking Camp coffee. It was only then that Nellie remembered about the solicitor. 'Where's Grandfather?' she asked. 'Did the solicitor come? Did everything go according to plan?'

Francis nodded. 'Once I'd assured Grandfather he could be trusted everything was agreed. Once it's drawn up all he has to do is sign it. The solicitor had another appointment and had to leave. I thought I'd stay and see you.' He rubbed his jaw with his hand and yawned.

'You tired?'

'I'm always tired. I don't sleep very well.'

She knew the feeling. 'Memories?'

He grimaced. 'Too many bad ones. The sights I saw in the blitz ... having to identify Mam and Aunt Josie. It'll be a year soon.'

'I bet you never thought your faith would be tested in such a way when you went into the priesthood,' she said softly. 'Have you ever doubted or had regrets about the life you've chosen?'

'By regrets I presume you mean never having a wife and children? Is that what you're trying to say, Nellie?'

'I suppose I am.'

'I'll let you know that at the end of my life.' His large hand grasped her small one and squeezed it. 'Remember when we were young?'

'Young? We're not old, Francis.'

'I feel old. When I do sleep I have terrible nightmares. I question how I would cope on a battlefield. I wonder sometimes whether it's another testing ground where God wants me.'

'No!' cried Nellie, her fingers tightening on his. 'I've lost too many. I don't want to lose you as well.' Her voice sank to a whisper. 'Surely it says in the Bible that God does not test us beyond that which we are able to bear?' He stared at her. The moment was fraught with emotion. 'Don't volunteer! You're needed here,' she insisted.

He took a deep shuddering breath. 'Perhaps. I'll stay for a few more months at least, and will see how things go after that.'

Nellie knew that she had to be satisfied with those words for now. Neither of them moved straight away but stayed grasping the other's hand as if it were a lifeline.

Lottie came through the door and they drew away and looked at their younger sister. Nellie said, 'Have you heard anything from Dad, Francis?'

'No. I thought you might have. I did write and tell him about Teddy and the baby.'

'I haven't heard a word. I'm sure if anything had happened to him one of us would have heard.'

Francis nodded and stood up. 'I'd best be going. But first would you like me to give you a blessing, Nellie?'

She nodded, thinking that perhaps he needed to do this more than she did. He placed his hands on her head and asked God to comfort her in her grief, heal her pain, guide her for the future and bless her that night with peaceful sleep.

She thanked him. He kissed the cheeks of both his sisters and then picked up his hat from the dresser. 'I'll see myself out.'

There was a silence after he had gone.

Nellie made herself a cup of tea and sat at the table. She sensed her sister was dying to ask what they had been talking about and wondered if Lottie knew about their grandfather having a will drawn up. She realised that she didn't want to talk about it but there was something that needed saying. She repeated what Francis had said about it almost being a year since their mother and aunt had been killed.

Lottie cried in horror, 'How could I have forgotten?'

'So much to do,' said Nellie. 'If you think you can manage, we'll visit the grave on the anniversary of their death.'

Lottie said, 'We can pick the bluebells under the fruit trees and cut some hawthorn blossom and put them in water in a jam jar.'

So they visited Ford cemetery together. Afterwards Nellie wished that Lottie had stayed at home. She had watered the grave with her tears. The next day Nellie felt duty-bound to visit Bootle cemetery where Teddy's parents were buried. They

184

had died some years before. She was not the only one there because so many had died that week in May just over a year ago.

Nellie began to have strange nightmares about Sgt McElroy arresting her for having stolen a baby. Perhaps it was because she had bumped into him coming round the side of the house. He'd told her that he was just keeping an eye on the place because of the reported break-ins.

'I haven't heard of any,' Nellie had said.

'That's because we don't want to worry people,' he'd replied.

She'd thought his answer was too glib, not to mention peculiar in the light of his having told Lottie to warn their grandfather about them. She'd been so irritated that she asked how his wife's paralysis was with a knowing look. He had turned a funny colour and hurried away. Afterwards she felt ashamed of herself, and the nightmares had begun. In one he arrested her for being drunk and disorderly!

This state of affairs might have persisted if it were not for a visit from Babs. Nellie was sitting in a deckchair, relaxing for once while Lottie and Billy worked in the garden, when a familiar voice whispered in her ear, 'What's this? You skiving off?'

Nellie started and opened her eyes and smiled up at her youngest sister. 'Why didn't you say you were coming?'

'I wasn't sure if I'd make it. As it was I got a lift.' Babs' heart-shaped face was alight with excitement. 'I wish you could have seen him, Nell. He was the spitting image of Cary Grant. I think I'm in love,' she said dreamily.

'Who was?' asked Nellie, amused.

'The Yank who gave me a lift to Warrington station in his jeep.'

'Oh!' Nellie stared at her lovely sister, thinking about her flirtatious ways and remembering what had happened with their mother. 'Don't you get carried away and do what you oughtn't,' she warned.

Babs' expression changed. 'You're a right one to talk about getting carried away. What about the way you rushed into marriage?'

Nellie was not to be diverted. 'At least I'd known Teddy for years before we took the plunge.'

Babs pouted. 'Don't be a such a fuddy-duddy, Nell. You're sounding like my mother. I suppose you don't believe in love at first sight?'

'I've never given it much thought.'

'Think about it now. This love I feel could be the real thing. It could last for ever,' she said, striking a dramatic pose.

Nellie said, 'It depends on what you mean by real love. I suppose people can be instantly attracted to each other but it didn't happen that way for me and Teddy. It grew on us. I suppose if he hadn't been on disembarkation leave, we mightn't have realised how much we cared about each other and got married in a rush the way we did.'

'So you weren't desperate to go to bed with him?'

Nellie fixed her younger sister with a stare. 'You shouldn't be talking about such things.'

'Why not?' Babs flushed. 'That's nearly all

some of us talk about after being out on a date. So did you enjoy sleeping with him?'

Nellie smiled and then realised Lottie was present and straightened her face. 'You're not married, so get such thoughts out of your head.'

Babs giggled. 'Your expression said it all, Nell. A bit of all right, was it?'

Nellie said severely, 'Sex outside marriage is a mortal sin for a respectable Catholic girl like you!'

'I don't know why you have to sound so scandalised and talk about mortal sin to me. You eloped and were excommunicated.'

'Was I? I've yet to receive a written notice saying so. Anyway, I don't want you ending up in trouble just because an airman has Cary Grant looks.'

'Yes, Nell,' said Babs, her voice subdued and her eyes downcast.

Nellie wished her mother was there to reinforce the pitfalls of sex outside marriage. Although, on the other hand, perhaps it was just as well that she wasn't. 'Now you're here, how about the three of us going the flicks together? It's ages since we've done that.'

Babs hesitated and, for a split second, Nellie wondered if her sister had made a date with the Yank until she said, 'Why not?'

Nellie then thought that perhaps they should ask Grandfather, but he shook his head and said, 'Someone has to stay here on guard. There might be spies.'

Babs rolled her eyes and said as they went upstairs, 'Why's he talking about spies?'

Nellie told her about Billy's father warning them that there had been some break-ins. 'For some reason Grandfather has it fixed in his head that they're spies.'

Babs looked thoughtful. 'I suppose it makes some kind of sense with there being a war on.'

They went to see Gracie Fields in a re-showing of *Shipyard Sally*. The newspapers had panned the star for divorcing her comedian husband and marrying an Italian-born director, Monte Banks. She had further displeased them by exchanging England for Canada, according to the press, so he wouldn't be interned. However, her fans had remained loyal, especially as, recently, she had returned home to perform live in front of factory workers and troops.

When they got back, it was to find that Grandfather had locked all the doors. It was only by persistently knocking and calling to him that he eventually allowed them into the house. 'You shouldn't have gone out,' he complained querulously, 'leaving me all on my own for the spies to torture me.'

Nellie hugged him and kissed his cheek. 'Sorry, Grandfather, but you're perfectly safe. There are no spies here. I'll go and make you a nice cup of cocoa.'

He appeared soothed by her attentions and Nellie determined not to leave him alone in future. Perhaps she should think of having the local bobby to keep an eye on the place if she and Lottie were to go out at any time and let Grandfather know help was at hand.

The warmer weather arrived and Polly insisted

on their young charges spending more time out-doors. Polly and her helper took the smaller ones to the park, while Nellie went with the older ones along the canal where they could watch the barges bringing coal from Wigan to the gasworks in Bootle and Liverpool. Nellie enjoyed these outings. The weather was beautiful and being outside made her feel more hopeful about life. She knew Polly so much better now and dis-covered that her husband had been in the RAF, and had been shot down over the Channel. Nellie asked how she had coped with his death.

Polly answered simply. 'What else could I do?'

Nellie told her about the baby. They discussed whether it would have been easier for Nellie to cope if she had been able to hold her child in her arms. Polly said that to hold him and then have to let him go would have been unbearable.

Then she went on to say, 'We'll be losing some of the children in September to big school.'

'I know. Jimmy for one. Will you advertise for more?'

'We've got a waiting list. Although, I'd give it all up if I got the chance of working in a council nursery. I wouldn't have to worry about the mothers forgetting to hand over their money some days. We must keep a look out for any news of a nursery being built in the area.'

Nellie remembered what she had been told a few months back when she had called at the council offices but decided not to say anything until she had more information. In the meantime, she had plenty of other things on her mind; not only would they be losing Billy soon but Babs had

189

not written since her last visit when she'd had a lift from an American. Could it be that it was time Nellie took a trip to Warrington one Saturday, while Billy was still around to keep an eye on Grandfather and Lottie; see if she was getting up to anything with that airman. She would write a letter to Babs and post it that evening.

Chapter Ten

Babs pocketed the letter from Nellie, thinking she would read it later when she had time. No doubt her sister was wanting to know why she hadn't heard from her recently. Well, that was OK because she had good reason for not having written. She was worked off her feet but this evening she had a date with Luke, the Cary Grant look-alike, and was late already. She was meeting him in the village and no doubt he would give her chocolates and suggest they went for a walk. He approved of the countryside around Culcheth and it seemed to have slipped his mind that, as a land girl, she saw enough of fields, trees and farm animals.

She outlined her lips with an orange-red Max Factor lipstick she had bought from one of the other girls, and then smiled at her reflection in the mirror. She thought she looked pretty good. Reaching for her shoulder bag, she remembered how she had believed herself in love with Luke when they'd first met because he looked the stuff a girl's dreams were made of: tall, dark, handsome. He was also kind and had good manners. Trouble was, last week he had told her that he didn't approve of make-up and had asked her to wipe off her lipstick. It seemed he was a Baptist and didn't approve of tobacco, alcohol or any of the other activities she considered fun. She had told him that she was Catholic and he had immediately begun to talk about the Bible. Discussing religion was the last thing Babs wanted from Luke but she had agreed to another date and made up her mind if he was not prepared to do a few things to please her, such as going into Warrington to a dance or to see a film or a variety show at the theatre, then she would call it a day.

Babs knew she was more than three quarters of an hour late as she approached their meeting place under a chestnut tree, near the parish church. There was a jeep parked at the kerb and she expected the waiting Luke to be a little cross with her. It was not until the airman in the olive green uniform turned round that she realised he was not her date. He removed his cap and she saw not only was his hair fair but that he wasn't handsome either. His nose was crooked and his mouth too wide and he looked to be a few years older than Luke.

'Miss Callaghan? Miss Barbara Callaghan?' he drawled.

'That's right. Who are you? Where's Luke?' Her voice sounded snappy.

'Name's Jake. Sergeant Jake O'Donnell. Luke couldn't make it.' He held out a hand.

She took it, noticing that his eyes were blue and

191

fringed with dark-gold lashes. 'So he sent you.'

Jake's tawny eyebrows rose. 'You'd rather he'd just stood you up? I was beginning to think that's what you'd done but he did say you were often late, so I decided to wait exactly an hour.' He glanced at his watch. 'You just made it.'

Babs' cheeks pinked. 'I'm sorry. It's been a long day for me out in the fields.'

'Understood.' Jake squeezed her fingers gently before releasing them and replacing his cap. 'So where would you like to go?'

'Pardon?'

'Granted.'

'I meant ... what do you mean by asking me where I'd like to go?'

A lazy smile started in his eyes and dimpled his lean cheeks. 'I thought the question was a simple one,' he drawled. 'I'm Luke's replacement. If you'd rather not go out with me, then perhaps I'll just walk you home.'

Startled by the change that smile made to his face, Babs said, 'For goodness sake, it's Saturday night, the last thing I want to do is stay in.'

'So what would you like to do?'

'Make me an offer,' she challenged.

He looked her up and down, taking in the curves beneath the floral printed summer dress with its accompanying bolero, and the neat ankles and dainty feet in the low heeled court shoes, and gave in to temptation. 'Do you like swing?'

'Swing?'

'Jazz. Bopping?'

'I've heard of jazz and jive but not bopping?' It was as if he was speaking a different language.

'Do you dance?'

Immediately Babs smiled. 'Now you're talking, Sergeant O'Donnell. I'm not a brilliant dancer but I'm a quick learner. Although, I'll warn you now that I've heard there are dance halls that don't allow jive.'

'I wouldn't know that as I haven't been over here long ... no time to case the joints. One thing's for sure, they're gonna have to get used to it or we'll be holding our own dances back at the base,' he said, opening the passenger door of the jeep. 'Climb aboard.'

She did not need asking twice and, in no time at all, she was being whisked along the road in the direction of Warrington, having dismissed Luke from her thoughts.

The dance hall that Jake chose to patronise turned out to be strictly ballroom. 'Are you sure you're OK with this?' he asked, having found them a small table. She nodded and he went off to get them a drink. She watched the dancers circling the floor, wondering if he had volunteered for the job of taking her out or had had it thrust on him.

Jake returned after the next dance and placed a long glass in front of her before pulling up a chair. The band struck up another tune and she began to hum, 'Goodnight, Irene'.

'Now that number is from back home,' said Jake.

Babs nodded, sipped her drink and realised it was lemonade, refreshing but without a kick. 'There's no alcohol in this. I am over eighteen and allowed to drink in this country.'

'Sorry, Miss Callaghan, but I don't have it in

mind to get you drunk and have my wicked way with you.' He took a long drink of his beer.

His words startled her. 'Why not? Don't you find me attractive?'

A muscle in his jaw twitched but he did not answer her straight away and asked did she mind if he smoked. She shook her head and watched him take out a packet of Camel cigarettes. 'Can I try one of them?'

'Nope. Smoking is a bad habit and I don't want to lead you astray. To be honest, you remind me of my sister back home. She's always trying to push back the boundaries. Luke treated you right but I can see how a guy like him would eventually drive a girl like you nuts.'

Babs was annoyed. 'You don't know anything about me, so how can you say that?'

'You haven't mentioned his name since you climbed into my jeep.'

'If I remember rightly you haven't either. In fact we didn't speak at all on the way here.'

'I was waiting to see if you'd ask why he couldn't come.'

She flushed. 'You could have told me. Now *you* have mentioned him, perhaps I can say that Luke isn't the person I thought him, so I was going to end it tonight.'

'He'd come to the same conclusion about you, realised you didn't have much in common.'

Babs was hurt. 'He could have had the guts to say so to my face.'

'He was going to but had an accident this morning ... dropped a wrench on his foot. He gave me a note for you.' Jake reached into his pocket and held out an envelope.

The colour in Babs' cheeks deepened. 'Don't bother. You've said it all.'

He reached for her hand and placed the envelope in it. She stared at him and then ripped it up. 'My, you've got a temper, must go with the red hair,' said Jake mildly, shaking his head.

'None of us is perfect.'

He drawled, 'No. But you have got looks, so I can see why Luke fancied you.'

Babs was about to say that there was more to her than just a pretty face, when she remembered that it was Luke's handsome face that had attracted her. 'You obviously don't fancy me,' she said.

'I wouldn't say that but I'm older and wiser, so I don't believe in rushing my fences. Have some of your drink and if you're still in the mood to dance then I'll take you round the floor.'

Babs recovered her nerve. 'It's the only reason I came here with you,' she said, reaching for her glass, 'and I hope you don't tread on my toes.'

She was to wish those words back after he led her onto the floor because she was so nervous of making a fool of herself, she stumbled over his feet and found herself lifted into the air. He danced her round the floor in that position and she felt so embarrassed she wanted to hit him but that was impossible; clamped to his chest and with his shaven cheek against her smooth one she couldn't. Instead she gazed up at the twirling, glistening ball hanging from the ceiling, so that she didn't have to meet anyone else's eyes and experienced a sense of floating.

When that dance ended and he took her back to their table, she drank her lemonade down in almost one draft and then stared at him. 'Is that how you usually dance with women?'

'Nope! I usually dance with mature women who can dance. Another drink?'

If she hadn't drunk all her lemonade, Babs just might have flung what was left in his face but as it was she had to make do with saying, 'D'you mean to insult me?'

'I was just speaking the facts as they are, Barbara. Drink?'

She nodded.

When he returned to the table and placed another lemonade in front of her, she made no comment but acted like he was not there, continuing to watch the activity on the dance floor. When the dance finished, she expected him to say something but he didn't. So she remained silent and reached for her glass, taking tiny sips of the lemonade. The next half hour was one of the most frustrating since she had moved from the farm near Ormskirk. He sat there as silently as she did and she could not help thinking that he was making her suffer because she had ripped up Luke's note. It had been a childish thing to do. She wondered if Jake was a close friend of Luke's and whether he came from middle America. With a name like O'Donnell there must be some Irish in him, so most likely he was Catholic, but that didn't say she and he would have anything else much in common. He was too old for her, anyway, and besides, she didn't feel the least bit attracted to him. It would be a relief when they

196

said their goodbyes.

When the interval arrived and he asked her if she would like to go, she said yes and strangely felt near to tears. Despite her telling him to drop her at the entrance to the drive, he drove her to the front door of the house. As she was about to let herself out of the jeep, he left the driving seat and helped her down. 'Thanks,' she said. 'Although, you didn't have to.'

'Sure, I didn't.' Abruptly he seized her shoulders and brought her against him and kissed her long and hard.

When he released her she stared up at him from blazing eyes. 'I beg your pardon!'

'Again. Think before you say yes in future, Barbara.' He saluted her and climbed back into the jeep. 'Goodnight. Sleep tight.'

She watched him drive off, wishing she had thought to slap his face. Then she skipped into the house, thinking she was free of Luke and could now do damn well anything she wanted to do. It was not until she was in bed that she remembered Nellie's letter, but decided she was too sleepy to read it. Tomorrow would do and she'd reply to it the same day.

Nellie pounced on the letter and hurried with it into the kitchen. She slit it open and spread the single sheet of paper on the table.

Dear Nellie,
This is just a quick scribble as I'm up to my eyes. It would be lovely to see you but it's just not worth your while coming here at the moment. We get sent off

places where we're needed and sometimes we stay there, so I can't guarantee I'd be here even if I gave you a date. You mustn't worry about me. I'm fine. I've finished with the Cary Grant lookalike and at the moment I'm fancy free and have no intention of getting serious with anyone. I hope you and Lottie are fine, and Grandfather, too. Seen anything of Francis? I had a letter from Dad but he didn't ask after you, which surprised me because I'd told him about Teddy and the baby. Having said that, a lot of the letter was blacked out. At least we know when he sent it he was still alive and kicking.

Lots of love,
Babs.

Nellie was disappointed about not seeing her sister but accepted that, because of the war, things weren't easy for anyone. She was hurt by her father's failure even to send his condolences via Babs. Still, nothing he did that was hurtful should surprise her but it did depress her. She realised that she really was in need of a break.

There was a sound at the kitchen door and Nellie looked up and saw Lottie in her pyjamas. 'You not gone to work yet?' she said.

'In a minute,' said Nellie, smiling. 'There's some tea in the pot. I've a letter from Babs. I had thought of going to see her but she says not to bother because she can't guarantee when she'll be there.'

Lottie poured herself a cup of tea and said sadly, 'Billy'll be off soon. He's had his call up papers.'

'We're going to miss him, aren't we?'

Lottie nodded and then rested her chin in her

hands, causing her lank hair to flop about her face. 'There's only one good thing about him going and that's we'll see less of his father.'

Nellie nodded. 'Although, he might still come round because of the break-ins.'

Lottie muttered, 'I don't know one person around here who's been broken into. I think he only comes to keep an eye on me and Billy. At least Grandfather won't be sacking him now.'

Nellie stared at her. 'What d'you mean "keep an eye on you and Billy"? And why should Grandfather sack him?'

Lottie hesitated. 'Nell, is it wrong to kiss someone you like?'

'Why, have you been kissing Billy?'

'Only once,' said Lottie, flushing. 'He kissed me first and it was only a little kiss but when his dad caught us he said Grandfather would sack Billy if he knew about it. So I made sure it didn't happen again.'

Nellie said tactfully, 'It could be that Sgt McElroy thinks Billy's too young for you and, with him going away, doesn't want either of you getting hurt.'

Lottie's face brightened. 'It could be that. It was really nice being kissed. I never thought any boy would want to kiss me.'

Nellie was glad that she had a happy memory. Eying Lottie from head to toe, she realised that she had lost weight. She had good legs and shapely ankles and, although she could never be classed as pretty, she was growing into a handsome woman. She had an air of innocence about her that some men might find attractive.

'Well, you know different now, Lottie, so let it boost your confidence and don't let anyone pull you down,' said Nellie.

Lottie blushed. 'Thanks, Nell.'

'My pleasure. Anyway, I've work to go to. You relax and stop worrying about Grandfather and Sergeant McElroy. You're probably right about there not being any break-ins.'

'Does that mean we can have a night out? There's a film on in Liverpool I'd like to see.'

'You think you can manage a trip into Liverpool on the bus?' asked Nellie.

Her sister nodded. 'It's on at the Paramount and is called *Moonlight in Havana*. It stars Allan Jones, the American tenor. You know the one. He sings "Donkey Serenade".'

'He's the one with blond wavy hair and a lovely voice, isn't he? OK! As long as you don't end up complaining because of the walking and Grandfather doesn't mind.'

'I won't complain,' said Lottie cheerily, 'and we could ask him if he'd like to come with us.'

But when they approached their grandfather, he first asked what the film was about and when they said it was a musical, he shook his head. 'Not my kind of thing. Anyway, someone's got to stay home and keep guard.'

'I don't think there's anything to fear, Grandfather. Neither of us has heard of anyone being broken into, so you won't lock us out, will you?' she teased.

He scowled. 'I'm not a fool, girl. You give the password and I'll let you in.'

'What is the password?' she asked.

'V for Victory,' he said.

She nodded and left him sitting in front of the fire with the *Liverpool Echo* on his knee, listening to the wireless.

The film was as enjoyable as the sisters expected and, for a couple of hours, they were transported to Cuba and taken out of themselves. Nellie told herself that it was as good as going to Warrington. But by the time they arrived home, Lottie's limp had worsened and her mouth was tight with pain.

'In future we'll stick to the Regal,' said Nellie firmly.

They went round the back of the house but the washroom door was locked. She banged on it loudly but there was no response so she banged again and shouted, 'V for Victory!' Still no answer.

'Perhaps he's fallen asleep on the parlour sofa,' said Lottie. 'You go round the front and he might hear you better. I'll sit on the step and wait here.'

Nellie nodded and retraced her steps. She not only banged on the front door but called, 'V for Victory!' through the letterbox. She also knocked on the parlour window but without any effect.

'Hello, hello, hello! What's going on here?' called a voice out of the darkness.

Nellie jumped and turned round; she could just about make out a dark shape looming behind the torch. 'Is that you, Sergeant McElroy?' she asked.

'Yes.' He shone the torch in her face.

'Lower that!' said Nellie, half-blinded. 'What are you doing here? You didn't half give me a fright.'

'Sorry about that. What's up?'

'We can't get in. Grandfather must have locked

all the doors and fallen asleep.'

'Where's your sister?'

'Waiting round the back.'

Immediately he set off round the side of the house. Nellie hurried after him, arriving seconds later. The first thing he did was ask Lottie if she was OK.

'I'm tired and in pain and I want to go to bed,' she said fretfully.

'All right, love, we'll soon get you inside.' He tried the handle but it didn't open. He shone his torch up at the first-floor windows. 'There's a window open up there.'

'You'd never get up there,' said Nellie. 'You're too large. And I'm not shinning up the drainpipe in my best stockings.'

He returned to the washroom door and tapped a small window pane with his truncheon. The glass broke and, carefully, he slipped his hand through the gap and turned the key.

Nellie was surprised that the door was not bolted. She hurried inside, followed by Sgt McElroy. A limping Lottie brought up the rear. Nellie could feel her heart beating heavily, not knowing what she would find inside. She clicked on the electric light and led the way into the kitchen. She stopped abruptly as she saw her grandfather lying on the floor with his stick beside him.

'Oh God,' she whispered, hurrying over to him. She looked into his ashen face and knelt down to search for a pulse; his skin was still warm.

'Oh dear, oh dear, oh dear!' said Lottie.

Nellie looked up at Sgt McElroy. 'I can't find a pulse. I think he's dead. Could you fetch a doctor? I'd rather stay with him.'

'Let me try.' The sergeant knelt down and fumbled for the old man's wrist and then felt the vein in his neck. Slowly he shook his head before getting to his feet. 'You're right. He's dead. You wouldn't like me to look around before I go for the doctor? Make sure there's no one here? That window upstairs...'

'Please, the doctor. If anyone got in, they've probably got out by now.'

He nodded and left the house.

Nellie told Lottie to sit with Grandfather. 'Where are you going?' she asked, looking scared.

'I'm just going to check that nobody is here.' She picked up the poker.

'Why didn't you let Sgt McElroy search? If Grandfather's dead, there's nothing a doctor can do about it,' said Lottie.

'I was surprised to find him hanging around here when Billy's not working,' said Nellie.

Lottie's brow puckered. 'Could be that there really have been break-ins. Don't go up, Nell! Stay here.'

Nellie hesitated but then shook her head and left the kitchen, switching on lights as she went, checking Lottie's room and the parlour, thinking she'd need to go through the latter again before she could be sure nothing had been stolen. She went upstairs and into the bathroom and closed and locked the window. Then she crossed the landing to her grandfather's room and opened the door. It swung silently open and she switched on the light.

To her relief the room was empty but in the

middle of the floor was a black tin box with the lid flung open and envelopes beside it. She looked inside, expecting to find it empty, but there were a heap of half-crowns and several sepia photographs. She gathered the coins together and pocketed them. Then she picked up the papers and placed them with the photographs in the tin box and shut it. She took a blanket from her grandfather's bed and checked the other bedrooms but found no sign of them being turned over. She returned to the ground floor and covered her grandfather with the blanket, swallowing a tightness in her throat. Then she sat beside her sister to wait for the doctor.

'We shouldn't have gone out,' said Lottie, gazing down at the covered body. 'I suppose I'll miss him despite his being a moaner.'

'He's left me something in his will,' murmured Nellie.

Her sister gave her a sidelong glance. 'How d'you know?'

'Francis told me. I suppose he died of a heart attack.'

She got up and felt the kettle. It was hot enough to make tea. She was trying to analyse how she felt about her grandfather's death. Although she had known that he would die one day, somehow she had expected him to last longer. Was she upset? Yes, but the way she felt could not compare to her grief over the loss of Teddy or her baby.

She made tea and handed her sister a cup. 'Did he have much money, d'you think?' asked Lottie.

'I've no idea. I did find a bag of half-crowns upstairs. We can use them for anything we have to buy until the insurance money comes through,' said Nellie, wondering what had happened to disturb her grandfather while rooting in his box. Perhaps he had heard a noise and come downstairs. Maybe it had been fear of attack, alone in the house, that had killed him. Just like Lottie, she felt guilty for having left him but there was nothing she could do about that now.

A few minutes later the doctor arrived with Sgt McElroy and pronounced her grandfather officially dead. In answer to Nellie's question about it being a heart attack, he said, 'Yes. Not surprising in a man of his age and with all the stresses of wartime. My sympathies, Mrs Lachlan and Miss Callaghan.' He scribbled on a slip of paper all that was necessary and handed it to Nellie. 'Perhaps the sergeant and I can help move your grandfather out of the kitchen.'

A relieved Nellie thanked him.

'Perhaps to his bedroom,' said the sergeant, teetering on his heels, his arms behind his back. 'I'd like to look around upstairs with that window being open.'

'There's no one up there, I've looked. You can put Grandfather on Lottie's bed in the old dining room, that would be the simplest thing,' said Nellie.

'Makes sense,' said the doctor, slapping the policeman's back, adding, 'Come on, man! Let's do it so we can leave the young ladies to sort themselves out.'

As soon as the two men left, Nellie wiped the urine off the kitchen floor and then, looking at Lottie, knew she needed to be in bed. 'Can you manage the stairs?' she asked.

Lottie nodded. 'Can we sleep together, Nellie? I feel cold and a bit shaky.'

'Of course,' said Nellie, putting an arm round her. 'I'll take the shelf out of the oven and wrap it in newspaper and pop it in the double bed. Then I'll help you upstairs.'

'You'll have to get the priest to say absolution and what about Francis? You'll need to get in touch with him to arrange the funeral.'

'That can wait until the morning,' said Nellie.

Once Lottie was in bed, Nellie went back downstairs. There was something she felt she must do. She fetched clean clothes for her grandfather, as well as soap, hot water and a towel. She went into the parlour and, taking a deep breath, she did for him what she hadn't been able to do for her mother. She stripped, washed and changed him before his limbs stiffened. Only when she had performed that act did she go upstairs and run a bath. She lay in the water, tears in her eyes, thinking about the old man. What would her father's reaction be to his own father's death? This house would be his now and no doubt he would expect her to look after it. She must speak to Francis. Tomorrow she would tell Polly that she needed a few days off to arrange things.

Polly was understanding. 'Of course you can have time off. I don't know how I'll manage without you,' she said seriously, 'but I'll have to cope.'

Nellie apologised and wasted no time in heading for her brother's parish. Francis was not at the presbytery but the housekeeper told Nellie that she would most likely find him at the boys' club in the church hall. So Nellie went in search of her brother. She had once expressed her disgust to him and Joe about what some men called the art of boxing. Both had told her that boxing was popular in the deprived parishes of Liverpool because lads knew that there was a chance of escaping the streets by making money in the ring. She thought she knew what to expect when she walked into the boys' club but no one was using the ring, there were only a couple of youths hitting punch bags and another was skipping with a rope. She saw her brother's black-clad figure at the other end of the hall speaking to a man. She waved and Francis spotted her.

Immediately, he excused himself and made his way towards her, a concerned expression on his rugged face. 'What is it, Nellie? For you to be here at this time of day it must be something serious.'

She told him what had happened and he placed an arm about her shoulders. 'It sounds like you've done as much as you can. I presume you've spoken to your parish priest?'

'Not yet. I thought I'd speak to you first.'

'Perhaps that's just as well. I know Grand-father's wishes. He wanted to be buried at sea.'

'Why didn't I think of that?' murmured Nellie, surprised. 'How do we go about arranging it?'

'There's no need for you to worry, Nell. I spoke to Father Waring at Atlantic House after Grand-father made his will. He agreed to arrange every-thing when the time came.'

'That's a relief!'

'Did you think to bring the papers that were in

Grandfather's black box?'

'Yes. I haven't opened anything.' She handed several long, narrow brown envelopes to him.

'I can tell you what's in his will right now, Nellie. He left the house and its contents to you. Any money that's left after funeral expenses is to go to the church.'

Nellie rocked on her heels. She must have misheard him. 'Say that again?'

'Grandfather left the house and its contents to you,' repeated Francis with a faint smile.

'What about Dad?'

'Dad was a fool. That's what the old man thought and not only a fool but a selfish, opinionated one, who drank too much and took things for granted.'

'Goodness!' exclaimed Nellie. 'I never thought he felt that strongly about him.'

Francis nodded. 'He appreciated you returning to the house and taking responsibility for the family. Of course, if Joe had been alive, he would have got everything.' He grimaced. 'As it was you were second in line favourite after your husband was killed.'

Nellie shook her head. She felt positively odd, remembering her mother banning her from the house which now seemed to belong to her. 'I can't believe it. Dad'll have a fit. He'll say I wormed my way into Grandfather's good graces,' she babbled. 'I'll have to make the house over to him. It's only right. He was his son.'

Francis said sternly, 'Pull yourself together, Nellie. Don't rush into doing anything of the sort. You need a cool head to make any big decisions. Carry on just as you are.'

Nellie gulped and a shudder went through her. 'You're right. Dad's not here, so there's no rush.'

'Exactly. You need to think hard before considering going against Grandfather's wishes.'

'I told Lottie he had left me some money, I never imagined this. Do I tell Babs?'

'I suggest you keep mum for now. A will does reside with Grandfather's solicitor. He'll not be getting in touch with Dad because he's not a beneficiary. I'll write to Dad about Grandfather's death but, for the moment, I won't mention his will. If you decide to keep the house and Dad cuts up rough when he comes home, if I'm not around then the solicitor will help you.'

A ripple of fear raced along her nerves. 'Why shouldn't you be around? Don't you go enlisting in the Forces as a padre, Francis. I've told you before, I don't want anyone else I love dying on me.'

He hesitated and said gently, 'If I feel it's God's will and not just my own guilt, then I'll have to go. In the meantime, our next move is to comply with Grandfather's wishes. In the meantime his body will have to be taken to the undertaker's.'

After Nellie had written to Babs telling her about their Grandfather's death, Nellie thought a lot about her grandfather's wishes. Several times she considered making an appointment with his solicitor after the burial at sea was over. Then she would wander through the rooms of *her* house and down the garden, feeling a strong sense of possession. An idea started to grow in her mind about how she could put the house to good use for the war effort but she didn't tell anyone about her plan because it needed a lot more thinking out.

Ten days after his death, Grandfather's body was carried aboard a pilot boat that would take it to the Mersey estuary. There, Nellie, Lottie and Francis would say their farewell to the old man. Babs could not get away so it would just be the three of them. Although only a short voyage, it was not without its fraught moments. There was the danger of floating mines, and buoys marked the numerous wrecks where ships had sunk during the blitz. Just like the shifting sandbanks, they needed the navigation skills of an experienced pilot.

At last they reached the spot deemed the right one to launch Grandfather's body into the deep. Francis said the words of committal and the old man's earthly remains slipped into the sea. Nellie and Lottie dropped a wreath of lilies and roses on the surface of the water. It was a moving moment. The old man had not always been easy to live with but both sisters would always be grateful to him for providing them with a home when they needed one.

Part Two

1943 to 1944

Chapter Eleven

January 1943

Dear Nellie,
Sorry I couldn't make Christmas but I'm about to go
off to a New Year's Eve party. You wouldn't believe the
changes the Yanks have brought to the area. Lively is
not the word for the place these days. The airbase at
Burtonwood is growing. It's going to be huge with
shops and cinemas and dance halls ... oh, and they do
have runways, hangars and warehouses, too. It'll be
like a little town in itself. They call it Little Detroit or
Little America. The natives are already calling it

Babs paused and chewed on the end of her pen.
She had been about to write *Sodom and Gomor-*
rah but decided that might bring her eldest sister
running to see for herself if the rumours about
the American servicemen being over-sexed were
true. Instead she wrote, *other names.*

I doubt they have anything to complain about. The
Yanks are spending money around here like there's no
tomorrow. I'd really love for you to visit but now is not
the right time. It's real bleak out here at this time of
year because the winds blow icy across the flat fields
from the Mersey. Wait until the spring and then we'll
have a good time. In the meantime don't worry about
me. I have got a head on my shoulders and no man in

213

uniform is going to sweet talk me into doing something daft. By the way, I had a letter from Dad. Has he written to you? Seems his ship was hit but managed to limp into Greenock in Scotland and he's up there now. Maybe you'll get a visit. It's been ages since he wrote but he seems to think that Grandfather's death was a blessing. Hope to see you when the weather gets better,

Love and kisses,
Babs.

She blotted the letter and slipped it into an envelope and addressed and stamped it. Then she placed it, with the one she had written to her father, in her shoulder bag. She looked up as a couple of young women entered the lounge. One was Flo and the other, a tall blonde, was Heather, who had initiated Babs into the workings of a tractor's innards. She was wearing a kilt and a frilly cream blouse beneath a tartan waistcoat, because although she had not been born in Scotland she was of Scottish descent.

'You ready yet?' asked Heather, without a trace of a Scottish accent.

Babs nodded. 'I needed to get a couple of letters written. I'll post them in the morning. Nobody else going from here?'

'No,' said Heather. 'Some have still got hangovers from last night's celebrations in the village.'

Babs had missed out on last night but was raring to go out that evening. Captain Stuart McGregor, a Yank and officer of Canadian and Scottish descent, had invited her to the dance, which was to take place in the hall where he was

214

billeted. He had told her to bring a couple of friends. She was hoping to see him in a kilt. She put on her hat and waterproof coat over her frock and followed the other two outside.

It was pitch black and raining but, fortunately, Heather was driving the farm truck and knew the area well. Soon they were heading towards the hall a few miles from Burtonwood. Babs marvelled at how quickly the Americans had extended the base in the last nine months or so. It had been Stuart who had told her of its attractions and she hoped one day to have the opportunity of being set loose in the shop. She knew that pleasure would have to be deferred but tonight she was intent on having fun.

Heather parked the truck in the driveway alongside several jeeps and cars, and the girls hurried through the rain into the hall. Lights blazed inside and they were directed to a room where they could leave their outdoor clothes. They did not need to ask directions to the ballroom because the sound of a big band led them to it. The noise reverberated round walls festooned with streamers and there were already couples on the dance floor.

Stuart must have been looking out for Babs because no sooner had the three girls entered the room than he came over to them with two other airmen, one of whom Babs recognised with mixed feelings.

Stuart seized her hand and pulled her towards him. 'It's great you made it, honey. I was just starting to think the weather had put a kibosh on things.'

'No, a bit of rain wasn't going to keep me away.'

She smiled up into his pleasant, fresh-skinned face and then eyed him up and down. Yes! He was wearing a kilt and looked OK in it. They had met a fortnight ago in a pub in Warrington. He had been with another airman and she'd been with Flo. The men had bought them a drink and they'd got chatting.

'You've met Chuck,' he said. 'Let me introduce you to Jake.'

'We've met,' she said, thinking that if Jake had been invited for Heather she was going to top him by at least four inches.

'Barbara.' Jake inclined his fair head.

She turned to her friend. 'Heather, this is Jake O'Donnell. You'll have gathered the other two are Stuart and Chuck.'

Chuck nodded in her direction and then whispered in Flo's ear. She said something in a low voice and the next moment the two of them were heading for the dance floor.

Heather stared after them before turning back to the other three and giving Jake the once over. 'I suppose it's me and you then, if Stuart's Babs' date.'

Jake drawled, 'I really appreciate that gracious invitation to dance.'

Babs suppressed a giggle but Heather said, 'Are you trying to be funny?'

He raised his eyebrows. 'Perish the thought. Shall we give it a go?'

'That's what I've come for.' She seized him by the shoulder and almost yanked him onto the floor.

'Why is it I think they're not going to get on?'

said Stuart.

'No comment,' said Babs, watching the other couple and wondering why she was glad Jake and Heather weren't hitting it off.

'You ready to dance?' asked Stuart.

Feeling confident of making a good impression on the dance floor this evening because she had been practising, she turned to him and smiled. 'When you are.'

He took her hand and led her onto the floor but they'd hardly got into the rhythm of the dance when the music stopped. Stuart grimaced. 'Bad timing. Drink?'

She nodded and watched him hurry away, kilt swinging as he dodged between people. 'Left you already, hey?' whispered a voice against her ear.

She did not need to look round to know who had spoken, but did anyway.

'He stood on my foot,' complained Heather.

Babs gave Jake a severe look. 'Is this true?'

'I'm saying nuthin'!' he said, straight-faced.

Heather glared at him. 'If you're saying it was my fault then that's not true. If you'd been paying attention, you'd have realised the music was coming to an end and stopped dancing.' She slipped off her shoe and made a painful show of wriggling her toes.

'OK! I admit that my mind was on other things,' said Jake.

'Now there's a confession. I'm going to have to sit out the next few dances if I'm to be fit for the Gay Gordons,' said Heather.

'Perhaps you'd like me to find us a table,' said Jake.

Heather smiled. 'Now you're talking.'

The two girls watched him disappear into the throng before exchanging glances. 'Do you think he'll come back?' asked Heather.

'Why shouldn't he?'

Heather wiggled her toes, replaced her shoe and walked a few paces without any sign of a limp.

'That got better quick,' said Babs.

Heather said, 'I need a taller guy. See you later.' She went in the opposite direction from Jake.

Babs stood waiting for Stuart and Jake to reappear, knowing there was nothing for it but to tell Jake the truth. She doubted he would care about being ditched if his earlier comments were anything to go by.

He was the first to arrive at Babs' side and smiled when he saw her standing alone. 'I reckon I've been ditched,' he said. 'As for you...'

'I could lie and say she's gone to rest her foot but...'

'Let's stick to the truth. Tall women are not my cup of tea.' His blue eyes took in Babs' appearance in one sweeping glance as the band launched into a boogie and she began to tap her foot. 'Do you want to dance?'

She was tempted to accept his offer, so she could show him how good she'd got since their last meeting, but said, 'I'm waiting for Stuart.'

'If he's gone to the bar he could be some time. Come on,' he said. 'Admit you're dying to dance with me.'

'After the last time when you made a show of me! Don't make me laugh.'

'Could be fun.'

She glanced at the dance floor and wanted to be on there amongst the boogying couples. 'OK!'

He wasted no time leading Babs onto the dance floor and whirling her around before launching into an energetic jitterbug. His enthusiasm was infectious and she had no trouble matching his every step and coming up with a few of her own when he held her by the waist and lifted her up in the air before swinging her down between his legs. She managed to retain her footing and do a bit of a step dance before he turned to face her. She laughed. He grinned as he grabbed her by the waist and pulled her close. They still danced fast but now they were cheek to cheek. When the music ended she was out of breath and had to cling to him while she recovered. She could feel the heat of his body against her hand and thought how useful he would be in bed as a hot water bottle. She giggled, thinking it wasn't a romantic thought.

'What's so funny?' he asked, gazing down at her.

She noticed the smile in his eyes and the sweat glistening on his face. 'You don't want to know.'

'Yes. I do. A dollar for your thoughts.'

She shook her head. 'Not this one.'

'What about when we get to know each other better?'

She did not answer because out of the corner of her eye she noticed Stuart standing on the edge of the dance floor, staring at them. 'Time to go. Thanks for the dance.' She freed herself and made her way over to her date.

Close up she could see that Stuart was not pleased. 'What happened to your friend, Heather?' he asked.

'Jake stood on her foot.' She reached for one of the glasses he held. 'This one mine?'

'Sure. So how come you're dancing with him?'

'He said you'd be some time and could see I wanted to dance.'

'You said you wanted a drink.'

'You asked if I wanted a drink. I just didn't expect you to be away so long.' Babs was thirsty and thought this exchange might go on for some time. She lifted the glass to her mouth and gulped down half the shandy.

'How well d'you know Jake? He hasn't mentioned going out with you.' There was suspicion in his voice.

'I know him hardly at all.'

'It didn't look like that to me.'

'It's true. This is only the second time I've met him.' She was getting annoyed by his possessive attitude and knew she wouldn't be accepting any more invitations from Stuart. 'Can we change the subject now? You asked me to come. I'm here. So let's not waste time arguing. Let's down our drinks and dance.'

Grudgingly, he agreed.

They danced on and off for the rest of the evening but exchanged little in the way of conversation. Several times Babs gazed about her for Jake but he was nowhere to be seen. She had to admit that the fizz had gone out of the evening without him around.

As she climbed into bed that night, she wondered whether she would see Jake again. Trouble was she could hardly go asking for him at the base, so it seemed she was going to have to wait until he came looking for her. She thought of Nellie, wondering what she would make of Jake, and remembered that she must post those letters tomorrow.

Nellie seethed as she re-read that part of Babs' letter referring to their father. She could understand a son calling his father's death a blessing if he had been gaga or in terrible pain and bedridden from some horrible disease, but that couldn't be said about Grandfather. The truth was that the two men had never got on and whether that was because they'd spent so much time apart she just didn't know. She guessed now that her father's only interest in Grandfather's death was what he would get out of it. She could only pray that he would stay in Scotland and not come south. She glanced at the clock and realised she should be on her way to work. Pocketing the letter, she left the house.

As Nellie walked, she thought about the number of women on Merseyside who had husbands, sons or brothers in the navy. The Battle of the Atlantic was still being waged and the deaths of so many sailors must surely be having its effect on the morale of their women. Yet like herself, they had to come to terms with their loss because life went on, but the end of this terrible war couldn't come quickly enough for all of them.

At least up here on the north-west coast of England they were not suffering like those in

London, which was being bombed again. Still, there were a lot of less worrying things to think about. The government had warned that there would be coal shortages and the British Gas Company was urging people *To save Gas, to smash the Axis Powers.* The local press said shortages of fish and green vegetables were likely during the rest of winter. The nation was being urged to tighten its belt to give give, give, save, save, save. There was hardly an iron railing to be seen anywhere. Regular collections of waste paper were made and the *Crosby Herald* was urging people not to hoard their Christmas cards and old calendars but to take them to the post office.

Even the libraries were at it now; thousands of books had been destroyed in the blitz and they wanted people to give books purchased at Christmas to their local branch. She was in favour of that because she borrowed books to read to the children. While all this was going on, the Anglican bishop of Liverpool was concerned that women and girls were turning to alcohol to calm their nerves. Nellie, for one, did not blame them. She thought of Mrs McElroy and wondered whether she had lost a father or brother in the Great War as well as a child. Perhaps if she'd had more children, she would never have turned to drink.

Nellie was thinking about her own son when she spotted a notice on the waste plot of land close to the lift bridge. Her curiosity was roused and she went and read it. As she did, her spirits lifted and, singing a Cole Porter number under her breath, she hurried across the bridge and along Linacre Road. She came to the bicycle shop and climbed the stairs and burst into the room above.

'Polly, guess what?' she blurted out.

Her friend looked up from the register. 'What?'

'The council nursery is being built on the waste land the other side of the canal, near the lift bridge. It'll be a single-storey prefabricated building and should be opening the first week in April.'

Polly's eyes shone. 'So they've finally got down to it.'

'You know why, don't you? Now the Allies have almost won the war in Africa, the next stop will be Europe. It'll be more men in the Forces, more bombs, bullets, guns, tanks, uniforms.'

'Poor sods,' said Polly softly.

Both were silent, remembering their own husbands.

A mother and child stopped in front of the table. Polly took the woman's money and ticked off the child's name. As soon as she had gone and the toddler had settled with chalk and a board with a handful of other children, Polly asked Nellie what else she knew about the nursery.

'Nothing,' said Nellie. 'But I'll go into the council offices and find out on the way home.'

'Great,' said Polly. 'Now Margaret's started school, I'll apply for a job there as a nursery nurse. I'd best do it straight away because there could be any number of children's nurses applying.'

Nellie glanced about her. 'What about our children?'

Polly frowned. 'Depending on the cost and what the nursery is offering, we could lose most of them.'

'There'll be more wanting to fill their places,' said Nellie with conviction. 'The other day I passed a woman with two little ones. I remembered them from Ambleside. She told me that she wasn't the only one who's back. They all reckon it's safe to come home now and are keen to earn money. She told me that she'd apply for a job in an Ordinance factory, filling shells and things if she could get someone to look after her kids.' Nellie added ruefully, 'Would you believe, Polly, that the government are promising not only good money to get them into the factories but a canteen, stockings and make-up at special prices? It's shift work, mind, and that includes working part of Sunday. I think we're in the wrong job.'

Polly shook her head. 'It'll only last while the war's on. Us widows need jobs that'll pay us a regular wage for life.'

Nellie knew she was right and, on the way home, dropped in at the council offices to discover that the only jobs available were for trained nursery nurses. She found that disappointing but it made her plan all the more appealing. She wrote down the details for the nursery nurses' jobs for Polly and hurried home.

When Nellie woke the next morning, she could hear the wind whistling in the eaves and rattling the windows. She wanted to snuggle down in bed but had to drag herself up. In such weather her plan seemed all the more attractive. She went downstairs, shivering as she lit the fire, and then went out to see to the hens and collect the few eggs they produced at this time of year. Soon there would be work to be done in the vegetable patch and she would have to ask around or advertise for a replacement for Billy.

Polly was excited when Nellie gave her the information about the nursery. 'This is great. Sister Mary Moore's to be matron. She worked at the First Aid Post in Litherland during the blitz, so she's well known in the area. You're a true friend, Nellie.'

Nellie shrugged. 'It's the least I can do. Unfortunately they only want trained nursery nurses and I have no medical background.'

Polly sighed. 'It's a shame. You're so good with the kids. If I do get the job, then perhaps you'd like to take over here.'

Nellie hesitated, knowing it would take capital to get her own nursery up and running. 'I'll think about it,' she said.

'Do. There's no rush. I mightn't get one of the posts.'

'The hours'll be longer. It's going to be open from seven in the morning to seven at night six days a week.'

'Probably be shift work. What do you think of their charges?' asked Polly.

'Incredible. A shilling a day and the children will get three meals for that and medical care. They plan to take fifty children from six months to five years. With staff and meals to pay for, the government must be subsidising it.'

'We'd have trouble competing,' said Polly.

Nellie agreed, wondering if her plan was sensible after all, but she still believed there would be a demand for more pre-school childcare in the area. Fifty nursery places wasn't that many considering the number of families in Litherland. She really had to give it serious thought.

It was in her mind to mention the possibility of taking over Polly's nursery to Lottie as soon as she arrived home but, when she walked into the kitchen, it was to find her brother sitting alone in front of the fire.

'Hello, Francis,' said Nellie, pleased to see him. 'Where's Lottie?'

'She's forgotten something for supper and gone out to see if she can get it.' He rose to his feet. 'You look tired. Lottie thinks you're working too hard.'

'I'm no different from most of the country. What are you doing here?'

'I had a phone call from Dad.'

Nellie's smile faded. 'He's not coming here, is he?'

'No.'

'Thank God for that.' She sat down at the table and eased off her shoes.

'But he did ask me to come and check the house, see if anything needed doing and get it done. How he expects me to make that happen when there's a shortage of materials and man-power beggars belief.'

'He's presuming a lot like we thought. He didn't say how this work was going to be paid for, did he?' asked Nellie.

Francis tapped his thumbs together. 'He suggests you sell some of Grandfather's stuff ... but that's not all he said. He thinks you and Lottie should be paying him rent.'

Nellie gasped. 'You are joking! Who does he

think is paying the rates?' She poked her breast bone. 'Soft pot here! Ooh, I can't wait to see his face when I tell him the house is mine. You didn't tell him, did you?'

Francis shook his head. 'He just might have had an apoplexy and we don't want that, do we, Nellie?'

'Oh I don't know,' she said, tongue in cheek.

'Nellie!' Francis shook his head at her but with the faintest of smiles in his eyes. 'He is our dad.'

She nodded. 'A pity he doesn't remember it and do the nice things dads are supposed to do for their children. Our lives would have been much easier if he hadn't spent so much time in the pub when he was home. I bet Mam never saw much of the money he got when he cashed his advance note before a trip. So what's he up to?'

'He's signed on another ship. Says he's going to the Americas to pick up supplies but once they're loaded his destination is hush-hush.'

'Doesn't trust his son enough to tell him?'

'I honestly think he doesn't know,' said Francis.

'OK. So it's unlikely he'll turn up on the doorstep in the next few months, so I'm free to do what I want,' said Nellie casually.

Her brother stared at her hard. 'What have you in mind?'

'Hot drink?' She did not wait for his answer but put the kettle on.

'Nellie, come on. Tell me! You've got that look on your face.'

'What look? Like I'm plotting something?' She chuckled as she spooned Camp coffee into cups. 'I should really put my idea to Lottie at the same time as you but that will mean my telling her that the house is mine.'

'Come on, Nellie, get to the point,' said Francis.

She sat and stared at him because she wanted to see his expression when she unfolded her plan. 'Polly, who runs the nursery group, is applying for a job as a nursery nurse at the new council nursery being built. If she gets the job she's asked if I would like to take over her group.'

Francis frowned. 'You mean work there full-time? You'll be exhausted, Nell. I mean, it takes time getting there and back everyday and then there's the house and garden. Lottie might be a lot better now but she couldn't possibly cope with the work involved on her own. She'll be lonely, too, here all day on her own.'

Nellie smiled. 'Exactly, that's why my own plan is better than Polly's.' She paused.

He looked at her warily. 'Go on.'

'I want to open a nursery school here in the house.'

Francis' jaw dropped.

'No need to look like that. It's for the war effort. Now the desert war's won, there'll be a big push to get into Europe. That's why the government is desperate to get more women into the factories. You can imagine the guns and ammunition that are going to be needed.'

'And men,' murmured Francis, with a tortured expression.

Nellie nodded and could not continue for the lump in her throat, thinking of the suffering so many would experience in the coming months and possibly years, but what could they do? Britain and America were committed to defeating Hitler and Mussolini and winning this war.

The kettle started steaming, so she made coffee and took Francis a cup. Then she picked up her own and sat across the fireplace from him. 'The mothers will be paid good wages. I've spoken to at least one who would jump at the chance of nursery care. Some of these poorer women have hardly two pennies to rub together. You must know what it's like in your parish. Holes in the kids' shoes and trips to the pawnshop.'

'All right!' Francis eased back his broad shoulders. 'You don't have to lay it on with a trowel. But what happens when their husbands return from the war?'

Nellie said softly, 'I believe most mothers want to be with their children but they'll make sacrifices for what's best for them. Anyway, some of the mothers won't have husbands coming home and will need to work to support themselves and their children. Not everyone has family to help them out and, even though I now own this house, I have to work to support myself and Lottie. It isn't easy. I can't save anything and every farthing is accounted for.'

'But surely you'll need money to have a nursery school here?' said Francis, glancing round. 'You'll need equipment and toys. Where will you get them from and how will you pay for them?'

'What Dad said about selling some of Grandfather's stuff has given me an idea. If Polly does get the job at the council nursery, I'll have a sale and raise cash that way. I can't rely on Polly's nursery closing down and my buying stuff from her. I can take the toys that are mine back but I'll need money, not only for equipment, but to pay myself a wage. I mightn't get in enough money from the mothers at first.'

A reluctant smile lit up Francis' face. 'You've got some guts, Nellie. Dad will probably go through the roof like a rocket when he eventually gets home.'

Nellie did not doubt it. 'I'll worry about that when he arrives.'

During the next few weeks, Nellie made enquiries at the council offices as to whether she needed planning permission and whether she would be entitled to a grant if she opened a nursery school in her house. Her proposal was welcomed, which proved to her just how advanced the government's plans to get a foothold in Europe must be. No grant was promised but she was ready when Polly next asked her whether she was prepared to take over the nursery group above the bicycle shop.

'I need an answer from you, Nellie,' said Polly, as they cleared equipment and toys away so the room was ready for the dancing class that evening. 'I've been waiting until now to talk to you, so we wouldn't be disturbed. I've got the job in the council nursery.'

'That's great,' said Nellie, smiling with delight. 'So when do you start?'

'April. Towards the end of Wings for Victory Week.'

'They're really pushing up the target this year, aren't they? Eighty thousand pounds to fund two

Lancaster bombers,' said Nellie, thoughtfully.

'Don't change the subject,' said Polly. 'If you don't want to carry on here then say so. It's just that I need to tell the mothers to make other arrangements for their kids.'

Nellie popped the piano key in its jar on the window sill. 'No. I won't be staying on here. I have a plan of my own.'

'What plan?' asked Polly, looking taken aback.

'I've decided to use the house for my own private nursery school. I never told you but Grandfather left it to me.'

Polly's eyes almost popped out of her head. 'You jammy thing. But that's marvellous.'

Nellie smiled. 'I couldn't believe it. Nobody else knows. I haven't even told my sisters ... or my dad. He thinks the house is his and I know there'll be trouble when he eventually gets home and finds it isn't. He's been known to be violent when he loses his temper.'

'Bloody hell, Nellie! I just hope you've got someone big and strong in the house when he does.'

'Don't worry,' she said, 'I'll make sure my brother's there.'

Polly nodded. 'Makes sense. Anyway, back to your plan. How much room have you got? What about lavs? Equipment? Toys?'

'I've got more space at home than here. I've also got outdoor space for the children to play and a washroom to hang their outdoor things. There's an outside toilet and one upstairs. I've a lovely big kitchen, too. As for equipment and toys... I'm going to have a sale to raise the money. Grandfather might have left me the house and its contents but cash ... no! I'm going to have to advertise for children's toys.'

Polly grimaced. 'You'll be lucky if you can get more toys. The council nursery's having a problem. They've made an appeal but there hasn't been much of a response. People could do with searching their attics ... or it would be great if some of the old ladies could knit some small dolls, teddies or golliwogs.'

Nellie agreed but she was of the mind that most old ladies thought that knitting socks, balaclavas and gloves for the troops was of far more importance than toys. She felt certain, though, that she could persuade Lottie to knit some for her children.

'I'm sure some of the mothers here will be interested, others might consider your house too far away. You're going to need an assistant,' said Polly.

'I'll think about that when my nursery school is up and running,' said Nellie. 'In the meantime my sister can help out.'

'Naturally you'll take back the dolls' house and everything else you brought ... but if there's anything from here you want ... except for the rocking horse, which I've promised to the nursery ... take it.'

Nellie said, 'I'd like to buy your small tables and chairs.'

'No, take them. You've well earned what they cost me second-hand,' said Polly.

'Thanks.' Nellie was truly grateful. 'There's a piano at home so that won't be going in the sale. I need to get rid of some of the larger furniture:

a Victorian sideboard, as well as one of the dining tables.'

'They'll be snapped up. The old stuff is better than this utility furniture that's in the shops now.'

'There's loads of ornaments, china and porcelain that belonged to my great-great aunt, as well as mementos Grandfather brought back from his travels. They'll make nice presents with there being so little in the shops these days. I'll be selling clothes, too.'

Polly looked surprised. 'Surely you'll want to keep some of them ... and what about your family, won't they want something to remember your grandfather by?'

'I'll ask Lottie what she wants and I'd best write to Babs and tell her what I'm up to. It's time she visited. I was hoping to visit her but I just haven't had time.'

'How many children will you start with?'

'A round dozen? I'd rather they were made up of three- and four-year-olds ... although I'm prepared to make exceptions in special circumstances.' Nellie brushed back a strand of chestnut hair, thinking of Irene Miller, who wasn't yet two.

As they made their way out of the building, Polly said, 'We will keep in touch, won't we, Nellie?'

'Of course. You can always bring Margaret to tea one Sunday,'

Polly smiled. 'And I'll definitely be at the sale.'

Nellie arrived home an hour later, having done some shopping on the way. She had yet to tell Lottie of her decision about the nursery and knew that the time had come to tell her about the house, too. When she broke the news to her sister, Lottie stared at her from rounded eyes and then slowly smiled. 'It'll be one in the eye for Dad but I think you're doing the right thing.'

Nellie wished her sister had not mentioned their father but at least she genuinely seemed pleased about her idea. 'I'm planning on making you my assistant, Lottie, and your first job will be to knit some toys for the children.'

Lottie flushed with pleasure. 'Your assistant. Will it count as essential war work?'

'Of course,' said Nellie. 'It's much more labour-saving for just two people to look after twelve children instead of having, say, eight mothers.'

Lottie said eagerly, 'You get patterns and wool and I'll get cracking. When will we be opening?'

'I'm not sure yet. I thought we could have the sale on the Sunday at the end of Wings for Victory Week. I'm sure we'll get more people coming then and we can say we'll give a donation from what we raise to the appeal. As for wool for toys, you can use a couple of Grandfather's old woollies. We can unravel them and I'm sure we'll be able to find a pattern book in the library.'

Lottie wriggled in her chair. 'It's exciting! I've felt so out of things being home all the time and it's been worse since Billy left. I like kids. I'll be made up helping in any way I can.'

While she made a pot of tea Nellie told her sister what she expected of her.

Lottie added a few thoughts of her own. 'If I just had a couple of the older ones at a time, I could show them how to make jam tarts and things.'

'Of course, you could.' Nellie put an arm

around her shoulders and hugged her.

Lottie frowned. 'What about the vegetable patch, Nell? We'll be needing to plant soon and buy seed potatoes.'

'I'll see what I can do,' promised Nellie, whose mind was buzzing with ideas. 'Perhaps one of the mothers might know someone willing to barter their time for vegetables and fruit and a couple of fresh eggs a week.'

But help with the garden was to come from an unexpected quarter the next day. 'I believe you're looking for some help in the garden, Nellie,' said Mrs Wainwright, catching her as she walked home after visiting the library. 'Labour in exchange for vegetables, fruit and eggs?'

'Who told you that?' Nellie had been on her feet all day and couldn't wait to kick off her shoes and put her feet up. She just couldn't see their busybody neighbour being of help to her.

'One hears these things.' The old woman waved a be-ringed hand dismissively. 'I have a nephew, my widowed sister's only son. He's not got much upstairs,' she tapped her head significantly, 'but he is harmless and strong. I'm sure he'd suit you.'

'That's kind of you to offer his help.' Nellie would have sympathised with any nephew of Mrs Wainwright, but one who was backward she felt even more sorry for. 'Send him along.'

'Certainly, my dear.' Mrs Wainwright seized Nellie's sleeve as she made to walk away. 'And while we're talking, I really do admire you for the way you seem to be coping with everything. I suppose there's no news of Bernard coming home yet?'

Nellie shook her head. 'Last time he docked was in Scotland and then he was off to the Americas and then an unknown destination.'

'Well, let's hope he's safe. Perhaps he'll give up the sea once the war's over now your grandfather's dead. It's good to have a man around the place. I was really worried when those break-ins were going on.'

Nellie stilled. 'You weren't broken into, were you?'

'No, thank God. Terence McElroy probably frightened them away.'

'I believe this used to be his beat,' said Nellie.

'Yes. I remember having a reason to call upon him when your brother Joseph kicked a ball through my window.'

'I see. Thank you, Mrs Wainwright.' Nellie was about to walk away but then had second thoughts and turned back. 'I wonder if you could help me.'

'Help you!' The woman's pencilled eyebrows arched and she tittered. 'My goodness, fancy you asking me for help!'

'I thought you should be the first to know that I'm starting a nursery school in the house.' Nellie saw her expression change and added hastily, 'You'll find they won't make any more noise than the music teacher a few doors away. If you could spread the word that I'm having a sale to raise money for the children and that I'm giving a donation to Wings for Victory Week from the proceeds, then I'd be grateful.'

'Well! I don't know what to say,' said Mrs Wainwright, looking flabbergasted. 'What kind of sale?'

Nellie told her and her neighbour's eyes

gleamed and she rubbed her pale hands together. 'I'd be happy to help you price things. Adelaide had some very nice porcelain. You won't know the true value of it and I wouldn't like you to be robbed.'

Nellie could see the sense of having the help of someone who knew what was valuable and what was junk. Besides, if she was to help her, then she could hardly complain about the nursery. 'Thanks.'

'Just tell me when you're ready to do the pricing and I'll be there. And have you thought of making a charge and serving refreshments?'

Nellie had not done so but now welcomed the suggestion. Smiling, she thanked Mrs Wainwright again. 'I'll see if I can rope in some mothers to help.'

'Good. What date are you planning for your sale?'

'The Sunday at the end of Wings for Victory Week. It's my only free day.'

Mrs Wainwright patted her shoulder and hurried off in the opposite direction. Nellie hummed 'Sing as We Go' as she carried on into the house, thinking back over their conversation and what her neighbour had said about Sgt McElroy. So he'd been around here when Joe was a boy. Why didn't she remember him? Perhaps she had been too young. Francis might remember him, though. She dismissed him from her thoughts, remembering that she still had a letter to write to Babs about the sale.

Chapter Twelve

Babs watched intently as the farmer tied the pieces of string firmly into two separate knots round the umbilical cord before cutting the cord between the knots. The afterbirth was disposed of and within a short space of time, the calf was standing rather shakily on her spindly legs, a black and white replica of her mother.

'Do you ever get used to seeing calves being born?' Babs asked when she and the farmer left the byre.

'Never,' said the ruddy-faced woman easing her back. 'I'm just grateful when everything goes as well as it did today and I don't have to call in the vet. You can be off now. I hope you've learnt something here.'

'You can say that again,' said Babs on a laugh. 'I'm made up my first was a female calf. She won't become veal, will she?'

'You can't be sentimental in farming, girl.' The woman's expression was severe. 'But you're right. When the time comes, if I'm lucky, she'll be as good a milker as her mother.'

'Great,' said Babs, beaming.

'I suppose I'll see you on Sunday with your gang. You'll be bringing a tractor?'

Babs shook her head. 'Not me. I've managed to get a whole day off to go and see my sisters. My grandfather died and my eldest sister wrote to me about a sale she's having of some of his things and those of my great-great-aunt. Dad gave her the idea apparently. Anyhow, she wants me to go and choose something as a memento. Grandfather was a sailor and he brought home some interesting stuff. I'm bound to see you again, though. Bye.'

She raised a hand in farewell and walked towards the footpath that would take her across the fields to her billet. The sun was setting and she had forgotten her torch so she wanted to be back before it got dark. She was desperate for a bath and to get out of her working clothes which stank to high heaven.

Birds swooped and dived. Were they swallows catching insects on the wing? she wondered. Spring had arrived and the air smelt different. The countryside was full of cheerful sights and sounds. She had discovered a clump of primroses in a sheltered spot near a hedge the other day and they had smelt so sweet, unlike the pretty white flowers of wild garlic. The countryside was a revelation to a city girl like herself and she was beginning to love it, even when it seemed empty of human habitation, like now.

Ten minutes later she realised that she did not have it to herself. A man was coming along the footpath towards her and, for a moment, she was nervous because he was in shadow and she could not make out who it was. Then he raised his arm in way of greeting and she realised it was Jake O'Donnell. Her heart seemed to flip over as he came to a halt a few paces away. He was scowling.

'What do you think you're doing walking alone

in the country at this time of evening?' he demanded.

Her hackles rose. 'Hello, Barbara! How nice to see you, long time no see.' She mimicked his American accent.

The muscles of his face relaxed. 'I do believe you've missed me,' he said.

'Like I'd miss a nest of red ants,' she said, brushing past him and carrying on along the path, wishing he hadn't come along right now and caught her looking such a mess. God only knew what he thought of how she smelt.

He turned and followed her. 'I came looking for you.'

'How did you know I was here?'

'I hung around the entrance and asked anyone I saw if they could give you a message until I struck lucky. I have to admit to being as surprised as hell when I was told you'd gone to watch a calf birthing. If I had a dollar for every calf I saw born when I was a kid I'd be rich.'

She stared at him. 'Were you a cowboy like in the Westerns?'

'Glad you had the right schooling,' he drawled. 'I'm from Montana. My father has a herd there. I left when I was fourteen after we had a bit of a disagreement.'

'So how did you keep yourself?'

'Worked at anything I could to survive but it was machines I really liked, especially aeroplanes. Eventually I ended up in the air force as a mechanic. What work did you do before becoming a land girl?' he countered.

'Nothing exciting. I was an invoice clerk and

then I worked behind the counter in a dry-cleaners'. This war has plenty of downsides but at least I've had my horizons widened.'

'By seeing a calf born? Smelly business, calving.'

She flushed. 'I know I stink but it's an experience I'll never forget. New life after so many deaths.'

'You've lost folk?'

She nodded. 'My brother, my mother, my aunt. More recently my grandfather died, although, he was old. My sister's husband was killed in the Desert War and her baby was stillborn.'

Jake swore under his breath. 'You poor kid.'

'I'm not a kid!' She glared at him. 'I've had to grow up fast. Now why did you want to see me?'

'To ask you out but you must be whacked.'

She felt a tingle of pleasure, but this evening was just no good because she was worn out and wouldn't be good company. 'What about another time?'

'I've the whole day off on Sunday.'

A sigh escaped her. 'Sunday I'm visiting my sisters who live on the outskirts of Liverpool. I can't get out of it. Nellie's getting rid of some of my grandfather's stuff and she wants me to pick something to remember him by. I'll be out most of the day and can't say when I'll be back for sure.'

Jake looked thoughtful. 'I could tag along. Unless you don't want me to meet your sisters?'

She hadn't even considered him meeting Nellie and Lottie. How would they react after what Nellie had had to say about American servicemen?

'Your face says it all. You don't like the idea.' He sounded hurt, which surprised her because she saw him as a tough guy.

She looked up at him. 'My elder sisters have preconceived ideas about Yanks. I don't want Nellie thinking that...'

'I'll be on my best behaviour,' he said softly, taking her hand and toying with her fingers.

'Stop that!' She attempted to free her hand.

He drew her hand through his arm and continued walking. 'I can guess the kinda ideas they have.'

'You can?'

'Sure.'

'Good. I don't want them worrying that I might get hurt or end up in trouble. I don't want to get serious about a bloke. After seeing how Nellie suffered after her husband was killed, I can do without that kind of pain.'

Jake gazed down at her and kissed the tip of Babs' nose. 'I get the message but we can still have fun going places together. The movies, a meal, a dance. I'm sure your sisters won't begrudge us that and, if they cast an eye over me, that's surely better than imagining I'm some good looking fly-by-night guy.'

Babs wasn't so sure about that. He mightn't look like a movie star but there was definitely something about him that attracted her. 'OK! But best behaviour, mind.'

He raised a hand in a kind of salute. 'Scout's honour. And afterwards we'll take in a movie in Liverpool.'

Babs agreed, hoping she could trust him to keep his word.

Nellie was in the parlour, arranging a few things and considering going up to the attic to see what was in the back room, when she heard a knock on the door. She stopped what she was doing and hurried to open it. On the door step was a strapping young man she had never seen before. 'Yes?'

'Aunt Ethel told me to come,' he said, breathing noisily through his mouth, which seemed full of overlarge teeth. 'My name's David and she said you wanted me to dig.' To her astonishment he burst into song, 'Dig, dig, dig, dig, dig, dig, you dig the whole day through.' He stopped abruptly and beamed at her. 'Dwarfs! They were funny. You seen them?'

'I can't say I have.' She was amused by his partial rendering of the song from the Disney film, *Snow White*.

'They dug for diamonds. I don't suppose you've got any of them?' he said, with a twinkle in his eye.

'I wish I had but you'll have to make do with seed potatoes. Come round the back and I'll show you where everything is.'

She introduced him to her sister, who was polishing brasses in the kitchen. 'Lottie, this is Mrs Wainwright's nephew David. He's come to help in the garden. I thought we could give him a trial period. Do you want to show him everything?'

Lottie eyed David up and down and was impressed by his physique. 'I don't mind if I do. It'll be a nice change from doing these brasses.' She dropped her duster and told him to follow her out.

Nellie left her sister to it and went back to what

she was doing.

Lottie led David into the back garden. 'So have you done much vegetable growing?' she asked.

'A bit for Mum but she's getting on and gets angry when I do things wrong.'

Lottie looked at him. 'What kind of things?'

He shook his head. 'Don't want to talk about it.' He stared at her unwaveringly from hazel eyes. 'You limp. Something wrong with your leg?'

'My hip. I was buried during the blitz. These things, they're nothing to do with growing vegetables?'

She realised he had stopped listening to her and was looking about him. She saw his face light up as he spotted the hens scratching in the dirt. 'Chickens, you've got chickens! I wanted us to have some of them but Mum said, no, too noisy, too messy.'

'They're both that but what does it matter as long as they're not in the house because they lay eggs and one makes a nice roast dinner at Christmas. Come here now.' She took his arm and led him over to the outhouse where the gardening tools were kept. 'We need a trench digging for potatoes. You wouldn't want to make a start now, would you?'

'Don't mind.' He picked up a spade and grinned at her.

Lottie was astounded by his smile. *All those teeth!* she marvelled. And then asked herself what had his teeth to do with anything. They needed a strong man and he certainly looked that. She showed him where she wanted him to dig and then stood back and watched him. After seeing how fast he could shift soil, ten minutes later she decided he would do and went indoors to speak to Nellie about him.

She looked in the parlour for Nellie but she wasn't there or anywhere else downstairs. She shouted for her but, on getting no answer, climbed the stairs. She found Nellie in the back attic room, staring about her with a vacant expression. 'What are you doing, Nellie, standing like a statue? There's loads of work to do.'

Nellie started. She had been thinking about Teddy and children, but now her gaze focused on her sister. 'What is it? You should have shouted for me to save you climbing all the way up here.'

'I did but you mustn't have heard me. I think David will do. He's very strong.'

Nellie smiled. 'Good. Perhaps he can come up here and help me down with a few things.'

'You want me to ask him now?'

Nellie nodded. 'I'll come down with you.'

David was perfectly willing to do what Nellie asked and left his digging and went upstairs with her. He gazed about him with obvious interest and went over to the window and stared out. 'There's Aunt Ethel's garden. Mum says she's bossy and nosey and that's why she won't have her living with us.' He turned and looked at Nellie. 'She likes to know what Mum's up to and asks me but I won't tell her.'

'Good on you,' said Nellie, trying not to smile. 'Now these tea-chests. I want you to help me carry them down.'

He eyed them up, looked inside, placed his strong arms as far as they could reach around

245

one of the tea-chests, heaved, lifted it a few inches. There was a rattling sound and he shook his head and replaced the tea-chest on the floor. He started to remove the newspaper wrapped parcels before she could stop him but then she realised what he was about and so she began to do the same with the other tea-chest.

Half an hour later the chests had been emptied and everything was in the parlour. She thanked him and sent him out to carry on with the digging whilst she set about unwrapping the parcels. The first was a china plate with a pattern of dark red roses and had a stamp on the back saying Royal Albert. She unwrapped another piece and so on and so on, placing crockery, cutlery, glassware and ornaments that consisted of china figurines, brass bells and trays from India. She had also found rolls of wallpaper. A fortnight ago she had found a single roll of a different design of wall-paper in one of the chests in the front attic and had used the back of it to make notices advertising her sale.

With Lottie's help she set to washing and polishing their spoils, reflecting on the positive reactions she had received about her nursery school scheme and the sale. The old man who owned the bicycle and repair shop had offered to display one of her notices in his window, and so had the librarian, the lady in the sweet shop and the man in the post office. Even so, she could not help worrying that either enough people wouldn't come or that so many would turn up that she wouldn't have enough things to satisfy everyone. A banging on the door curtailed her reverie and she went to answer it, wondering who it could be this time.

On the doorstep stood Mrs Wainwright. 'Just come to see how David's doing,' she said, her head held to one side like a perky bird.

'He's only been here a short time but I'm sure he'll do fine,' said Nellie, guessing her nephew was not the real reason behind the old woman being there. 'Do you want to come in and I'll show you what I've gathered together so far?'

Mrs Wainwright's eyes gleamed. 'I was just waiting to be asked.'

She bustled inside after Nellie. So far nothing had been priced and Mrs Wainwright stood inside the parlour, assessing what was there.

'Just as I thought,' she said at last. 'Some really nice stuff amongst the bric-a-brac your grand-father brought home. Although, no doubt, that will go, too. If you like I could start pricing things now? Best not to leave it until tomorrow.'

'Thank you,' said Nellie sincerely, 'and please, Mrs Wainwright, tomorrow, after Babs has had her pick, I want you to choose something in appreciation of your help.'

The woman was obviously touched. 'You're very trusting, Nellie. How do you know I won't take something expensive?'

'I would expect you to take something decent.'

'Yes, but what will Bernard say?'

'It was Dad who gave me the idea for the sale,' said Nellie smoothly, 'so I wouldn't worry.'

Mrs Wainwright's face lit up with pleasure. 'Well, if you say so, dear.'

Nellie went and found paper and pen and gave

247

them to her neighbour and left her to the pricing, while she returned to the kitchen. Lottie had vanished but Nellie found her in the garden, helping David plant the seed potatoes. Smiling, Nellie left them to it and went to put the kettle on.

As she made tea, she thought of the mothers from Polly's group, who had enrolled their children. Among them had been Maisie Miller, who had lent her the pram to carry the dolls' house back home, anxious to ask if she would bend her rules for Irene. Nellie had become fond of the little girl with her blonde curly hair and big blue eyes, thinking, with a catch at her heart, that her own child would have been of a similar age if he had lived. Tears pricked the back of her eyes but she told herself that now was not the time to get upset. She had to be focused on raising money for her new venture.

On the morning of the sale, Nellie was up at six. She had been lying awake for ages, a dozen things running through her head. She prayed the rain would stay away so Maisie and another of the mothers who had volunteered to help with the refreshments could serve them in the front garden, so making the house less crowded if her sale turned out to be a success. But uppermost in her mind was what time Babs would arrive. In case she was late, Nellie had set aside a couple of pieces of porcelain that Mrs Wainwright had said were the genuine article, but even so Nellie would have preferred for her sister to make her own choice.

'So this is your home,' mused Jake, gazing at the people in the front garden, some sitting on child-

248

size chairs at child-size tables, while others stood chattering and drinking tea. Children played with toys on the grass and the buzz of conversation was loud enough to compete with several swarms of bees.

'It doesn't normally look like this,' said Babs, wondering what on earth Nellie was thinking of having all these people in the garden. She imagined their father would have a fit if he saw them crowding on the front lawn. 'She must be having a proper sale. I just thought she'd be taking things to the second-hand shop.' She tugged on his arm. 'Come on, let's find Nellie, so I can introduce you and find out what's going on.'

As they walked up the garden path, Babs would have had to be blind and deaf not to be aware of the attention Jake was attracting, but she told herself that she did not care what these people thought because she didn't know most of them from Adam.

She found Nellie in the parlour with a ferrety-faced man and Mrs Wainwright arguing over the price of the heavy, dark oak sideboard that had been there as long as Babs could remember. She was astounded, wondering what the hell her sister was playing at. So the sideboard was a monstrosity and she, herself, much preferred modern stuff, but it wasn't Nellie's to sell. It struck her that the room was almost empty of most of the furniture and ornaments that had been there for years. Then she saw that Nellie had spotted her and Jake. To say her sister looked surprised was an understatement. She whispered something to Mrs Wainwright and hurried over to them.

249

'So you made it at last,' said Nellie, smiling brightly. 'Any later and there might have been nothing left.'

'What are you up to, Nell?' demanded Babs. 'I presumed when you said you were getting rid of a few things, you didn't intend emptying the whole house.'

Nellie flushed and shoved a dangling lock of hair behind an ear. 'Don't be daft! We need the beds and furniture in all the bedrooms for when the war's over and you and Dad come home, but there is too much stuff in this house and I needed to raise money for my nursery school.'

'Your nursery school! What are you talking about?' asked Babs.

'The one I'm opening here, but never mind that now,' Nellie paused and looked at Jake and smiled. 'Introduce me to your friend.'

'You've gone off your trolley,' said Babs, her green eyes sparkling. 'You can't have a nursery school here.'

Nellie shifted her attention from the American, whom she considered no oil painting, back to her sister. 'I'm having one and nothing you say will alter that. It's my contribution towards the war effort.' She turned back to the airman and held out a hand. 'I'm Nellie Lachlan. Who are you?'

He shook her hand and said gravely, 'Jake O'Donnell. I don't know if Barbara will have my hide if I say it's a pleasure to meet you.'

Babs glared at him and then walked out of the room.

Nellie said ruefully, 'Oh heck! I should have said more in my letter but I wanted to explain to her face. Having said that, she hasn't mentioned you to me.'

'Shocks all around,' he said, with the faintest smile.

She nodded. 'You'd best go after her. I'll find you in a few minutes after I find out if Mrs Wainwright's got me a fair price for that sideboard.'

Jake said, 'See you later,' and left the parlour.

Nellie put him out of her mind and looked over to where Mrs Wainwright and the dealer seemed to have come to an agreement. He was in the act of removing a wad of banknotes from an inside pocket and was peeling several off. He counted them onto the old woman's outstretched hand and Nellie realised he had paid forty pounds for the sideboard. Hallelujah! She decided to talk to Mrs Wainwright later and sort things out with Babs.

She slipped out of the parlour and into the kitchen, where she found her sister whispering vehemently to Jake. She started guiltily when Nellie said, 'I do have a right to hold a sale of Grandfather's things and use this house for a nursery school, but you're not going to like it. If I tell you why you must swear on the Bible that you won't tell Dad.'

A rosy-cheeked Babs said, 'What right?'

'I want your promise first,' said Nellie.

Babs' curiosity was such that she cried, 'OK! I promise.'

Nellie took a deep breath before blurting out, 'Grandfather left the house and its contents to me. I want you to know, though, this will always be your home as long as you wish. There's also a couple of pieces of Royal Doulton upstairs in our bedroom that Mrs Wainwright says are worth something. They're yours if you want them.'

Babs gulped and then she swore, uttering words that Nellie had never heard her say before. She looked at Jake, who held up both hands and said, 'Don't look at me, Mrs Lachlan! She hasn't heard them from me. You have to admit, though, you've given her a helluva surprise.'

'No more than the surprise I got when she turned up with you. Anyway, the truth's out now and you heard her promise not to tell Dad,' said Nellie.

Babs turned on her with a furious expression on her lovely face. 'I'm taking my promise back. How could you steal Dad's inheritance?'

Nellie counted to ten, tapping her fingernails on the table. 'I am shocked that you could believe I'd set out to do such a thing. If you doubt me, speak to Francis. Grandfather asked him to arrange for a solicitor to call here. I was out at work. Francis had told me that Grandfather wanted to leave me something so I'd be secure. I thought he meant something like fifty pounds. He cut Dad out of his will because he...' She stopped abruptly, remembering Jake's presence. 'Enough said. This is family business.'

'And I'm not family,' he drawled. 'It sure is interesting, though, why you get it all and Babs gets nothing.'

'Lottie doesn't get anything either,' said Nellie. 'I think Grandfather believed I'd never marry again and that nobody would want to marry Lottie. As for Babs,' she glanced at her youngest sister and her face softened. 'Look at her. She won't have any trouble finding a husband.'

'What about Dad?' asked Babs, feeling calmer.

Nellie's face hardened and she folded her arms across her chest, thinking with half a mind that they were fortunate not to have been disturbed by anyone in the last five minutes. 'You know that Dad's first love is the sea. You might have been his blue-eye but you can't have forgotten the way he treated Mam or the time he spent in the pub. He's only ever used this house as somewhere to sleep when he docked. Well, Lottie and I will be here keeping the home fires burning and we'll try our hardest to welcome him.'

'Are you going to tell him you own the house?' asked Babs.

Nellie's mouth twisted in a smile. 'Only when I've a big strong man in the room to protect me.'

There was silence in the kitchen and faintly they could hear the sound of people talking, the cries of children and the clucking of hens. Then Babs stirred and went over to Nellie and put her arms round her. As they hugged each other there were tears in their eyes.

'I won't spill the beans,' whispered Babs. 'Now where's my inheritance, did you say?'

Nellie felt too emotional to speak and it was Jake who said, 'In *our* bedroom, I heard her say.'

Inexplicably his answering caused them both to laugh. 'That's right,' said Nellie. 'You go and get it while I collect my money from Mrs Wainwright.' She left Babs and Jake alone, thinking that he knew a family secret that even their busybody neighbour hadn't latched on to yet.

Babs stared at Jake. 'Well, what do you think of

my sister? If you were looking for a woman of property, she's the one to go for.'

Jake gave a crooked smile and placed a hand on the side of her face and caressed her cheek and chin. 'You're a nice person, Barbara Callaghan. You go and collect your inheritance. I'll be waiting here for you.'

His touch had its usual effect on her and for a moment she closed her eyes and kissed one of his fingers. 'Thanks. I won't keep you waiting long.'

She hurried out of the kitchen before her emotions completely got the better of her. She found the figurines where Nellie had said they'd be and, feeling they were a bit old-fashioned for her taste, she decided to ask Mrs Wainwright to sell them for her. After all, thought Babs, she didn't need something to remind her of her grandfather. He had been part of her life since her birth and she wasn't going to forget him. Money would be much more useful.

When Babs arrived downstairs, she found Jake still waiting in the kitchen for her and that was a comfort despite his not being alone. Lottie was handing him a cup of tea while Nellie was talking to a woman whom she introduced to Babs as Polly Perkins, her former boss from Linacre Road. Babs asked a few questions about Nellie's proposed nursery and when she listened to the answers, wondered if her sister had given any thought to what would happen if their father arrived home unexpectedly. She kept her thoughts to herself, though. Soon after, she and Jake said they'd have to go if they were to catch the first house at the pictures.

'You'll come again soon, Babs?' asked Nellie, following the pair out to the front gate.

'If I can. We're getting really busy now but you mustn't worry about me, I'll be fine.' Babs kissed her sister's cheek.

The sisters drew apart and Nellie looked at Jake with a smile. 'It was nice meeting you.'

'Same here, Nellie.' He tipped his hat at her, and drawing Babs' hand through his arm, walked away.

Nellie watched them go with mixed emotions. Part of her envied Babs for having a man in her life but another part of her felt it was disloyal to Teddy's memory to think in such a way.

She returned to the house to see how things were going but it was obvious the sale was a success. The weather had been a great help and so had people's curiosity. Neighbours, acquaintances and those mothers who had not helped with the refreshments had come to support the venture even if they had not bought anything. They had paid their entrance fee and had a tour of the house and gardens and every penny was appreciated by Nellie.

By the end of the day Nellie knew she had made more than a hundred and fifty pounds. It was a small fortune to her and she was over the moon because it was enough to get the nursery off the ground and keep her and Lottie for months, even after making a donation to Wings for Victory.

Mrs Wainwright was obviously pleased with herself. She had looked down her nose a few times at the accents of some of the mothers from the other side of the canal but, fortunately, she had refrained from making comment.

'A very satisfactory sum, Nellie, considering your sale came at the end of Wings for Victory Week and on a Sunday. Fortunately lots of people accept that while there's a war on there's no rest on the Sabbath.'

'Have you chosen something for yourself, Mrs Wainwright?' asked Nellie.

'I have.' The old woman took the brass ornament of the three wise monkeys from her bag.

Nellie stared at it in astonishment. 'I would have thought you'd have chosen a piece of porcelain.'

'No. My father served with the army in India and I remember him bringing one like this home ... but my sister was given first choice after he died and chose the monkeys because she knew I wanted them.' Her fingers caressed the shiny backs of the monkeys. 'It will help bring back happy memories.' She returned the ornament to her bag. 'Babs has asked me to sell her porcelain for her. I'll collect the pieces tomorrow. Thank you, dear. I've enjoyed myself. Bye.'

Nellie thanked her again and saw her out, thinking about what she had said about Babs wanting her to sell the porcelain for her. She hoped her sister wasn't short of money because if she was, then sometime in the future maybe, she was going to have to do some rethinking.

The following day, the dealer arrived with a horse and cart. David was in the garden, so Nellie roped him in to help the men to carry out the sideboard. The parlour was now empty apart from the piano, sofa and the small tables and chairs. The sofa would be ideal for either her or

Lottie to sit on to read to the children on cold, wet days. She would bring down the old nursery guard from the attic and have a fire in here. Her aim was to follow the routine she had kept as a kindergarten teacher as much as possible. She wanted *her* children to have the start in life that was seldom given to those of working-class parents. If most could begin school knowing their alphabet, numbers up to twelve and write their names, they were in with a chance.

Due to the paper shortage, she had decided to supplement her stationery supplies by giving the children cut-up sheets of wallpaper to practice their writing. There were items she would not be able to get due to the war but she did not doubt that she would be able to keep the children occupied. She had her round dozen and was looking forward to the time when the nursery was up and running and, like her sale, could be deemed a success.

Chapter Thirteen

Babs lay on the bed, gazing up at the ceiling with her father's letter held against her chest. It was short and to the point.

Dear Babs,
Hope you're keeping well. I haven't heard from you for some time and Francis and Nellie haven't been in touch either. I thought you, at least, would have

dropped me a line but maybe you're too busy to think of your old dad thousands of miles away out on the briny. Anyhow, I'm still alive and I want you to do something for me. If you haven't visited Nellie recently I want you to make time now. I want to know if what I asked to be done has been done. Let me know.
   Yours,
   Dad

Her first reaction had been annoyance and then guilt for having given him little thought in the last few months but then he hadn't written to her either. He must be referring to the sale but she had no idea what his plans were for the money raised. She groaned and eased herself over onto her side. Every muscle in her body seemed to be aching after being out in the fields all day. She would have to get in touch with Nellie and ask what she wanted her to say to Dad. It was months since the sale, so perhaps it was time she paid her sister a visit to find out for herself how the nursery school was doing. Nellie seemed happy with the way things were going, saying so in the letter, which had enclosed a postal order for the sale of the Royal Doulton. The amount had surprised Babs but she wasn't going to look a gift horse in the mouth. She wouldn't bother trying to get a day off as most likely it would be refused. The light summer evenings meant they were working most of the hours God sent but an evening visit was not out of the question. If she could persuade Jake to get the use of a jeep and take her there, she could be back in time for work the next day.
   Jake! She sighed, wondering if she was doing

the right thing by allowing herself to get so fond of him. It would have been wiser to carry on playing the field but, even if she had the time, she wasn't interested in finding someone else. He was generous, a great dancer and, inexplicably, considering he was no Adonis, she was attracted to him like a nail to a magnet. She would have to drop him a line and arrange a date.

The door opened and Heather entered, still in her working dungarees. 'Babs, Jake's at the gate.'

Babs sat up, wincing and smiling at the same time. 'Great! But talk of the devil, I was just thinking of him.'

Heather winked. 'Like that, is it?'

'Never you mind what it's like,' said Babs, her feet searching for her shoes.

'You've done it then?' Heather giggled. 'Was it worth the risk? Some say it's a real disappointment and the men just want to satisfy themselves.'

'I wouldn't know,' said Babs, easing her feet into highly polished brogues and reaching for her shoulder bag. 'When I do it, I aim to have a wedding ring on my finger.'

'Good for you,' said Heather, flushing. 'I hope you get your wish but you know what they say about Yanks.'

'No, tell me,' said Babs in a mocking voice, taking out the compact and the Max Factor lipstick that Jake had purchased from the shop at the Burtonwood base. He would have given them to her but she had insisted on handing over the cost from her inheritance. 'You sure are one stubborn dame,' he'd said.

'You know exactly what they say and most of

it's true,' muttered Heather.

Babs made no comment because she was applying lipstick. Her green eyes smiled at her reflection in the small mirror, and she found herself humming 'Look for the Silver Lining', thinking Jake had not pushed his luck in trying to get into her knickers and that couldn't be because he didn't fancy her. He could undo her bra single-handed and for a moment she dwelt on the hungry kisses he had lavished on her and felt hot all over. She dusted the freckles on her nose with the powder puff and said, 'Did he have a jeep with him?'

'Aye. He must be hoping to take you somewhere,' said Heather.

Babs replaced her lipstick and compact in her handbag and took her hat from a wardrobe shelf. 'See you later,' she said. 'But if I'm not back, don't worry, I'm hoping to persuade Jake to take me to see my sisters and that will take some time. Bye.'

She hurried out of the hall and down the drive to the gates where she found Jake, sitting in the jeep, smoking a cigarette. Immediately he saw her, his face lit up and he stubbed out the cigarette and opened the passenger door for her. 'Hi, honey. I was praying you could make it. I've news.'

Her heart flipped over as she seated herself. 'News! What kind of news? You're not going away?'

Jake grimaced. 'Me and my big mouth. I shouldn't have broken it to you so soon. I should have waited until later.'

Babs' throat felt tight and she had to swallow before she could speak. 'You're not going on a bombing raid over Germany, are you?'

He smiled. 'Do you listen to anything I say? I'm an aeroplane mechanic. I don't fly the darn things.'

She touched his arm, caressing his sleeve. 'I do listen. I just wasn't thinking straight. So what's your news?'

'Shall we get away from here first?'

'Yes. Go somewhere quiet where we can talk.'

'Sure.' He drove off along a country lane.

A warm wind tugged at her hat and automatically she put up a hand to hold it in place as her gaze fastened on his craggy profile. 'So you're going away?'

He nodded. 'You know the Allies have taken Sicily and Mussolini's quit.'

'No, I didn't. I don't read newspapers or listen to the news. Grandfather was forever wanting to know what was happening with the war. Not me. I do know the Battle of the Atlantic's being won because one of the girls mentioned it.' She smiled. 'I've told those who follow what's going on just to tell me the good news.'

He thought of those in her family who had been killed and said 'Understandable. But getting back to what's going on now. The next stop for the Allies will be the Italian mainland and more experienced aeroplane mechanics are going to be needed in the south of England.'

Babs was torn between relief that he was not going abroad and a sense of loss because he would be hundreds of miles away from her. 'I don't know what to say,' she murmured.

He placed a hand over hers without taking his

eyes off the road. 'You could say you're going to miss me.'

'Of course I'm going to miss you,' she said vehemently. 'I mightn't have wanted to get serious but you caught me while my guard was down.'

His cheek creased into a smile. 'I'm kinda fond of you, too. What say we get wed?'

Babs felt a rush of warmth and happiness. 'I never thought you'd ask.' She flung an arm around his neck and the jeep swerved.

'Hey, hey, woman, control yourself or you'll have us in the ditch.'

'Sorry.' She kissed his cheek and resumed her former position.

'Do I take that for a yes?' he drawled.

'No, a no.' She chuckled. 'Jake, you'll be able to get me some parachute silk, so I can have a wedding dress made from it, won't you?'

'I was hoping to dispense with the fancy stuff,' he said wryly. 'I want to marry you before I go away, take you with me, even. We'd have to do it within the week.'

The excitement in Babs' face died. 'You mean no white wedding in church? I've dreamt of a white wedding in church.' She saw the expression on his face. 'OK!' she said hastily. 'There's a war on and we can't all have what we want. I'll do without the white wedding but you're forgetting, I'm under age. I need Dad's permission to marry.'

The expression on Jake's face this time would have been comical if the subject under discussion had not been so serious. 'Hell! Your dad's at sea. How long will it take to get in touch with him? How long before he writes back?' He stopped the jeep and stared gloomily through the windscreen and then his face lit up. 'We could send him a wire.'

Babs' concept of how a radio telegraph worked was nonexistent but perhaps it was possible to find her father's ship in such a way. Then she thought this was her father they were talking about and she knew that even if he received the wire, he wouldn't say yes. She groaned and dropped her head on Jake's shoulder. 'It won't work. I'm his favourite daughter. Even if you weren't a Yank, he'd want to look you over before giving his permission.'

Jake put his arm round her. 'OK. I suppose any father worth his salt wants what's best for his daughter, but there's a war on and some things just have to go by the wayside. I reckon we'll just have to elope. What's that place up north in Scotland?'

'Gretna Green! You must be joking.' Babs thought it might sound romantic to elope but she didn't fancy tying the knot over an anvil. She wouldn't feel properly married if it wasn't in church. It occurred to her that to suggest such a thing Jake mightn't be Catholic. 'You are Catholic, aren't you?' she asked.

He shook his head. 'Grandpa was but he married a Protestant and Dad was brought up in the Episcopal church. He met Ma at a church social. I didn't suppose it mattered to you what I am.'

A dismayed Babs nodded glumly. 'I'm sorry. It does.'

He rubbed the back of his hand over his jaw. 'I never realised you felt so strongly. You don't talk religion. I'll convert. I'll get married in your church.'

'You will?' Her spirits yo-yoed again. 'But that still means I'll need Dad's permission.'

Jake swore long and hard.

Babs said, 'What's the point of swearing? What are we going to do?'

He stared at her from hopeful blue eyes. 'We could always jump the gun and hope you get pregnant. Then your father would have to give his permission.'

'No way!' Despite understanding the way his mind was working, all the talk about her father reminded her of what Grandfather had said about her parents having to get married and she did not want a marriage like theirs. She drew away from Jake. 'If you want me, then you're going to have to wait for me. It's not as if you're going off to fight.' Her pretty mouth set firm.

'Sure, but we are going to be parted. After this evening, we probably won't see each other for months.' His voice had deepened and he reached out for her.

She knew he wanted her but she placed a hand against his chest. 'You were listening to me, weren't you, Jake? No going too far. I've got strong doing the job I do now and I wouldn't want to hurt you if you really tried it on.'

He frowned and then the muscles of his face relaxed. 'I'm really scared, honey, but I sure get the message.' He took her hand and drew her closer. 'Isn't there any way we could get married this year?'

'I'll have to think about it,' said Babs, remembering Nellie running off to marry Teddy, but that was a no-no. Even so, thinking about her sister reminded her that she had been going to ask Jake to take her to see Nellie but now was not the right time. If he was to leave within the week, she wanted to spend that time alone with him, so decided her sister would have to make do with a letter.

'Nellie, you don't ever wonder if the nursery wasn't a good idea, do you?' asked Lottie anxiously, eyeing the boy that had just snatched a sheet of paper from Irene, who had been happily scribbling until that moment.

Nellie did not answer because she was reading Babs' letter, which had just arrived. The news that her father had asked Babs to find out whether Nellie had done what he'd asked annoyed her but she was more worried about what her sister had to say about wanting to marry Jake. For a moment she felt a pang of envy that Babs was in that wonderful state of being in love, which probably accounted for the letter being so garbled and Babs forgetting to say whether she had received the postal order. Nellie hoped it hadn't gone missing because she had added a few pounds to the amount Mrs Wainwright had handed to her from the sale of the china. As she read the last paragraph, Nellie frowned. Babs seemed to want her to write to Dad and persuade him to give his permission so Babs could marry Jake.

'She must be mad,' murmured Nellie, 'thinking he'd listen to me.'

'What did you say?' asked Lottie.

Nellie looked at her sister. 'Babs. She wants to marry Jake and expects me to get Dad to agree to it.'

'You'd be better getting in touch with Francis and see what he thinks,' said Lottie. 'But what *I* want to know now is are you going to deal with Tommy? He's just ripped up Irene's paper.'

'OK!' said Nellie, pocketing the letter and squeezing her way between two tables to where the young miscreant was scattering the paper like confetti. She still marvelled that even the most cherubic looking child could be an imp in disguise. She supposed that as children even Hitler and Mussolini hadn't looked like the monsters they turned out to be. Thinking of the Italian dictator reminded her that a short while ago twenty-two thousand Italian POWs had been landed at a north west port. Probably Liverpool but the press had to be discreet. Recently the Ministry of Information had let it be known that Italy had now surrendered unconditionally. Their declaration of war on Germany had followed soon after. She wished the Italians had realised earlier who was the real enemy. Perhaps if they had, Teddy might have still been alive.

Nellie took Tommy by the shoulders and turned him round to face her. 'That wasn't kind, Tommy.'

'It was rubbish she was doing,' he sneered, trying to wriggle free.'

'Not to Irene. You can go in the garden and help David dig up potatoes. I want you to try and count as many as you can and write down the number for me when you've done that.'

His sullen expression lifted and he would have

266

run out of the parlour if she had not darted after him and told him to slow down. 'We don't want any accidents, do we?' she said, smiling down at him.

He nodded and she let him go before returning to where Irene had already taken another square of wallpaper and was scribbling on the back of it. She rested a hand on the girl's fair curls, feeling a strong affection for her. Another child might have attempted to snatch the paper back but not this one. Nellie thought of Maisie, who was worried sick about her brother fighting with the Allies in Europe. The feeling in the country was that there were still tough days ahead but the tide of war had turned. Africa was in the hands of the Allies, and thanks to Captain Johnny Walker, who had led his U-boat destroyers out of Gladstone Dock in Seaforth to a band playing, 'A-Hunting We Will Go', more Allied ships were reaching their destinations.

She left Irene and returned to the table where she had originally been showing the four-year-olds how to write the letter s. Having the children in her home was a real joy. They had brought the old house alive and she hoped that if her grandfather could see her now, he would approve of the way she was using her inheritance. She wasn't making much money but at least she was doing something worthwhile and, although not completely happy, she was content.

The only fly in the ointment was Mrs Wainwright who, when it came to music time or the children playing in the front garden, complained of the noise they made. Nellie was disappointed in her, having believed after the sale that the old woman was on her side. Still, there was no use worrying about her as she had enough on her plate.

Later over a cup of tea, Lottie said, 'I forgot to mention that I saw Billy's father when I went looking for our cat last night.'

'Did you ask him about Billy?'

'He's up in Scotland and enjoying being a soldier. Sgt McElroy was really friendly, asked how we were and whether the nursery was doing well.'

Nellie smiled. 'And what did you tell him?'

'I said it was great and that I was learning a lot about children.'

'You're doing really well.'

'David likes the children, too. They accept him for what he is,' said Lottie. 'Grown ups can be too judgemental.'

'I noticed Tommy was happy to go and help him.'

There was a pause before Lottie said, 'So what about Babs' letter? Will you be going to see Francis this evening?'

'This evening!' Nellie screwed up her face, thinking about that.

'No time like the present. David will keep me company. He's whittling something from wood for the children. He's really good with his hands,' said Lottie eagerly. 'You don't mind him staying on a few hours, do you?'

Nellie shook her head, and decided if David was staying then she could safely leave Lottie in the house. He was so big and strong that a burglar would think twice before breaking in.

Nellie almost changed her mind when the time came to catch the bus to Francis' parish. The wind had got up and it was threatening rain.

'If you put it off, the weather could be the same tomorrow and the day after that,' said Lottie, who was settled by the fire with the cat. David was sitting opposite her, whittling a piece of wood, whistling while he worked.

'OK! I'll go but don't be worrying about me if I'm late,' said Nellie, putting on her outdoor things. 'See you later.'

By the time she was making her way to the presbytery near Byrom Street, it was dark and pouring with rain and Nellie was wishing she had ignored what Lottie had said and stayed at home. With her coat collar turned up and the brim of her hat pulled down as far as possible, she focused her torch on the ground a few feet in front of her, worried in case she fell into a hole. As she passed the looming bulk of the darkened church, she heard what she thought was a groan. She paused and spun her torch round but could not see anything unusual so continued walking, only to hear the sound again.

She retraced her steps and shone her torch into the porch. The beam fell upon the shivering, huddled shape of a man, who had one leg thrust out. His breathing was laboured and his clothing looked soaking wet. She reached out a tentative hand and touched him. He jerked back causing her to almost jump out of her skin. With a heavily beating heart, she waited for any more sudden movements, but when he remained still, she touched his shoulder. 'Are you hurt?'

He did not answer.

She shone her torch on him and saw a large rip in his trouser leg, exposing bloodied flesh beneath. 'Nasty,' she said. 'Are you hurt anywhere else?'

He did not speak and she shone the beam of the torch on him and saw that, despite the heavy boot he was wearing, his left ankle was swollen. She was going to need help.

'I'll go and fetch the priest,' she said.

Without further delay she hurried to the presbytery, praying that her brother was not at the boys' club or out visiting a parishioner. As it was, she did have to knock several times before she heard the sound of hurrying footsteps and her brother's voice informing her that he was coming.

Nellie's shoulders sagged with relief as the door was flung open. His dark bulk was a reassuring presence. 'There's a man in the church porch, Francis. He needs help.'

'Nellie! Is that you?' He peered out.

'Yes! Hurry! He's injured and he's soaking wet.'

'OK! I'll come. You must be soaked yourself. Come inside. I'll just get my coat and a torch.'

Nellie stepped inside and closed the door on the filthy evening. 'Perhaps you'd prefer to wait here while I go and take a look at him,' said Francis.

'No. You'll need my help to get him up.'

'I'm not an eight-stone weakling,' he said, sounding amused.

'I know that! But you'll need someone to hold the torch because you'll have your hands full.'

'You're right! Father would have helped but he's away at a conference and I've given Mrs Riley a couple of days off to go and see her sister.

So why are you here, Nellie? What can I do for you?' asked Francis, putting on his coat and reaching into the drawer of an ornate umbrella stand. He took out a torch.

'Babs and Dad. *She* wants to marry a Yank. *He* wants to know if I've done what he's asked.'

'Dad's written to you?'

'You're joking! He's wrote to Babs.' Nellie almost blurted out, 'Bloody cheek!'

He opened the door. 'So what do you want me to do?'

'Speak to Babs, see her fella, write to Dad,' she said, following him out. 'You've got your key?'

He felt in a pocket, sighed and went back into the house, reappearing a few minutes later and closing the door.

Nellie held onto her hat as she walked alongside him, taking two paces to his one. 'So will you do it?' she asked.

'Do what?'

'Speak to Babs, see Jake, write to Dad. Although, she didn't ask me to speak to you. She wanted my opinion because he's not Catholic but says he'll convert,' panted Nellie, trying to keep up with him as they turned a corner and felt the full force of the wind.

'Good. But instruction will take time. She'll have to wait.'

She was indignant. 'You can tell you've never been in love.'

'Good thing, too, from what I've seen of what it does to people.'

Nellie opened her mouth to say something good about love but they were now nearing the porch. Francis flashed the beam of his torch onto the man. He had moved and Nellie could now see his face clearly. One side of it showed heavy bruising and there were scratches on his cheeks and nose. His eyes were closed and, although his eyelids flickered, they remained closed. If he'd had a hat then the wind must have whipped it away because his dark hair shone wetly.

'He's completely out for the count,' said Francis.

'I'm sure he was conscious before. One of his legs is bloody and he's hurt his ankle.'

The stranger opened his eyes and muttered indistinctly.

'Did you hear what he said?' asked Nellie of her brother.

Francis did not answer but handed his torch to her. She kept its beam on the man as Francis lifted him upright. 'Be careful of his ankle,' she warned.

The man groaned as Francis heaved him upright and hoisted him over a burly shoulder. 'You light the way, Nellie.'

She did as told, flashing the torch on the ground in front of them, aware every now and then of the painful hiss of the man's breath. She wondered who he was and where he had come from.

Francis told her to take the key from his pocket and open the door. She did so and held the door open while he carried the man inside. Once the door was closed, she switched on the light. Now she could see the man's damaged face more clearly. At some time he had been in the sun because his skin was tanned, his cheeks were thin and his nose was swollen, his dark eyebrows were thick, sooty slashes. She placed his age at twenty-six or seven.

'I'll take him into the study, there's a fire there,' said Francis. 'Could you put the kettle on and make some tea? The matches are on the shelf near the cooker.'

Nellie headed for the kitchen, knowing what to expect. Unlike the one at home, the room was freezing with no friendly fire in a black-leaded range. She had no trouble finding the matches and lighting a gas ring. She filled the kettle and put it on before removing her wet hat and coat and hanging them on the back of the door. She was hungry but considered it good manners to ask her brother before making herself something to eat. Besides, the injured man might be in need of food.

She made the tea and carried it into the study. Francis was not there but the stranger was sitting in an armchair in front of the fire. All she could see of him was the top of his dark head and steam rising from his clothing. She placed the tray on the desk, poured the tea and carried a cup over to him.

His injured foot was resting on a stool and the trouser leg had been cut away, exposing a nasty gash on his shin. He stared up at her from eyes that were almost black and she had trouble reading his expression. Her heart fluttered beneath her ribs and she felt breathless. She thrust the cup and saucer at him, wanting to get away. As he took it, his fingers brushed hers and her skin tingled. She hurried back over to the desk and picked up her cup of tea and gulped down a mouthful.

To her relief, Francis entered the room, carrying a bundle of clothes, a blanket and towel. As if in answer to an unspoken question, he said, 'The church jumble. Not given by the local poor, I might add, but from a richer parish in South Liverpool. Comes in handy at times like this.'

She burst out, 'Do you recognise him?'

'I don't know everyone in this parish.' Francis placed the clothes on a chair and reached for his cup of tea. 'I want you to look at his leg; best sort that out before he puts on a clean pair of trousers.'

'Me!'

'You look after children so you must know something about cuts and bruises,' said Francis.

'OK,' she said reluctantly, 'but I'm no Florence Nightingale. He looks like he's had a good clout to the head. He could be suffering from concussion. He should see a doctor.' The man's head turned and she saw the apprehension in his eyes. 'He understands English OK,' she murmured.

'Were you thinking he mightn't?' asked Francis.

She hesitated. 'He's got real dark eyes and hair, and his skin...'

'That doesn't mean a thing, Nellie. There's plenty of men in this parish with those same dark eyes and hair.'

'Maybe. But why isn't he knocking on his family's door?'

'He could be from Holy Cross parish; been away and not realised the church there was bombed and that's why he's turned up here.' Francis drained his cup and placed it on the tray. 'Anyway, I'm not about to start questioning him. He came to the church for help. No doubt he's hungry.'

'I'm hungry, too. I thought of making myself a jam butty.'

Francis smiled. 'I can do better than that ... there's the remains of a pie, a gift from a grateful parishioner in the larder. It's tasty, although I'm not sure what's in it.'

She left the study, thinking of that grateful parishioner, guessing that half the women in his congregation were in love with him. She found the pie and cut it into wedges and put it on plates.

Back inside the study, she found the man had changed into a flannelette shirt and Fair Isle pullover and he had a blanket draped over his shoulders. Francis had pulled up a chair next to him and was talking to him in a low voice.

'Has he told you anything yet?' asked Nellie.

Her brother shook his head.

The man's dark eyes washed over Nellie's weary face. Then he noticed the plates in her hands and she saw that he was hungry. 'I wonder when he last ate,' she said, going over to him.

'Never mind that. Give him his pie,' said Francis.

Nellie did so and then handed another plate to her brother before sitting in a shiny leather arm-chair to eat her pie. It had an unfamiliar flavour but was as tasty as her brother had said. She only hoped it wasn't somebody's moggy; these days, people were eating meat they wouldn't normally touch.

Francis polished off his slice in no time. 'I'll just nip upstairs for the first aid box. If you could get some hot water and there's clean rags in one of the kitchen drawers.'

Nellie nodded but did not rush to do what he said. She was tired and, besides, the man was still eating. She watched him surreptitiously, wondering how he'd got his injuries. He looked as worn out as she did; how far had he travelled before finishing up in the church porch? She swallowed the last bit of pie, rose from the chair and went into the kitchen.

She ran hot water into a bowl and took the clean rags from a drawer. When she entered the study, her brother still hadn't returned. She placed the bowl of hot water on the hearth and knelt on the rug. Blood had crusted over the wound on his shin at some time but something had happened to cause the injury to open up again. She picked up a clean rag and dipped it in the hot water and gripped the man's calf. She felt him tense and then relax, only for his calf muscle to tense again when she began to clean the wound.

She was unaware that Francis had entered the room until he said, 'There's no Dettol or iodine.'

'Have you any whiskey?'

'Whiskey?'

'Remember the parable of the Good Samaritan?'

Francis looked pained. 'You're not suggesting using good Irish whiskey as an antiseptic?'

As her brother moved into her line of vision, she was aware that the man was watching her. 'I only want an eggcup full,' she said.

'That's approximately a dram. That whiskey came to me at great cost.'

'Illegally, I bet,' she said dryly.

'I'm a priest, Nellie. How can you accuse me of

breaking the law?' His expression was one of mock horror.

'Come on, Francis, you don't want this poor man ending up with septicaemia, do you?'

With a sigh he fetched the bottle from the sideboard cupboard, found three small glasses and poured out the whiskey.

'Is one of them for him to drink?' she asked.

'You're the nurse. Would it do him good?'

Nellie looked at the man. 'What do you say?' she asked.

He gave her a ghost of a smile. Goodness! He'd be quite nice looking if it weren't for the bruising and the swollen nose, thought Nellie. 'Give him some,' she said, 'and while you're at it, I wouldn't mind a dram.'

'You drink whiskey, Nellie, what would Dad say?' He handed her a glass and gave one to the stranger. Francis raised his. 'Good health and may God bless us all.'

'Ditto,' said Nellie, taking a cautious sip.

The stranger gave a sharp nod and downed his drink in one go.

'Do you think he's used to whiskey? Perhaps he's an Irishman, who's been in the sun,' said Nellie.

Francis smiled and took the man's glass from him and half-filled it. 'Here's your antiseptic, Nell. Don't let it evaporate.'

Nellie tossed off her whiskey and felt it burning a path down her throat. She gave a small cough before reaching for a piece of cotton wool and dipping it in the whiskey. She hummed beneath her breath as she swabbed the wound. It was deep and she felt the man tense again and considered suggesting Francis give him another shot to drink. His warm breath stirred her hair and, for a second, her fingers faltered but then she told herself not to be so bloody silly and finish the job.

She got to her feet and turned to her brother. 'I think that cut needs a few stitches.'

'I'm sure it'll be fine. That whiskey's powerful stuff. What about his ankle?'

'Cold water compress?'

'I'll get fresh water,' said Francis, lifting the bowl and carrying it out.

Nellie eased aching shoulders and glanced at the clock on the wall. It was a shock to see that it was ten o'clock.

When Francis re-entered the room, she said, 'I should be going.'

'It's still throwing it down outside. Stay. You can have Mrs Riley's bedroom.'

She shook her head. 'Lottie will be worrying about me. Besides, the kids will be coming in the morning.'

'It's Sunday tomorrow.'

'Is it?' Nellie put a hand to her head. 'I'd forgotten what day it is.'

'Lottie's not stupid. She'll realise you've stayed here because of the rain.'

Nellie eased tired shoulders. 'You're probably right. I just hope she's not frightened in the house on her own.'

'She's not a child, Nellie.'

'I feel like she is at times.' She glanced at the stranger. 'What about him? I take it you'll be putting him up here?'

'I can hardly throw an injured man out in the rain.'

She relaxed. 'OK, I'll stay but I want a hot water bottle in my bed.'

Francis shook his head and said in a droll voice, 'I can see you're going to be a troublesome guest. You'll find the hotties in the kitchen. Fill three.'

'So you're going to be Florence Nightingale now while I fill hotties?' She glanced down at the wounded man and he smiled back at her from drowsy eyes. She felt a similar thrill to when a troublesome child surprised her by behaving well, and hurried out of the study.

She boiled water and filled the stone hot water bottles, forcing her thoughts away from the two men in the study and thinking, instead, about Babs and Jake. He had seemed OK to her but whether he was the right man for Babs Nellie did not know. Perhaps Francis was right in thinking that there was no rush to sort out Babs' problem and that her having to wait until she came of age to marry him could be the wisest course to take.

She returned to the study with two of the hotties. The man had his foot in the bowl of water and a glass in his hand; his eyes were closed. She realised that his leg between his ankle and just above his knees was dark in comparison to part of his thigh. 'He's been wearing shorts and has been in the sun,' she said.

'What did you say, Nell?' asked Francis, who also had a glass in his hand and was sitting in the leather armchair.

'I think he's been abroad.' She thrust the hotties at him. 'You'll have to take these up. I don't know where they go.'

'I'll show you Mrs Riley's room,' said Francis, getting up. 'Have you done the other one?'

Nellie nodded. 'I'll fetch it. I'll go to bed now if you don't mind. I'm whacked.'

She went over to the door but paused to glance back at the man. His eyes were open and he was staring at her. He looked anxious and who could blame him? He must be in trouble to have sought out the help of the church. She watched as he turned his head away and gazed into the fire. Then she went to bed and wasted little time worrying about him, or anything else for that matter, but fell asleep, clutching the hot water bottle wrapped in her vest.

'So did you find out anything about him after I went to bed?' asked Nellie the following morning. She placed toast on a plate and handed it to her brother.

'I can't answer you,' said Francis, crunching into his toast with strong teeth.

'Can't?'

He nodded.

She thought about that and murmured, 'I see.' Her mind buzzing with possibilities, she reached for the teapot. 'Nothing more I can do to help?'

'No. You've been a good Samaritan and can leave things to me now. He needs to rest, so I won't wake him yet. You can go home and check Lottie's OK.'

'Thanks.' Nellie knew it was pointless being annoyed with him but after the part she'd played in the drama last night, she felt that she was owed an explanation. Yet she knew her brother well enough to know it was not going to be forthcoming, so she let it go and finished her breakfast.

When she was ready to leave, she said, 'Will you let me know how he gets on?'

He nodded. 'I'll come and see you and Lottie soon.' He opened the front door.

She had the impression he couldn't wait to get rid of her, which surprised her as she had thought he might have tried to persuade her to attend Mass at his church. Obviously the man's needs were more important. But before she was prepared to say her goodbye, she had something else to ask him. 'Dad and Babs, anything further to say?'

'Let me think about it. As I said, I'll come and see you soon.'

Nellie had to be content with that and so she said her goodbye and left.

The rain had dried up and the sun was peeping through clouds which scattered before a stiff breeze. She decided not to worry her head about the man. It could be that he was a soldier who had gone AWOL, but he was not her problem. So what if she had felt something towards him? She was a woman, after all, and was not immune to the opposite sex.

When Nellie arrived home, she was surprised to find Lottie in the kitchen peeling potatoes, talking to David. 'You're here early for a Sunday morning,' she said.

'I didn't hear you come in, Nellie,' said Lottie, looking flustered and dropping a potato.

'Obviously, you weren't worried enough to look

281

out for me.'

'I was a bit worried about you,' said Lottie, darting a glance at David, who had picked up the potato. 'But-but when I saw the weather, I guessed you w-were staying with Francis.'

'Good. I'm glad you weren't frightened on your own.'

'No. I was fine,' said Lottie, her face scarlet. 'So what did Francis have to say?' She took the potato from David who stood awkwardly, his head turned away from Nellie.

'He wants time to think about it. We had a bit of excitement, so we didn't talk about it much,' said Nellie, sitting at the table.

'What excitement?'

'I found an injured man in the church porch and Francis has taken him in.'

'What was wrong with him?'

Nellie told her. 'Anyway, Francis didn't need me anymore, so I came straight home.' She smiled. 'If you don't mind getting on with the dinner, I'll go and have a bath.' She turned to David. 'I suppose you've seen to the hens?'

He nodded jerkily.

'Thanks. You can go home now if you like.'

David glanced at Lottie. 'Will I go?'

She hesitated. 'It's up to you.'

He stood there indecisively. Nellie sighed and left them to it.

As she lay in the bath with her eyes closed, she could see the man's face against her eyelids. 'Man of mystery,' she murmured, wondering what his name was and where he had come from.

During the days that followed, he haunted her

dreams and on wakening, she felt guilty for his doing so. She gazed at Teddy's photograph and felt a mixture of sadness and guilt but realised that she was no longer heartbroken. She replaced the photograph, wondering whether love really could last a lifetime.

A week later Francis called with the news that his unexpected visitor had left.

'Where's he gone?' asked Nellie, her heart quickening.

'To find his family.'

'Oh! So we won't see him ever again?'

Francis shook his head. 'I doubt it, Nellie. Best to forget that you ever met him and concentrate on Babs' problem.'

Nellie felt depressed and knew that she did not want to be bothered with Babs' love life. Yet she knew she had no choice. Jake was not the first fella in Babs' life and it could be that he wouldn't be the last. She was still young and perhaps their not rushing into marriage would test whether he was the right one for her or not. In the meantime, she listened to what her brother had to say and made up her mind to visit her sister.

Chapter Fourteen

The decision to speak to Babs face to face having been made, Nellie wasted no time in getting in touch. She wrote that she didn't believe their father would take any notice of what she had to say but that she'd spoken to Francis and he was going to write to him. In the meantime, perhaps it would be a good idea if she visited Babs.

Nellie received Babs' answer by return post, consisting of a few lines telling her which bus to catch and promising to meet Nellie on her arrival. She began to look forward to the outing, relieved to have the anniversary of Teddy's death and the loss of her baby behind her.

When the day came for her visit, Nellie put on her best frock and twisted her hair into a knot on top of her head. Unfortunately she was delayed by a traffic jam in getting to the city centre and had to run for the bus. She was greeted with a resounding cheer as she jumped aboard.

'Yer just made it,' said a blonde, touching Nellie's arm as she swayed up the aisle.

'Not that yer'd have had long to wait,' said another girl, giving a wriggle of excitement. 'They've laid on extra buses for the big dance tonight. They've a real swing band over from the States.'

'What!' exclaimed Nellie, startled.

The girl patted the seat next to her. 'Sit here.'

Nellie thanked her in a breathless voice. She'd have to be blind not to notice that nearly every place on the bus was taken by her own sex. 'You – you don't mean this bus is going to Burtonwood base?'

'That's right. Where did you think it was going?'

'Warrington.'

'Wrong bus.' The girl looked at her sympathetically. What are you going to do?'

Nellie fiddled with the strap of her handbag,

284

imagining what Francis would say if he knew she was on a bus heading for the airbase. Perhaps she should get off but Babs had told her to catch this bus and would be waiting for her at the other end. She must have meant for her to go to Burton-wood, perhaps to show her that there was nothing for her to worry about. She glanced about her at the young, excited faces and couldn't blame them for wanting some fun, to dance with one of those glamorous GIs when there was such a shortage of home-grown young men around. As long as they kept their heads, she thought, relieved that Jake was a couple of hundred miles away, which surely meant Babs would stay out of trouble.

'Well, have you made your mind up?' asked the girl, smiling.

Nellie nodded. 'I'm staying put. My sister's meeting me at the other end and she'd only wonder what had happened to me.' She sighed, wondering what she was letting herself in for.

'Great! I'm sure you'll have a smashing time even if you can't dance.'

'I can dance OK,' said Nellie affronted.

'Then you're in for a treat,' said the girl.

Nellie smiled and kept quiet, feeling certain Teddy would not begrudge her enjoying herself. In fact she was beginning to look forward to the prospect of being asked onto the dance floor.

Babs kissed Jake's letter and placed it under her pillow. She wondered why she had doubted him, just because he had not been in touch as soon as he had arrived at the base in Essex. Well, she need not have worried. The poor love had been up to his eyes in work since he got there and she had to remember that winning the war was uppermost in most servicemen's minds. She wished they could be together. Perhaps she should have eloped with him as he'd suggested. After all, she had the money that Nellie had sent her in her post office saving account. A sigh escaped her and then she mentally shook herself and, reaching for her bag, walked slowly out of the room. She must not forget the trouble Nellie marrying Teddy had caused in the family. She wondered what her sister would do when she realised that she was heading for Burtonwood. Maybe she'd get off the bus and go back home, but hopefully not. Nellie could do with a bit of brightness in her life and, with her love of dancing and music, what could be better than dancing to a swing band?

A bus had just pulled up and passengers were disembarking when Babs arrived at Burtonwood. Almost immediately she spotted Nellie and was relieved to see that her eldest sister was wearing a brightly coloured frock of red and blue. Her cheeks were rosy and her chestnut hair shone as if it had been polished with a silk handkerchief. Babs hurried forward with a skip in her step to greet her.

'Hi, Nell, long time, no see,' she said, flinging her arms around her.

'Not since April,' said Nellie, returning her hug.

Babs' jaw dropped. 'That long! Where does the time go?'

'Being busy helps,' said Nellie, holding her sister at arms' length. 'You've lost weight.'

'Hard work, and I haven't eaten much the last

week or so.'

'Why is that?'

'No letter from Jake, but I got one today.' Babs' green eyes sparkled. 'He's not the best of letter writers but then neither am I. Still, he said all that needed to be said.'

'So marriage is still on the cards,' said Nellie, releasing her sister. 'Because if so, what are we doing here?' She glanced about her at the crowds and the buildings, which her sister had once referred to as 'Little America'.

'I thought you could do with having some fun,' said Babs, linking her arm through her sister's. 'You haven't sworn off men completely, have you?'

'No, but that doesn't mean I'm looking to hop into bed with one.'

Babs gaped at her. 'I should think not. Who gave you such an idea?'

'Listening to some of the talk on the bus. Not for them a walk down the aisle first,' said Nellie dryly.

Babs grimaced. 'Hopefully you'll trust me to use my nous.'

Nellie nodded. 'You seem serious enough about Jake, so I can't see you chancing ruining what the pair of you have. Although, Dad will probably refuse his permission for you to marry until he sets eyes on him. Could be you might have to wait until the war's over.'

Babs nodded. 'You could be right. Although, I'll be twenty-one in forty-five, so I'll be able to do what I want then. It seems ages away.'

'It'll probably go over quicker than you think,' said Nellie, smiling. 'Now where's the dance hall?

I can't wait to hear the swing band.'

Babs' face brightened up and she hugged her sister's arm. 'All we have to do is follow the crowd.'

So that's what they did. Nellie had never seen such a large ballroom or so many men in uniform, except in a war film. Couples were already on the dance floor and she felt excitement and pleasure as she recognised 'Lullaby of Broadway'. Memories of dancing with Teddy caused her a moment's sadness but then her feet began to tap to the rhythm of the music and she hoped someone would ask her to dance.

Babs insisted on their finding a table first but, no sooner had they sat down than two men appeared. 'I didn't think I'd see you here, Babs, with Jake gone.' The younger airman's sarcasm was evident.

Babs stiffened. 'I'm surprised to see you here without Heather, Stuart.'

He flushed. 'She didn't tell you it's over between us? I caught her with another bloke. I wasn't putting up with that. I can't see Jake putting up with it from you, either.'

'Jake and I trust each other,' said Babs, her eyes flashing green fire. 'But if you want to go telling tales, don't forget to mention I was chaperoned. This is my sister, Nellie. Nell, Stuart McGregor.'

Before Nellie could even offer her hand to shake, he turned on his heel and stalked off. 'What's wrong with him?' she asked.

'Sorry about that, ladies,' said the remaining airman. 'Stu can be a bit touchy. I'm Ray Jones, by the way.' He held out a hand.

Babs barely touched his fingers but Nellie

shook his hand firmly because she liked the look of him. He had a pleasant face and his uniform was spotless. 'Nice to meet you.'

'Likewise.' He smiled. 'Are chaperones allowed to dance?'

Nellie glanced at Babs. 'Will you be OK?'

'Of course!' Babs rolled her eyes. 'I brought you here to dance. You deserve some fun after spending most of your time looking after kids.'

Ray looked startled. 'You're married?'

'Widow,' she said hesitantly, hating the word. 'And they're not my kids. I'm a nursery school teacher.'

'Now that's what I call heroic,' smiled Ray. 'I've a couple of boys back home and my wife says two's enough of a handful for her.'

'I've none of my own.' Nellie wondered if he would have been honest with her if Babs hadn't mentioned children. Still, he hadn't had to tell her he was married. 'Shall we dance?'

'Sure.' He led her onto the dance floor to the strains of 'Don't Sit Under The Apple Tree'.

Babs watched them dancing a speeded-up quickstep and thought if Jake had been here they'd have been jitterbugging. Of course, she had no intention of dancing but, even so, she couldn't prevent her foot tapping.

A clean-shaven, gum-chewing airman stopped in front of her. He was tall, dark and had surprisingly vivid blue eyes in a square-jawed face. 'I spotted you from across the floor and thought you looked kinda lonely. So I thought I'd mosey on over and see whether you'd like to dance with me,' he said.

'I'm not dancing,' she replied.

He stopped chewing. 'Why? It can't be that you don't fancy dancing with me, so you must have broken your foot or something.'

Her lips twitched. 'No. But my boyfriend isn't here, so I'm just watching.'

'Why did you come?'

'I brought my sister. She deserves a good time.'

'She the one dancing with Ray?' He took out a packet of gum and offered it to Babs.

'Yes. Thanks.' She tore off the wrapper and popped it into her mouth. It was cinnamon flavour and one of her favourites.

They chewed companionably for a few moments before he said, 'Name's Pete Rand. You want a drink?'

'Thanks. Lemonade.'

He nodded and left her. Babs looked for Nellie and Ray and spotted them still on the dance floor, talking animatedly. The two had certainly clicked but she doubted that would lead to a date. She bet they were talking about kids. She thought of Jake and wondered how many kids he'd like. She considered two boys and two girls were the perfect family. She wondered what he was doing right now. Would he be off duty? If he was then maybe he had gone out with some of the other guys. Perhaps even now he was dancing with a girl somewhere. She frowned.

'So where's your chaperone?'

Babs groaned and looked at Stuart. 'None of your business,' she said.

His face hardened. 'I saw you talking to Pete.'

'Is it against the law to talk to someone now?' said Babs.

'No, but Jake might not like it.'

Babs felt her temper rising. 'Go and find yourself another girl to annoy.'

'Annoying you, am I? Good.' His expression was ugly. 'I'm going to carry on doing it. Because you sure as hell annoyed me the way you threw me over for him.'

'Something wrong?' said Nellie.

Babs had not noticed her sister approaching the table and flashed her a grateful look. 'Nice dance?'

'Great. Our steps matched perfectly.' She smiled up at Ray. 'Thanks. Perhaps we can dance again later. Right now I'm going to sit this one out.'

'Sure.' He glanced at Stuart and was about to speak when Pete arrived with his and Babs' drinks. Stuart glared at him and then deliberately brushed against him, almost knocking one of the glasses out of his hand as he walked away.

'What's up with him now?' demanded Pete.

'Ignore him,' said Babs. 'Give me that glass. I'm really thirsty.'

He handed the lemonade to her and glanced at Nellie. 'You're the sister. I'm Pete.'

'Nellie.'

'D'you want a drink, Nellie?' asked Ray.

'Thanks. I'll have a shandy.'

He went off to the bar as the band launched into 'My Heart Belongs to Daddy'. A female singer sank huskily into a microphone. Pete put down his drink and looked at Babs.

Nellie said with a smile, 'Why don't the pair of you dance. I'll keep my eye on you both from here and if there's any shenanigans, I'll be on that floor separating the pair of you before you can say Jack Flash.'

'Thanks, Nell,' said Babs, who was longing to dance.

Pete grabbed her hand and led her onto the dance floor.

Nellie sang along with the singer as she watched them. She had so much enjoyed her dance with Ray and him being married meant she didn't have to worry about him making a pass at her.

'So she's dancing after all. I knew she wouldn't be able to resist flirting with another guy,' said Stuart.

Nellie stared at him. 'Not you again. You really are a pain in the neck.'

'Don't you care that your sister's a flirt?' he said, sitting on Babs' chair.

'Go away!' said Nellie. 'She's not engaged to Jake, so if she chooses to dance with someone else that's none of your business. You've no right to pester my sister the way you do.'

'God, you're as bad as her. Ray's married you know?'

'I do know. Now get lost.'

'Are you here again, Stu?' said Ray, appearing at his shoulder. 'There's plenty of other girls around, so go find someone else.'

Stuart got up and walked away silently.

Nellie took her shandy and thanked him. 'He must have really had it bad for Babs.' She looked for her sister and Pete. The music had changed and they were both giving their all to 'Jeepers Creepers'. She was pleased to see Babs enjoying herself.

'She's a lovely girl but it really got his goat that

she preferred Jake. They'd only been on a couple of dates. He needs to move on.'

Nellie agreed. They dropped the subject and talked about music until they got up and danced again.

For the next few hours Nellie and Babs enjoyed themselves, dancing with a variety of partners but Babs happened to be dancing with Pete again to 'The More I See You' when Stuart made another appearance. He forced himself between Babs and Pete and managed to fasten his mouth onto Babs'. She thumped him on the back but the next moment Pete had him by the back of his collar and dragged him off her. Stuart struggled but Ray seized one of his arms and he and Pete marched him away between them.

Couples nearby had stopped dancing to watch what was going on.

'He's made a complete show of me,' seethed Babs. 'Let's get out of here, Nell.'

'Yes, I agree! Show's over,' cried Nellie, waving the curious away. 'I'd best be getting home anyway.' She took her sister's arm as they walked off the dance floor. 'You OK?'

'Yuk! He put his tongue in my mouth. It was just like I imagined a slug would taste. I felt as if I was choking,' said Babs. 'I won't be coming here again.'

The sisters left the dance hall, arm in arm, and walked to the gates. Nellie thought that the air smelt lovely and took deep breaths of it. There was a bus waiting outside with Liverpool on its destination board and she could see quite a number of women and girls already inside. It seemed they weren't the only ones who'd had enough. Nellie felt a spurt of anger every time she thought of Stuart and was worried for her sister.

'You working in the morning?' asked Nellie.

Babs said wryly, 'When don't I work mornings? Why, what had you in mind?'

'You're coming home with me. I think you've had a shock and need a bit of spoiling.'

'That sounds lovely,' said Babs wistfully. 'Although, normally I can handle Stuart, you know? He just took me by surprise.'

Nellie was not convinced. 'You could do with a break. Come home. I'll give you breakfast in bed and then you can catch an early bus.'

Babs hesitated and then smiled. 'What the hell! I'll probably get into trouble for not starting work at the crack of dawn but it'll be great to get away and be spoilt just for a few hours.'

'Then let's get aboard before someone comes looking for us,' said Nellie.

'You mean Pete and Ray,' said Babs.

Nellie nodded as they settled themselves on a seat. 'You seemed to be enjoying yourself with Pete.'

'He's a great dancer but I told him straight off that I had a boyfriend,' said Babs. 'What about you and Ray?'

'Nice guy but that's it.' Nellie yawned. 'My feet are tingling. I haven't danced so much for ages.'

'You enjoyed yourself, though?' said Babs.

Nellie nodded and closed her eyes.

They were almost asleep on their feet by the time they reached home and it was past the witching hour. They crept into the house via the washroom, and Nellie pushed open the kitchen door only to freeze when she saw her father sitting in front of the fire.

'What time d'you think this is to be coming home?' he rasped.

'Is that Dad's voice?' asked Babs, wriggling past Nellie.

Bernard's expression changed and a smile creased his face. 'Is that my dearest, darling daughter, Babs?'

Babs blinked. 'Are you being funny, Dad?'

Bernard's smile wavered. 'Why should you think that?'

'You don't generally call me your dearest, darling daughter even when you've been drinking.'

'So I've been drinking,' growled Bernard, holding out his arms. 'Come and give your ol' dad a kiss.'

Babs glanced at Lottie. Her face was fixed and her lips were pressed together in a thin line as she sat at the table, knitting. She wondered what he had said to put that expression on her face. With a sigh, Babs went forward and succumbed to her father's embrace. He smelt of beer, tobacco and sweat and she did not like it when he smacked her bottom before releasing her. She stood, looking down at him, considering how best to approach the matter of getting him to agree to her marrying Jake. It seemed providential that she should have come home with Nellie and found him here. 'So what are you doing here, Dad? It's not so long since I got a letter from you and you made no mention of coming home.'

'Didn't know I'd be home, did I? And I'm only

on turnaround, girl. Just in dock while some minor repairs are done. Be off again tomorrow.'

'So where will you be sailing next? Or shouldn't I ask?'

'Good God, girl, if I can't trust my own daughter, who can I trust?' He laughed. 'The Americas for supplies and then the Italian coast. The Eyeties might have signed the Armistice but the Allies have still got to get the Jerries out of Italy. I've heard there's some nasty things going on there. The Jerries aren't pleased with their former allies. I won't upset you by mentioning some of the things they're rumoured to have done.'

For a moment there was silence and Nellie paused in spooning tealeaves into the teapot to glance at their father. Her imagination ran riot, thinking of bombings, rape and the shooting of innocent people.

'So-oo,' said Bernard, scraping his unshaven chin with a fingernail. 'It doesn't look to me like you've done anything in the way of decoration, Nellie. Instead, I hear you've got rid of stuff and now run a bloody children's nursery school in the house. You've got no right, girl. You should have asked me first. Not that I'd have given permission.'

Nellie could feel her heart beating. Was it confession time? She could imagine what Babs was thinking. Here was the perfect opportunity to tell their father about Jake and ask his permission to marry him. Could she, herself, risk putting her father into a filthy temper and so spoil any chance of his saying yes to her sister? She decided to keep her secret a little longer. 'I had to do something for the war effort, Dad, as well as earn money to pay the household bills. As for getting work done in the house, no chance of that with the shortage of materials and manpower.'

He looked put out but didn't persist and instead said, 'The kids bring in money, do they?'

Nellie's fingers curled into her palms. 'How else could Lottie and I keep ourselves?'

'You don't expect me to send you money, do you?' he muttered. 'You're living rent free as it is.'

'I pay the rates,' she said, hanging on to her temper.

'I should think so, too!' His eyes narrowed. 'Wouldn't surprise me if I'm stuck with you and that slob of a sister of yours for life now your husband's dead!'

Nellie felt like hitting him. 'Thanks for the sympathy. I was really glad to receive your letter of condolence when I lost Teddy and the baby.'

He flushed but only said, 'By the time I got the news what was the use of writing. Anyway, it was a marriage that should never have taken place.'

Babs took a second look at Nellie's face and said, 'You really have a gift for saying the right thing, don't you, Dad? Our Nellie's suffered.'

He turned on her. 'Keep your mouth shut, girl. It's God's punishment on her that she lost that baby for marrying outside the faith.'

His daughters gasped.

Nellie's eyes glinted and the truth hovered on her lips but she held back for Babs' sake. 'I'd watch what you say, Dad, or you might find you're the one on the sharp end of God's punishment.'

He got to his feet and raised his hand as if to hit her. Nellie reached for the poker. 'Just you dare!'

Babs cried, 'Back off, Dad. Use your head. I can't be here looking after this place while you're away. Our Nellie's the only one fit to do that. Isn't that right, Nell?' she said, not looking at her sister. 'I might be getting married. There's an American airman who's popped the question.'

Bernard swore. 'You've been seeing a bloody Yank without a word to me?'

'Probably knew what you'd say,' muttered Lottie. 'You want to be the only man in her life.'

'Shut up, bitch. I don't want to even look at you,' he said.

'I've noticed,' said Lottie. 'It's as if you think the gypsies brought me.'

'Don't you give me lip, girl,' he yelled, 'or you'll be out on your ear. I'm going out. Don't wait up for me.' He stalked out of the kitchen.

Babs glanced at her sisters and then hurried after Bernard, catching him up at the front door. 'Jake. Can I marry him? He's a good bloke.'

'Sez you! I'll not have a Yank in this house. Forget him, girl.' He opened the front door and slammed it after him.

For a moment Babs stood there, staring at it, and then she returned to the kitchen. Nellie handed her a cup of tea. 'I take it the answer was no?'

Babs nodded. 'He's selfish and unreasonable.'

'I know what I'd do,' said Lottie. 'Tell him to go to hell.'

Babs stared at her. 'What's got into you? I've never known you so lippy.'

Lottie smiled. 'I'm not scared of him anymore. I know the ten commandments and that I should honour my father but I can't. Anyway, all I can say is that I'm glad he's only on turnaround: our gain is Italy's loss. The sooner he goes back to his ship, the better I'll like it.'

Nellie nodded. 'Let's forget him. I'm whacked and want my bed.'

She did not wait for them to answer but went upstairs. She did not expect to sleep straight away because she was feeling so angry but having cleaned her teeth and undressed, she fell asleep within minutes and did not even remember Babs getting into bed with her.

Bernard did not return to the house until the following morning and by then Babs had left. She said that she didn't see the point of hanging around waiting for him to make an appearance. Nellie agreed. When he did arrive, he had an almighty hangover. She almost wished it wasn't Sunday, so the children would have been there making a din. He asked after Babs.

'She left early,' said Nellie. 'Had to get back to the land.'

He swore and went upstairs to shave and put on a clean shirt. That done, he said to Nellie on his way out: 'Things had better be different here when I get home again, or I'll be making changes myself.'

'Yes, Dad,' she said calmly. 'Say hello to Italy for us.'

'Those kids will have to go for a start,' he warned, giving her a dirty look before striding down the path without a backward glance.

'We'll see about that,' said Nellie, and closed the door, knowing she mustn't pray that a torpedo would sink his ship.

Chapter Fifteen

'Polly!' Nellie's eyes lit up as she spotted her former employer outside the Co-op. 'Long time no see. How are things with you?'

'Fine! I was thinking of coming to visit you to see how you were getting on but what with Christmas and the dark nights...' Her voice trailed away.

'I know what you mean. Anyway, we're OK. Although, we lost half of our intake to school in September. We've taken on four three-year-olds but I'm still not making enough money to pay me and Lottie a decent wage.'

Polly looked concerned. 'How's your sister doing?'

'Not bad actually. She's good with the kids and there's David, he helps out, too.' Nellie told her a little about him.

Polly listened before saying, 'Do you think they could cope without you? Because if they can, you might be interested to know that the nursery's expanding in April and they're looking to employ a nursery teacher for the older ones. If you like, I could put your name forward and they'll probably get in touch with you bearing in mind your experience. What d'you say?'

Nellie felt a buzz of excitement. It seemed ages since her outing to Burtonwood and Babs had not written for a while, so it would be good to get away from the house, and as for getting a proper wage, that really appealed. 'I don't mind giving it a go.'

'I'll do that, then.'

After Nellie finished the shopping, she went home with her head in a whirl but she decided not to mention having met Polly and the job in the nursery until she knew more.

A week later Nellie received a letter, asking her to write to the matron at the nursery detailing her experience and qualifications. It was then that she told Lottie about the job and asked if she thought she could cope with running their little nursery school herself.

Lottie looked anxiously at David, who was eating an apple, and said in a trembling voice, 'I honestly think, Nellie, that only a few of the mothers really care whether their kids know their alphabet and can write their names before they go to school. As long as they're getting looked after while they're at work that's all they care about. I'd still carry on with the older ones doing what you want me to if you think I'm capable.'

'Of course you're capable,' insisted Nellie, putting an arm around her sister's waist. She realised Lottie had gained a few inches during the winter months. 'I wouldn't even be thinking of applying for the job, if I didn't believe you were.'

'I can carry on helping Lottie,' said David eagerly, rocking backwards and forwards on his heels.

Nellie's forehead creased. 'I'm sure you'd be a great help with the music and games but once spring comes, you'll be working in the garden more. We could do with roping in a volunteer as well. I'll speak to the mams and see if they can suggest anyone.'

She took the opportunity of doing that the next day and was delighted when Elsie, one of the mothers, said that her fella had been home and she was expecting again. 'I'm going to have to give up me job but I'd hate to be home all the time. I wouldn't mind helping out a couple of afternoons, if I don't have to pay for our Mo.'

Nellie accepted the offer and applied for the job at the nursery. Within a month she had an interview and a week later was informed she had the job.

In the intervening weeks before she started at the council nursery, she made sure that Lottie and the mother worked out a schedule of activities for the children. David's input was logged, as were the times he would be spending in the garden. Nellie suggested that the children might enjoy having a little patch of land of their own to plant seeds and watch them grow. 'You'll have to make sure they don't dig them up to see what's happening to them, David,' she said.

He nodded vigorously. 'You bet I will.'

Having done as much as she could to help them, Nellie had to trust that they would cope without her when she started her new job in April.

It was difficult at first getting up at the crack of dawn to be in work before seven in the morning. Most of the mothers would already be there, waiting for the doors to open. Nellie was glad that she had not started in the depths of winter and decided not to think what it would be like getting up next November. Most of her class were eager to learn but there were always those who just wanted to muck about. Generally it was boys who didn't want to keep still. She stuck to the plan she had adopted when teaching the children in the Lake District: prayers, learning their letters, writing, numbers and colours. Then it was story time, music, and she even started a nature table, taking the children for walks in the park or along the bank of the LeedsLiverpool canal. It was almost the same as dealing with the children in *her* nursery school but with the added pleasure of nipping into the nursery and seeing the babies in their cots.

The hours were longer and, of course, she had to take orders from Matron and give account of herself, the children and the progress they were making. She would have preferred not having to obey orders and explain such things but at least she had more money and that was a relief. She did not see as much of Polly as she had thought she would, though. Her friend looked after the smaller children while they played, making sure they had an afternoon nap on the foldaway, washable canvas beds provided and that they drank their milk, orange juice and cod liver oil daily.

Absorbed in her new job, Nellie had little time to worry about Babs, from whom she had received only a scribbled note saying that Jake was not happy about their father's reaction. He wanted her to try and visit him in the south, but that was impossible at the moment as she could not get the time off. She just wished the war would end but that appeared some way off still.

At the beginning of June, Nellie woke up to the news that the invasion of France had begun. She felt for the thousands waiting anxiously to hear the outcome, fearing that their menfolk would be amongst the fallen or seriously wounded. During the weeks that followed she took an avid interest in the progress of the Allies across Europe, especially as a couple of the mothers had husbands with the army. She soon realised that it was going to take months rather than weeks before the Germans were defeated.

Nellie's every hour was filled with activity or sleep so that the weeks flew by. She noticed that Lottie had put on more weight but perhaps that was because she was contented and was eating more now she wasn't there to watch her. She stopped worrying about how Lottie and David were coping with the nursery because nobody complained to her. Then one sunny morning in August, Nellie was roused by screams from a dream about a dark-haired stranger reaching out to her through mist and rain. She fell out of bed and for several moments just lay on the floor, winded, wondering what the hell was making that noise. For a second she thought it might be the cat, only to hear Lottie screeching her name.

Nellie pushed herself up and not bothering to throw on a dressing gown, ran downstairs. Before she reached the ground floor she caught sight of her sister writhing on the floor in the lobby. She was panting and both her legs were drawn up onto her fat belly beneath the cotton nightdress. Nellie could see Lottie's private parts and watched in astonishment as her sister groaned, gasped and panted. When she realised what was happening, she was so astounded that she could not move but felt glued three steps from the bottom. Then she saw the crown of the baby's head appear and flew upstairs and into the bathroom.

'Oh my God,' she muttered. 'Oh, my God!' She flung open the cupboard and grabbed a couple of towels and thundered downstairs. Just in time to put a towel between Lottie's legs as the baby slid out covered in mucus.

Nellie stared blankly at the little girl. Having been out for the count when her own dead baby had been delivered, she did not know what to do and had to rack her brains. She had to make the baby take its first breath. Wrapping the towel round her, she carefully turned the child upside down and hit her gently on the back. She was rewarded with a choking noise.

'What's going on, Nellie? What's happening to me?' asked Lottie weakly.

Before she could answer, there was a banging at the front door. Nellie could only hope it was someone who had come in answer to her prayer.

'Don't move!' she croaked, placing the baby on Lottie's belly. She opened the door and to her horror saw that it was Mrs Wainwright. 'What's going on, Nellie? What's all that screaming? I mean it's bad enough hearing those children during the week when they're playing outside but today's Sunday and I was just on my way to church when...'

Nellie made to close the door in her neighbour's face but Lottie groaned and the old woman thrust it wide open and forced her way past Nellie. If the sight of Lottie giving birth had been a shock to Nellie it came as an even bigger shock to Mrs Wainwright to see the afterbirth arrive.

'I don't want to believe this,' she said weakly.

'You're going to have to,' said Nellie, deciding to make use of her neighbour. 'You go and fetch the midwife.'

Mrs Wainwright said in a trembling voice, 'Your sister is unmarried. It would be kinder to let the baby die.'

Nellie was furious. 'Don't ever say that!'

'What's going on?' interrupted a second voice.

Nellie whirled round in surprise to face her youngest sister. 'Babs, you're not going to believe this!'

'I'd like not to,' said an amazed Babs, taking in the scene, 'but it can't have been an immaculate conception.'

'I don't suppose you can help?' asked Nellie.

Babs hesitated and then knelt down besides Lottie. 'Scissors and some string, Nell.'

Nellie asked no questions but rushed into the kitchen. As she searched for the required items, she counted back nine months. When she returned to the scene in the lobby it was to the sound of the baby's cry. In delight and amazement she watched Babs deal efficiently with the umbilical cord. Once that was, done the baby was wrapped in another towel and handed to Lottie.

'You're marvellous!' cried Nellie.

Babs stood up, easing her back. 'You'd better get some rags to bind her.'

'I know that much,' said Nellie, wanting to hug

her youngest sister. 'How did you know what to do? I'm sure you saved their lives.'

Babs shrugged and smiled. 'I've helped deliver calves. I never thought it would come in handy here, though.' She looked down at Lottie, who was gazing into the baby's tiny face in disbelief. 'We're aunts,' said Babs. 'Who'd have ever believed our Lottie would have a baby before me?'

'It's a disgrace,' said Mrs Wainwright, tight-lipped. 'She's just like her mother.'

The sisters had forgotten the old woman but now stared at her. She was standing in the door-way, dressed in her Sunday best suit, clutching her missal.

'Yes, I can see how you'd think that,' said Nellie, her eyes sparkling. 'But I'd think twice before you go spreading the word. There's only one person who can be the father, in my opinion, and that's David.'

Mrs Wainwright's face reddened. 'Prove it!'

Babs and Nellie looked at each other and then both got down on their knees beside their sister. 'Think back nine months, Lottie,' said Babs.

'Did you do something you'd never done before with a fella?' asked Nellie. 'Something that in-volved removing your knickers and getting very close to David?'

Mrs Wainwright spluttered, 'You're putting words into her mouth.'

The sisters ignored her.

Lottie lifted her eyes from her perusal of the baby's face and, if there were to be a competition for whose face was the reddest between her and the old woman, it might have been a draw. 'It was when you stayed overnight at Francis'. I was scared being in the house on my own, so David stayed with me. I didn't know what I was doing,' said Lottie hastily. 'At least I didn't know it would make a baby. It was just so comforting being together and loved.'

Babs and Nellie exchanged satisfied smiles and looked up at Mrs Wainwright. She did not speak but retreated in a hurry.

'Wedding on the cards or not?' asked Babs, grimacing.

'Not if she has anything to do with it,' said Nellie, getting to her feet. 'But at the moment, she's the least of my worries.'

Babs nodded. 'Let's make Lottie and the baby comfortable. The rags, Nellie, and we'd best try and get her to bed and call in a midwife to check that she and the baby are OK.'

With a concerted effort, Nellie and Babs managed to get Lottie into bed. While Nellie dressed and then fetched the midwife, Babs saw to her sister's basic needs. Lottie was grateful. 'You do surprise me, Babs. I never thought you'd be so kind and not say how terrible I am for committing a mortal sin.'

'What's the use of that. It'll be punishment enough you're having to put up with the consequences of being an unmarried mother if David doesn't marry you. Now shut up and put this lovely little baby to the breast.'

Lottie's cheeks were rosy as she unbuttoned the top of the nightgown. 'Mam and Aunt Josie would have killed me. They'd have sent me away for bringing disgrace on the family. They'd have said I was a sinner and I'd go to Hell.'

'I'd stop worrying about that,' said Babs. 'They're not here, are they? Dad will have a fit, though, so let's hope David will marry you. That's if you want to marry him?'

Lottie did not answer because she had managed to get a nipple into her baby's mouth and when her daughter began to suckle, she felt such a feeling of warmth and love that she could think of nothing else. Babs shrugged and moved away, deciding that it was pointless worrying about what was going to happen to Lottie and the baby right now.

When the midwife arrived, her manner was brisk and non-judgemental and she complimented Babs on her actions and told Nellie that she would look in again on Lottie and the baby tomorrow. Then she left.

After she had gone, Nellie made tea and toast and, after taking some in to Lottie, she sat down at the kitchen table with Babs. 'So what brings you home? Any news from Jake?'

Babs brushed back a strand of red hair and sighed. 'Would you believe he's been sent abroad. I don't know where. Something to do with keeping the planes flying. I tell you, Nell, I'm really fed up. I'm wondering if we'll ever get together again. I should have eloped with him when he suggested it. At least I could have had his baby by now and be done with working on the land.' She scrubbed her face with her fingernails. 'I almost envy our Lottie.'

'Me too,' murmured Nellie, reaching for the milk jug. 'A perfect healthy little girl. Anyway, I'll need to have words with David when he arrives.'

'You think they'll get married?'

'The baby needs a name and the pair of them get on well. He might be a farthing short of a shilling but he's a hard worker and is genuinely fond of her. I'll put it to them both. They can live here.'

'Dad will be made up with that.'

Nellie shrugged. 'He'll just have to lump it if he wants to carry on using this house as a base when he gets shore leave.'

Babs toyed with her fingers and said, 'Do you want me around when you tell him?'

'I'd appreciate some moral support but don't worry about it. I'll make sure Francis is here.' She paused, thinking suddenly of the mystery man she had met at the presbytery and wondering where he was now.

Babs interrupted her thoughts. 'I haven't told you about Stuart.'

Nellie reluctantly dismissed the mystery man from her mind. 'He hasn't been pestering you, has he?'

'Nothing that I can't handle.' She paused. 'Our Lottie's not the only one who surprised me recently. My friend Heather had a baby. Don't ask me how she managed to keep it a secret so long but she did. She said it's Stuart's but he's denying it. I told him he was a right heel. I just thank God I finished with him and got together with Jake, even though we've spent more time apart than together.'

Nellie topped up their tea. 'You're in the same boat as thousands of others. It's hard but you just have to bear it.'

'I know, I know.' Babs sighed. 'So getting back to our sister. The baby's going to need clothes.'

Nellie nodded and said softly, 'At least I can help there.' She drained her cup and went up to the attic. She had stored the shop-bought layette and knitted garments Lottie had made in an old chest of drawers. As she removed them she experienced that pain of loss and tears tingled the back of her eyes, but she thought of the baby downstairs and wasted no time on regrets.

Lottie was sleeping and Babs had placed the baby, still cocooned in a couple of towels, in a sideboard drawer. As she took the items from her, she said, 'You might marry again, Nell, and have babies.'

For once Nellie did not shrug off the idea. Who knows? I'd have never have believed our Lottie would end up in trouble, so there's no use trying to foretell the future.' She glanced at the clock. 'David's generally here by now; I wonder what's keeping him?'

But David did not turn up that day and he had not arrived the next day when Nellie had to leave for work. Babs said that she would stay and have a word with him when he turned up and speak to the mothers.

'Do I tell them Lottie's had a baby, Nellie? I don't see how we can keep it quiet with them bringing the kids here,' she said.

Nellie agreed. 'One of the mothers stays and helps on a Monday; she's having another baby. You can tell her what's happened and leave it to her to spread the news.'

Babs nodded and Nellie left her to it. Later she explained to Polly what had happened. Her friend tried not to look shocked and offered the services of her cousin. 'She's having her third child and I'm sure she'll help Lottie out for a few days as a favour to me ... until Lottie's on her feet.'

'Thanks. I can't pay her but I'll give her some vegetables and she can help herself to apples from the tree.'

With that settled, Nellie got on with her work but she could not concentrate, uneasy about David not having turned up yesterday. She determined if he didn't arrive that day then she would call on Mrs Wainwright that evening.

When Nellie arrived home it was to find Lottie alone with the baby. 'Babs had to leave. David hasn't arrived, Nell. What am I going to do?' she asked, tears rolling down her cheeks.

'Right!' said Nellie, storming out of the house and up Mrs Wainwright's drive. She banged on the front door but got no answer, so went round the back. The curtains were drawn and the door was locked.

A voice the other side of the fence, said, 'She's gone on holiday. She went yesterday. I was told she'd be away a fortnight.'

Nellie's heart sank. 'Did you see David with her?'

'I only saw him briefly. She had him in and out of the house in no time. She mustn't have gone to church after all.'

Nellie realised she had no choice but to concede defeat for the moment. She returned to the house. 'He's been whisked away by that old witch,' she

312

said to Lottie in a seething voice.

'What do we do, Nellie?' asked Lottie, sniffing back her tears.

'Wait,' she replied. 'There's nothing else we can do. We'll register the baby's birth as Callaghan. Have you thought of a name for her, Lottie?'

She nodded and murmured, 'Lucia Helen Barbara.' She looked up at her sister. 'You and Babs are the best sisters in the world.'

Nellie was so touched she could not speak for a moment, and then she squeezed her sister's shoulder and said huskily, 'Word's bound to get around and, if you ask me, Mrs Wainwright hasn't done herself any favours by going off the way she did. The neighbours know David's always round here. They'll put two and two together and guess he's the father. If she and David's mother insist on keeping the two of you apart, I think it'll rouse people's sympathy.'

'I hope you're right, Nell,' said Lottie.

Nellie hoped she was, too. One thing was for sure, there would be no placing this child in an orphanage. She was a little love with dark curls and the sweetest little mouth.

By the time the fortnight was up and Mrs Wainwright was a visible presence in the neighbourhood once again, Lottie had convinced herself that David did not want her; she was too ugly, too fat and, besides, neither of them had any money to look after a child. Even so, she hoped that he would visit just so he could see how lovely his daughter was. But he did not come and it was only when Nellie went round to visit Mrs Wainwright that the truth came out.

313

'His mother needs him,' said the old woman defiantly. 'It's all right for you, Nellie, you're young and strong and can cope without a man about the place. My sister can't. She's got a weak heart and so the pair of them have gone to live in the country with our cousin.'

Nellie was angry. 'Does David know about the baby?'

Mrs Wainwright flushed. 'Don't be silly. You think we'd have told him? Best he doesn't know in case he gets any stupid ideas about marriage. They'd have more children and how would they cope without help? You tell me that, Nellie. You mightn't like the idea but my sister and I have done the sensible thing and you'll realise that sooner or later.'

'You should have given him a choice. You and your sister will rue the day you made your decision. Lucia is a lovely baby. Your sister could have found a lot of pleasure in being a granny but that's her loss. Good day, Mrs Wainwright.' She walked away, wishing that she knew the whereabouts of the cousin.

Lottie greeted the news bravely and said little. She accepted that David's mother needed him but she wanted to scream that she and the baby needed him too. Not knowing where he was meant there was nothing she could do about it. David wasn't strong-willed and bossy like some men, so she could understand why his mother and Mrs Wainwright could have such a hold on him that he would fall in with their wishes. So she accepted life as it was and got on with it. Somehow she managed without complaint to cope with the baby and run the nursery school with the help of the volunteer mother.

Several weeks passed before Nellie decided Francis should know about the baby. Telling him was something she was not looking forward to but she couldn't put it off indefinitely. Lottie wanted the baby baptised but was too ashamed to go to the parish priest.

Francis looked rightfully stunned when Nellie told him the news. 'I can't believe it. Lottie of all people. Now if you'd said Babs had got herself into trouble...' He shook his head in bewilderment. 'I can imagine what Mother would have said.'

Nellie leaned back in the leather chair and stared at him from beneath drooping eyelids. 'So can I, but she was in no position to judge having been pregnant herself when she got married.'

He looked shocked and several moments passed before he said, 'So that's what you meant about her being no angel. Dad'll have Lottie out.'

'Over my dead body,' said Nellie fiercely.

'Let's hope it doesn't come to that,' said Francis, riffling his fingers through his hair. 'He wrote to me about Babs and Jake. You didn't let me know he'd been home and knew about them.'

'Sorry, but my life's so busy.'

'You're too busy. You need to be careful you don't crack up, Nellie.' He twiddled his thumbs. 'You must keep me up to date with what's happening with you girls.'

'Women, Francis, not girls,' she said firmly, getting to her feet. 'Anyway, you know everything I know now, so what do I say to Lottie? She wants

315

the baby baptised.'

'She hasn't visited her parish priest?'

Nellie shook her head. 'Lottie hasn't been to church since Lucia's birth. She's too ashamed.'

Francis met her gaze squarely. 'Get her to go to English Martyrs' and make her confession. I'm sure the priest will baptise the child as she's an innocent in all this.'

She nodded and stood up, fiddling with her gloves. 'She'll find it difficult.'

'Tell her to look upon it as a penitence and let's pray David turns up.'

Nellie nodded. 'I hope so for Lottie and the baby's sake. It will be easier for Lucia if she has her father's name as she grows up.'

She returned home and told her sister what Francis had said. Lottie closed her eyes briefly. 'Will you come with me, Nell?'

Nellie nodded, knowing it was essential to Lottie's well being that her spiritual needs were met. She only hoped that Lottie would not go all religious on her again because she did not want to have to cope with that. She reckoned her mother being overtly religious was due to her sense of shame in having sex before marriage and, sadly, she must never have really felt forgiven. It was taking Nellie some time to get back on friendly speaking terms with God, and perhaps that wouldn't come about until the war was over.

Part Three

1945 to 1946

Chapter Sixteen

Babs climbed down from the tractor and eased her aching shoulders. A bath, a meal and bed, she thought. Her breath misted in the frosty air as she made her way across the farmyard. Then she spotted an airman leaning against the barn wall, smoking a cigarette. Only for a second did she think it might be Jake because he had written saying he was coming home but then she recognised Stuart and swore inwardly. Could she get away with ignoring him?

He killed that idea stone dead by dropping his cigarette stub in the mud and coming towards her. 'I'd almost given up on you,' he said.

'What are you doing here?' She did not pause but carried on towards the footpath that would take her across the fields to her digs.

'I've got news of Jake.'

Her stride faltered and she glanced at him. 'What is it?'

'He's missing.'

She felt the blood drain from her face. 'I don't believe it,' she whispered.

Stuart shrugged. 'Please yourself, but the plane flying him home never arrived. Radio contact was lost and nothing has been heard since.'

She croaked, 'Where did it go down?'

He took out a packet of cigarettes and offered her one. She shook her head, not wanting to take anything from him. In a fever of impatience, she watched him light up, knowing he was deliberately keeping her waiting.

'Most likely they ditched in the sea. The same kind of thing happened to Glenn Miller on his way to Paris. His plane just vanished. I'm really, really sorry, Babs.'

'Don't be such a hypocrite. You're not sorry,' she said in a trembling voice. 'Now, if you don't mind going away, I'd like to be alone.'

His eyes narrowed. 'That's not very friendly or sensible. We don't want you doing anything silly now, do we? I'm perfectly happy to provide a shoulder for you to cry on.'

Babs looked at him in disgust and walked away. She didn't want to believe what he had said was true but surely even he wouldn't lie about such a terrible thing? Her eyes filled with tears and her throat felt as if it had a plum blocking it. She wanted to howl, but with Stuart still in earshot, didn't want to give him the satisfaction of hearing her give way. She began to run as if she could escape the terrible news she had been told.

'Hey, wait! Don't run away,' shouted Stuart.

She ignored him, running along the frost-hardened ground and remembered it was on this path that she had met Jake one beautiful spring evening. Tears trickled down her cheeks. She could hear Stuart shouting and he sounded closer. She spun round and saw him a few feet away. He stopped and smiled. 'You're being silly.'

Despite her tears she could see him clearly and without hesitation she walked towards him. Before he could realise her intention, she drew back her arm and then let fly with her fist and hit him smack on the jaw. His body seemed to crumple as he slid to the ground. She left him there and carried on back to her digs. She needed Jake still to be coming home but if she couldn't have him, then she wanted Nellie.

Nellie hummed 'Brahms' Lullaby' as she carried the sleeping baby into Lottie's bedroom and placed her in her cot. She tucked the blankets in around her niece and then kissed the top of her head before tiptoeing out of the room.

She was halfway to the kitchen when the knocker sounded and hurriedly she made for the front door, not wanting the baby to wake. She opened the door and to her surprise saw Babs standing there. Immediately, her sister's wan features told Nellie something was terribly wrong.

'What is it?' she asked.

Babs gulped. 'Jake's missing. His plane lost radio contact and vanished.'

'Oh, Babs,' breathed Nellie, seizing hold of her sister and drawing her into the house. 'You poor, poor thing,' she added, putting her arms around her. Babs burst into tears and wept on Nellie's shoulder. She felt helpless in the face of such grief and could only pat her sister's back and whisper, 'There, there now, get it all out.'

She had no idea how long she stood there, nursing her sister, before a drowsy voice asked, 'What's wrong? Where's the baby?'

'In her cot. Put the kettle on, love,' said Nellie, glancing at Lottie.

Lottie blinked. 'Is that our Babs?'

Babs sniffed and wiped her damp face with the back of her hand and drew away from Nellie. 'Yes, it's me.'

'You look terrible,' said Lottie, concerned.

'Jake's missing,' said Nellie. 'Will you put that kettle on?'

'OK, OK, I'm doing it,' said Lottie, leading the way into the kitchen. 'When did it happen?'

Babs shook her head. 'I don't know.' She stood in the middle of the kitchen, gazing about her as if she had never seen the place before.

Nellie helped her off with her coat and hat and ushered her over to a chair by the fire. Babs stared into the flames and gulped convulsively.

Lottie glanced at Nellie. 'Shall we have cocoa?'

She nodded. 'Put an extra spoonful of sugar in Babs'.'

Lottie said, 'It's a terrible shock. Us three don't half seem unlucky when it comes to men.'

Nellie made no reply but drew a footstool close to Babs' chair and reached for her sister's hand. She held it firmly but did not speak, not wanting to say anything that would upset Babs further.

Lottie made the cocoa and took the tray over to the fireplace. She handed a cup to each of her sisters before sitting down herself.

Babs stared at her and said in a vague voice, 'You've lost weight.'

Lottie was gratified and said, 'You think so? It must be chasing round after kids and looking after Lucia.'

Babs sighed. 'I suppose I'll never have kids.'

'You don't know that,' said Nellie. 'Drink your cocoa.'

They drank in silence and only when the empty cups were placed on the tray did Babs say, 'I don't know what to do.' Her lovely features were pale and drawn. 'It was Stuart who told me. He said he was sorry but he wasn't really.' Her green eyes darkened. 'A couple of the girls think he'll start pestering me to go out with him again but I told them that I'd punched him on the jaw and he'd be a fool to try.'

Nellie said, 'Good on you, but if I was you, I'd think of making a move.'

'I feel I need to get away. Go where nobody knows about me and Jake.'

Nellie stood up. 'Makes sense. What d'you say to a glass of sherry? I've some left over from Christmas. I presume you'll be staying the night?'

Babs nodded, slipped off her shoes and tucked her legs beneath her. 'Do you remember the pea-pod wine I brought that first Christmas I was away?'

'It went down a treat,' said Nellie, going over to the dresser.

'If you'd stayed at that first place you would never have met Jake,' said Lottie.

Babs' eyes filled with tears. 'I'm glad I met him. I'm just bloody sorry I never married him.'

'It's no use thinking like that. Get that down you,' ordered Nellie, handing her a tumbler of sherry.

Lottie gasped. 'You'll get her drunk drinking all that.'

'It'll help her sleep,' said Nellie, taking a generous mouthful of the sherry herself. 'Anyway, missing doesn't mean that he's dead, just presumed dead.'

Babs stared at her from dull eyes. 'Stuart said it went missing over the Channel.'

'How does he know that if radio contact was lost?'

'I – I presume that's where the plane was when contact was lost.'

Nellie nodded. 'Of course. I was just trying to give you some hope.'

Babs' eyes brightened. 'You think there is hope?'

'I can't say.' Her tone was sad. 'But if there is a chance he's survived, then they'll find him, won't they, and you'll get to know? I mean, even if they ditched in the sea, it has been known for sailors to have been found alive weeks after going missing. If it was me, then I'd want to believe Jake would turn up again.'

Silence.

'Nellie found a man that went missing,' said Lottie, yawning.

Babs stared at Nellie. 'What man?'

'Didn't I tell you about him?'

'I can't remember. Tell me again in case?' She downed half the sherry.

So Nellie told Babs about discovering the stranger in the porch of St Joseph's and how she had dealt with his injuries but that she had never seen him again.

'So what happened to him?'

'Francis said that he'd gone in search of his family. I never knew his name,' said Nellie.

Babs swallowed the last of her sherry. 'Was he young? Was he good looking?'

Nellie smiled. 'He was in his twenties and, yes, I think that if his face hadn't been bruised and his nose swollen then he wouldn't have been half bad.'

'So who do you think he was?'

Nellie shrugged. 'Either he was a soldier who'd gone AWOL or...' she hesitated, 'an escaped POW. He looked like he had Italian blood.'

'An Eyetie! And you helped him? You do surprise me,' said Babs, 'although, we're supposed to be mates now. There's a couple of camps not far from us that have Eyeties prisoners and they've helped on the land.'

Nellie nodded. 'It could be that he wasn't one of the enemy. There's hundreds of immigrants of Italian descent in Liverpool and some were put in POW camps at the beginning of the war and later were freed to fight. I remember Francis mentioning it ages ago.'

'If he was from Francis' parish, he should have known his name and where his family lived,' said Lottie.

'I know. Anyway, it's unlikely I'll ever see him again.'

The light in Babs' eyes died. 'Just like I'll never see Jake again,' she muttered. 'Why is it men like Stuart survive and the Jakes and Teddys of this world are lost?'

'It's useless thinking like that.' Nellie fetched the sherry bottle. 'So where are you thinking of moving? Somewhere nearer home?'

'But what if...' began Babs.

'What if what?' asked Nellie, draining the sherry bottle.

'Jake turns up and I've moved?'

'He'll come here,' said Nellie. 'So chin up and think of doing what I said.'

She nodded and no more was said on the subject.

Babs waited a little while before putting in for a transfer and by then, she had given up hope of ever seeing Jake again, convinced she would have heard from him by now if he had survived. It was a struggle to carry on but what else could she do? Nellie had survived double heartbreak losing her husband and baby, so could she do less?

Spring came to Merseyside and Nellie and Lottie planted seeds, both thinking that this time last year David had been there to help them, and before him there had been Billy.

'Remember Billy?' said Nellie.

Lottie nodded. 'I hope he's still alive.'

During the previous weeks there had been Allied victory after victory and the latest news was that Cologne had fallen. 'If one of us sees Sgt McElroy, we should make a point of asking him,' said Nellie. 'Although, Maisie Miller will probably know.'

So Lottie asked Irene's mother. 'As far as I know, he's still OK,' said Maisie.

Babs visited. Despite having a healthy colour with spending so much time outdoors, it was obvious to her sisters that she was still grieving. How Nellie wished that the war would be over, not next week or next month, but now!

In April, President Roosevelt was succeeded by President Truman. Nellie received the news with sadness, thinking it was such a shame that he should die when victory was in sight.

Within weeks American and Soviet forces met in Germany and the horrors of Hitler's death camps were discovered. Shock vibrated through Nellie, wondering how men could be so cruel to their fellow man. Yet she was avid for more news that spoke of the war coming to an end.

In Italy, the Allies captured Bologna, and the following day Mussolini was shot dead by partisans. Venice was taken and Nellie was reminded of her father and she worried about him coming home. Not only did he need to know she owned the house but also about Lottie and Lucia.

On the thirtieth of April, Hitler committed suicide. The news of his death created wild expectations of an immediate end to the European war with Germany's unconditional surrender; a two-day holiday was promised.

Nellie was weeding in the garden when Lottie called her in to say that Churchill was about to speak to the nation. It had started to rain, so she was more than happy to stop work and run inside. Lottie had been in the middle of making a cake while Lucia crawled about the place. She picked her up and settled her on her knee. Nellie turned up their grandfather's old wireless and the unmistakable tones of the Premier came over the airwaves, announcing that the war in Europe was over. The sisters cheered and danced round the kitchen. Within minutes, ships' hooters on the Mersey blared out a cacophony of sound and church bells began to ring. There was no mistaking what that noise meant; it was time to celebrate.

Nellie's throat tightened with emotion. How

327

many others would be feeling as she did? They had survived the war but, having lost loved ones, their lives would never be the same again. There would always be a tiny core of sadness in their hearts. She wanted to sit quietly and let the thought of peace sink in but such stillness could not last long. The neighbours had decided on a party.

Lottie popped her cake in the oven, while Nellie made meat paste sandwiches. Once ready, they were carried outside to where trestle tables were erected and spread with cloths. People chattered and sang as food and drink were placed on the tables. When she looked at the amount of food displayed, Nellie wondered where it had all come from. There were meat paste and sardine sandwiches, ham and egg, cakes, jellies, custard, chocolate and lollipops. There was a barrel of beer, as well as bottles of sherry port, ginger ale and lemonade.

Nellie noticed Mrs Wainwright was missing and asked the neighbour who lived the other side of the old woman whether she knew where she was. Nellie had not spoken to Mrs Wainwright since she had told her David and his mother had gone to live with a cousin.

'Gone to celebrate with her sister. She said that she hadn't been too good. Heart. Pity you couldn't have followed them, you might have seen David.'

What heart! thought Nellie, still angry that the two women had kept David away from Lottie and his daughter. Perhaps she should have thought of shadowing Mrs Wainwright. She smiled wryly. What would be the use? She and Lottie were coping and Lucia was a contented baby and that's what mattered. She thought about her other sister. Poor Babs! It would be great if she could make it home. No sooner had she thought that than she heard someone say, 'Here's Babs Callaghan.'

Nellie turned and saw her youngest sister coming towards them. She was dressed in her land girl uniform but still managed to look feminine and attractive. 'So you made it,' said Nellie, her face lighting up.

Babs forced a smile. 'It wasn't easy but I managed to get a lift. So when do we eat? I'm starving. And what about a drink?'

The children were seen to first and then drinks were poured for the adults and food was handed round. The three sisters sat together on the chairs that Nellie had brought from the house. 'We should toast the valiant dead,' she said.

So that's what they did and there was many a tear shed when Nellie said, with a break in her voice, 'Without their sacrifice we'd never have won this war.' She was conscious of that feeling of unreality that had held her in its grip on previous occasions and wished that the victory in Europe had not cost so many lives.

Afterwards there was dancing and singing and Nellie admired Babs for joining in because she must have given up hope now of ever seeing Jake alive again. She could only pray that her younger sister would find someone else one day.

If Nellie had believed everything would change overnight now the European war was over, she was soon proved wrong. Rationing remained and the mothers still worked long hours, but at least lighting restrictions were lifted, so they were able to take down the black-out curtains and go out in the evening without torches. But Babs continued working as a land girl and the troops did not immediately come marching home.

In July, an election was held and the Labour party won a resounding victory. Churchill was out and there were many who thought it was a slap in the face for him. It was said that it was the soldiers' vote that had won the socialist victory. Nellie could understand why they had wanted a change and it was the reason she voted for a Labour government. They were determined to improve the lot of the working classes and promised new homes, jobs and, most of all, a health service, where nobody would need to pay to see a doctor or to go into hospital. Lottie still suffered from the injuries she'd received during the blitz and Nellie hoped that, one day, something could be done to help her.

The following month the Americans dropped two atom bombs on Japan, bringing the war in the Far East to a speedy end. VJ Day followed with more parties to celebrate. The numbers said to have been killed when the two bombs were dropped astounded Nellie. She realised that such explosive power would change the way war was waged in the world for ever, but at what price?

Happily, Lucia had her first birthday towards the end of August. She was a bright-eyed, lively child and was toddling everywhere. Lottie had saved some rations and made her a cake. Nellie bought her niece a pink sun-bonnet and she looked a picture in it.

Lottie had her hands full but said to Nellie, 'I'm glad we've still got enough mothers interested in the nursery, because it means she has other children to play with.'

'Numbers could start going down, though,' warned Nellie. 'Once the men start coming home, most won't want their wives out at work but looking after them and the house and kids.' She was reminded that Bernard's homecoming was something she really must give more thought to but until she heard from him, she could not really make any arrangements to sort things out.

It was October before Nellie heard from her father. The letter informed her that he was in hospital in Italy after falling through a hatch into the hold. He had broken several bones but said that his life was not in danger, so they were not to worry as he was in good hands. She breathed a sigh of relief, glad that his homecoming was to be delayed for a while longer.

The first Christmas of the peace was to come and go before Nellie heard from her father again. She had written to him, wishing him a happy Christmas and hoping his bones were healing, but had not received an answer. Francis was the first to get up-to-date news of Bernard having been moved from hospital to a villa further down Italy's western coast to convalesce. His bones were taking longer to mend than the doctors had predicted but, hopefully, he would be home some time in January.

'I would have thought his bones would have healed ages ago but I have been praying he'll stay away longer,' said Lottie. Her knitting needles were going ten to the dozen. 'I can imagine what he's going to say about Lucia.'

Nellie tapped the letter against her teeth. 'I suppose we can expect him any day now, seeing that we're halfway through January.'

She was right. Two days later a telegram arrived saying that Bernard would be with them by the end of the week and that he was bringing a surprise with him. Immediately Nellie wrote to Babs, asking her to get some time off, so she could be there when Bernard arrived. She also wrote to Francis but she was still waiting for an answer to her letter, or for him to call, when Babs turned up the following evening. 'It's dull, dull, dull on the farm,' she said. 'I hope the surprise he's got is a good one. He never even sent me a card for my twenty-first. I hope it's something I can wear.'

'It won't cost much that's for sure,' said Lottie, not looking up from her knitting. 'He's even more tight-fisted than Grandfather was. Anyway, he's not the only one about to spring a surprise, is he?' She grinned at Nellie.

'I wish Francis was here. Dad mightn't believe Grandfather left the house to me but he'd have to believe Francis.' Nellie closed her library book and put coal on the fire. 'Of course, I could always speak to the solicitor.'

'Dad'll probably try and force you to make the house over to him,' said Lottie.

Nellie sighed. 'You mean contest the will. Francis said that if I made the house over to Dad, I would be going against Grandfather's wishes. He trusted me to make this a place where all the family could feel at home.'

'You really believe that?' asked Babs.

Nellie said softly, 'He didn't tell us to go away when we needed somewhere to live. We had our disagreements but this house has been a refuge to all of us in times of trouble.'

Babs said, 'It's going to be tough on Dad but I'll never forgive him for not giving his permission for me to marry Jake.'

'He doesn't care about your feelings,' said Lottie. 'As for the house, he only needs somewhere to hang his cap when he's on leave.'

'Yes. This will still be his home,' said Nellie. 'For all his faults he is still our father.'

'OK! You've made your point,' said Babs, her brows knitting. 'Are we going to do something special to welcome him home? I can guess the first thing he'll say is that you haven't had the place done up.'

'He never handed over any money.' Nellie gazed at the dingy eggshell-blue painted walls and smoke-stained ceiling. 'I wouldn't have used it if he had. It's my responsibility. The whole house needs a lick of paint and hopefully I'll get some of it done this spring.'

'So we can't paint the walls but we could write a big notice saying Welcome Home, Dad,' suggested Babs.

'And where do we get a clean sheet of paper that big?' asked Lottie. 'There's been a war on, you know.'

Babs made an exasperated sound and turned to Nellie. 'Can't you get some paper from the nursery?'

'There's a paper shortage.'

333

Babs persisted. 'How about crepe paper? Remember making red, white and blue paper roses for the coronation and twining them through a trellis round the front door?'

'Don't start getting nostalgic. I haven't got any crepe paper, but what I have got is bunting,' said Nellie.

'Bunting?' said Babs.

'Upstairs in the attic.' Nellie got up. 'And there might be some other stuff we can use. Anyway, I'm going to take a gander through what was left over after the sale.'

'I'll come with you,' said Babs, her eyes alight. 'It's ages since I've had a nose up there.'

Immediately Lottie said that she'd like a root around as well. 'I'll just check that Lucia is sleeping OK. She's been a bit fretful lately because she's teething.'

'Won't you find it difficult climbing all those stairs?' asked Babs.

Lottie sniffed. 'Don't you worry about me. I'm tougher than you think.' She put down her knitting and followed them out of the kitchen.

Once in the attic, Nellie dragged out yards of bunting, triangles of red, white and blue flags.

Lottie entered the room a few minutes later and immediately delved into another tea-chest. She lifted out a couple of gowns, dropped one and held the other against her. 'What d'you think?'

'Holy Mary, mother of God, Charlotte Callaghan, you're not thinking of wearing that? It's touching the floor and goes up to your neck,' said Babs.

'I like it.' Lottie tilted her chin. 'Lots of lovely

material in it and I love the flowery pattern in orange and brown and that it'll fasten to my throat … as for the length, I'll shorten it a bit.'

Her sisters exchanged looks but made no comment. Nellie remembered how she had thought of altering some of the frocks for dressing-up clothes for the children, but she had never had the time.

They continued to root in the tea-chests and eventually, with a triumphant shout, Babs dragged out a remnant of a roll of wallpaper. 'The back of this will do for a notice.'

Nellie looked at it in surprise. 'I thought we'd used up all the wallpaper.'

'Obviously not this bit,' said Babs, waving it in the air.

Carrying their spoils between them, the three sisters went downstairs, discussing whether to put up the bunting outside or in the kitchen. Babs was all for hanging it on the chestnut trees but Nellie said, 'It could rain or even snow at this time of year … best inside.'

Babs gave in and said she would hang it up in the morning after Nellie had gone to work. 'I'll do the welcome notice, too. It's a pity we haven't got any paint. The words won't show up much in ink or pencil.'

'Try the outhouse,' said Nellie, spooning cocoa into a jug. 'You just might be lucky and find some dregs in a tin.' It seemed strange to her that in a day or two her father would be home and she would have to face his wrath, not only over the house but also for allowing the unmarried Lottie to get pregnant and bring up her daughter here without a word to him. If only it had been Teddy coming home instead of her father, but there was no chance of that and so she had to make the best of what she had.

Chapter Seventeen

Less than twenty-four hours later Nellie came out of the nursery to the sight of falling snow. To her surprise, standing at the gate was Irene Miller. 'What are you doing here?' asked Nellie, thinking that Maisie should have collected her daughter from The Chestnuts an hour or so ago.

'Mam didn't come for me, so I decided to walk home on my own,' said the little girl who would be five that year. 'Your sisters were arguing, so I sneaked out. Then I saw you and wanted to say hello.' She smiled up at Nellie.

'I don't think you should be going home on your own in this weather and in the dark,' she murmured.

'But the snow's lovely,' said Irene, looking skywards.

Nellie's face softened, remembering as a child she had found the snow magical. Sadly, what with the war and all that had entailed, life had lost much of its magic. Suddenly she had a deep longing to feel carefree, to sing and be happy and to have that childish sense of wonder about life. She felt the cold kiss of a snowflake on her flushed cheeks and another one stung her chapped lips.

A small hand slipped into hers. 'Do you like it, too?'

'I love it!' said Nellie. 'I'll see you home.' If Bernard had arrived then their talk was going to have to wait.

As they trudged towards the lift bridge, fat snowflakes continued to pirouette lazily from an overloaded sky in what seemed like a never-ending stream. The child tried to catch them in her mouth and Nellie smiled, recalling doing the same thing with her sisters.

'Mrs Lachlan, look! The snow's melting in the canal.'

Roused from her reverie, Nellie gazed at the oil-streaked surface and saw that indeed the snow-flakes were being swallowed up by the mass of water. Strangely, it reminded her that she was one of millions in the world, all in the same boat, weary after a war that had taken so much from and out of them. They crossed the lift bridge, passed the smithy and the Red Lion pub; ahead lay Lither-land library and the factory where Maisie worked. On its wall hung a model of a perky pig, carrying a meaty sausage on a fork. She noticed the figure of a boy making his way towards them.

'It's Jimmy!' cried Irene, jiggling about. 'It's me big brother.'

The boy slithered to a halt a foot away and Nellie saw that the thin face of the eight-year-old was not only pinched and flushed with cold but was tight with distress too. Her heart sank. 'Oh, Mrs Lachlan, Mam's acting crazy and I don't know what to do,' he said.

Nellie's heart flipped over. 'What d'you mean

crazy, Jimmy? You just calm down and explain yourself.'

'She threw the potatoes at me and smashed the teapot. Then she picked up our only saucepan and began to bang it against the fireplace, screaming at the top of her voice.'

'Has she been drinking?'

'I couldn't smell it on her breath. I think she's just gone off her nut.'

Nellie took the boy's hand and began to hurry the two children in the direction of Linacre Road. 'Couldn't the woman you share the house with help?'

'She's gone. She married a fella. She lives across the water now.'

'Have you any idea what it's about?'

Jimmy shook his head. Nellie asked no more questions.

The front door was ajar and Nellie paused only to give Maisie warning that she was there by knocking and announcing herself before walking in. She found Maisie sitting in front of a fire struggling for life in the grate. Her shoulders were bowed and she was sobbing as if her heart would break. Nellie signalled to the children to sit on the sofa and went over to her. She placed a hand on her shoulder. 'What is it, Maisie? What's wrong?'

The woman did not answer at first and Nellie waited for her to gain control of herself. After a couple of minutes she raised a tear-stained face and said in a wobbly voice, 'Our Marty's gone and got himself married without a word to me. I thought he'd come and live here ... get his old job back and I could work part-time and we'd cope fine. Me and him were always there for each other when we were kids,' she said, biting back a sob. 'We never knew our dad and, as for me mam, she wanted rid of us as soon as she could. Now he's married this girl in the ATS. I just don't know how I'm going to manage with all the rent to pay on this house.'

'He's alive, Maisie! You be thankful for that. You want him to be happy, don't you?'

'I wanted him to be happy here with me ... that's what we planned,' she said angrily.

'You're not the only one whose plans have been wrecked,' said Nellie. 'For the kids' sake, pull yourself together. You can get a lodger to help you with the rent.'

'I suppose I can. I didn't think of that. I had me mind set on our Marty living here.' Maisie wiped her eyes with the back of her hand.

Nellie signalled to Jimmy to put on the kettle. 'Well, you've got your children and I'm sure they're a blessing to you, Maisie. At least you have part of your husband to love.'

Maisie sniffed. 'I suppose you're right. Marty's survived the war and I should be thankful for that. I just hope this girl and I will get on.'

'I'm sure if you meet her half way, things will be fine,' said Nellie, bending to pick up a potato. She motioned to Irene to help her gather the rest together before taking off her coat and peeling the spuds. Maisie thanked her and said that she would be all right now and wasn't she wanting to get home.

'Yes. My father's coming home. He could be at the house when I get there.' Nellie hugged the

339

children and said that she would call again soon.

'Well, yeah, thanks, luv. Jimmy, see Mrs Lachlan out.'

The boy walked with Nellie to the front door. She stepped outside and then turned and looked into his young face and saw the anxiety there. It touched her heart. 'Don't be worrying. If your mam gets upset again then come to me. In case you've forgotten, the house is called The Chestnuts; Irene knows where it is if you ever need help.'

His face brightened up. 'Yes, Mrs Lachlan.'

'Bye, Jimmy.'

'Tarrah!' He waved his hand and then turned and went back inside the house.

Nellie put her head down and hurried towards the main road. She did not see the figure looming ahead through the whirling snowflakes until she almost walked into him.

'Watch where you're going,' said a rough voice.

Looking up and blinking snow from her eyes, she realised it was Sgt McElroy. 'Oh, it's you! I haven't seen you for ages.'

'I didn't realise it was you, Nellie. My wife died, you know?'

'Oh, I didn't know. I'm sorry.' Here was something that Maisie hadn't mentioned, but then she had not asked. 'How's Billy?'

'He's in Germany. Won't be coming home just yet.'

Nellie said, 'I'm so glad he survived the war. I'll never forget what a help he was to me when I needed it.'

'Aye. He's a good lad.' He hesitated. 'How's

Lottie? I did hear she had a baby.'

Nellie flushed. 'Yes. She was a bit of an innocent was our Lottie. I must rush. My father's due home.'

'Is he now? If he stays for long that would be something new.'

'You remember my father, then,' said Nellie.

'I remember your mother more than him. I remember her saying when she had a bit of trouble that he was never there when she needed him.'

She knew he was right but only said, 'Mam wasn't alone, although, I agree that a woman needs a man about the house. I must go. Nice seeing you again. Sorry about your wife and give my love to Billy when you write.' She hurried away, thinking that her sisters would be wondering what had happened to her.

But Lottie and Babs were more worried about the telegram they'd just received than Nellie being late home.

'I don't believe it,' cried Babs, her green eyes glinting with anger as she paced the floor. 'Dad wouldn't go and do something like that ... not without telling us first.' Her shapely figure, clad in a navy blue skirt and jumper with a blue cardigan on top, was stiff with outrage.

'Read the telegram for yourself.' Lottie waved the yellow slip under her sister's nose. It had come while Babs was at the shops. 'I found it hard to believe, too. But he's a man and most of them generally do what they like without consulting us women.' Her face flushed with annoyance. 'You think I'm not upset? He's always behaved like I'm

341

a changeling. A child the gypsies placed in a basket and left on the doorstep. I'd be the first he'd have out of the house if it was what *she* wanted.'

Babs said impatiently, 'Don't be daft. Nellie won't allow it.'

Lottie groaned. 'I know you're right but I'm still worried. He-he's so aggressive. I wonder what Mam's thinking of him right now. Perhaps she's looking down from Heaven, saying he's run mad.'

'You still believe in Heaven?' Babs shook her head as if in disbelief. 'I bet this woman isn't the first he's had. You know what they say about sailors. Maybe she's the reason he's stayed away so long. She could be a nurse who's looked after him.'

Lottie clutched the towel turban that covered her curler-clad head and cried, 'But he'll expect her to live here and how can Nellie say no after her talk of this being a family home? And what about the nursery? She might hate kids.' She limped over to the oven.

'Talking of our Nellie ... she's late,' said Babs, lighting a cigarette.

'It could be because of the snow.' Lottie opened the oven door. 'I just hope this woman remembers to bring her ration book. Imagine what it's going to be like when he goes back to sea, leaving *four* women in this house. I'm going to have to pass off Lucia as an orphan that we've taken in,' she said gloomily.

'Don't be daft! The neighbours know she's yours. Still, another woman in the house...' muttered Babs, sitting in the armchair and kicking off her shoes.

There was a noise at the washroom door and Nellie walked in. She eased off a sodden glove and hung it over the open oven door without taking her eyes from Babs' face. 'What's this about another woman in the house?'

'Dad's bringing a woman home and he says they'll be here this evening,' said Lottie bluntly.

Nellie dropped her other glove on the hearth. 'You're joking!'

Babs raised her eyebrows. 'Would we joke about something as serious as Dad being married?'

'Yeah! It's no joke,' said Lottie, taking a pie dish out of the oven and placing it on a cork mat on the table. 'Although Babs jokes about things, I never would.'

'I want to see the telegram. I need to see exactly what he's written,' said Nellie, white-faced. 'Some surprise! What's he playing at getting married at his age?'

'We knew you'd hit the roof,' said Babs.

Nellie stared down at her sister sprawling in the armchair, her stocking feet resting on the brass fender. 'You're taking it in your stride, are you?'

'No, but...' Babs reached for the telegram on the alcove shelf beside the chimney breast and held it out to her.

Nellie read, *Thought I had better tell you my surprise. I am bringing a new mama for you. Be with you Friday evening. Dad.* She swore and flopped onto the sofa. 'A new mama. How old does he think we are? We don't need another bloody woman in this house. In fact, I won't have it.'

'He'll hit the roof,' said Lottie, dishing out the

fish pie. 'He might start smashing things, including us.'

'In front of her? I don't think so,' said Nellie, a glint in her eye.

'We'll soon know,' said Babs, glancing at the clock on the mantelpiece. 'I'm surprised they haven't arrived already.'

'I suppose with Dad being captain, he has to sort things out with the Mersey Dock and Harbour Board,' said Nellie.

'I'll have to feed them and there's barely enough fish pie left here for us three, despite Lucia refusing to eat any earlier,' sighed Lottie. 'She's gone to bed after only having bread soaked in warm milk and sugar.'

'Never mind feeding them. I'm hungry. I can always run the chippie if they want something,' said Nellie.

'I wonder what she looks like?' said Babs.

'I don't want to think about it,' muttered Nellie.

Lottie said, 'Would you believe there's an article in the *Echo*, saying Britain's so drab at the moment we women should be dressing in shades of myrtle green and the like. Apparently the servicemen returning from the near East and the Med have learnt to like the lovely soft dyes worn by the natives, so we're supposed to brighten ourselves up for the men.'

Nellie flinched. 'I don't wish to know that. It's going to be hard enough for Babs and me to cope when the men come home as it is.'

'Sorry,' muttered Lottie. 'You can't hide from it, though. The men will soon be everywhere wanting their old jobs back. You can bet a pound to a penny they won't find it easy, either, having to cope with everyday life after living on a knife-edge for so long.'

'I only hope to God that Dad doesn't decide to get a shore job,' said Nellie, pulling a chair up to the table.

Lottie gasped, 'He'd be complaining about Lucia running around the place. I'll have to get another job and find myself somewhere else to live.'

'You'll do nothing of the sort,' said Nellie. 'Just calm down.'

Lottie forked fish and potato into her mouth and mumbled, 'I suppose they'll sleep in Mam and Dad's old bedroom.'

Nellie nodded. 'I can't see them sleeping any-where else.'

'I wonder why he got married again,' said Babs. 'I mean it's not as if he had a happy marriage. Surely it can't be for sex? He's a sailor and they know where to find it when they want it.'

'You're terrible talking of such things,' said Lottie.

Babs gave her a speaking look. 'Don't be com-ing the innocent with me, Lottie. I was there when you gave birth.'

Nellie looked at Lottie's face. 'Enough said, Babs,' she murmured. 'Get on with your supper. They're going to be here soon and I don't know about you but I'm going to put on my best bib and tucker to face the enemy.'

'D'you mean her or Father?' asked Lottie.

Nellie did not answer because her mouth was full. It was Babs who said, 'We could be wrong

345

about her. She could be a nice woman, all motherly.'

'She might also be like the wicked stepmother in *Snow White*,' said Nellie. 'Whatever, we've got an ace up our sleeve.'

'*You* have, you mean,' said Babs.

'Should we light a fire in the parlour?' asked Lottie.

Nellie shook her head. 'It'll take ages to warm up. Now let's get finished and wash the dishes and get changed.'

Once the dishes were out of the way, Nellie made do with a wash down before changing into a blue and green tweed skirt and blue jumper. She found a darned pair of lisle stockings and pulled them on, folding the tops over garters, hoping they wouldn't wrinkle at the ankles. She hesitated only briefly before slipping her narrow feet into a pair of court shoes. Her breath came out as a sigh as she looked at the photo of Teddy and traced the outline of his face with a fingertip. She imagined him massaging away the stiffness in her shoulders and she rolled her head round one way and then the other, hoping and praying that her father would not decide to find a shore job. As it was, she could imagine the names he'd call her when she told him the house was hers.

Her grandfather had created a difficult situation for her because Nellie knew deep down she could not turn her father and his new wife out of the house. The housing situation was horrendous. Grannies, grandpas, aunts and children were having to share homes, sleeping in the parlour or kitchen on sofas or a couple of chairs put together. If her father was to give up the sea, then somehow they all would have to learn to rub along together.

As Nellie entered the kitchen, she saw Babs balancing on the brass fender on one foot so she could see herself in the mirror above the fireplace.

'You'd better get a move on. Although, I can imagine what Father's going to say when he sees you wearing lipstick.'

Babs' mouth formed a moue at her sister's reflection. 'I've had this lipstick for ages. Jake got it for me.' She could now say his name without getting too upset. 'It's Max Factor from the American stores.' She turned away from the mirror and said seriously, 'I don't mind giving you a bit, Nell. You could do with a dab to brighten yourself up. It might help with your chapped lips, too.'

Nellie smiled. 'OK. But I don't want you making me look like a painted doll.'

'Of course I won't. A bit of lippy is good for a woman's morale, though. You can have a dab of my face powder, too. Close your eyes.'

Nellie did as she was told and felt a featherlight touch on her nose, chin and forehead, accompanied by the delicate sweet perfume of the face powder. It was lovely. Then came the greasy feel of lipstick on her chapped lips.

'That'll do you,' said Babs briskly.

Nellie opened her eyes and glanced at her mirror image. She did look better. Lottie limped into the kitchen and her sister's lips twitched. She had removed the pipe-cleaner curlers from her mousy hair and brushed it into a frizz. She had also changed into the brown and orange floral dress that was buttoned up to the neck and floated down to her surprisingly shapely ankles. The style was completely unlike the skimpy skirts and dresses worn by most women due to shortages of material.

Lottie returned their stares. 'Don't look at me like that. At least I'm decent. That neckline plunges too much, Babs, and as for that skirt of yours, Nellie, I can see your knees, and you're wearing make-up.'

Babs said mischievously, 'Want a dab, Lottie?'

She shook her head. 'I don't know what you want to put that stuff on your face for. It doesn't do your skin any good.'

'Is that why you've got spots?' taunted Babs. 'From using the finest face powder?'

Lottie turned a dull red. 'You think yerself so funny.'

'I do try to give people a laugh.'

'You'll be laughing the other side of your face when Father sees you're wearing nylons. He'll know where they've come from.'

Babs' smile ebbed away. 'So what? I bet he'll be so full of this woman that he won't even notice unless you draw his attention to them.' She adjusted the sweetheart shaped neckline of her turquoise taffeta dress. 'You know what's wrong with you? You're jealous of me.'

The atmosphere in the room was suddenly charged with tension. Lottie's face turned ugly and she made a swipe at Babs, catching her a stinging blow on the ear.

'That hurt!' Babs lunged at Lottie and managed to seize a handful of frizzy hair.

Nellie cried, 'Stop it! We haven't time for this. I don't know what's got into the pair of you. You're not kids anymore and we've got to present a united front. If we can't get on how can we expect to get on with this woman?' She was ignored. Both her sisters panted as they struggled to get the upper hand. Suddenly there came the ring of a bell. 'That must be them,' whispered Nellie.

Her sisters froze. 'You go, Nellie,' urged Lottie, frantically smoothing her hair.

'Yes, you go,' gasped Babs, adjusting the neck of her frock.

Nellie noticed a scratch on her cheek. 'You're bleeding.'

She touched it gingerly. 'You bitch, Lottie.'

'Cover it with face powder,' suggested Nellie, and left the kitchen. She felt as if a hundred moths were re-enacting the Battle of Britain in her stomach and wished she did not have to face her father and the woman on her own. Yet, if she was to give Babs and Lottie time to tidy themselves up, there was no choice. The bell sounded again.

She clicked on the light and almost ran down the lobby, only to pause on reaching the door because she could hear Bernard muttering under his breath. She bit hard on her lower lip to stop it trembling and then flung the door open.

It was no longer snowing but the light from the lobby reflected off the fallen snow so that Nellie was able to see her father's tall figure clearly. He was wearing his seaman's cap and a heavy navy blue duffle coat and, to her surprise, he was alone. 'Where is she?' she asked.

349

'She'll be along,' he said. 'Has Babs managed to get here?'

'Yes.' Nellie heard the sound of footsteps to the rear of her and quickly got out of the way to allow her younger sister her first look at their father. Bernard stared at her and then Nellie caught the white flash of teeth from beneath his Clark Gable moustache. 'How's my girl? Come and give your ol' dad a spanking kiss.'

Babs hesitated, remembering his refusal to allow her to marry Jake, then she leaned forward and kissed Bernard's cheek. 'How are you, Dad? Broken bones healed?'

'What kind of welcome is that?' he growled. 'You're not sulking because I wouldn't let you marry that Yank still?'

'That Yank is dead.' Babs' voice was unemotional. 'You didn't answer my question, Dad. How are you?'

He frowned. 'Not too bad. Nothing like a nice long holiday in the sun to get a man on his feet.'

The sound of someone clearing their throat caused Bernard to look beyond Babs to Lottie standing at her shoulder. 'You,' he said. 'Still lazing about the house?'

She stiffened. 'I don't laze. I'm in charge of the nursery and I cook, clean and look after the hens.'

'Don't back answer me. You're just like your Aunt Josie. She always had too much to say for herself.'

'I wouldn't argue with you about her. There were times when she frightened the life out of me but I don't think you should be disrespectful to the dead, Dad. Anyway, where is she? You said you were bringing us a new mama,' said Lottie.

Bernard's mouth tightened and he reached for the kitbag he had placed carefully on the ground. 'Let's get inside.'

'But where's our new mother? You said you were bringing us a new mother,' insisted Lottie.

'Inside,' hissed Bernard. 'I don't want to be discussing my business in front of the neighbours.'

'Hardly in front of the neighbours,' Lottie bridled as she limped up the lobby.

'You wouldn't have spoken to me like that before the war,' he muttered, following his daughters to the kitchen.

He placed his kitbag in a corner and his gaze roamed the bunting decorated walls with the Welcome Home, Dad notice. 'Still no improvements, I see, Nellie. You're going to have to do something about this place.' Bernard removed his cap and riffled his greying hair with stubby fingers. 'But first things first. We've hardly eaten a thing all day, so what's there to eat?'

His daughters stared at him. 'What made you do it, Dad?' asked Babs.

'And where is she?' asked Lottie.

'The bottom of the road. I thought it best if I came on ahead and put you more in the picture.' He glanced at the clock on the mantelpiece, 'She'll be here in five minutes.' But the words were no sooner out of his mouth than the doorbell rang.

Lottie clutched the cheap rosary beads about her neck and muttered, 'Mary, mother of God, help us.'

Bernard scowled at her. 'Adriana's been through

a hard time, so you're to make her welcome.'

'Adriana! What kind of name is that for a stepmother?' asked Babs.

'It's a fine name for a stepmother because she sure is love and joy to me. So listen, the three of you ... you'll be out on your ear if you don't do and say the right thing to her.' The bell rang again and he left the kitchen, slamming the door behind him.

'That's what he thinks,' said Lottie with a grim smile. 'When are you going to tell him this is your house, Nellie?'

'Let's just wait a while,' she said, a tiny pucker between her eyebrows. 'I want to see if he'd actually kick us out.'

Babs said, 'I never thought I'd see the day when Dad would threaten to turn me out. I'm glad Grandfather left you the house.'

Nellie wondered if the old man had ever considered his son might marry again after their mother was killed. It made sense his leaving her the house if he had. She caught the sound of a woman's muffled voice and strained to hear what was being said but was defeated by the thickness of the door. Then it opened and Bernard stood in the doorway holding a woman by the hand. Nellie drew in a breath that positively hurt, whilst Babs and Lottie just gaped at their stepmother.

Adriana was no middle-aged mama. Nellie judged her to be about her own age. She had smooth olive skin, dark eyes and shoulder length black hair on which perched a maroon beret. Her face was oval and from her expression, Nellie guessed she was a tough cookie. She wore a navy blue duffle coat and trousers tucked into Wellington boots. The sharp brown eyes reminded her for a moment of someone else as they rested on the three sisters. *'Buona sera!'* she said in a husky, accented voice. 'Good ee-vening, la-dees.'

'You're foreign,' gasped Lottie.

'Give that woman a medal for observation,' murmured Babs.

He's taken leave of his senses, thought Nellie.

Bernard placed his arm about his wife's shoulders. 'Adriana, let me introduce you to my daughters, Nellie, Babs and Lottie.'

The sisters inclined their heads stiffly but Bernard's fixed expression resulted in Nellie holding out a hand to the woman. 'How d'you do?'

Adriana looked amused and said something to Bernard in her own language before taking Nellie's hand and shaking it. His expression altered. 'How understanding you are, *cara mia*. It is a shock to them but that's no excuse for such formality.'

'What do you want me to say, Dad? Welcome, Mama, you're just what we need?' asked Nellie.

Bernard snapped, 'Don't be rude. She's what *I* need and you either like it or lump it.'

'That's no way to endear her to us. I take it *she* is Italian?' said Nellie.

'Don't refer to her as *she* in that tone. You'll either refer to her as Adriana or Mama.'

'Adriana it'll have to be then,' retorted Nellie with a distinct lack of warmth.

'So be it.' He turned to Babs and his face softened. 'Now, come on, sweetheart. Adriana's going to need all the friendly faces she can find when I go back to sea.'

Nellie experienced a flood of relief. 'So you are going back to sea and leaving her here alone with us?'

Babs said, 'Is that wise?'

'What d'you mean by that?' An angry flush darkened Bernard's face.

Nellie jumped in quickly, 'She means ... how much English does she speak? How will we understand each other?'

His expression lightened. 'She speaks some English ... not much, though. She'll learn soon enough.'

Lottie said, 'Has she been to Rome? Has she seen the Holy Father? I'd love to hear about it if she has.'

For once Bernard viewed her with approval. 'It's a question I never thought to ask ... but I can see that you've got the right attitude for a change.'

Such praise astounded Lottie so much that she was struck dumb.

Nellie said, 'She looks cold. Perhaps she should sit by the fire. It must be terrible for her coming from a hot country to an English winter.'

Lottie found her voice and said, 'I feel sorry for her.' She held out a hand to Adriana, who hesitated only a moment before grasping it and allowing herself to be led by her limping stepdaughter to the armchair by the fire.

She sat down and stretched out her legs before glancing up at her husband. To his daughters' astonishment, he got down on one cracking knee and proceeded to remove her Wellington boots. Babs looked at Nellie and shook her head with a barely perceptible movement. Nellie raised her eyebrows, only to start when Bernard said, 'So what about rustling up some grub, Lottie, seeing as how you're the chief cook and bottle-washer here.'

She looked at Nellie in dismay. 'We decided it would be best to get you something from the chippie,' said Nellie.

'Good idea, girl. It seems ages since I've had home-grown fish and chips. I've told Adriana that Liverpool has a Little Italy and the best chippie is run by Italians.' Bernard smiled as he dug into a pocket and produced a ten shilling note. 'Two portions of fish and chips and an extra portion of chips if you three are feeling hungry as well.'

A surprised Nellie thanked him and put on her outdoor clothes and left the house, wondering if the ten shilling note meant that Adriana's influence on her father was a good one and had led to a loosening of his purse strings. But his mention of Little Italy reminded her that some of the old streets that had made up that area had been pulled down in the Thirties and corporation tenements built in their place. The neighbourhood had changed even more since the Blitz. She decided that perhaps she should telephone Francis from a telephone box as soon as she could and tell him about their brand new Italian stepmother.

As Nellie waited in the warm steaminess of the fish and chip shop, she wondered if her father could possibly have fallen in love at his age. It was the only reason she could think of for his marrying Adriana, but it also raised the question: why had the Italian woman married a foreigner so much older than herself? He wasn't exactly the sort of man that women's dreams were made of. Could he have boasted of owning a large house in England?

As she trudged back to the house through the snow with the newspaper wrapped package of fish and chips stuffed inside her coat to keep warm, she thought that if Adriana was a gold digger, then she was in for a big surprise.

She found Babs standing in the washroom doorway with the cat in her arms. 'So why do you think she married him?' Nellie asked.

'She saw Dad coming and conned him into marrying her. They say, *There's no fool like an old fool*. A young woman making out she wants him? He'd feel flattered.'

'So you think she married him for what he could have in the way of money?'

'He might have a Clark Gable moustache but he's no film star.'

Nellie smiled. 'Should we feel sorry for her? There's no doubt that Italy's one of the big losers from the war. It'll be in a heck of a mess with the Nazis and Allies having fought over its ground.'

'I wouldn't argue,' said Babs. 'But I'm going to wait and see before giving her my sympathy.'

Nellie entered the kitchen and was taken aback to find Adriana perched on Bernard's knee. She had removed her duffle coat and wore a seaman's jumper that clung to her breasts. Her dark head was bent over his and she was kissing his ear. A mixture of emotions tore through Nellie. Uppermost was the pain caused by knowing she would never again sit on Teddy's lap or hear him whisper sweet nothings in *her* ear.

Her father lifted his head, and looking slightly embarrassed, eased his wife off his knee. 'Hurry up and dish out them fish and chips, Nellie. We're starving.'

She tore open the newspaper and placed the fish and chips on two plates and the extra portion of chips on another one. Her ears caught the sound of Bernard murmuring to his wife. The next moment Adriana came over to the table and was about to pull out one of the chairs when Nellie stopped her. 'That one's got a wonky leg.' She called over her shoulder, 'Dad, explain to her what a wonky leg is. You could do with fixing it.'

He looked at her as if she had suggested that he sprout wings and fly, and walked over to his kitbag and removed a couple of bottles from its interior.

As he approached the table, Adriana patted the chair beside her. Before he could sit down, Lottie entered the kitchen, carrying a hot water bottle. She glanced at the Guinness and the wine bottle in his hand and her mouth turned down at the corners. Before Lottie could put her foot in it by voicing her disapproval, Nellie said that she would get the bottle opener.

Babs picked up the wine bottle and looked amused as she read the label. 'Aussie White's! I would have thought you'd have brought us something from sunny Italy. Is this to toast you and Adriana?'

'Indeed, it is,' he said, taking the bottle from her with a smile. 'Besides, it's not always sunny in Italy, girl. Fetch us some glasses.'

'I don't want any, thanks,' said Lottie, tightening the top of the hot water bottle. 'I'll put this in your bed.'

Nellie tried to imagine what her grandfather would have thought of his son and this woman sleeping between his sheets. She glanced at Bernard as he poured the wine and then shifted her gaze to Adriana. The Italian was stuffing chips into her mouth as if she hadn't seen food for a week, and then she caught Nellie's eye. 'The foo-od on the shee-p of your poppa...' She shrugged expressively.

'The cook's fault for almost severing his thumb,' said Bernard apologetically, placing a glass of wine next to his wife's plate.

'You don't have to explain, Adriana,' said Nellie, trying to sound friendly as she made chip butties. 'We all know what it's like to go hungry.'

'Of course you do,' said Bernard heartily. 'But now the war's over things can only get better. You girls and Adriana will soon learn to rub along. I'll have a word with Francis and see if he can find me someone to talk to her in both Italian and English.'

Nellie thought that her brother shouldn't find that too difficult but she'd like to see his face when he set eyes on Adriana. No doubt he would disapprove as much as they did. She raised her glass. 'Cheers!'

'Congratulations,' said Babs.

Adriana regarded her stepdaughters with a smile. '*Salute!*'

Babs drained her glass and licked her lips. 'I doubt I'll get halfway merry on that but it was a

358

nice change.' She ate her chip buttie and then glanced at the clock. 'My bedtime and yours, Nellie, if you're to be up in time for work and I'm to get an early train to Ormskirk. I'll use the bathroom first if you don't mind?'

Nellie said that of course she didn't but, before she could leave the kitchen, her father said, 'D'you have a nightie you can lend Adriana, Nellie? She doesn't have much in the way of clothes.'

Nellie glanced up at the drying rack where that week's washing was being aired and smiled. If her father was imagining his wife in a sexy nightie, he had another think coming. She dragged a pair of pink winceyette pyjamas, patterned with teddy bears, from the rack and held them out to her stepmother. 'Best I can do.'

To Nellie's surprise, a smile eased the corners of the Italian woman's mouth, making her face almost beautiful and her thin fingers stroked the fleecy material. *'Orso.'* She pointed to one of the bears. 'Cute.'

Cute! thought Nellie. Not a word that sprang readily to mind, taking into consideration her father's use of the English language. 'Glad you like them.'

'Grazie. Thank you. I ... follow ... you,' said Adriana in careful English, clutching the pyjamas to her chest and hurrying out of the kitchen.

'Follow me where?' asked Nellie, hastening after her.

Her stepmother was moving at a fair lick but she halted at the bottom of the stairs and faced Nellie. 'I desire *gabinetto!* You understand?' She mimed pulling a lavatory chain.

'*Si*,' said Nellie, having heard that word for yes in an American film set down Mexico way.

The smallest room was empty and Adriana scuttled inside and closed the door in Nellie's face. Not a way to endear yourself to me, she thought, crossing the landing to switch on the light in her parents' former bedroom. She wandered inside to check everything was OK. She felt for the hot water bottle that Lottie must have placed in the bed and thought how she would have to go without that night.

She returned to the lavatory and found the door open but noticed the bathroom door was closed. From inside came the noise of running water. She knocked on the door but there was no response. Then came the sound of splashing. She was convinced her stepmother was having a bath. How dare she? Nellie remembered how she had made do with a quick wash earlier when a hot bath would have been bliss. She swore under her breath and used the lavatory before running downstairs to wash her hands at the kitchen sink.

Bernard glanced at her. 'Adriana OK?'

Nellie managed to swallow her anger. 'She's having a bath.'

Bernard smiled. 'It'll do her good. I don't think she realised how bloody cold it can get at sea. It's going to take her some time to get used to our weather.'

'So where does she come from in Italy?' asked Nellie, wanting to know as much as she could about the Italian woman.

'I'm not sure exactly where she was born and brought up but I do know she spent some of the war in Rome. I've picked up some of the language but they speak so fast, the Eyeties.'

'We wondered if she was a nurse at the place where you convalesced?'

He ignored the question. 'The Amalfi coast? Lovely place, sheer drops to the sea.' He got to his feet. 'Time I was getting to bed.' His eyes were bright and his cheeks rosy. 'Don't wake us when you get up in the morning, Nellie. We both need the rest.'

'Wouldn't dream of it, Dad,' she murmured, thinking that was surely a polite way of saying he wanted to spend time in bed with his wife. The thought of the pair of them at it made her feel slightly sick. She forced herself not to dwell on the prospect, wondering if Lottie had gone to bed. She hoped Lucia would not wake up in the night and disturb the household; at least that was less likely with her sleeping downstairs in Lottie's room. She wondered how long it would take for the news of her father's Italian wife to spread over the neighbourhood. She could guarantee as soon as Mrs Wainwright got wind of it, it would only take hours. She noticed the bathroom door was ajar and went inside. The green painted walls showed signs of condensation and on the floor was a wet towel. She hadn't stayed in the bath long, thought Nellie, picking up the towel and dropping it in the bath. Already her stepmother was making her mark. Two extra people in the house, one of them a young foreign woman and the other a father who believed he owned the place. She had no doubt that, in seamen's terms, there would be rough waters to navigate in the days ahead.

Chapter Eighteen

Nellie crept downstairs in the dark, only to pause as she heard a sound. Then she realised the noise she could hear was Lucia singing her babyish version of 'Pat-a-Cake'. Nellie smiled, thinking that it would not be long before her niece's speech improved in leaps and bounds. She frowned, thinking that could be a problem if her father and Adriana were to hear Lucia address Lottie as Mam. She saw that her sister's bedroom door was open and peeped inside, making out the humped shape of her sister in bed. She decided to leave her sleeping for the moment as Lucia wasn't there and went into the darkened kitchen. The singing was clearer here and accompanied by the growling of the cat. Nellie clicked on the light switch and child and cat blinked up at her from the hearth rug.

'What are you doing up so early?' asked Nellie quietly.

'Dinkies,' said Lucia, releasing the cat and toddling over to her aunt.

Nellie swung her up into her arms and kissed her before plonking her on the sofa and going over to the sink. She half-filled a cup with water and handed it to Lucia. Then she lit the fire, thinking of her father and the mothers and children that would be arriving in a couple of hours. She heard a noise behind her and turned

362

to see Babs. Her red hair was in a tangle and she was still wearing pyjamas.

'Did I disturb you?' asked Nellie.

'I had to get up.' Babs curled up on the sofa next to her niece. 'So d'you think Lottie'll be able to keep secret that Lucia's hers for long?'

'No. Impossible. I'd suggest to her that she pretends to have married the father and for him to have been killed in the war, but one of the neighbours could let the cat out of the bag.'

'I don't see why. The only one I can think of is Mrs Wainwright and I can't see her talking to Dad about it. What would you do about a wedding ring for her?'

Nellie barely hesitated. 'I could lend her mine if you really believe it could work.'

'It's worth a try, and better than Dad threatening to throw her and Lucia out of the house,' said Babs. 'Not that you'd allow him to do it. How long d'you plan on keeping quiet about the house being yours?'

'I'm playing it by ear. If you're hungry, you'll have to make do with bread and jam and a cup of milk. Sorry.' Babs nodded and nothing more was said on the topic of the house.

After Nellie had told Lottie her plan and handed over her wedding ring, she and Babs left the house, the latter to make her way to Ormskirk and Nellie to the nursery. Several times throughout that day they were to think about their sister, wondering how she was coping with their father and his Italian wife in the house.

The nerves in Lottie's stomach quivered as she

limped over to the pantry, carrying a half-empty jar of homemade plum jam. As she tried to open the door, the knob came away in her hand. She had mentioned it needed fixing to her father but he had ignored her. It was not the only thing that needed mending in the house but she had decided it was a waste of time pointing them out to him. It was only because he had complained about Nellie not having done any of the things he had asked her to that had got up her nose and made her mention the knob. That and the language he had used when she had asked for his and Adriana's ration books. 'Use your bloody nous,' he'd said. 'We've only just bloody set foot in England.'

She had yet to tell him about Lucia and her fictitious marriage, and prayed she wouldn't go red when she did. Lying did not come easy to her and she hoped God would forgive her. Her father hadn't even noticed the wedding ring and had made no mention of her having lost weight. Probably that was because he seldom bothered looking at her. Fortunately, when he'd glanced into the parlour, most of the children had been listening to a story so there had been no cause for him to complain to her about any noise.

A short while ago he had gone upstairs, carrying a breakfast tray of Camp coffee, toast and jam for Adriana, despite it being almost noon. As soon as he had disappeared to the bedroom, Lottie had put her assistant in charge so that she could go shopping. She could not understand why her father got so mad with her but decided not to mention ration books again. Somehow she would manage to produce a really tasty supper without his contribution. If he asked why there was so little meat, she would tell him exactly why.

She put on her outdoor clothes and slipped out of the house. She was halfway down the front path when she heard her father calling her name. For some reason that panicked her and she put on a spurt, only to slip in the snow. Her leg gave way beneath her and she fell heavily to the ground.

'Hell's bells, what d'you think you're doing, you bloody fool of a girl?' demanded Bernard from the front doorway. 'How d'you think I'm going to get you up? I'll need a crane to lift you.'

Lottie tried to get herself up but collapsed in pain. Her brother's welcome voice said, 'What have you done to yourself now, Lottie?' And slipping his strong arms beneath her armpits he heaved her into an upright position.

She clung to him, balancing on one foot, remembering the shame of his knowing about her fall from grace. He patted her shoulder and looked to where Bernard stood in the doorway. 'If you could give me a hand here, Dad, we could get her into the house and off her feet.'

'Did our Nellie get you on the blower?' rasped Bernard, walking gingerly down the path. He seized one of Lottie's arms and dragged it about his neck, causing her to gasp in pain.

'No. I had an interment at Ford cemetery and thought I'd kill three birds with one stone by visiting a former parishioner in Seaforth and dropping in on my sisters, too. Why, what's wrong if she did?' asked Francis.

'Nothing. I can make use of you now you're here. Let's get this one inside.'

Before they could make a move towards the house, there came the sound of hurrying feet and the next moment Adriana appeared in the doorway. Her dark eyes flickered in her husband's direction before passing over Lottie to Francis. For several seconds her gaze lingered on his face and then she gestured with her hand. *'Buongiorno, Padre.* Come!'

Lottie whispered to her brother. 'This is our new "mama".'

Francis almost dropped her but she managed to cling onto him and he made a quick recovery. 'What did you say?'

'Our new mama,' said Lottie. 'Her name's Adriana and she's Italian.'

Francis glanced at his father but Bernard avoided his eyes and said, 'Let's get her inside.'

'OK. You can tell me about your wife later,' said Francis in an undertone.

Adriana hurried ahead to the kitchen and opened the door wide. The two men settled Lottie in a chair close to the fire. Francis fetched a stool for her to rest her foot on and inspected the damage. 'It looks badly swollen, Lottie. I hope it's not broken.'

'Me too,' she said shakily, her face white with pain. 'I don't want to go to hospital, Francis. I've the children. I can't expect my helper to do all the work.'

'You might have no choice, love,' said her brother.

Bernard said, 'They'll have to go home. I don't

like the idea of having a nursery in my house, anyway.'

Francis opened his mouth but Lottie gave a tiny shake of her head. 'I'll speak to my assistant,' she said. 'What about some cold water, Francis? I'm sure Nellie would say putting my foot in some would help bring the swelling down.'

'You're probably right.' He glanced at Adriana, who appeared to be searching the shelves. Suddenly she pounced on a bottle of Camp coffee and then looked at Francis and waggled the bottle at him with a smile.

Hurriedly, Francis switched his attention to Lottie's ankle and undid her laces and eased off her shoe before saying to his father, 'Could you ask your wife to run some cold water in a bowl and fetch it here?'

'I'll get it,' said Bernard.

As he walked over to the sink, Lottie said, 'He wants you to find someone who speaks Italian to teach Adriana English.'

Bernard glanced over his shoulder. 'It can wait until I go back to sea. I want her spending time with me and nobody else right now.'

'Please yourself,' said Francis.

'Padre!'

He looked up and saw Adriana holding out a steaming cup to him and realised he had no choice but to accept it from her. He thanked her in a cold, polite voice and saw the smile die in her dark eyes and experienced an unfamiliar sensation beneath his ribs. As she turned away, Francis gulped a mouthful of the coffee before rattling off several questions to Bernard.

'Has she any family, Dad? Where is she from? How did you meet her? When and where did you get married?'

'What is this? An inquisition?' demanded Bernard, slopping water onto the floor as he carried the bowl.

Francis' eyes glinted. 'I'd say they're natural questions to ask when a father turns up with an Italian wife young enough to be his daughter.'

Bernard flushed a dull red. 'OK, OK!' He placed the bowl on the stool and straightened. 'Her brothers died in the Desert War. The rest of her immediate family was slaughtered by the Nazis after the Allied landings. She doesn't want reminding of the past, so don't pester her with questions.'

'That would be a bit difficult as I don't speak Italian, just some Latin ... and in my experience the past isn't so easily forgotten,' said Francis.

'Well, she wants to try and forget it,' muttered Bernard.

Lottie said, 'I agree with Francis. The past isn't easily forgotten. I'll never forget the explosion that crippled me and killed Mam and Aunt Josie.'

Bernard turned on her. 'Don't start on about your mother! You've no idea what I had to put up with from her.'

'OK, Dad, that's enough,' rasped Francis. 'We won't mention Mam. Now if you'll step out of the light, I'll see to Lottie's foot.'

But before he could do anything, Adriana suddenly knelt down and seized the injured foot. Lottie screamed with pain and slapped Adriana's hand away. 'You're stupid!' she gasped.

Bernard was furious. 'Bloody hell, girl, don't be such a baby. She was trying to help you.'

Adriana stepped back and a furious stream of words burst from her and she stabbed the air with a finger.

'There, sweetheart, don't take it to heart,' Bernard said, placing an arm round her and ushering her from the room.

Lottie turned to Francis. 'He doesn't know the truth about Lucia or Nellie owning the house yet. He's threatened to have us out of the house if we're not nice to her. Nellie said she's waiting to see just how far he'll go before she tells him. His marrying this woman has really put a cat among the pigeons.'

'I can see how it's made things difficult.' Francis gently lifted Lottie's swollen foot and placed it in the cold water. A shiver ran through her. 'Keep it there for a while, Lottie. Regard it as a penance for hitting our stepmother. What have you told him about Lucia?'

'Nothing yet. Nellie's given me her wedding ring and has told me to tell him that Lucia's father was killed in the war.' Lottie bit her lip and stared hard at her brother to see what he thought of the suggestion.

He lowered his head and said, 'I didn't hear that, Lottie.'

She was about to repeat what she had said when she realised what he meant. Instead she said, 'I was going shopping, now I can't.'

'Write a list and I'll drop it off at the shops and explain the situation. I'm sure they'll deliver what you want. I'll also drop by at the nursery and

369

leave a message for Nellie, telling her what's happened.' He placed his cup on the hearth and produced a pencil and a small notebook from an inside pocket and handed both to her.

As Lottie wrote she said, 'I'll need to speak to my assistant, Francis. Could you pop your head in the parlour and explain to her what's happened?'

He nodded and ten minutes later the woman came in and she and Lottie discussed what was the best thing to do. They came to the decision that until Lottie was up and about again, and her father back at sea, the assistant would run the group from her house. 'It won't be as good as from here but it means the other mothers won't have the worry of no one to look after their children.'

Lottie thanked her and then said her goodbye to Francis.

He left without seeing his father or stepmother again but could not get either out of his mind as he called in at the shops before heading for the nursery to speak to Nellie. However, he did not get that far as he saw her on the other side of the road with a child clinging to each hand and in company with more children and another woman. He hurried over to them.

Nellie spotted Francis and her face lit up. 'Have you been to the house? Have you seen her?'

'Yes!' He drew his sister aside and said in a low voice, 'Without wishing to be disrespectful to our father, he must be mad. She's far too attractive and young to be left behind when he returns to his ship. She's trouble, Nellie. I can feel it in my bones … and talking about bones, Lottie slipped in the snow and has damaged her ankle.'

Nellie's face crinkled up with dismay. 'Poor Lottie! Is it bad?'

'You can decide that for yourself. The woman who helps her is going to have the children at her home for now. Lottie was worried about the shopping, so I've arranged for it to be delivered.'

Nellie was glad about that. 'Did he tell you anything about Adriana?'

'Not much. Her brothers fought in the Desert War and were killed. The rest of her family were murdered by the Germans.'

Nellie was shocked. 'He said she'd suffered. I should feel sorry for her. I *do* feel sorry for her losing her family … but why did she have to marry Dad and complicate our lives?' she said ruefully.

Francis gave a ghost of a smile. 'Security probably. Italy's in a mess. I think you're doing the right thing at the moment not mentioning about the house being yours.'

'I'm glad you agree. I need to get to know her better before I decide what to do. If we can't get on, then I'm going to have to make some difficult decisions.' Nellie sighed. 'By the way, did he ask you to find someone to teach her English?'

'Told me to leave it until he goes back to sea. I'd best be going. See you soon,' said Francis, squeezing her arm gently.

The rest of the day could not go fast enough for Nellie. She was weary by the time she arrived home and not looking forward to having to be polite and friendly to her father and his wife. She pushed open the kitchen door expecting to find them both there, but only Lottie was present.

'Where are they?' whispered Nellie.

'They went out ages ago before the nursery finished so they don't know yet that Lucia lives here. She's asleep in her cot now. I'm going to have to tell Dad about her tomorrow.'

Nellie nodded. She knelt, feeling her sister's ankle with gentle fingers. 'It doesn't feel broken but I'm no expert. You should have it X-rayed.'

Lottie shook her head. 'No hospitals.'

Nellie did not argue with her. 'Then you'll have to rest and keep putting on cold compresses.'

'I know. It was a good job Francis arrived. I think *she* was impressed by us having a priest in the family. He was cool with her, though.'

'He says she's trouble. Mind you, he'll have more difficulty than us in accepting her in Mam's place with him having been so close to Mam.' She stood up. 'Where have they gone, by the way?'

'Dad's taken her into town for a meal and a dance at Reece's.'

Nellie's eyebrows shot up. 'A dance! What on earth did she wear?'

Lottie hesitated. 'I told her to go up to the attic and look in the tea-chest.'

Nellie giggled. 'And?'

'She looked OK.'

'I bet.'

Nellie was still smiling when she took her supper out of the oven. After she washed the dishes, they discussed the rest of their day but it was not long before their stepmother became the subject of their conversation again.

'How do you think she'll cope with you being laid up?' asked Nellie.

'She'll have to do the housework. What choice has she?' Lottie shrugged.

'What about Lucia? I can't see Dad allowing Adriana to look after her.'

Lottie agreed and her eyes looked worried. 'I doubt I'll manage her with my ankle the way it is.'

Nellie agreed. 'I could ask Matron if I could bring her to the nursery with me just until you're on your feet again.'

'Would you, Nell? I'm sorry to cause you so much trouble.'

'You're no trouble,' said Nellie, kissing the top of her head.

Any sympathy Nellie might have for her step-mother being landed with the housework over the next few days was misplaced. Bernard did not want his young wife getting her hands chapped and sore and insisted on the washing being sent to Kwok Fong's laundry. He also hired a woman to come in daily to do the housework and cooking.

Nellie remembered how hard her mother had worked and was exasperated with his molly-coddling his young wife. She, herself, had to see to the hens before leaving for the nursery, as well as in the evening. Fortunately, Matron had agreed to Lucia attending the nursery until Lottie was on her feet again. Both sisters saw little of the newly-weds as they did not get out of bed until halfway through the morning and were out gallivanting every evening.

373

'It can't last,' said Nellie when she arrived home one Saturday evening in early February to find Bernard and Adriana out yet again. 'He'll run out of money.'

'She's been buying clothes,' said Lottie, holding out her arms to her daughter. Her father and stepmother were still unaware that Lucia was hers, despite the little girl's presence in the house on Sundays, as they had seen no reason to explain with them rarely seeing the child. Bernard's only comment was that he hoped that Nellie was getting extra pay for looking after the child on a Sunday. The sisters had exchanged looks and smiled.

'I didn't know she'd registered for clothing coupons,' said Nellie, easing off her shoes and putting her feet up on the fender.

Lottie leaned towards her sister and said in a whisper, 'Who says she has? Some poor Hindu draper in Everton was robbed of thousands of clothing coupons. I bet they've been sold on the black market.'

Nellie stared at her. 'You think Dad...?'

'He'd do anything for her. Anyway, she's bought a corset. A real lovely one. It's red and black and made of real whalebone with satin and cotton elastic,' said Lottie. 'She showed it to me. I'd love one like it. I'd feel safe in it.'

'Safe from what? Or from whom, should I say?' asked Nellie.

'Men. A good corset can match a suit of armour,' said Lottie with a twinkle.

Nellie laughed. 'I doubt that was her reason for buying it.'

'No. She'll look glamorous in it, unlike me.'

Nellie took a hard look at her sister. 'Don't pull yourself down. You have nice skin and eyes and a neat pair of ankles once the swelling's gone down, you've lost weight and now curve in the right places.'

Lottie blushed. 'Thanks, Nellie. You've done me the power of good, but I can't see a bloke wanting to take me on with Lucia. There must be more women than men in this country due to the war. They'll have their pick of the best.'

Nellie said, 'You're doing it again. Who says you're not the best. Any decent bloke would accept Lucia if he loved you enough. Anyway, any news of when Dad's going back to sea?'

'Shouldn't be long now. I think I heard him mention the ship was having a complete overhaul and it's nearly ready.'

It was to be another fortnight before Bernard finally left with the promise that he would be back in a couple of months. In an aside to Nellie, he told her to get some work done on the house, as well as keep a close watch on Adriana. 'She's an attractive woman and the young men are coming home now. It's not that I don't trust her, Nellie, but some men will make a beeline for her.'

Just like you did, thought Nellie, wondering how her father could imagine she would be able to spy on his wife while she was out at work all day. Even so, with him away, she was bound to see more of Adriana and have the opportunity to get to know her better.

Chapter Nineteen

Nellie crept downstairs, intent on not waking the household. But as she neared the kitchen, she realised that the wireless was switched on to the shipping forecast. She opened the door and, to her dismay, saw Adriana sitting in front of a glowing fire, still clad in pyjamas, and Lucia on the rug, looking at a book. The girl was so absorbed in the pictures that she did not lift her head. Adriana was smoking a cigarette and, in her other hand, she held a cup. Nellie's nose caught the distinct smell of chicory. Adriana's expression was sombre and it did not change as Nellie, dressed in her working green blouse and dark skirt, took the tea caddy from a shelf and spooned tealeaves into a brown teapot.

The kettle was on the hob and steam was coming from its spout so she infused the tea, cut a couple of slices of bread and reached for the toasting fork. Lucia lifted her head and smiled. She pointed a finger at the picture of a dog. 'Dog,' she said.

'Yes, dog,' said Nellie, holding the bread to the bars of the grate. She was aware that her stepmother was watching her. Should she say something? The question she wanted to ask was what was Adriana doing up so early. Until the Saturday just gone, Nellie had left the house with Lucia without her stepmother being any the wiser about her being Lottie's daughter. Today would be different because the nursery was starting up again in the house. How would she explain to Adriana that Lucia was Bernard's granddaughter when they didn't speak each other's language? She puzzled over it and was no nearer to solving the problem by the time the bread was toasted and spread with margarine. She offered half a slice to the Italian woman.

'No... *Grazie!*' Adriana waved the toast away and flicked the cigarette butt into the fire. She stood up and left the room.

Despite being glad to have the kitchen to herself, Nellie would have welcomed the opportunity to try and make friends with Adriana. She would have enjoyed asking her about Italy and how she and Bernard had met but that was impossible. What was her father thinking of leaving his wife here without arranging for her to have English lessons? As she ate her toast, listening with half an ear to the shipping forecast, she wondered whether she should arrange the lessons herself. According to Lottie, Francis had not visited since she had damaged her ankle, so maybe she should call on him at the weekend. Nellie went over to the window and drew back the curtain to see what the weather was doing. It was not quite light and she could make out a few faint stars in the sky, which boded well for a dry day. She decided that she had best get a move on or she was going to be late for work.

'Me come?' asked Lucia, scrambling to her feet as Nellie put on her coat.

'Not today, sweetheart.' She picked her up and

carried her into Lottie's bedroom and woke her sister before leaving the house.

Lottie watched as Adriana put on the new scarlet woollen coat with the black fur collar and wondered where her stepmother was going. It was no use asking her, of course, because neither could understand what the other was saying. At least she was going to be out of the house when the mothers and children started arriving in half an hour's time. Something was going to have to be done soon about Adriana having English lessons. It would be of help to Lottie if Adriana could do the shopping and contribute to the household budget, but so far she hadn't turned over any money. Of course, lessons would cost money, too, but then perhaps her father had provided for them out of his advance money. She and Nellie had no way of knowing without Adriana telling them. She was going to have to speak to Nellie about it later.

When Nellie arrived home that evening, she was surprised to find Babs digging in the garden, despite it being almost dusk. 'Who's got you doing that?' called Nellie.

'Our Lottie!' Babs straightened up. 'It's not what I planned to do when I got here, but I'd only put my foot inside the kitchen when she begged me to make a start. She said you two had enough on your plate. As for our dear step-mama, I doubt she'd know where to begin growing food. There's talk of a wheat shortage, you know. She'll soon be wishing she'd stayed in Italy when bread goes on ration.'

'Have you seen her?'

'No. Which is just as well because I wouldn't know what to say to her.'

Nellie frowned. 'I wonder where she is?'

'God only knows. Lottie said she went out early wearing her best coat.'

Nellie wrinkled her nose. 'Who would she know? Anyway, don't do any more digging. Come inside.'

Nellie went indoors while Babs put the spade away, thinking about Adriana and how they could pay for English lessons for her. There was no sign of Lottie or Lucia in the kitchen, so she went upstairs to get washed and changed and was on her way downstairs when the knocker sounded. She hurried to open the door, wondering if it was Adriana.

It was, but she was not alone. Nellie darted a look at the man standing beside her. He wore a cap, and due to it being almost dark, she could not see his face clearly. She looked at Adriana, expecting her at least to make some attempt at introducing her companion, but she only took a shopping bag from him with a muted *'Grazie,'* before brushing past Nellie and going inside the house.

For a moment she wondered if the man was a taxi driver and she was expected to pay him, but then he removed his cap, revealing a head of dark hair, and said, 'Good evening, Mrs Lachlan. I am happy to meet you again.' He had a slight foreign accent that was pleasant to the ear.

She was mystified, certain she had never heard his voice before. 'I'm sorry. Do I know you?'

'We met only briefly but I have never forgotten

the help you gave me at the padre's house.'

The breath caught in Nellie's throat so that she couldn't speak for a moment. She clutched the door lintel for support because her knees seemed to have turned to water and her heart was racing fit to beat the band. 'You can't be... Francis said I'd never see you again.'

'I, too, believed that at the time, but the war destroyed so many lives.' He gestured with both hands. 'I returned to Liverpool. The padre knows I need work, so he asks me to teach Mrs Callaghan English. Also he says that there are things that need mending in the house and walls that need painting. I will also work in your garden and see to the chickens.'

'That would be marvellous but I'm not sure how much I'll be able to pay you.'

'I do not ask for money. The padre, he say that we can agree terms that will be of benefit to us both.'

Relief flooded her. 'What terms are they?'

'I need somewhere to stay. The padre, he suggests that I lodge here for the time the work takes.' He hesitated. 'I also have a small son and hope that he'll be able to stay here, too?'

Nellie's spirits plummeted. 'You have a son?'

'*Si!* The padre, he says that is no trouble because your sister, she has children here.'

'Of course, he'll be no trouble but-but what about your wife?'

He twisted his cap between his hands and she sensed his dismay. 'I would not be standing here on your step, Mrs Lachlan, if my wife was alive.'

Her spirits rose mercurially, causing her to feel

dizzy. 'Sorry. Of course you wouldn't. I don't know what I'm doing keeping you out here on the step. Come inside!'

He shook his head. 'No, I must go now because my friends are looking after Tonio, but I will return tomorrow if you are in agreement.'

'Yes! *Si!* I mean. Please come. I really do need a man about the place.'

She caught the gleam of his eyes and thought he smiled. 'That is good. I want to be of use to you. But for now I say *buona sera*, Mrs Lachlan, until tomorrow.' He replaced his cap and walked away.

She watched him go and then remembered she did not know his name. 'Wait!' she called.

He turned and she hurried down the path. She could see his face much more clearly now by the light of the street lamp. Finely drawn lines were etched between his nose and mouth and at the corner of his eyes. The marks of suffering, she thought, hating that the war had aged them all beyond their years.

'You have not changed your mind, I hope?' he said anxiously.

'No! I want to know your name.'

His hesitation was barely noticeable. 'Michelangelo Gianelli. When I come tomorrow, I will bring my ration book and identity card.'

She smiled. 'Good.'

'*Arrivederci!*' He lifted a hand in farewell and went on his way.

Nellie hurried back into the house and found her sisters in the kitchen. She noticed a bulging shopping bag on the table. 'Where's Adriana?'

381

she asked.

'Upstairs,' said Babs, who was washing her hands at the sink.

'Guess what she's got in this bag,' said Lottie, placing a hand on it.

Nellie was momentarily distracted from what she was about to say. 'A mutilated body?' she suggested flippantly.

Babs raised her eyebrows. 'You seem different.'

'That's because we're going to have a man about the house. A man who will not only fix things and decorate the house but also dig the garden, care for the hens and teach our stepmother English. Would you believe she went to see Francis herself about English lessons?'

'Bloody hell! Who'd have believed she'd be able to find her way there?' said Babs.

'Perhaps Dad took her to show her Little Italy and Francis' church,' said Lottie.

'Anyway, who is this superman?' asked Babs.

Nellie's eyes sparkled. 'My mystery man! But now I know his name is Michelangelo Gianelli.' The name rolled off her tongue and it sounded vaguely familiar.

'Another Italian,' said Lottie.

'He speaks good English.'

'Why didn't you bring him in?' asked Babs.

'He had somewhere to go but he'll be back tomorrow.'

Babs' face fell. 'That's no good to me. I'll be gone.'

'You'll see him again. He's going to stay here in lieu of wages. He's also bringing his son.'

'His son! You mean he's married?' said Lottie.

'A widower. Thank God Adriana's married to Dad, although if he were to set eyes on Michelangelo Gianelli, I don't think he'd be too happy about his teaching her English.'

'Good-looking, is he?' said Babs, looking amused.

'Hmmm. I just hope Adriana doesn't start fluttering her eyelashes at him.'

There was a sound behind her and Nellie turned and saw their stepmother standing in the doorway, and was relieved that she didn't speak English. Even so, there was an uncomfortable silence as she walked over to the table and picked up the shopping bag. She began to remove its contents, placing them on the table.

When the bag was empty she hung it on the back of a chair and faced the sisters, waving a hand over the newspaper wrapped packages and jars. 'Good Italian food.'

'Lottie does the best she can and she's yet to see your ration book,' said Nellie.

Adriana shrugged and muttered something in Italian. She began to unwrap a package. 'Pasta. *Fresca.*' She sniffed it and the expression on her face was one of such bliss that Nellie was reminded of the Bisto kids. She watched as Adriana took a saucepan from a shelf and half filled it with water.

Nellie's stomach rumbled, reminding her that she was hungry. 'What are *we* having for supper?' she said.

'Liver and onions,' answered Lottie, 'and it's in the oven.'

'Lovely. I'm ready for it now,' said Nellie,

although she would have loved a change from liver and onions, but she knew it was an economical meal.

Lottie's face brightened. 'I'll serve up. We might as well scoff Adriana's share seeing as she doesn't want it.'

The sisters ate with half their attention on their stepmother, as she sliced and grated ingredients. 'I wonder where she got that cheese from?' muttered Lottie. 'There seems a lot of it. We only get a tiny bit on the ration ... and what's that thing she's peeling? Can you smell it? It stinks.'

'It's garlic,' said Babs. 'It grows wild in some parts of Lancashire. I bet she bought it from an Italian shop in Francis' parish.'

'Same with the cheese, then,' said Nellie, pushing away her empty plate. 'I remember Italian ice-cream makers had cows in their backyards. Some probably still do.'

'D'you think Adriana knows how to make ice-cream?' whispered Lottie. 'I'd forgive her preferring her own cooking to mine if she could make Italian ice-cream like it tasted before the war. Look! She's got tinned tomatoes! Where did she get them?'

Babs stifled a giggle. 'This is crazy. We've become obsessed by food.'

Nellie smiled. 'That's not surprising given that we've just come through a war and there's still shortages.'

'If the harvest this year is as bad as it was last year here and in Canada, then she won't be getting her pasta either,' whispered Babs. 'It'll be potatoes, potatoes and potatoes – that's if we're lucky.'

They groaned in unison.

Adriana seated herself at the table and began to eat her pasta. The three of them watched her until Nellie could stand it no longer and began to collect their empty plates. She carried them over to the sink and was soon followed by her sisters.

'It makes me hungry watching her,' said Babs.

Lottie agreed. 'I wouldn't mind having a taste of what she's got. I wonder if they have pancakes in Italy?'

'Is that a reminder that Lent starts the day after next?' said Nellie.

Babs chanted, 'Pancake Tuesday's a very happy day, if you don't give us a holiday we'll all run away.'

'We'll be able to have lemon with them this year,' said Lottie. 'It says so in the *Echo*.'

Babs winked at Nellie. 'If it says it in the *Echo* then it must be true. Just a shame I won't be here to enjoy them and say what I think about Michelangelo Gianelli.'

'I can't wait to see him,' said Lottie, looking forward to tomorrow.

'Pancake Tuesday? What name ees this?' asked Adriana, lifting her eyes from darning a stocking and gazing at Lottie and Lucia. The little girl was kneeling on a chair at the table and clattering a spoon inside a small bowl.

'So you don't have pancakes in Italy,' said Lottie with a satisfied smile, pausing in beating batter and glancing in Francis' direction.

He stood over by the window, talking in a low voice to Michelangelo Gianelli. What a name for such a good-looking man, thought Lottie. Had his mother taken one look at him and thought of the Archangel Michael? His son was a nice-looking lad, as well, although he hadn't opened his mouth since his father had brought him into the parlour, where she had been reading to the children. She waited until there was a lull in the men's conversation and asked Michelangelo to explain what Pancake Tuesday was to Adriana.

He turned his dark head and spoke in Italian, causing Adriana's face to brighten as she answered him in the same language. He looked at Lottie and said, 'She will make supper this evening because you are cooking the pancakes. I tell her today is also named Shrove Tuesday and is the day before Lent begins here in England, but that you have no carnival beforehand.'

'But there is the Exposition of the Blessed Sacrament,' said Francis, glancing at the clock on the mantelpiece. 'I must go. You're quite satisfied with the arrangements, Michelangelo?'

'Si. I have brought all I need.'

Francis nodded. 'And you'll be strict with Mrs Callaghan, won't you? We don't want her babbling on in Italian because you understand her. No one knows better than you that to fit in she needs to be fluent in English.'

Lottie flashed both a startled look and then lowered her eyes as her brother turned to her. 'I'll see myself out, Lottie. Enjoy your pancakes,' he said with a smile.

Instantly Adriana tossed her darning aside and rose gracefully from the chair. 'You go, Padre?'

He said stiffly, 'Yes. I go.'

She gazed up at him from soulful eyes. 'You return, how you say … soon?'

'That depends.'

'Depends?'

Francis hesitated. 'Michelangelo, explain that it depends on how busy I am in the parish, which is likely to be very busy,' he said, avoiding looking at Adriana directly again and hurrying out.

Michelangelo said something in Italian to Adriana. She jerked her head in Lottie's direction and sat down in front of the fire and took up her mending. He fired a short burst in Italian at her but she ignored him and dug her needle into the fabric.

He turned to Lottie. 'I have heard that many repairs need to be done in this house, furniture and door knobs which are broken or damaged. I will need a bedroom for me and Tonio.'

Lottie said, 'Did Nellie say which bedroom you were to have? There's Grandfather's old room and Great-great-aunt Adelaide's on the first floor. Although Adelaide's is really Nellie's, but there's no bed in there at the moment, so she has the bedroom we sisters shared when we were younger.' She added hastily, 'Babs, my younger sister, is in the land army and will be coming home sooner or later. I suppose she'll have to have Grandfather's room if she wants one to herself. At the moment I sleep downstairs because of my hip … and Lucia.' She indicated her daughter with a fluttering hand. 'I – I didn't want her disturbing Dad while he was home.'

His brow knitted. 'There are no other bed-rooms?'

'There's two rooms in the attic but they're in a bit of a mess.'

'Perhaps Mrs Lachlan wishes me to clear out one of the attic rooms for myself and Tonio?'

Lottie said with an air of helplessness, 'I've no idea. There is a bed up there but it's in pieces.'

'I will have a look.'

'You don't need me to show you, do you? Only my hip's a bit painful today and you should be able to find the attic rooms with no trouble.'

'I will manage,' he said, hoisting a well-worn haversack over his shoulder. 'Come, Tonio, you will watch and learn.' He held down a hand to him and father and son left the room.

Nellie entered the house over an hour later. The kitchen was deserted but something smelled good. Her nose twitched and her mouth watered. Then she heard hammering and, realising the sound was coming from overhead, she hurried upstairs and glanced in her grandfather's old room, but it was empty. She was puzzled when she realised the hammering was coming from the attic. She climbed upstairs and managed to squeeze past the paraphernalia on the landing, and saw Michelangelo doing something to an iron bedstead inside the front bedroom.

The air struck chill when she went inside. 'You've come,' she gasped, attempting to tell herself that her breathlessness was due to her rushing upstairs. 'What are you doing up here?'

'Mrs Lachlan, how pleasant to see you again.' Searching brown eyes took in her appearance. 'You did not say where we were to sleep. It is good that Tonio and I sleep up here. It means you ladies will have your privacy.' He shoved a screwdriver into the breast pocket of his shirt.

Her eyes searched the room, taking in the damp patch in the corner, and she shook her head. 'You don't have to sleep up here. In fact...'

He cocked an eyebrow. 'You would prefer we sleep on the roof?'

Her lips twitched. 'Of course not. You said "we". Where is your son?'

He turned his head and said, 'Tonio, come here, please.'

A small, dark-haired boy stepped out from behind the door. Nellie stared at him and her heart felt as if it was being squeezed. He was beautiful. Tears filled her eyes, thinking of the mother who would never have the joy of rearing such a son. 'He's the image of you,' she said huskily.

'Yes. His name is Antonio but his pet name is Tonio.' He hesitated. 'The padre, he told me about your losing your baby son. I am sorry.'

'Thank you,' she murmured, lowering herself so that her face was level with that of the boy's. 'Hello, Tonio. Welcome to my home.'

He flashed her a shy smile before burying his head against his father's trouser leg. Michelangelo protested, 'Tonio, that is not the way to thank a lady.'

'He gave me a lovely smile,' said Nellie, her expression tender as she straightened up.

'Payment in smiles, you would be happy with this?' he teased.

She laughed. 'Why not? After years of war there were times when I felt I might never smile again.'

His expression sobered. 'Much has happened to make you sad and yet this house it...' His hand painted a circle in the air, 'it is not an unhappy house.'

Nellie nodded. 'Having the children here has changed the atmosphere. Grandfather was miserable after my brother Joe was killed. Then when he died, I felt the house was too big for just Lottie and myself, and could be used for a nursery. You don't mind having to put up with the noise of children while you work?'

He shook his head. 'Of course not.'

'I'm glad.' She changed the subject. 'There is a bedroom downstairs that you and Tonio can have. I'm surprised Lottie didn't tell you.'

'She mentioned several bedrooms but I found what she had to say confusing. When she told me of these attic rooms, I decided to have a look.'

Nellie sighed. 'I understand your confusion. We lost several family members during the war.' She hesitated, 'Has Lottie told you about Lucia?'

'Only that she sleeps in her room. Mrs Callaghan had spoken of a little girl doing so and thought that perhaps she was an orphan.'

Nellie hesitated, not wanting to lie to him, but if she told the exact truth it could get back to their father. 'Lucia is Lottie's daughter but her dad was killed in the war.'

He nodded. 'So many men killed. If there is nothing else you wish me to do up here, I will come downstairs with you.'

'Right,' said Nellie, leading the way.

She took the stairs sedately, aware of the man and boy following her. Life was no longer humdrum and she did not know how she was going to handle the excitement that bubbled inside her when in the company of this man. She was unsure which bedroom would be best for them. Grandfather had slept in a single bed and there was no bed in the room that she still thought of as Adelaide's. She decided it would be more sensible to give him and Tonio the room she was using because of the double bed. She would move into Grandfather's old room, and if Babs should visit while Michelangelo and Tonio were here then the bed in the attic could be moved into Adelaide's old room.

Having worked that out, Nellie explained to him what she intended doing. Immediately, he offered to help her move her things. 'It's mainly clothes,' she said, switching on the light. 'You can carry the statue of the Madonna and Child, if you would. The furniture's pretty much of a muchness, so it's not worth changing that around.'

Clicking on the lamp beside her bed, she turned and saw him hovering in the doorway with Tonio and it took her a moment to realise he was waiting to be invited inside. 'Come in.' She pointed to the Madonna and Child and then, noticing the book next to it, suggested that the boy carry that for her.

As Michelangelo lifted the statue, the photo propped against it fluttered to the floor. He bent and picked it up and glanced at the man in the picture. 'This is your husband?'

'Yes. That's Teddy.'

'The padre said that he was killed in the Desert War.'

'Yes!' She avoided looking at him. 'It seems to me that my brother told you a lot about me.'

'That is because I asked. I wanted to know more about the woman who helped saved my life.'

'Saved your life?' She lifted her head as she pocketed the photograph. 'I'd say that's an exaggeration.'

'That is because you do not know all there is to know about me.'

Before she could ask what he meant by that, he left the bedroom, carrying the statue, with his son trotting at his heels.

Nellie gathered her clothing and shoes, bundling them in her arms, and followed them. She wanted to know more about him but didn't know how she could begin to ask him personal questions.

He held the door open for her. 'If you will give me the bedding, I will make up the bed.'

She looked at him in surprise. 'You will?'

'I have managed such things for myself for several years.'

'When you were abroad during the war? I remember how sunburnt you were when I found you.' She dumped her clothes on the bed.

'I spent some time in India.'

'India! It was 1943 when you turned up wounded; I'm surprised they brought you home instead of sending you to fight in Burma.'

He flushed. 'The tides of war had changed and a large number of us were brought to England.'

She was puzzled but before she dared question him again, Lottie called upstairs to tell them supper was ready.

'We must not let it spoil.' He lifted his son up in his arms and followed her downstairs.

Nellie was in for another surprise when she saw the concoction of pasta and mince in a delicious smelling sauce heaped on plates. She glanced at Adriana, who was wearing a Cheshire cat smile. 'You've cooked for us all?'

'I cook good. You enjoy.'

Amused, Nellie said, 'I bet we have Mr Gianelli to thank for this. They do say the way to a man's heart is through his stomach.' No sooner were the words out than Adriana stiffened. 'What do you mean by the heart and the stomach and Mr Gianelli? Are you suggesting I have my eye on him?'

Her reaction amazed Nellie. 'Your English has improved. He must be a brilliant teacher.'

'*Sciocca!*' Adriana's tone was scornful.

'Translate,' snapped Nellie.

Adriana turned to Michelangelo and said something in Italian.

'What's she saying?' asked Nellie suspiciously.

He hesitated.

'The truth,' demanded Nellie.

'*Sciocca* means idiot. She says your father is mad about her and you would be wise not to forget that.'

Nellie glared at her stepmother. 'Tell her if that is meant as a threat then she'd better think again. Things in this house are not as they seem.'

He looked puzzled. 'What is that supposed to mean?'

She hesitated. 'You don't need to know. Tell her that I want to be her friend. If she feels the same then threatening me is not the right way to go about it. Even so, I'm surprised she understood what I said, although I didn't mean it the way she took it.'

He said carefully, 'It is possible that she already understands more English than your father gave her credit for, but she has not had the confidence to use it.'

'OK. I can accept that. I don't want to make an enemy of her. This house is big enough for all of us if she remembers that we're her family now and this is our home as well.'

He nodded. 'I will tell her that.'

Turning to Adriana he spoke to her first in Italian and then in English. She nodded and wagged her finger at Nellie. 'I no enemy.'

'Good,' said Nellie.

She reached for her cutlery and glanced across the table to see what her sister thought of what had taken place, but Lottie, who had allowed Lucia to stay up late for once, appeared oblivious to what had just happened and was staring at the window with an odd expression on her face. 'What is it?' asked Nellie. 'You look like you've seen a ghost.'

Lottie slowly brought her gaze to focus on Nellie. 'What did you say?'

'It doesn't matter,' said Nellie. 'You and Lucia eat your supper before it gets cold.'

Adriana placed a plate of pasta on the table in front of Michelangelo and a smaller plate for Tonio, who was sitting on his father's knee. 'But before I eat, I will hand over my ration book and show you my identity card, Mrs Lachlan,' said the man.

'You don't have to,' said Nellie, plunging her fork into the pasta. 'If Francis has vouched for you, that's good enough for me.'

'I insist,' said Michelangelo, reaching into a pocket.

Nellie glanced at the identity card. 'Michelangelo Gianelli,' she read.

'Does it make you happy, Mrs Lachlan, to know I belong here?' His dark eyes were intent on her face.

She smiled. 'Yes, Mr Gianelli, it does.'

Nellie spoke the truth, although, it did not really matter to her anymore what his name was: it was the man himself who was making her feel things she had never thought she would experience again.

Chapter Twenty

Nellie breezed into the house, waving a newspaper. She was fit to burst with the news that the Labour government had promised free medical treatment from the beginning of 1948. That was still some way off but it did mean that there was hope of something being done for Lottie. It had never been made clear to them exactly what was causing the pain she endured some days. If they could have afforded doctors' fees, Nellie had always believed something could have been done to ease her sister's suffering.

She pushed open the kitchen door, only to stop short in the doorway. The smell of the distemper he had used on the walls was strong in her nostrils. Michelangelo was over by the sink cleaning brushes and belting out 'Come back to Sorrento' at the top of his voice.

'Have you ever been to Sorrento?' she called.

The singing stopped and he whirled round. He had flecks of distemper in his dark hair and splattered on his face. 'You like this song, Mrs Lachlan?'

She smiled. 'I play the piano and enjoy most music, but I especially like love songs.'

'Ahhh, that is good. Perhaps I will sing one evening and you can accompany me on the piano? Although, I will not sing "Sorrento" because it did not start out as a love song.' His dark eyes twinkled.

'I like the idea of a musical evening but explain what you mean about "Sorrento" not being a love song,' said Nellie, perching on the edge of a chair and gazing up at him.

Michelangelo folded his arms across his chest and leaned against the sink. 'It was written by a fresco painter and dedicated to Italy's prime minister at the beginning of this century. Parts of the city were run down and it was hoped that, having seen the deprivation for himself, he would set in motion plans for improvements. The song urged him to return to Sorrento in better days.'

'And did he?'

Michelangelo shrugged expressively. 'Alas! He died the following year.'

'That's sad.'

'It is life.'

'True.' She gazed at the newly painted walls.

'You think I do a good job?'

She smiled. 'I think you're fishing for compliments. It's great. No runs. Have you done much painting before?'

'When I was young. I am glad it pleases you.' His smiling dark eyes met hers.

She felt the colour rise in her cheeks. 'I'm sure my stepmother and sister have already admired your work,' she said lightly.

'Of course. Mrs Callaghan is in the garden. She wishes to grow the herbs oregano and sweet basil for the Italian cooking. The padre, he bring the plants but only stays long enough for coffee. This does not please her because she believes he hates her for taking his mother's place.'

Nellie protested. '"Hate" is too strong a word. He's a priest and takes his calling seriously. I wish I'd been here. I wanted to speak to him.'

'He wishes to speak to you, too. He suggested you might like to attend Mass at St Joseph's this Sunday and share a meal with him afterwards.'

Nellie's eyes lit up. 'That'll make a change. Where's Lottie and Lucia? Were they invited as well?'

'She refused. After the mothers collect their children, she went out with Lucia.'

Nellie was surprised. Lottie seldom went out in the evening. 'Did she say where she was going?'

'Not to me but perhaps she tell Mrs Callaghan.' He changed the subject. 'The *bambini*, they have been good for you today?'

She presumed by *bambini* he meant children.

'On the whole, although, some of them can be holy terrors. Where's Tonio?'

He grinned. 'I ask myself why is it that Mrs Lachlan asks where my Tonio is after mentioning *holy terrors?*'

Nellie laughed. 'He's an inquisitive little boy, so naturally he gets into mischief sometimes.'

'I am glad you say that because he is in the garden. Hopefully he is not chasing the hens and pulling out their tail feathers.'

'I'm sure he'll think twice about doing that again after getting a peck from the cockerel.' She rose to her feet and put on the kettle. 'Tea? Coffee?'

He shook his head and carried on cleaning the brushes. She gazed at his back, thinking how broad and strong it was and wondered what it would feel like to be held in his arms. The more she saw of him, the more she felt that strong tug of attraction. Occasionally she felt guilty for feeling the way she did, as if her feelings were a betrayal of the love she had felt for Teddy. She was usually sensible, so why was she allowing herself to fall for him? He was the reason why she wanted to speak to Francis. She needed to know a lot more about Michelangelo's background. It was obvious from his having a British identity card and ration book that he was a nationalised British Italian, but she was still puzzled about his being brought back from India in 1943; and what about the family he had gone in search of? Where had his wife lived and when did she die? What about his parents? She decided to chance her arm and ask him about the latter at least.

'Are your parents still alive?'

He did not answer immediately but placed the wet brushes on a sheet of newspaper before turning to face her. 'Poppa was killed in the Great War. Mama was a companion to a rich old lady, a Mrs Simpson. I was brought up in her house. Sadly they were both killed in an automobile accident in 1937.'

'That's sad. Do you have other relatives?'

'I had an aunt and uncle. They lived in Liverpool but were killed in the Blitz ... but this I did not know until the padre told me.'

'So when I found you in the church porch, you'd been looking for them?'

'Yes. But the house was not there, so I search for the church, knowing the padre would help me.' He smiled, showing even teeth. 'And I was right. Now if you will excuse me, Mrs Lachlan, Tonio and I go to visit friends this evening so I must fetch him from the garden and get ready.'

She wanted to ask who his friends were but thought she had pried enough into his private life that evening. She wondered where Lottie had gone and whether she would be out long. It could be that she was visiting the mother who hadn't brought her child to the nursery the last few days, possibly because the father had been demobbed and wanted his wife at home. Nellie could see the numbers dwindling away and Lottie having to close down. Still, their nursery had served its purpose and it had done a lot to bring Lottie out of her shell and give her confidence.

Michelangelo and Tonio entered the kitchen but went straight upstairs. Adriana followed them inside and surprised Nellie by saying, 'Lottie said she and Lucia would not be back until late, so I wonder, would you like to go to the cinema with me?'

Nellie could not conceal her astonishment and, although she would rather have been asked out by Michelangelo, said, 'Thanks. I'd like that. I'll have a look at what's on at the Regal. Do you know where Lottie and Lucia have gone?' she added, reaching for the *Liverpool Echo*.

'She did not say.' Adriana spooned Camp coffee into a cup. 'I have not made supper. I thought maybe you like fish and chips?'

'Fine,' said Nellie, guessing she would be paying for the fish and chips and feeling a tiny spurt of irritation. She ran a finger down the list of cinemas on the front page. 'How about Tyrone Power and Linda Darnell in *Blood and Sand*? I've seen it before but I don't mind seeing it again.'

'It is good?' asked Adriana.

Nellie nodded. 'Rita Heyworth and Anthony Quinn are in it as well. I remember they do this marvellous dance number. I saw it with my husband. He was a good dancer.'

'You must mees him?'

'I do. Although, we spent more time apart than together,' said Nellie.

Adriana's expression was sympathetic. 'That is sad. One day you meet someone else and be happy again, *si?*'

Nellie flushed. 'Perhaps. I'll go and get the fish and chips and change into a frock when I get back.'

Adriana was to surprise her again by paying for the cinema tickets. The film was as good as Nellie remembered and if she shed a few tears at the end, then she was not the only one. They left the cinema with Adriana still dabbing her eyes with a handkerchief. 'I am glad you did not tell me that the handsome Tyrone Power dies.'

'That's Hollywood for you. He sinned by committing adultery, so he had to be seen to be punished.'

'But he had confessed and the lovely Linda Darnell forgave him,' protested Adriana, tossing back her long black hair. 'I thought we would have the happy ending but no, the bull, it keells him.'

'It's only a film,' said Nellie. 'You're English has really improved.'

'Mr Gianelli is a good teacher,' said Adriana.

'He must be. It's come on in leaps and bounds.'

Adriana looked at her with a hint of suspicion in her eyes. 'What does this "leaps and bounds" mean?'

Before Nellie could answer, from behind them came a voice, 'Did you both enjoy the film?'

The women's heads turned and they saw Michelangelo with Tonio astride his father's shoulders. Nellie felt the colour rise in her cheeks. 'I thought you said you were visiting friends.'

'It is true. I am with my friend Salvatore and his wife Teresa.' He indicated the couple at his side.

Nellie noticed Teresa was heavily pregnant and that Salvatore was holding out a hand to her. 'You're Father Francis' sister,' he said. 'Pleased to meetcha! I grew up in St Joseph's parish but my wife and I live in Seaforth now.' He was a tough looking man with a broken nose and a scar on his cheek.

'It's nice to meet you,' she said, shaking his hand.

'I used to work out at Father Francis' boys' club, and now I teach lads boxing at a couple of clubs in Seaforth. I've roped in Mick to help out.'

'That's nice,' said Nellie, hoping Michelangelo wouldn't end up with a broken nose or a cauliflower ear.

Introductions made, the five of them stood apart from the crowd while Adriana asked Teresa when her baby was expected and whether she wanted a boy or a girl. The other woman answered in Italian and Adriana's face lit up. Nellie's attention wandered as the two rattled away in that language. She noticed Tonio's head drooping and mentioned it to his father in a low voice. 'He should be in bed.'

'You are right,' replied Michelangelo.

They said their goodbyes to his friends and returned to the house, where they found Lottie sitting in front of the fire, gazing into the flames. Michelangelo did not linger but took Tonio up to bed.

'You're late in,' said Lottie, glancing up at Nellie. 'Where've you been?'

'The pictures. Where've you been?' Nellie placed a hand on her sister's shoulder.

'Out.'

Nellie smiled. 'Where's out?'

'To see a friend.' Lottie rose from the chair. 'Was it a good film?'

'*Si!* I cry at the end,' sighed Adriana. 'Then Nellie and I meet Mr Gianelli and Tonio outside the cinema and we are introduced to his friends. They both speak a little Italian and Teresa has invited me to dinner on Sunday. Lottie, if you cook that day, I cook on Monday.'

Nellie had been unaware of the invitation. 'I won't be in on Sunday either, Lottie. I'm going to see Francis.'

'I know. Mr Gianelli and Tonio are going to be out as well. He told me this morning.'

Nellie could only presume that he had arranged before that evening to have Sunday lunch with his friends. She hoped there really wasn't anything developing between him and Adriana and, worrying, went upstairs, chiding herself for already being too fond of a man she still knew little about.

Michelangelo was coming out of the bathroom as she reached the top of the stairs. 'Tonio is asleep. I think that perhaps next time I take him with me to the cinema then it will be to see a film more suitable for a four-year-old,' he said ruefully.

'Mickey Mouse or Donald Duck. You could take him to the Tatler in town,' she suggested. 'They only show cartoons and newsreels.'

'That is a good idea. Perhaps you would like to come with us?' There was such warmth in his dark eyes that she could not believe there was anything going on between him and her stepmother. 'I'd enjoy that.'

'Then we will make a date, but first, if you permit, may I call you Elena? And you could call me Michelangelo.'

She loved the way he pronounced her name, presuming it was the Italian version of Helen. 'Why not? I've been thinking for days that Mrs Lachlan and Mr Gianelli sounds so formal.'

His eyes twinkled. '*Si!* Good night, Elena.

403

Sleep well.'

You can guarantee it, thought Nellie.

On Sunday, Nellie left the house early to reach her brother's church in time for the service. She found it intensely moving and when it ended ran out of the church. She hurried not in the direction of the presbytery but towards the main road. The first lines of the Lenten preface repeated itself in her head: *Passer invenit sibi domum, et turtur nidum, ubi reponat pullos suos:* The sparrow hath found herself a house, and the turtle a nest, where she may lay her young ones. She had seen several pregnant women with their husbands in the congregation and had found herself grieving afresh for her dead husband and child.

She wiped her eyes and gazed at a bombed site situated at the end of a row of shops. Amongst the rubble children played and already a haze of green showed where seeds had blown in the wind and taken root. She thought in a few months the purple flowers of fireweed would bring colour to bombed sites throughout the country. She wondered how long it would be before new housing was built to provide homes for the thousands of couples starting families, who were going to have to make do for now with maybe just one room in a parents' house.

'Elena, what are you doing? You are supposed to be having lunch with the padre. He is worried about you.'

Nellie started and looked up at Michelangelo, dressed in a pinstriped suit and wearing a trilby on his dark head. To say that she was surprised to see him was an understatement. 'What are *you* doing here? Where's Tonio?' she asked.

'With the padre. I saw you leave the church.' He removed a handkerchief from his breast pocket and, taking her chin between his fingers, he wiped her damp face with the linen. She was touched by the gesture and a sob broke from her. 'Shush,' he murmured. 'The time for tears is over. You have lost much but there comes a time when we all must look to the future.'

'Why didn't say you were planning on coming here?'

'Because I thought if you knew then you might not come.'

'Why should you think that?'

'Did you not want to question the padre about me?' His dark eyes smiled into hers.

She returned his smile. 'I'm not going to answer that. I know how good he is at keeping secrets. He never did tell me how you came by your injuries. I did wonder if you were a soldier who'd gone AWOL at one time.'

'Close. I was an escaped prisoner of war.'

She could not take her eyes from his face. 'I did wonder about that, too. Escaped from where?'

He hesitated. 'Many Italian immigrants were interned at the beginning of the war because the British government saw them as a threat.'

'I know that. Some went to the Isle of Man. You said you were in India.'

He nodded. 'That is true. Perhaps we talk of this another time. The padre will be waiting for his dinner.' Michelangelo put away his handkerchief and reached for her hand. 'Tell me, Elena, what caused you to train to become a kinder-garten teacher? Did you not believe you would marry one day?'

'I was in no rush to marry.' She was aware of the calluses on the palm of his hand as they crossed the road that was Sunday quiet. 'My parents' marriage was not a happy one and my great-great aunt knew I loved children, so she encouraged me to train for the job. Mam was far from pleased but Francis thought it was a good idea.'

'Your mama listened to him, of course?'

Nellie nodded. 'He was her favourite.'

'So when your father married again a much younger woman, what were your feelings?'

'Shock, horror,' said Nellie. 'I still ask myself why she married him.'

'For security.'

She gave him a sidelong glance. 'Francis gave that as a reason. You sound very sure about it.'

'A young woman marries a much older man, a foreigner, who is away most of the time. A young woman living in Italy, who believes all her brothers dead and saw her own mother taken by the Germans. Naturally she needs security,' he affirmed.

Nellie felt a rush of jealousy. 'She's talked to you about her past?'

'Only yesterday. The padre thought it would be helpful for her to speak of it to someone in her own language.'

'So she's spoken to Francis as well as you?'

'Yes. He is concerned for her but does not want to get too involved. Besides, he says that the Brit-ish have no idea what it is like to live in terror of someone banging on their door at night,' he said softly. 'So much fear that a person could faint away with the strength of the horror. To be dragged from one's home and taken where one does not want to go, knowing most likely one will never return but be tortured, raped or killed.'

Nellie shivered. 'It would be a living nightmare. Poor Adriana.'

'*Si!* Poor Adriana. That is why we must be a friend to her.' His hand tightened on Nellie's. 'Forgive me. I did not mean to upset you. I am glad the Allies won the war but now let us speak of something else.' He asked her whether he should ask Adriana about doing up one of the attic bedrooms. 'Who is to say that there might not be another *bambino* in the house one day?' he said.

'You mean Adriana and Dad?' asked Nellie, not liking that thought at all.

'You have not considered it?'

She shook her head, thinking if Adriana did get pregnant then things would become even more complicated. She suggested that he just went ahead with the room and to give her the bill for the paint and anything else he needed.

He looked at her askance but dropped the subject.

Nellie was quiet at the dinner table, choosing to listen to the men's conversation as they discussed not only the youth of the country whose fathers wouldn't be coming home, but also what the Pope had said about the need for Britain to move more swiftly in repatriating its Italian prisoners of war.

'He says this perhaps because he believes the British are using them for cheap labour,' said Francis' superior. 'He has a point. Despite thousands of our own men being demobbed there will still be a shortage of labour when it comes to rebuilding our country.'

'It could also be because there are soon to be elections in Italy,' said Michelangelo. 'There is a need for true representation from its people.'

'Surely it's possible for Italy to do what our government did last year in the lead-up to the General Election?' said Francis. 'They provided all servicemen abroad with a postal vote.'

Nellie could not resist murmuring, 'Don't forget the women. Their votes count as well. What about Bessie Braddock MP? She's done a lot for the poor in Liverpool.'

'It would be a big mistake to forget the role women played in winning the war and the new society we need to create for justice for all,' said Michelangelo gravely.

'Which reminds me,' said Francis. 'I'm glad you spoke up, Nell, because I want a few words in private with you before you go.'

She nodded and took no part in the rest of the dinner talk, thinking of what Michelangelo had said about being an escaped POW and wondering what her brother was going to discuss with her.

'Well, what did you want to say to me?' she asked once seated in the study.

Francis steepled his hands and rubbed his fingers against his chin. 'The house, Nellie. I think Adriana should know it belongs to you.'

She was astounded. 'Why? I still haven't told Dad yet.'

'She became very emotional last time she was in my company. She said that she feels as if she's a lodger, not the mistress of the house.'

Nellie sat bolt upright. 'She said that to you? She should have come to me.'

Francis reddened. 'I'm sure you can see her point.'

'Yes,' she said through gritted teeth. 'But Adriana should have spoken to me. I've tried to make her feel at home but it's not easy when I'm out working all day and it's me paying the bills. Dad must have given her some money before he left if she can afford to buy Italian food and cinema tickets. She might need security after the lousy time she had in Italy but I need to feel safe just as much as she does. I lost loved ones during the war, too.' Nellie rose to her feet. 'I'll tell her the truth when I get home.'

'No,' Francis said hastily. 'I want your permission to tell her. I can explain how it came about without getting angry and feeling guilty about it.'

'You're saying I feel guilty?' said Nellie, smoothing down her skirt. 'I don't see why I should feel any such thing these days.' She met her brother's gaze squarely. 'You tell her the truth and don't forget to add that I have more right to Grandfather's house than she has if anything should happen to Dad. Bye, Francis. Thanks for the meal. It was lovely.' She walked out of the study before he could say anything more.

'Something has vexed you. Is it something I have said?'

Nellie switched her attention from the busy pavement in Stanley Road to Michelangelo. 'Sorry. No, it isn't. It's something my brother told me.'

'About me?'

She shook her head. 'You didn't come into the conversation. We were talking about my father and stepmother. There's something they both need to know and I'll have to tell him when he comes home and I'm not looking forward to it.'

'Is it that you are thinking of leaving home?'

'No, never! But what I have to say will make him hit the roof.'

'Hit the roof?' His dark eyes were puzzled. 'What does this mean?'

'He'll explode ... be furious.'

'Is it to do with my presence in the house? Mrs Callaghan thinks I should leave before your father returns.'

'That probably would be best,' sighed Nellie. 'When you do, you won't go without saying goodbye, will you?'

'Of course not,' he said gravely. 'But I would hope that it would not be goodbye but only *Arrivederci!*'

Chapter Twenty-One

Nellie woke, blinking at the shaft of sunlight shining through a gap in the curtains. Her heart was pounding. She had been chasing Michelangelo Gianelli along a winding lane and had almost caught up with him when she was seized from behind and dragged backwards and her father's voice hissed in her ear, *'What do you think you're doing falling in love with a wop and giving him my house?'*

She glanced at the clock and shot out of bed. It was Grand National Day, the first since before the war. Not only that but her father was due home any day now. Her spirits plummeted. She wished Michelangelo and Tonio were not leaving but his work was finished here for now and Salvatore and Teresa had offered to put the two of them up for the time being.

She washed and dressed and went downstairs to find Michelangelo in the kitchen making toast. 'You're up early,' she said casually, delighted to see him.

'I wanted to catch you before you left for work.' His gaze rested on her neat figure in green and white. 'You look *chic*.'

'Thank you, kind sir,' she said, her cheeks rosy. 'You don't look so bad yourself.' He was wearing his pinstriped suit and she wondered if he was going for an interview for another job.

'It is a beautiful day,' said Michelangelo. 'As the poet said, "Oh to be in England now that April's here".'

'I must admit it's my favourite time of year and the mini heat wave we're having makes it even better.' She reached for the teapot. 'I suppose in Italy this wouldn't count as warm.'

'It is warm enough for me.' He scraped butter on a couple of slices of toast and handed one to Nellie.

'Thanks. Are you going for a job interview today?'

He nodded. 'Salvatore has recommended me to the owner of an Italian marble company. He says it will be hard work but I'm not afraid of that. I must earn money to support myself and Tonio.'

'I was reading in the *Echo* that there have been demonstrations in Italy against unemployment.'

His eyes darkened. 'I read that too. They are ex-servicemen, who demonstrate also against the high cost of living. There were clashes with the Carabinieri and many people were injured. Two old women Fascists were hanged.' His expression was grim. 'Italy is paying a high price for having allied herself with Germany.'

'Wasn't there trouble before the war between the Communists and the Fascists in Italy?'

He sighed. 'This is true and why I prefer to live in England.'

'I'm glad you're happy here and I'm sorry you're having to move out of this house. We'll all miss you both.'

'But your lives will be so much more peaceful without us,' he said with a twinkle.

'It'll be dull. You must come and see us.'

'Of course. We have yet to take Tonio to the Tatler and we have not had our musical evening.'

Nellie was pleased that he had remembered those suggestions. 'I love a good musical.'

'I too. We will arrange it next time we meet. It will be a treat to look forward to. Now I must waken Tonio and so must say *arrivederci* until the next time.'

Before she could be alerted to his intentions he bent his head and kissed her. She did not resist and the kiss lasted for perhaps half a minute before they drew apart. Neither of them spoke but stared at each other, a question in their eyes. He stroked her cheek with the back of his hand and then kissed her lightly on the lips again before leaving the kitchen.

Nellie could still feel the imprint of his mouth on hers and she felt like singing. She finished her tea and toast and reminded herself that when she returned to the house later that day, it was possible that her father would be here. She didn't know whether her brother had raised the matter of the house with Adriana but, if he had, she was keeping quiet about it. Hopefully she would carry on keeping quiet until Nellie had a chance to speak to her father.

'So who's done this?' asked Bernard, his eyes scanning the kitchen walls and ceiling.

Adriana wagged a finger at him and pouted prettily. 'Do you not read my letters, Bernardo? Francis finds a man to speak Italian. We converse and that is why my English is so much better. He also paint and mend things, so now this house is much brighter. Is it not good?'

Bernard said grudgingly, 'It's not bad and I have to admit your English has improved. We'll have to celebrate by going to a dinner dance at Reece's tonight.'

'You'll be lucky getting in. Unless you've already got a ticket from somewhere,' said Lottie, looking up from the picture book she and Lucia were perusing. 'It's Grand National Day and everywhere will be booked.'

He scowled down at her. 'You don't know that

413

for a fact. Anyway, what's that kid doing here? I thought I told you, I wanted no kids in this house.'

'Nellie and Adriana don't mind children in the house,' said Lottie, not planning on telling her father that Lucia was her daughter right then.

'Well, I bloody do,' he growled.

Adriana said hastily, 'What is this Grand National Day?'

He explained.

'It's a pity we couldn't pick a winner,' she said with a smile.

'Too late,' said Bernard. 'But we can still go out and celebrate. We'll need to get changed.' He rubbed his hands together and his eyes ran rapidly over Adriana's figure in the tight-fitting floral frock. 'Lottie, you can go and get the *Echo*.'

'No,' she said, without looking up. 'I've had a hard day and my hip's killing me.'

'What did you say?' he said, colour flooding his face.

Lottie looked up at him. 'I've had a hard day and my hip's killing me,' she repeated.

He swore. 'You'll bloody do as you're told, girl, or you're out on your ear! You and that bloody kid.' He flicked her cheek with a finger.

It stung, angering Lottie. 'It's not your house!' she blurted.

'What was that you said?' asked Bernard, placing a hand behind his left ear.

Adriana said loudly, 'The nursery will be closing for the Easter holidays soon and while you're home it will move to another place. Is this not so, Lottie?'

414

She nodded.

'You must not get yourself excited, Bernardo. It is not good for the heart,' said Adriana.

'There's nothing wrong with my heart,' he said irritably. 'She has too much to say for herself. If she still wants to carry on living here, then she'd better do what I say.'

Like hell I will, thought Lottie, a cold knot of resentment settling in her chest, but she kept her mouth shut as Adriana ushered Bernard out of the room.

Nellie strolled along the pavement, enjoying the warm breeze and the sight of the spring flowers blooming in the neighbouring gardens.

'Nellie!'

She jumped and glanced around her to see where the voice had come from and spotted Mrs Wainwright waving to her. She was so astounded that she should speak to her that, instead of ignoring the old woman, she obeyed her summons.

'What can I do for you, Mrs Wainwright?'

The old woman grabbed her arm. 'David! You know where he is, don't you?'

'I beg your pardon! I haven't seen him since before Lucia was born. You saw to that.' She wrenched her arm free.

Mrs Wainwright's lips trembled. 'I don't believe you! He's gone off, leaving my sister to fend for herself. She'll be wanting to come here and live with me and I just couldn't cope with that. She's not as sprightly as she used to be and would expect me to wait on her hand and foot.'

'Poor you,' said Nellie with mock sympathy.

'Sorry, I can't help.'

'I don't believe you! You just want to get back at me. Anyway, what's happened to your lodger? It seems fishy to me that he's beetled off just as Bernard arrives home.'

Nellie stared at her coldly. 'I don't see what business it is of yours but Michelangelo finished the work he came to do and left for another job.'

The woman's baby-blue eyes sharpened. 'On first name terms with him, I see. He's a workman! You need to be careful, Nellie, those dark-eyed Mediterranean types can't be trusted.'

'I think you've said enough,' said Nellie. 'Pity you don't imitate the three monkeys I gave you: see no evil, hear no evil, speak no evil.'

She walked away with a sinking heart, knowing that she was going to have to face her father in the next few minutes. The front door was ajar, so she went straight inside but had only just started rehearsing what to say to him when she heard her sisters talking. She pushed open the kitchen door and found them sitting at the table with a heap of coins in front of them.

'Hi, Babs! Where did you spring from? And that money, where did you get it?' asked Nellie.

'I had a couple of days due and one of the other girls suggested we go the races,' said Babs.

A smiling Lottie answered, 'She backed the winner and the horse that came second in the National.'

'Backed them both ways,' said Babs, her eyes dancing as she looked up at Nellie.

'You lucky duck! Good odds were they?'

'The winner came in at twenty-five to one and

416

the second a hundred to one,' said Lottie. 'She's quids in and is taking us the pictures and buying us an oyster supper.'

Nellie let out a whoop. 'I can't believe it!'

'True,' said Babs solemnly. 'I thought I might as well spend some of the money on pleasure. I want to see Deanna Durbin in *Lady on a Train*. The reviewer said it was a screwball murder mystery and she's been allowed to grow up in this one. It should be good.'

Nellie agreed and then remembered her father. 'Mrs Wainwright said Dad was home.'

Babs' expression tightened. 'I'd only been in the house ten minutes when he said they were going out. I don't mind Adriana but she's all he can think about. He was in such a rush to go gallivanting with her that I'd be surprised if we exchanged more than a dozen words. Didn't have time to tell him about my winnings, so I thought *pot on him*.'

'Don't blame you,' said Nellie, sitting at the table opposite Lottie. 'What did he have to say to you?'

'Gave me orders as usual. Swore at me, flicked me in the face and told me he didn't want any kids in the house. He threatened I'd be out of the house on my ear.' A grim smile played round Lottie's mouth. 'I told him that it wasn't his house.'

Nellie gasped, 'You what?'

'Don't worry. He didn't hear me properly. I think he's going deaf in his old age. Adriana jumped in and told him I'd said something else. I wondered if she knew something.'

Nellie rested her chin in her hands. 'Francis told her about my owning the house but it looks to me like she doesn't want Dad to know yet. Was anything said about Michelangelo?'

'Not by name and nothing was said about him staying here.' Lottie's eyes gleamed. 'I wish I'd thought to mention how good-looking the painter and language teacher was. He'd be as jealous as hell, although he'd have no cause to be. It's you Michelangelo fancies, isn't it, Nell?'

'Maybe,' said Nellie casually. 'Anyway, what about the pictures? Where's this Deanna Durbin film on?'

'Town,' said Babs.

'Town!' echoed Lottie in dismay. 'I don't think I'm up to getting into town this evening, my hip's really been giving me gyp and I'd have to wake up Lucia, anyway, and take her with us.'

Nellie's and Babs' faces fell.

Lottie said, 'No need to look like that. You two don't have to stay with me. You go and enjoy yourselves.'

Nellie looked at her youngest sister. 'It's your decision.'

Babs hesitated and then her face brightened. 'I'll tell you what, Lottie. I'll give you the money I would have spent on you and you can use it for whatever you like. What d'you think of that?'

Lottie's face lit up. 'Thanks! I hardly ever have money to spend on myself. You two go and get ready and don't worry about me. I'll enjoy having the house to myself for once.'

Her sisters hugged her and went to get ready.

Nellie washed and changed into a yellow, green

and white patterned frock before giving her chestnut hair a good brush. She would have loved to be dressing up for Michelangelo but it was a while since she had been out with Babs and was looking forward to spending time in her company and seeing the film.

By the time they reached town it was dusk and there appeared to be people everywhere enjoying themselves. They linked arms and set off along Lime Street in the direction of the Futurist cinema, passing the American Bar. It must have been packed inside because people with drinks in their hands had spilled onto the pavement. Amongst them were several Yanks, enjoying a cigarette with their beer. A couple of them wolf-whistled but Nellie pretended not to notice. Babs raised a hand behind her head and fluttered her fingers in their direction.

'You surprise me,' said Nellie.

'Why? I have to accept that Jake's dead and I don't want to remain a spinster all my life. Besides, they mightn't follow us,' said Babs. 'Not with full glasses in their hands.'

'Obviously you haven't seen how fast some men can down a pint of beer, but I admit they'd have to be really keen to follow us into the pictures. Thank God, there isn't a queue. We've probably got the Grand National celebrations to thank for that.' She made to go up the steps but Babs dragged her back.

'If we go in now we'll see the end of the film, and as it's a murder mystery, I don't want to do that or we'll know who-dun-it.'

Nellie sighed. 'Listen, Babs, I've been on my

feet most of the day dealing with kids. I can't be doing with standing outside. Besides, if we stay here, those Yanks might just come and try to get off with us.'

Babs rolled her eyes. 'For God's sake, the way you talk you'd think they were rapists.'

'I'm sure they're not but even so...'

'Not all Americans are after one thing,' said Babs. 'Mine wasn't.'

'You don't know how the pair of you would have gone along if he hadn't gone away,' said Nellie, glancing at the men in the drab green uniform. One winked at her and she thought the other looked vaguely familiar. 'I think we should go and buy the tickets and wait in the foyer for the film to finish,' she added.

Babs scowled and with a toss of her flaming red hair, said, 'I'm never going to get married if I don't go halfway to encouraging a fella.' The words were hardly out of her mouth when the Americans made a move in their direction.

Immediately Nellie said, 'Please yourself. I'm going inside to rest my feet.'

A rebellious Babs stayed outside. One of the airmen backed off but the other taller one came towards her and, on closer inspection, she came to the conclusion they had met before. He had vivid blue eyes and the smell of his chewing gum took her back to an evening of dancing at Burtonwood.

'Hi, doll! How are you doin'?'

'I'm doing fine. How's yourself?' said Babs, fiddling with a strand of hair.

'You don't recognise me, do you?'

'I do. I've forgotten your name, though.'

He grinned. 'Wow! I thought I hadn't made any impact on you at all.'

'We jitterbugged.'

'We sure did. We were good together too.'

'Until Stuart interfered.'

'He sure was mad but he got his comeuppance eventually. Heather's menfolk caught up with him and worked him over.'

Babs experienced a spurt of pleasure. 'I'm glad to hear that.'

'My aim is to please,' he said, sweeping her a bow. 'Name's Pete by the way.'

She held out a hand. 'Babs.'

He claimed her hand and held it firmly. 'You moved away. I heard that your guy ditched in the sea. Shame.'

'Yes.' Babs knew that she would never forget Jake but she could not spend the rest of her days wishing that she had married him. If her sisters had taught her anything, it was that life went on and one had to make the best of things. 'We were just going the pictures to see Deanna Durbin,' she said.

'Good film.'

'You've seen it?'

He nodded. 'But I wouldn't mind seeing it again.'

Babs' smile deepened. 'Perhaps I'll see you inside then.'

'You can count on it. I'll just have a word with my buddy and finish my drink.' With a show of reluctance he freed her hand.

She tripped up the steps and went inside the

cinema, still smiling.

Nellie had been watching Babs through a windowpane and demanded to know what the American had said to her and had she remembered him.

Babs' eyes sparkled with excitement. 'Yes. His name's Pete and we've danced together.' She headed for the ticket kiosk.

'So what's happening?'

'He's finishing his drink and then coming to see the picture.' Babs bought two tickets and handed one to Nellie. 'I hope you don't mind sitting on your own but you'll cramp my style.'

'As long as we go home together,' said Nellie, not wanting to spoil her sister's chances. She noticed Pete approaching and smiled. 'Here he comes. Good luck and see you here afterwards.'

Babs turned to face him. 'Rear stalls?' he asked.

'Yes, but I have my ticket.'

'Golly, a girl that pays her way. I like that,' he joked.

As they walked into the auditorium, she asked how long he had before returning to the States. 'Long enough for us to get to know each other better, Babs.' As they sat down he drew her hand through his arm and began to ask her about herself.

By the time they stood for the National Anthem after the performance, their knowledge of each other had developed rapidly. They both enjoyed dancing, liked Bob Hope and Bing Crosby *Road* movies, hot sunshine, chocolate, chewing gum and growing things. She had told him she'd like a place in the country with a big garden and he told her that he lived in California. During the interval, he had asked her how she felt about kids.

'Four ... two boys, two girls,' said Babs.

'Perfect,' said Pete. 'Pops has his own canning business and I'll be working for him when I get back.'

'Sounds good,' said Babs, crossing her fingers and hoping Pete was Catholic, but decided that question could wait until their next date.

As Nellie waited in the foyer, watching Babs and Pete come towards her, it was obvious from their expressions that they would be seeing each other again. She felt a little sad that her sister's future might be in America but she wanted her to be happy. Babs re-introduced them to each other and Pete suggested that they join him at Gianelli's fish and chips bar in Christian Street.

Nellie started at his mention of the name Gianelli but thought they couldn't be related to Michelangelo or he would have mentioned them. She smiled at Pete. 'Thanks, but we've left our other sister at home alone and I think we'd best skip supper here in town and be on our way.'

'Sure,' he said, obviously trying to hide his disappointment. 'Another time perhaps?'

Nellie nodded and walked on ahead so as to give them time to say goodnight. On the way home she talked about the film and it was obvious from Babs' responses that it had not held all her attention. 'When will Pete be going home?'

'He reckons six weeks.'

'You don't have much time then.'

Babs agreed. 'Don't mention him to Dad. I don't want him coming the heavy father. I know

I'm over twenty-one and I can do what the hell I like but I don't want any hassle from him.'

'I won't breathe a word,' said Nellie.

When they arrived home, there was no sign of anyone in the kitchen. Nellie was making cocoa for them both when Lottie wandered in.

'So did you have a good time?' she asked.

Nellie nodded and Babs told her about Pete. 'Don't mention him to Dad, though.'

'As if I would. Anyway, the pair of them are in bed.'

'Already!' said Babs, surprised.

Lottie nodded. 'I went to bed early but I heard them come in and him staggering upstairs.'

'How d'you know he was staggering?' asked Babs.

'I recognised the sound from when I was a kid.'

Her answer silenced Babs and in that lull, they heard the sound of heavy footsteps descending the stairs. Bernard lurched into the kitchen and almost fell into a chair.

'Hello, Dad,' said Nellie, knowing that now was definitely not the time to tell him about the house.

He gazed bleary-eyed at his daughters. 'Where've you three been until this time of night?'

'Babs and I have been to the pictures,' said Nellie, eyeing him warily. 'I'm surprised you're in before midnight.'

'Everywhere decent was crowded, so we had a few drinks and then came home and went to bed early.' He yawned widely.

'So what have you come down for?' asked Babs.

He scrubbed his face with the back of his hand and stared into space. 'This Gianelli, who did the decorating an – and helped Adriana with her English, I want to get in touch with him to pay him. She said she didn't give him any money. I asked her for his whereabouts but – but I couldn't make sense of what she said.'

'Probably Adriana's brain couldn't cope with translating what she had to say into English because she'd been drinking,' said Nellie casually.

He squinted at her. 'I get what you're saying but I still want answers. This – this Gianelli bloke, what's he like?'

'A good man, a hard worker.'

'Were-were he and Adriana ever alone in the house?'

Nellie shrugged. 'I wouldn't have thought so, not with Lottie and the children here.'

He reached up and prodded a finger in her cheek. 'You've got your answers all pat. They'd be in another room.'

Nellie felt like prodding him back but made do with moving out of his reach. 'Mr Gianelli is a gentleman. He wouldn't carry on with a married woman.'

'You really believe that?'

She nodded. 'I don't think Adriana would betray her marriage vows either.'

'You think?'

'She's your wife, Dad. You should trust her.'

He stared at her and then struggled to his feet and left the room.

The sisters glanced at each other but did not speak just in case their father was listening outside. It was not until they heard the door slam upstairs that Babs said, 'It's started already. He doesn't trust his own wife.'

'He didn't when he left,' murmured Nellie. 'He asked me to spy on her.'

'As if you would,' said Babs.

'As if she could,' said Lottie, getting up. 'I'm going back to bed. Let's hope he'll be sober in the morning.'

'I probably won't see him. I'll have to be up at the crack of dawn to get back to the farm.'

When Nellie entered the kitchen the following morning, to her relief there was no sign of her father. Babs had already left and not bothered to light the fire. Nellie decided she wouldn't either and made do with a slice of bread and jam and a glass of water. She sat at the kitchen table, thinking about Lottie and David. She had forgotten to mention to her about Mrs Wainwright asking about him. On hearing a sound at the door, she turned to see a wan-faced Adriana standing there.

'Without preamble, her stepmother said, 'We've got to talk.'

Nellie noticed a bruise on her cheekbone and her heart sank. 'Did Dad hit you?'

Adriana's eyes smouldered. 'He drink too much and I scold him. Then he accuses me of being unfaithful. I know why this is so because he told me that his first wife was unfaithful.'

Nellie was stunned. 'He told you that?'

Adriana nodded. 'Bernardo is a dull lover but my expectations were not high when I married him. It came as a great surprise to me that he could be so suspicious and jealous but I understand now it was because your mother betrayed him.'

Nellie sprang to her mother's defence. 'You only have his word for it. Mam was religious. She wouldn't break her marriage vows.'

'You would want to believe that but to have a husband who spends so much time away is not easy for a woman.' She smiled wryly. 'But I do not regret marrying Bernardo. It was fate we met.'

'Fate?'

She nodded. 'I would not have met Francis and through him Michelangelo if I had not married Bernardo.'

Nellie's stomach seemed to turn over. 'What are you saying? It sounds like you believe that *you* were meant to meet Michelangelo.'

Adriana's dark eyes gleamed. 'That is the truth. I feel respect and gratitude towards him and that is why I will not tell Bernardo where he is but I have no doubt he will still try to find him.'

'He'll ask Francis.'

Adriana nodded. 'But he will not tell him. Now I have something to give you. I came down earlier and I speak to Babs but when I look in Lottie's room to see if she is OK, she and Lucia are not there.'

'What d'you mean, they're not there?'

'There is a note addressed to you.' Adriana reached into a pocket and withdrew a folded sheet of paper. 'It is as you say in England, an eye-opener.'

Nellie almost snatched the note out of Adriana's hand and unfolded it swiftly.

Dear Nellie,
I will be gone when you read this. I've been keeping

427

something from you. My little secret. David turned up at the house several weeks ago. It was a real shock but I was glad to see him. We had a good talk and I learnt that he didn't know about Lucia being his daughter. They'd whisked him away to some relatives miles away but now he's back. He was so upset but I said that just being upset wouldn't get us far. I told him what he needed was a regular job and us to find somewhere we could be together. I know that won't be easy. We've been writing to each other and now Dad's home, I've decided we should get married. We mightn't be able to be together as a family just yet but at least Lucia won't be illegitimate anymore. I pray that God will forgive me for being so deceitful and that you will, too.

May our Saviour bless you,
Your loving sister, Lottie

Nellie reread the letter and laughter bubbled inside her. She hadn't thought Lottie had it in her. 'You've read this?'

'As much of it as I could understand. I was worried for them both.' Adriana's brown eyes showed no shame. 'Bernardo, he does not know Lucia is his granddaughter. He thinks no man wants Lottie. I, as a woman, knew!' She hit herself on the chest. 'I tell him she run away to be married. I will like doing so. You go and work. If mothers and children come, I say Lottie gone away. *Bambini* have holiday.'

The laughter died in Nellie's face. 'What if Dad loses his temper and hits you again?'

'I will leave.'

'Leave! Is that because you know this house

428

belongs to me? You don't have to go because of that. You're welcome to stay, we can both gang up on Dad.'

Adriana's face softened. 'You are a kind woman, Nellie, but you worry about others too much. I will leave because since coming to England, I learn something that gives me much happiness.' Her sudden smile dazzled Nellie.

'What is it?' she asked.

Adriana placed a finger to her lips. 'I tell you soon. You go to work and not worry.'

Nellie nodded. 'OK! Keep your secret. A warning, though, Adriana, keep Dad away from Mrs Wainwright.'

'Mrs Wainwright?'

'Baby-blue eyes, white hair, looks like butter wouldn't melt in her mouth. You might think she's a sweet old lady but she's a gossip and has told me she thinks it's suspicious Michelangelo left just before Dad arrived.'

'Ahhh! I know the woman you speak of.' Adriana's face hardened. 'She is polite to me but I know she is thinking I have no right to be here. When she speak to me, I pretend not to understand and when I leave her I make the sign of the cross to protect myself from her evil eye.'

Nellie was amused. 'Let's hope it works.'

Later that day, as she washed paintbrushes and pinned up the children's pictures to dry, she wondered what Michelangelo had done for Adriana to make her so happy. Was she being honest when she had said that she felt only respect and gratitude towards him? She thought of her own feelings towards him and tried not to compare them with what she had felt for Teddy: then she had been a starry-eyed romantic and she was a different person now.

When Nellie arrived home that night, it was to find Adriana sitting in an armchair with her eyes closed, smoking a cigarette. To all appearances she was at ease, but Nellie took one look at her father standing over by the fireplace and knew that it had to be an act. He was fiddling with the jar of spills used to get a light from the fire, and his hand was shaking.

'What's going on?' asked Nellie.

'I'm waiting for your stepmother to tell me where that impostor is!'

'What impostor?' asked Nellie.

'The Eyetie who supposedly taught her English,' snarled Bernard.

His wife opened her eyes and fixed him with a stare. 'You tell me you see the Gianelli brothers in their fish and chip shop. They tell you their cousin Michelangelo Gianelli killed in Blitz, so you think one who worked here is impostor. If true, what does it matter? We not pay him, so we lose nothing.' She gesticulated with her hands, causing the cigarette smoke to spiral jerkily upwards.

'I don't believe it,' said Nellie.

Bernard ignored her and thumped the mantelpiece with his fists, causing several spills to drop onto the hearth. 'Maybe he's someone you knew back in Italy and he's followed you over here!'

Adriana's mouth tightened. 'It not true. He was a stranger to me. Francis introduce us. Speak to him if you wish to know more.'

Bernard drew in his breath with a hiss. 'Who do

430

you think I bloody asked? He's out to cause trouble between the pair of us. He was always Carmel's favourite and is furious because I've put you in his mother's place. Every time I came home from sea he resented my being in the house and that's why he sent that Eyetie here. He doesn't approve of my having married you.'

Adriana gazed at him incredulously. 'How you think this of your own son? A priest! A holy man! I think it is you who resent him because your first wife loved him.' She jumped up from the chair and stalked out of the kitchen.

Bernard turned on Nellie. 'Tell me the truth! What the bloody hell was going on between Adriana and this impostor?'

'I don't know.'

Anger twisted Bernard's face. 'You're in it, too. You and Francis were always close. Neither of you could see what your mother was. She was a tart, plain and simple. I couldn't have been Lottie's father, the months didn't add up.'

'What?' Nellie stared at him, scarcely able to take in what he had just said. 'You can't believe Mam really had another man?'

'Of course she had another man. I only wish I bloody knew who he was,' he rasped. 'I tell you, the months didn't add up.'

Nellie began to doubt her mother herself. 'Perhaps you should have asked Mam why she needed to find affection elsewhere. You were never there, Dad, for any of us.'

He caught her a stinging blow on the ear. 'How dare you say that? I had to work, didn't I?'

She put a hand to her ear. 'Yes, but you weren't

431

there for us even when you were home.'

He loomed over her and she thought he was going to strike her again. Stretching out a hand, she grabbed a fork from the table and held it in front of her. 'Try it!'

He glared at her and then walked out. She dropped the fork on the table and took a deep breath. There was the sound of hurrying feet on the stairs and the next moment her stepmother entered the kitchen. 'Where is he?' she asked.

'Gone.' Nellie felt her throbbing ear gingerly.

Adriana's face softened and she dragged a clean tea towel from the drying rack and dampened a corner of it. 'You are brave, Nellie.' She pressed the wet material against her ear. 'You miss your mama?'

'Yes. I only wish we could have made up our quarrel before she died.'

'I, too, miss my mama. She sacrifice her life for me. She say, "Run, run, my angel". I do not wish to leave her but she push me away. So I run and hide. I see the German soldiers capture her and it hurt me here what they do to her.' Adriana placed a hand in the vicinity of her heart and tears filled her eyes. 'I never see her alive again but when a German do bad things to me, I stick a knife between his ribs and kill him for my mama. Then I run again.'

Nellie wondered if she had misheard her. 'You killed a Jerry?'

Adriana's dark eyes glinted. 'It not easy to kill someone but is lot easier when they not expect it.'

Nellie knew that she'd find it almost impossible

to kill anyone. 'What happened next?'

'The Americans come, have food and chocolate. It is good to be free of the oppressors. I learn a leetle English and then I meet your father. I think his liking me so much is good. I would like to escape the – the misery in my country, so I marry him. I not know Michelangelo before but he is a good man, believe me.'

Nellie wanted to believe her and have faith in Michelangelo. 'Dad says he's deceived us.'

Adriana hesitated. 'You need to know the truth. You – you must speak to him. I see him, tell him what happen and you meet.'

Nellie wondered why Adriana could not give her Salvatore and Teresa's address so that she could go there herself, but agreed to her stepmother's plan.

Chapter Twenty-Two

Bernard did not return to the house until after Nellie was in bed and the next day, Saturday, the house was empty when she returned from the nursery. Jimmy and Irene Miller surprised her by appearing on her doorstep, so Nellie got them to help her plant seeds. Jimmy told her that his uncle and new aunt had been to visit them last week and this afternoon Sgt McElroy had dropped in to see them. 'He told me about the boys' club at Our Lady, Star of the Sea, and said I might like to join. They do different things for different ages.'

'Sounds fun,' she said.

Later, when she saw them over the lift bridge and across the main road, she wondered if the church boys' club was one of those Michelangelo and Salvatore were involved in.

Nellie was to be proved right when she arrived back home to find Adriana in the back garden, smoking a cigarette. 'Where's Dad?' asked Nellie.

'He says he get in touch with the police,' she said in a low voice. 'I am angry with him but I could not stop him.'

'He's a fool,' said Nellie angrily. 'What good will that do?'

'He was drinking and will not listen.' She scowled.

'Did you get in touch with Michelangelo?'

Adriana nodded and dropped her cigarette stub on the soil. She glanced in the direction of the neighbouring garden. 'We go inside. Even trees might have ears and I don't want anyone else knowing about my brother.'

Nellie stared at her in amazement. 'Your brother? I thought all your brothers were killed in the Desert War.'

Adriana's dark eyes glistened with tears but she did not speak until they were inside the house. 'Not Alphonso. I have seen him. He went missing. This Mama and I knew but we not know he found by the British and made prisoner of war and shipped to India. We believed him to be dead but no, he blind for a while and very sick. By the time they discover who he is and he manage to-to write to Mama, it was too late.'

'I see ... but how ... what has Michelangelo to do with this? Oh, I see, or I think I do.' Nellie's head was buzzing. 'He went to India.'

Adriana nodded. 'I say only a little more and leave the rest for him to tell you. I did not know im-immediately the truth about Michelangelo. It was only when I talk to Francis about my-my grief and anger, my brothers and mother and I confess the b-ee-g sin I committed, that I discover Michelangelo was a prisoner of war in India. He asks my family name and Michelangelo recognises that of Alphonso. It seems like a miracle to me that he should do this out of lots and lots of names but then he explain. His English is so good, unlike most Italian prisoners, that he act as an interpreter.'

'Stop right there,' said Nellie, holding up a hand. 'What do you mean *unlike most Italian prisoners?*'

Adriana sighed. 'That is what he was and when Alphonso very ill, he speaks to him and the doctor and that is how he remembers him.'

'It's wonderful for you,' said Nellie, trying to take in that Michelangelo had been a different kind of Italian prisoner of war to the one she had believed him to be. 'So what happened next?'

'Italy signs the...' she paused as if searching the right word in English, 'ar-armistice and those in India are asked if they like to go to Britain and help with the war effort. Many want to do this, and so Michelangelo and Alphonso come to England but they are put in separate camps.' Adriana sighs. 'Do you know, Nellie, how many POW camps there are in Britain?'

Nellie shook her head. 'Fifty, maybe.'

'More than a hundred and fifty. But Michel-

435

angelo, he write to my brother. Alphonso being so young when captured, only eighteen, and so ill, Michelangelo had compassion for him.' Adriana gave a beauteous smile. 'I meet my brother and we are so happy to find each other.'

Nellie imagined how she would feel if Joe had not been killed but only missing and then found like the lost sheep in the Bible. 'I'm so pleased for you, Adriana,' she said sincerely. 'Have you told Dad about this?'

Adriana frowned. 'You know Bernardo's jealous heart. It will not please him that Alphonso is alive, so I stay silent. It is possible that soon Alphonso will repatriated but that means we will be separated again and we do not want that to happen.' She fell silent.

Nellie stared at her worried face and instantly guessed why she was so concerned about Bernard getting in touch with the police. 'I'd like to see Michelangelo!'

'Of course. He sent a message asking if you could meet him this evening at Our Lady, Star of the Sea. He helps with the younger boys at the church club but at seven he will be free. He will wait in the church. You know where this church is?' asked Adriana.

'Yes,' said Nellie firmly, 'and I'll be there.'

Nellie dipped a finger in the bowl of holy water and crossed herself before slipping into a rear pew and kneeling down. She prayed for Michelangelo and Tonio, Adriana and her brother, Lottie, Lucia and David, Babs and Pete, Francis and herself. She even tagged on a reluctant prayer for her father and Mrs Wainwright and her sister before rising and going over to the statue of Our Lady, Star of the Sea. She smiled up at the calm face and touched the painted blue gown before reciting the Hail Mary.

She waited, staring dreamily into space and knowing she looked her best, having enjoyed dolling herself up for this meeting. The frock she wore was primrose yellow cotton scattered with white daisies, its bodice buttoned up the front and its waist was fitted and the skirt fluttered just above her knees. White sandals, white gloves and a matching handbag completed her outfit. She wished that she'd had time to give her chestnut hair a bit of a curl but had made do with tying it back with a yellow ribbon.

She did not have long to wait before Michelangelo made an appearance. The expression in his eyes caused the colour to flood her face. '*Bella*,' he said, taking her hand and lifting it to his lips.

She guessed that was a compliment and, trying to keep her voice light, said, 'Nice of you to say so.' Her fingers quivered in his grasp. 'Now I'd like you to tell me why you deceived me.'

Immediately he looked grave and his hand slid down her arm and caught her fingers. 'It is a complicated story.'

'I'm all ears. First of all, what is your real name?'

'My baptismal name *is* Michelangelo but my family name is Riccio.'

She was glad that she would not have to begin thinking of him by another name. 'Tell me more?'

'That is my intention. But first, if you are not too tired, perhaps you would like to walk as far as Cremola's Corner for an ice-cream?'

'Sounds good to me,' she said brightly.

They began to walk in the direction of the Mersey. 'Explain how you became Michelangelo Gianelli?'

'The padre found the ration book and identity card on the offertory plate. He presumed they had been stolen because he knew that he had buried the owner. So the padre puts them away in a drawer, intending to hand them over to the authorities, but forgets.'

Nellie burst out, 'I remember now his telling me of an Italian couple who had lost their son. He had been imprisoned at the beginning of the war but then released. So Francis remembered them when you turned up and told him your story. Which was?' She fixed him with a stare.

'Some of it you already know from Adriana's lips.'

'I still want to hear it from you.'

He took a deep breath. 'Mama was English but married an Italian.'

'So you're half-English?'

'Yes. My father was killed in the Great War and she died, as I said, in an automobile accident. I joined the navy when I was seventeen. The war broke out while I was at sea. I did not want to fight the English because of my mother but I had no choice.' He sighed. 'Later my ship was torpedoed in the Mediterranean and I was rescued and taken prisoner and shipped to India. I was in company with thousands of others and

438

was to spend almost three and a half years in the Bengal. When Italy capitulated, we were asked if we wanted to help the Allies in the final defeat of Germany. Of course, I jumped at the chance of coming to England. I had a wife and I was determined to escape. I do so but I have to cross the English countryside in winter and I fall climbing over a fence. I thought that if I could reach my aunt and uncle in Liverpool, then they might help me to get on a ship sailing for Italy. I was desperate to discover what had happened to my wife who was expecting our first child.'

Nellie gasped. 'So when you disappeared you went to Italy?'

He nodded. 'The padre, he arranged it.'

She said wryly, 'Francis really knows how to keep a secret. Wasn't it dangerous?'

He shrugged. 'It is true that I had no illusions what the Germans would do to their former allies once the Armistice was signed, but I still felt I had to find Maria. It was not easy. Eventually I discovered that she had died of a fever and my son had been placed in an orphanage.'

She squeezed his arm gently, guessing how he most have felt. 'Were the conditions bad in the orphanage?'

He nodded. 'I did not find Tonio immediately and am sick with anxiety. By then the German soldiers were wreaking a terrible revenge on Italy. The orphanage was bombed and if it had not been for the nuns, I might have lost my son. But I will not dwell on those times. I find him and he looked like what my mother used to say of an underfed child, a skinned rabbit. So I take him

439

and feed him. I hide him inside my greatcoat and I bring him to England.'

'Did you go by the name of Michelangelo Gianelli when you were on the ship?'

'Yes. I took on his identity. The war, it is over and a small boy is not so difficult to smuggle aboard a ship and keep in a cabin. When I reach Liverpool, I go to the padre. He is willing to help me again, despite I am officially an escaped POW and my son is in England illegally.' He paused. 'My mother, she often talked of England and so, although I miss the sun and the sea, the food and wine, I want to stay in her country.' His face softened. 'Besides, I remember a woman with hair like a polished chestnut and blue-green eyes, who was kind to me and who had suffered herself. I hope maybe we can help each other forget the past.'

Nellie was moved. 'I suppose you didn't tell me the truth immediately because my husband was killed fighting the Italians?'

'This is true. But also I am still an escaped POW and wanted by the police. If I was to give myself up to the authorities, I could be sent back to Italy.'

'But surely you'd be able to return to England?' she said earnestly.

'I could apply to return here but Italian bureaucracy being what it is we could be parted for years.' His eyes darkened. 'I have strong feelings for you, Elena, and I fear if I was to leave England I might never see you again.' He drew her into his arms and, despite their being in full view of passers-by, he kissed her.

She enjoyed the kiss and when it ended she

remained in his arms with her head resting on his shoulder. 'That was nice,' she murmured.

'Only nice?' he mocked.

She smiled. 'More than nice, then.'

'I enjoy kissing you very much.'

With obvious reluctance he released her and she slipped her hand through his arm. 'So what are we going to do?'

'I have a new job. I will work hard and save money and then I will ask you to marry me,' he said. 'Perhaps, by then, I will be allowed to stay in England.'

Nellie had a better idea but did not voice it, guessing that his pride might cause him to turn it down out of hand. Besides, she had to sort out her father first, because she had no intention of waiting for years to marry Michelangelo. 'Adriana said that Dad decided to visit the police, so you're best keeping your head down until he goes back to sea.' She hesitated before adding, 'and the same goes for Alphonso if he's not gone back to his POW camp.'

'Adriana has told you about Alphonso?'

She nodded. 'But she's not telling Dad because she's already got him sussed out.'

'Sussed out?'

'She knows the way his mind works. He's a very jealous man.'

He frowned. 'I cannot understand your father. He has a young Italian wife and three lovely daughters and a son to be proud of! He should be happy for Adriana that she has found her brother. Why does he have to be like this?'

Nellie could have told him what Bernard had

441

said about her mother as a way of an explanation, but surely there was more to her father being the way he was than that. 'I doubt Dad's ever been a happy person. It's just the way he is.'

'It is a pity.'

She agreed.

The Seaforth Naval Hospital came in sight and they turned onto the main road heading in the direction of Waterloo. 'How is Tonio? As soon as Dad leaves you must bring him to the house. Now Lottie's left, we won't have the nursery, but Jimmy and Irene Miller sometimes come and see me and he could play with them.'

'A Jimmy Miller came into the club this evening. He seems a nice boy.'

Nellie smiled. 'He's improved a lot since he was a four-year-old.'

She talked about when she first saw him and of the first months after she had lost her baby and Teddy had been killed.

'You are a strong woman, Elena. I admire you greatly,' he said.

She blushed. 'Shucks! I had to pull myself together. There was Lottie and Grandfather needing me.'

At last they arrived at Cremola's. The waitress seemed to know Michelangelo and in no time at all, dishes of ice-cream were placed in front of them. 'I sometimes bring Tonio here,' he said, dipping his spoon into the confectionary.

'I thought you might, the way that waitress smiled at you.' She spooned ice-cream into her mouth and winked at him.

'I would like to kiss you right now,' he whispered. 'Your lips would be cold and creamy, real tasty.'

Nellie giggled. She felt slightly naughty and young all over again. 'You shouldn't say such things.'

His mouth made a moue. 'OK! I will give all my attention to the ice-cream. What do you think of it?'

She spooned some into her mouth and let it trickle slowly down her throat. She remembered buying ice-cream from an old Italian who used to sell it from a cart down by the Pierhead in the Thirties. 'Lovely, but not as...'

He leaned towards her and said in a conspiratorial whisper, 'good as that which you remember eating as a young girl.'

'You're a mind reader. Tell me more about yourself and where you come from.'

'I was born in Castellammare di Stabia, a seaside town, which is situated opposite Vesuvius in the bay of Naples, about ten miles from Sorrento.'

Her eyes widened. 'So you lived opposite a live volcano. Didn't it ever worry you?'

He shrugged expressively. 'One becomes accustomed. It is thousands of years since 'Stabia was buried, along with Pompeii and Herculaneum, by the eruption of Vesuvius. It is famous for many things and many ships sail from there to America and England. Before the Great War visitors come from Britain to see the glorious scenery, its cathedral and archaeological sites. Some came to visit the spas, to drink the waters. Mama was a companion maid to a rich, widowed lady from Liverpool and she meets Poppa down by the harbour because he worked in the shipyard.'

Nellie was enchanted. 'Tell me more about your parents.'

'They did not consider marrying each other at first but the rich lady decides that the climate is to her taste and decides to stay. She rents a villa and so Mama and Poppa they get to know each other better and wish to marry, but the rich lady will not give her permission unless Poppa works for her. So he leaves the shipyard and becomes her servant, doing what is needed. The war comes and he goes off to fight and is killed. Fortunately, Mama is expecting me. She often say I am her little miracle because she did not want to live after Poppa died.'

Nellie sighed. 'It's a sad story. But it was good that the old lady took your father on and they were able to get married.'

'She saw to it so that I had a good education and I do lots of sports, javelin, discus and basketball. I win medals for the women in my life.'

'Was your wife from the same area?'

Michelangelo shook his head. 'I met her in Sorrento but she was from Caiazzo, a small town further south. We have ... what you say ... a whirlwind romance, get married in her church in Caiazzo and I return to my ship. She remains there with her grandmother. Like myself, her parents are dead and she has no family except for the old woman. Unfortunately, the Germans committed many atrocities in Caiazzo as they retreated before the Allied invasion and Maria's grandmother was killed.'

'So much sadness,' said Nellie softly. 'It's strange how some families seem to suffer more than others.' She glanced at the clock on the wall and realised that it was time she was going home.

'I will walk with you,' said Michelangelo, helping her to her feet.

'Only so far. I don't want you bumping into Dad,' she said. 'Now tell me about the new job?'

'I think I will like working with marble and doing tiling. It is creative and I am told that sometimes we do work on the liners. I will find that interesting.'

'You wouldn't go back to sea?'

'No. I would not like to leave Tonio or be away from you.'

It was the answer she needed.

When they reached the corner of Litherland Park, Nellie insisted that he leave her there. Michelangelo shook his head. 'I do not fear your father.'

'I'm sure you don't but I'd still rather that you didn't meet yet. I've still something to say to him that he's not going to like.'

'OK. But we will see each other soon? Perhaps we go and see a film?'

She nodded. 'How about Wednesday? I'll meet you outside the library at eight o'clock and we can decide where to go.'

He nodded and they kissed goodnight.

Chapter Twenty-Three

Nellie was singing 'Look for the Silver Lining' as she entered the house the following Wednesday evening. She had three quarters of a hour to get ready and be at the library to meet Michelangelo. She had seen nothing of her father and Adriana in the past few days and wondered what they were up to. She was going to have to face her father before he went back to sea but when would that be? She entered the kitchen and immediately the song died on her lips.

Bernard was standing in front of the fireplace, drumming his fingers on the mantelpiece. His hand stilled when he saw her and his expression darkened. 'So you know nothing, do you? Why didn't you bloody tell me that impostor was living under my roof while I was away? If that wasn't bad enough, the old bitch told me that she saw Adriana kissing him on the doorstep only two days ago.'

Nellie could only presume that Mrs Wainwright's resentment towards Lottie and herself had caused the woman to say such things. 'Where's Adriana?'

'Is that all you've bloody got to say?' he roared. 'I expected to find her here waiting for me but she's probably bloody gone off with him.'

Before Nellie could tell him how wrong he was, the washroom door opened and Adriana entered.

She was smiling but then she spotted her husband and her smile faded. Nellie waited for the explosion but before Bernard could open his mouth Adriana said brightly, 'Happy news, Bernardo, you are going to be a Poppa again.'

For a moment no one spoke and then Bernard moved swiftly. 'You whore!' he yelled, and hit her.

The blow sent her flying and Nellie went to her aid, falling on her knees and putting both arms round her. But her father was not finished. He seized his daughter by the hair and attempted to separate the two women. Both screamed and Nellie tried to ward him off with one hand but he managed to get in a couple of blows to her face. 'Stop it, Dad, stop it!' she cried.

'Don't you tell me what to do. I'll beat that baby out of her,' he snarled. 'I should have seen from the start that she was just like your mother.'

'Let go of my hair,' said Nellie. Unable to prise his fingers apart, she resorted to sinking her teeth into the back of his hand.

He swore and let go of her hair, nursing his hand.

Both women managed to scramble to their feet and backed away from him. Adriana reached for the bread knife and held it in front of her and Nellie pulled open a drawer and took out the rolling pin. Bernard stood there, his chest heaving, staring at the pair of them. Then he turned and stormed out of the kitchen. They heard the front door slam and sagged with relief.

'Where d'you think he'll go?' asked Nellie.

'To get drunk,' said Adriana.

Nellie realised that if he went to the Red Lion

and drank outside, as men did sometimes on a warm evening, he might see her meeting Michelangelo and realise who he was. 'I'll have to go out.'

'Where are you going?' asked Adriana, massaging her swollen cheek.

Nellie explained. 'I need Salvatore's address.'

Adriana told her and added, 'I will not stay here alone. I will go and tell Francis what has happened. He must speak to Bernardo.'

Nellie did not argue but headed for the front door with Adriana hot on her heels. Nellie told her what her father had said just before Adriana had come in. Her stepmother shook her head in disgust. 'It was Alphonso. He risk coming to see me here and I insist he must not do so again until Bernardo is back at sea.'

'It was your saying you were having a baby that did it with Dad.'

'It is his baby. I have not cheated on him.'

Nellie was glad to hear it and nothing more was said because they had reached the bus stop where they parted. She decided to take a shortcut to Salvatore's house, praying Michelangelo would not have left early for their date. She crossed the canal by the footbridge and followed a dirt path to Beach Road and past Lewis' clothing factory to another path that skirted the allotments. It was not a shortcut she would care to take on a wet and windy night because it was low-lying and given to flooding, but this evening was dry. She came to Sandy Road and ran up the street where Salvatore's house was situated. Her heart was beating with heavy thick strokes by the time she knocked on the door of the terraced house. To her relief it was opened by Michelangelo who was changed ready for their date. She saw the start of pleasurable surprise in his eyes and then shock.

'What are you doing here? What has happened to your face?' He reached out a hand and drew her towards him and ran gentle fingers over the bruising on her chin and cheek.

'It was Dad! I must talk to you,' she said urgently.

A spark of anger lit his eyes and he placed his arm around her. 'We will go into the parlour.' He ushered her into the tiny front room and sat her down on a sofa. 'Tell me everything before I go and find him and beat him into pulp.'

Right at that moment Nellie would have enjoyed seeing her father beaten into pulp but she knew that violence was not the right way to handle the situation. 'No! There are other ways of dealing with my father and it wasn't only me who suffered but Adriana too.'

'Was this to do with me?'

Nellie slipped her hand into his and held it tightly. 'Yes. Mrs Wainwright told him that you stayed at the house and that she saw you kissing Adriana. Of course, I knew it wasn't you because you wouldn't behave in such a way, but then Adriana told me it was Alphonso.'

Michelangelo swore softly in Italian. 'Once he hears that your father has hurt his sister, then he will be determined to confront him. We must stop him.'

'Adriana has gone to see Francis. She wants him to reason with Dad. I think she's wasting her

449

time. He's beyond reasoning and he's going to be worse once I tell him something I should have told him ages ago.'

His dark eyes were intent on her anxious face. 'What is this something that worries you so?'

She hesitated. 'It's the house. Grandfather left it to me instead of Dad. I looked after him and I suppose it was his way of saying thank you.'

Michelangelo looked stunned and then he nodded his head slowly. 'It will be a big disappointment for your father but perhaps your grandfather knew him better than you realised. Now I must ask you why did you not tell me of this wonderful news earlier? Is it that you thought I might want to marry you for your property?'

She said, 'It never occurred to me. I didn't tell you straight away because I thought your pride might get in the way of you marrying me sooner. You sounded so keen on supporting Tonio and me.'

He laughed. 'I am not that proud, Elena. One of my big concerns was where we would live. I would be a fool not to be relieved of that worry.'

'That's a relief,' she said, planting a kiss on his mouth.

He held her tightly and returned her kiss before saying, 'I cannot remain in hiding now. I will not have your father hurting you.'

She took a deep breath. 'Then you'd best come home with me. If Adriana persuades Francis to return with her this evening then, hopefully, Dad will have second thoughts before resorting to violence again.'

'I hope so. It is not good that I might have to hit

the father of the woman I wish to marry.' He drew her to her feet. 'I will tell Salvatore and Teresa where I am going. It is best you wait outside, otherwise they will keep you talking and we'll be delayed.'

When Nellie and Michelangelo arrived at the house, it was to discover Lottie in the kitchen with Lucia asleep on her knee and the wireless playing dance music.

'You're back! I didn't think I'd be seeing you so soon,' said Nellie.

'I told you me and David and Lucia wouldn't be able to live as a family just yet. Francis married us by special licence and...'

'He what!'

Lottie flushed. 'I would have liked you there, Nell, but I wanted the knot tied as soon as possible.'

'So where's David now?'

'With his mother. I've been to see her and we've had a talk. I've told her she has twenty-four hours to decide whether she wants to be friends. If she does then I'm prepared to move in there and look after her, so she can enjoy Lucia's company.'

Nellie shook her head in disbelief. 'You astound me. I never thought you had it in you to make so many decisions yourself.'

Lottie smiled. 'You helped me to do that, Nell. Anyway, where's misery guts and Adriana? And what's Michelangelo doing here?'

Nellie explained while she put on the kettle.

It was Lottie's turn to look amazed. 'I wouldn't have believed so much could happen in such a short time.'

451

'Well, it has, and as soon as Dad returns, I'll be having words with him.' She wondered whether she should tell Lottie what their father had said about her not being his daughter, but her sister said, 'Have you eaten, Nellie? I'm starving and there doesn't seem much in the larder.'

Nellie remembered she hadn't had anything to eat. 'I am hungry.'

'What about an omelette,' said Michelangelo. 'I make good omelettes. The hens, they are laying?'

Nellie said ruefully, 'I've no idea. I haven't seen to them this evening.'

'It is getting dark so I'll go and have a look,' he said cheerfully.

He had scarcely left the kitchen when Lottie said, 'I'm really glad to see the two of you together.'

Nellie nodded. 'I never thought I'd feel this way again, but I'm glad I do.'

'It seems that things are coming right for us at last, Nell,' said Lottie.

Nellie crossed her fingers. 'I hope so.'

A silence fell and Lottie closed her eyes. Nellie decided to leave mother and daughter to rest and went outside. Immediately she heard voices and realised they were coming from over the fence.

'Here he is, Sgt McElroy, and don't listen to any excuses from him,' shrilled Mrs Wainwright. 'He's up to no good, snooping round the garden.'

'Just you hang on. You've had me out on wild goose chases before,' said the sergeant.

'Nobody's snooping in my garden,' said Nellie, realising Mrs Wainwright must have spotted Michelangelo. She looked to see where he was but he wasn't in sight.

'Where did you pop up from, Nellie? I thought you'd gone out with your stepmother and the house was empty,' called the old woman.

'Well, I'm back now, Lottie's here and everything's fine,' said Nellie.

'I definitely saw a man,' sniffed Mrs Wainwright.

'It'll have been Dad.'

'No. I saw him go out a while ago, too. He looked in a temper and who can blame him with all the carrying on in your house.'

'What goes on in this house has nothing to do with you! You made that clear when you and your sister got David out of the way. Instead, you should have stood by the pair of them and done what you could to help,' said Nellie fiercely.

'Never mind that,' said Mrs Wainwright, sounding flustered. 'I was thinking about your lodger and Bernard finding kids in the house when he arrived home.'

'Were you? You surprise me.' Nellie's sarcasm was plain.

'Now, now, Mrs Wainwright, Nellie and Lottie have done wonders for the youngsters,' said Sgt McElroy. 'My friend, Mrs Miller, has told me all about it.' The policeman rested his elbows on the fence and smiled down at Nellie. 'How is Lottie and her little girl?'

'They're fine,' said Nellie bristling, remembering what Mrs Wainwright had told her father. 'In fact, Lottie got married the other day to Lucia's father, David.'

She heard a strangled noise and guessed it was Mrs Wainwright. 'Well, well, that is good news,' said Sgt McElroy.

'What's good news?' said a voice to Nellie's rear.

She almost leapt out of her skin and whirled round to see her father standing with his hand against the wall of the house. How long had he been there?

Bernard squinted at her and then looked up at the bobby leaning on the fence. 'Here! I want a word with you about aliens,' he shouted.

Nellie prayed that wherever he was hiding, Michelangelo would not choose this moment to make an appearance. The sergeant said heavily, 'You want me to come over there, Mr Callaghan?'

'Aye, I do. Inside the house.' He staggered over to the outside lavatory and went inside.

'I'll see you in a few minutes then, Nellie,' said Sgt McElroy.

Oh God, thought Nellie, wondering where Michelangelo was. Now was hardly the time for him to face her father.

'Well, I wonder how that meeting will go. He was in love with your mother, you know,' said Mrs Wainwright's disembodied voice, taking Nellie utterly by surprise. 'And his feelings were reciprocated. They were the talk of the neighbourhood.'

Nellie's stomach did a somersault and she hoped her father had not heard that. 'Why don't you go inside before you cut yourself on your own tongue, Mrs Wainwright,' suggested Nellie.

'Not polite, Nellie. Is my nephew inside your house?'

'No. He's at his mother's. You'll be pleased to

hear that Lottie and Lucia might go and live there. Goodnight, Mrs Wainwright.'

'What did you say, Nellie?' cried the old woman.

'I think you heard me,' said Nellie.

She glanced about her, still wondering where Michelangelo had gone.

The lavatory door opened and Bernard staggered outside. 'Where is he?'

'Where's who?' Nellie crossed her fingers.

'The scuffer. I'm going to tell him about that bloody impostor.'

'He's coming round the back, Dad. You go on ahead inside the house. I need to shut the hens in.'

'Naw, leave them. Come over here and lend me your arm.'

She hesitated, wondering if the drink had caused him to forget what had happened earlier that evening, and then decided she should be safe enough inside the house once Sgt McElroy arrived.

As they headed for the washroom, Nellie noticed out of the corner of her eyes that the outhouse door was open. Her heart began to thump and she forced herself not to look round as she helped her father over the threshold and steered him towards the kitchen. She pushed open the door and left it ajar, hoping Michelangelo would remember that Sgt McElroy would most likely come round to the back of the house and conceal himself somewhere. The light in the kitchen caused her to blink and she realised that Lottie must not have heard anything that had gone on outside because she and Lucia appeared to be sound asleep.

'So she and that bloody kid are back are they? Well, I won't have them in my house,' muttered Bernard.

'It's not your house,' said Nellie.

She began to withdraw her arm but he clamped it against his side. 'What do you bloody mean, it's not my house?'

She took a deep breath, hoping that Sgt McElroy would not waste time getting here. 'What I said. Grandfather left it to me. Now if you'll let go of my arm, Dad, we can talk about this later.'

Bernard made no move to release her but squeezed her arm even tighter. 'You conniving little bitch!' he roared.

Lottie started to wake up and Lucia whimpered. Nellie heard a sound behind her and Michelangelo's voice said, 'That is not the proper way to address your daughter. It would be best, Mr Callaghan, if you released Elena without any fuss.'

Nellie's heart was beating so fast now that her head felt light. Her father made no move to free her but turned and faced Michelangelo. The two men stared at each other. 'You'd better run, sonny. The police are on their way.'

The words were no sooner said than they heard the sound of boots in the washroom. Michelangelo moved towards Nellie. 'Let her go or it will be the worse for you,' he said in a dangerously low voice.

'Don't threaten me! You've been bloody carrying on with my wife. Where is she?' snarled Bernard.

'Hello, hello, hello,' said Sgt McElroy.

Nellie stared at him and saw his gaze pass

456

slowly from her face to Bernard before it grazed over Michelangelo and came to rest on Lottie and Lucia. His face softened. 'You'd best get the little girl out of here, Lottie. I think we have here what I'd call an incident.'

Lottie stood up with her daughter in her arms. 'You haven't come to arrest Michelangelo, have you? He did nothing but good while he lived here. I prefer him to my father any day of the week.'

'But he's not your father,' said Sgt McElroy. 'I am.'

Bernard's face suffused with colour and he looked from Lottie to the policeman and then to Lottie and Lucia and back to the policeman. 'I knew it!' he said. 'You're a bloody, bastard child!' He thrust Nellie from him and lunged towards the policeman. Michelangelo caught Nellie and cradled her in his arms.

For all his size Sgt McElroy was light on his feet and sidestepped the attack. Bernard landed up against the table gasping and tried to catch his breath before turning and launching himself at the sergeant again. Once more the policeman got out of his way but this time there was no table to halt Bernard's progress across the floor and he slipped on the rug and fell heavily, his head hitting the hearth.

He lay still.

For several seconds nobody moved, and then Sgt McElroy lowered himself onto one knee beside Bernard and inspected the skull where it had made contact with the brickwork. Nellie watched him feel for a pulse, aware of her blood rushing through her veins and of the throb, throb of Michelangelo's heart against her ear. 'Is he alive?' she asked.

The policeman did not answer but stayed with his fingers against her father's neck for what seemed an age before shaking his head. He stared at her and Michelangelo. 'You saw him go for me.'

'It was an accident,' said Nellie.

Michelangelo nodded. 'You didn't touch him.'

'Is it true what you said?' asked Lottie, staring at Sgt McElroy.

He did not answer but took a tea towel from the drying rack and placed it over Bernard's face. 'There'll be an inquest.'

'Will we all have to be there?' asked Nellie.

The policeman looked at Michelangelo. 'Little Irene and Maisie told me about you and your son and said you were OK, so as far as I'm concerned I haven't seen you,' he said woodenly.

Nellie sighed with relief. 'We're getting married so he'll be legal after that.'

'Shush, Nellie. I don't exist,' murmured Michelangelo.

Sgt McElroy's mouth twitched.

'You haven't answered my question,' said Lottie.

He went over to her and put a shaking hand on her head and stroked her hair. 'We never intended things to get out of control. I loved your mother and grieved terribly when she was killed.'

Lottie believed him. She knew all about losing control and, hearing the sadness in his voice, accepted that he had truly cared for her mother. Besides she much preferred him to the man she had believed to be her father all her life. 'I understand now why you didn't want Billy and me getting close.'

'Aye. It wouldn't have been right with his being your half-brother.'

Lottie was pleased that Billy was her half-brother. 'Will you tell him?'

'If that's what you want. Right now I'd best go and call an ambulance.'

The ambulance was just pulling away from the kerb when Adriana arrived with Francis. 'What's happened?' he asked Nellie and Michelangelo, who were standing on the path.

'Come inside and we'll tell you everything,' said Nellie, and led the way.

By the time she finished talking, Adriana was already making plans. 'Alphonso will return to the camp and be repatriated and I will return to Italy.'

Francis had been silent and stern-faced until then but now he seemed to come alive. 'You don't have to do that.'

'I must, Padre.' Adriana smiled at him sadly and, lifting one of his hands, she kissed it. 'It will make things easier for all of us,' she said softly. 'Nellie and Michelangelo will want to raise their family here in her house. I marvel at her being able to keep quiet about it for so long.'

'Perhaps I learnt something from Francis about keeping secrets,' said Nellie lightly.

'It is wonderful that he can do so,' said Adriana.

'People wouldn't trust me if I couldn't, but it isn't easy,' said Francis, gazing at Adriana, knowing he was going to have to live with his longing for her locked inside him for the rest of his life.

Nellie noticed the way Francis looked at their former stepmother and bit back the suggestion that Adriana should come and visit them after she had the baby. Instead she said, 'What about money? Italy's in a mess, so how will you manage?'

Adriana turned to her. 'You must not worry about us. Bernardo took out extra life insurance when we came to England. And Alphonso has friends he made in the POW camp. We will not starve. You and I will keep in touch and, perhaps one day, you will come to Italy and see your half-brother.'

'I'd like that,' said Nellie, glancing at Michelangelo.

'I will show you my home town and you can taste the waters,' he said with a smile.

'I'd rather make do with wine,' she teased.

'Perhaps I can officiate at the wedding this time?' said Francis.

'Of course,' said Nellie, gazing at him fondly. 'You might even have to officiate at two weddings. Babs is seeing an American she met at a dance a couple of years back and it looks like it could be serious.'

'I'm glad,' said Francis. 'I'd like to see her happy, too.'

Nellie thought, so would I. She wondered how Babs would feel when she knew about their father's death. Most likely she would not grieve for him as deeply as she would have once. He had caused her a lot of unhappiness when he had failed to understand how much she cared for Jake, just as he had shown the same lack of understanding when he had refused his permission for her to marry Teddy. If only her father had been a happier and more loving man, then his home-coming would not have cast a dark cloud over them all. But his death had lifted that cloud once and for all, and she and her sisters had a shining future ahead of them.

The publishers hope that this book has given you enjoyable reading. Large Print Books are especially designed to be as easy to see and hold as possible. If you wish a complete list of our books please ask at your local library or write directly to:

Magna Large Print Books
Magna House, Long Preston,
Skipton, North Yorkshire.
BD23 4ND

This Large Print Book for the partially sighted, who cannot read normal print, is published under the auspices of

THE ULVERSCROFT FOUNDATION